# MR RIGHT NOW

## MANDY BAGGOT

First published in 2011 as *Knowing Me Knowing You*. This edition first published in Great Britain in 2024 by Boldwood Books Ltd.

Copyright © Mandy Baggot, 2011

Cover Design by Alexandra Allden

Cover Illustration: Shutterstock

The moral right of Mandy Baggot to be identified as the author of this work has been asserted in accordance with the Copyright, Designs and Patents Act 1988.

A CIP catalogue record for this book is available from the British Library.

Paperback ISBN 978-1-83561-637-6

Large Print ISBN 978-1-83561-638-3

Hardback ISBN 978-1-83561-636-9

Ebook ISBN 978-1-83561-639-0

Kindle ISBN 978-1-83561-640-6

Audio CD ISBN 978-1-83561-631-4

MP3 CD ISBN 978-1-83561-632-1

Digital audio download ISBN 978-1-83561-634-5

Boldwood Books Ltd
23 Bowerdean Street
London SW6 3TN
www.boldwoodbooks.com

# 1

Bird poo and porridge were basically one and the same bloody thing as far as Kate was concerned. Well, at least they were when it came to stains. No matter how much you scrubbed, no matter what product you used, you were always left with a white residue that stood out a mile.

A pigeon had shit on her in the car park, all over the shoulder of her one decent work jacket. Old-style M&S she had picked up at a charity shop but still in good condition. That meant the first four chargeable units of the morning had been spent trying to get the mark off. And it was, as always, to no avail. You could still see it and now it didn't look like bird shit, it looked like a semen stain.

It was 2.00 p.m. now and she had just noticed another mark on her sleeve. This one was definitely porridge unless a bird had got very intimate without her knowledge. Judging by the hard, crusted, almost concrete look about it, it had possibly been there for weeks. She hadn't had a chance to get to the dry cleaners in ages. Giuseppe gave her a good discount and his mother's special recipes for everything Italian, pasta and tomato based, but dry cleaning was still something she considered a luxury. And, every time Kate went in to Giuseppe's, she suspected he knew she hadn't tried any of the recipes because she couldn't cook and she was sure he could smell that.

The M&S jacket was one of those wool mix ones that you couldn't just put in the washing machine, which was probably why it had ended up in Marie Curie. The last time she had risked the washing machine with a jacket like that, it had shrunk to something not even a size-six model could force herself into.

She hurriedly slipped it off her shoulders, ripped a paper towel from the wall and wet it under the tap. For the second time that day, she began dabbing and scrubbing and cursing under her breath, getting hotter and more frustrated by the second. It wasn't shifting; the paper towel was disintegrating until the only things rubbing the stain were her fingers. Tears began to well up in her eyes. She had spilt coffee on her desk this morning and had to share the lift with Smelly Milo from the post-room; the Ready Brek was the last straw. It felt like her world was ending. This couldn't be how it was going to be from now on. She didn't want to feel tired all the time, inadequate all the time and she didn't want to be sorting out soiled clothes all the time, especially her own. What was next? Incontinence and the nursing home? She was only just past thirty.

She was just about to give in to the emotion threatening to spill out when the door to the toilets swung open with a bang and in walked her boss, Miranda Marsh.

Blonde hair swishing, a reek of designer fragrance, and the familiar tip tap of her Jimmy Choo's introduced her. Now was no time for losing control. A stiff upper lip was required and more restraint than a stag party in a lap dancing bar.

'Oh there you are Kate,' Miranda remarked, standing uncomfortably close to her as only she could.

She was wearing a Jigsaw suit that fitted like a glove. No charity shop cast offs for her; she was a Per Una woman if ever there was one. Miranda was a size eight, petite, always smart, always organised, completely bloody annoying and unstained.

'Yes, here I am. Sorry, is Mr Coombs here already? I was just coming,' Kate spoke hurriedly, putting her jacket back on and crossing the damp sleeve behind her, out of sight.

'No he isn't. He's cancelled again! Silly bloody little man, that's the third time. And this time, he didn't bother to make up a plausible excuse, just muttered something about his granddaughter needing his professional opinion on buying an MG,' Miranda replied with a sigh, turning away from Kate and checking out her reflection in the mirror.

'Oh that's a shame,' Kate remarked, not meaning it at all.

She had a tonne of work on her desk already; she could do without meetings with clients until she had broken the back of it.

'He's a time waster anyway, that man. Too much money, not enough to keep him occupied in his retirement. I really don't know why we bother acting for him. A change to his will here, a bit of conveyancing there and that ridiculous trust fund he insisted on setting up. It isn't going to make us millionaires, is it?' Miranda continued, putting her hands in her long, blonde hair and preening it.

Kate didn't respond. She knew that the 'us' didn't really include her; it meant Randall's, the firm of solicitors they both worked for. Kate was a legal executive and Miranda was a solicitor. There wasn't much difference in their legal knowledge and ability, but being a solicitor and the head of the department meant Miranda had her eyes on the prize that was partnership.

Kate, on the other hand, didn't really know what she was doing practising law. It had been a choice between that and engineering, according to a very dodgy questionnaire she had gone through with her school careers adviser many years ago. There had been nothing else she had a yearning for. So she got on the study treadmill, looked at all the right books, attended all the necessary courses and passed all the exams for the heart-flipping excitement of drafting wills and dealing with dead people. Still, the pay was reasonable and she got the occasional bag of home-grown marrows from Mr Jarvis who seemed to change his will as often as he changed his fertiliser.

'You haven't forgotten Friday, have you Kate?' Miranda said in a way that was more of a statement than a question.

Kate watched her; she was still looking at herself in the mirror and pouting her lips at herself. She looked like someone with a horrendous facial tic.

'Friday?' Kate queried a chill running up her spine. Oh God!

She knew exactly what Miranda was going to say next and she was desperately trying to sound like she didn't for lots of reasons.

'Yes, the dinner at the Grand, Peterson Finance,' Miranda reminded.

'Oh yes, yes, Friday, of course. I hadn't forgotten, I just, couldn't remember what day it is today,' Kate answered lamely.

'Good! Perfect! I knew you wouldn't! I have finally found *the* dress after weeks of searching and I can't wait to wear it. It's just like the one Kate Winslet wore to the Oscars, you know the one, don't you?' Miranda spoke with a wide, red lipstick smile, turning her attention back to Kate and finally away from the mirror.

'Er, um, yes of course, *that* dress. I can't wait to see it,' Kate replied.

She didn't have a clue what Kate Winslet had worn to the Oscars on any year she had attended and she didn't really care that much either. The Oscars had no place in her life at the moment and in fact, never had. The only Oscar she knew of was a woolly-faced owl in one of Bethan's story books.

Kate smiled at Miranda and tried to ignore the extremely uncomfortable feeling that was creeping over her at the thought of a large social engagement she didn't want to attend. She hadn't been out much lately: a couple of dinners with some of her childminder Hermione's friends from the Medieval Fair Society and a pizza and vodka night with her secretary Lynn and some of the other very young secretaries who seemed to be able to drink their own body weight in shots.

'So, who are you bringing?' Miranda enquired, looking straight at Kate with her ice-blue eyes.

They were shark's eyes, large and emotionless, like a great white. They showed signs of ferocity but very little common sense.

Kate froze for a moment and gawped at Miranda as if what she'd said had been in a foreign language and she hadn't a clue how to translate. And then she realised Miranda was still staring at her, waiting for her to respond. She needed to speak to stop her mouth from hanging open. What to say? Try not to scream.

'I... haven't decided yet,' Kate said hurriedly, internally cursing herself.

'I see! Checking out that little black book. I like it! Perfect! OK, well, Collins deceased calls for me; how are you doing with the Slater case?' Miranda asked, turning the conversation back to business.

'Fine, yes, I'm doing fine with that,' Kate replied swiftly.

Yes, she was doing fine with that, not even registered the death certificates with the banks. Well, he'd only been dead three months and she'd been busy.

'Good! Perfect! Let me have the papers when you're done,' Miranda said and flashed Kate another pearly white smile before heading out of the door.

Kate smiled back, waiting for the door to close. As soon as it did, the smile fell from her face. Who was she trying to kid? She just couldn't cope. It was eight months on and she was as useless now as she was at the start. All she wanted to do these days was cry, cry and cry some more. Everything was hopeless; she had been a terrible wife, she was a terrible mother and a very extra terrible legal executive. And now today, she had terrible, terrible bird shite and porridge down her only good jacket. And if all that terrible stuff wasn't enough, now she had to find a man to take to a dinner on Friday night. She didn't know any men; she didn't really know how to go about getting one. What was she going to do? Let herself be humiliated by Miranda like always? Turn up alone and be a laughing stock for not having a date, or cry off and be a laughing stock for trying to avoid turning up *without* a date? There was no winning situation here.

She could feel tears pricking her eyes but quickly the door opened again and Kate fixed her smile back on like it was a pair of false lips from a Christmas cracker. She eked the smile wider, acknowledging the entrance of Dorothy from accounts, stretching her mouth so wide that it hurt. She had got used to conjuring up a happy expression now; she had practised at home in front of the mirror. She had the 'good morning' smile for when she came into the office first thing. Not too wide with the mouth, crinkling the eyes slightly. She had the 'yes, I'm absolutely fine, thanks for asking' smile. Slightly wider with the lips, showing teeth. And she had the 'life is wonderful, I'm getting on without him' smile which was as wide as her lips would allow and complete crinkling of the eyes until they were almost closed. Oh and laughter if required.

She waited for bouffant-haired Dorothy to close the cubicle door and then she hurriedly left the toilets before she started up a conversation while she peed. She always did that and Kate found talking while listening to someone else peeing quite unsettling. It just wasn't right.

She sat back down at her desk, determined to have a proper stab at the Slater file. It was a horrible case, a farmhouse (agricultural relief), two small companies (business property relief), and an argumentative family (no relief at all).

She looked at her screen and stared at her reflection. It was horrible. What was she doing worrying about pigeon shit on her jacket when she looked such a mess? Her hair was a state because she hadn't had time to shower and her straighteners were broken. It was also in desperate need of a cut. It was naturally dark and thick which had been an asset when she had time to brush and style it, but now it had started to resemble a Halloween witch's wig.

Today, she also had larger-than-normal grey bags under her eyes due to Bethan waking her up at 2.30 a.m. and 4.00 a.m., unable to locate her dummy. And to top it all off, this morning's lipstick, which she had scrawled on while reverse parking, was now just a thin line on her bottom lip.

She clenched her teeth together and swallowed another urge to cry. This was all Matthew's fault. It wasn't supposed to be anything like this. She should have been feeling confident, comfortable and settled in her life, not the complete opposite.

Matthew, her husband – well, ex-husband technically – had left her and a then sixteen-month-old Bethan, eight months ago. He claimed he hadn't taken to fatherhood, it wasn't what he wanted, it had never been what he wanted and she had pushed him into it. Kate hadn't known what to say the day he announced this. Coldplay's 'Fix You' had been playing on the radio, Bethan had been happily hammering on her highchair tray with a spoon and she had been standing in her dressing gown, milk down her front and Rice Snaps in her hair. He had mumbled something about going to his mother's and then left the room. She was still stood in the same position, staring blankly at her babbling daughter, trying to take in his words, when he had come back down the stairs carrying two suitcases, already packed.

She had absolutely fallen apart. She hadn't known what to do. She didn't know who to turn to or what happened next. For days, she lived some sort of half existence where day and night merged together around episodes of *In the Night Garden* and *Zingzillas*. She couldn't face work, she rarely got dressed and Bethan kept saying 'Daddy' at really inopportune times, like when she happened to let her eyes flit over the wedding photo on the dresser, or when she found an item of Matthew's clothing in the laundry basket. She needed help.

Help had come in the shape of Hermione Wyatt. Realising that you didn't get money in the bank by sitting around in your nightwear watching *This Morning*,

Kate knew she had to go back to work. But because in her misery she hadn't been able to face taking Bethan to nursery, she had lost her place there. At first, in angry tones, she had tried calling the manager a Nazi. Then when that hadn't worked, she had offered to pay for the time Bethan had missed. The manager said no and Kate broke down, sobbing until the hand piece was wet, trying to quote passages of law in an effort to frighten Mrs Hitler into giving her back her place, but even that had no effect on the hard-nosed manager.

So, she found the nearest childminder with a vacancy and got Hermione.

Hermione was eccentricity personified. She spent all day potato printing, hula-hooping and biscuit making with three of her own children, and a strange-looking, dark-haired boy called Cyrus who would only communicate by whispering.

Her house was filled to the rafters with toys, books and beloved clutter she and her husband Philip had picked up on the far-flung adventures of their youth. The couple were into dreams, feelings and controlling your own destiny. Hermione read tarot cards and did rune readings as a sideline to her childminding. At first, that made Kate question her suitability but Bethan had warmed to her immediately and that was the only reassurance she needed.

In a short space of time, Hermione had become much more than a childminder; she had become a firm friend. She had helped her get herself together after Matthew left and was determined to stop her from looking back. It was a good job Hermione had taken on Project Kate because there was no one else. Her parents were dead and her Aunt Jess lived in Scotland and they weren't exactly on the best of terms.

Hermione was her whole support network and she and Kate were all Bethan had.

* * *

It was almost 6.00 p.m. when Kate rang the doorbell of the Wyatt house. She let out a breath, glad she was there, glad she wasn't at work and glad she had stopped at the supermarket and bought a bottle of wine.

She had spent too long choosing the wine really. She had recently developed a liking for South African wine, primarily because it was cheap but also because she had found a brand that was 14 per cent and not too harsh on the taste buds. But they were sold out and that meant she had to investigate an alternative which in turn meant checking every price label for the best deal and finding one with the highest alcohol content. She had plumped for a 13.5 per cent Chilean.

There was screaming from inside the house and then thundering footsteps and growling. The door was thrown open and Philip grinned at her as he whipped a hairy troll mask off his face.

'Hello Kate, come in. We were just re-enacting "The Three Billy Goats Gruff", weren't we kids?' he spoke, letting out another roar and making all the children scream excitedly and run away from the front door and into the living room.

Philip was tall and lean with sandy-coloured hair that always seemed to flop down in front of his eyes. He had a permanent grin on his face that made him look like an oversized naughty teenager. He loved being with the children but was also equally at home burying his head in books about the lost treasures of far off tribal villages. Primarily, he worked at the university but he was also involved with lots of archaeological societies whose work took him all over the world.

'I think that's enough of the grumpy old troll now. Hello Kate, cup of camomile?' Hermione asked as she appeared from the kitchen and scooped Bethan up in her arms.

Hermione was almost fifty, although you wouldn't know it. She was one of those women who had sailed through pregnancy and childbirth and retained the figure she had when she was a young woman. She had skin that glowed, blonde hair that fell softly onto her shoulders and huge, kind, blue eyes. She was also capable and organised – annoyingly so. This was a woman who could wash up, change a nappy and make gingerbread men all at the same time. If she didn't love her so much, Kate would most probably detest her for being so perfect.

'Oh, I don't know if I have time for tea tonight. I—' Kate began, wanting to get home, crack open the Chilean wine and drown her sorrows.

'Of course you have time, doesn't she Bethan? Mummy has time for a cup of Aunty Hermione's camomile tea, doesn't she?' Hermione spoke, handing Bethan over to Kate and leading the way into the kitchen.

Bethan put her arms around Kate's neck and squeezed, hugging her tightly in agreement.

'Just a quick one then,' Kate agreed, kissing her daughter on the cheek and ruffling her hair.

'Come on kids, who wants to watch *The Jungle Book*?' Philip asked the four children.

There were squeals of approval and running foot-steps and they all thundered back into the lounge.

'Bethan has been an absolute delight today, haven't you sweetie?' Hermione said, tickling under the little girl's chin as Kate took a seat at the kitchen table and propped her daughter up on her knee.

'Have you? What have you been doing with Mione?' Kate asked, looking at Bethan intently.

'Painting,' Bethan responded with a smile.

Kate swallowed a lump in her throat; she was growing up so much. She was two, no longer a baby: a proper little girl.

'Good girl! Yes, we did painting and then we made biscuits and then we ran around the garden and played hide and seek, didn't we?' Hermione spoke as she made the tea.

'It sounds like you had a great time,' Kate answered, bouncing Bethan up and down.

'And did you have a great time at work? I would say probably not judging by those frown lines I can see,' Hermione said, turning her scrutiny to her friend.

'I have frown lines?' Kate exclaimed, her hands reaching for her forehead and pressing at the skin as if to iron out any creases.

'Beth, why don't you go and watch the DVD with

Philip and the others? I'm pretty sure they'll be dressed up as bears and monkeys by now. Mummy and I need to talk about secret things,' Hermione spoke, putting a finger to her lips and helping Bethan down from Kate's lap.

Bethan ran out of the kitchen towards the living room and as soon as Hermione could hear roaring, monkey noises and laughter, she closed the kitchen door.

'What's happened at work today? I sense more than the usual "too much to do, too little time" vibe,' she said, bringing the tea over to the table and sitting down.

'Nothing, it was the same as every day. I played my usual inadequate self, I didn't get half the things done I should have, Lady Dragon Miranda spent all day doing that really annoying laugh of hers and saying "perfect" every second word to anyone that came in contact with her. Oh yes, and I have to find a date to take to a function I'd hoped she'd forgotten about – this Friday,' Kate responded, taking a large swig of her tea.

'Would you like some sugar for the shock?' Hermione questioned.

'It isn't funny! It's one of our really big clients and

one that actually likes me. It's some banquet thing at the Grand. It'll be dressing up and looking nice and talking to lots of people I have nothing in common with. Oh, and did I mention I have to take a date. A date, Mione! I don't know any men! Unless? Yes, of course! I don't know why I didn't think of it before! Can I borrow Philip?' Kate asked, leaning almost excitedly across the table towards her.

'Afraid not, sweetie – Philip's off to Africa tomorrow. He's away for a week supervising digging for ancient artefacts,' Hermione replied.

'Then I'm well and truly buggered. What am I going to do?' Kate asked, putting her hands in her hair and leaning on the table face down.

'Don't you still have that business card I gave you?' Hermione questioned, drinking some of her tea.

'Oh no, I'm not doing that. That's for desperate people,' Kate said, lifting her head up and knocking her cup with her elbow, making some of the contents spill out on the table.

'And what are you if not desperate for a date – this Friday. I don't see you have any other option.'

'I cannot use an escort agency! Did you hear that? Even saying it sounds sleazy! It would be like using a male prostitute,' Kate exclaimed.

'Well, my friend Libby – you've met Libby – she

comes here for readings. She absolutely swears by this firm. She uses them all the time, purely for company; they go out for a meal or to the cinema. She's a professional just like you and she doesn't have time for a relationship. She's been burned in the past, just like you, but she loves male company. For her this is an ideal solution. I think her "friend" is called Jonny,' Hermione informed.

'I feel sick,' Kate responded.

'I think you should look at this a different way. You've created a negative vibe about this function. You think it's going to be dreadful, it won't be fun, you'll hate it and you know what I think about self-fulfilling prophecies. If you think it's going to be terrible then it will be,' Hermione told her.

'I still feel sick.'

'It's an opportunity to dress up, get your hair done, have a few drinks and some posh food with some gorgeous guy sat next to you. Wouldn't that stick it to the Lady Dragon?'

'I can't take a male escort; it just wouldn't be right. I don't do that sort of thing.'

'The card has the website address on it; at least have a look while you're trawling through your old address books, looking for an alternative,' Hermione suggested.

'D'you know, I don't think I have the card any more; what bad luck,' Kate remarked, drinking down the remainder of her tea.

'Isn't it? Luckily, I have another,' Hermione responded and she magically produced the card straight away from a large, towering pile of paperwork on her kitchen worktop.

'Are you sure you're not a witch?' Kate enquired, reluctantly taking the card from her friend's hand.

'Are you sure you haven't forgotten how to enjoy yourself?' Hermione retorted.

She looked at the business card, rolling it around her fingers.

'Perhaps I have,' she admitted with a heavy sigh.

'Then get back out there and start living your life again. *Your* life sweetie, not just Bethan's. You're a brilliant mum but even brilliant mums need a break and yours is long overdue. Ring the number, book yourself a date, buy something new to wear, and Friday night, leave work early, get your hair done and enjoy yourself! Bethan can stay the night here – my three love having sleepovers and with Philip away, I won't know what to do with myself. You'll basically be doing me a favour,' Hermione insisted with a smile.

'It sounds like I don't have a choice. Have you been reading runes for me again? Is this function something I have to attend for my greater good?' Kate asked.

'I'm saying nothing more; you don't believe any of that anyway,' Hermione replied and she pretended to zip up her lips.

## 2
---

By the time Kate had bathed Bethan, put her to bed and read her a story, it was almost 8.00 p.m. Her brain actually ached and she was completely exhausted. Although she should have known it before, she hadn't actually realised just how tiring having a child would be. Now she was doing it on her own and trying to hold down a job all at the same time. She was struggling with it, emotionally and financially. There were bills that needed paying, bills she had ignored for too long. Most months, she didn't know whether she was actually going to get through it just breaking even.

She thought about her delicate finances all the time and that meant she thought about Matthew a lot of the time and what a bastard he was for leaving her.

But knowing he was a bastard somehow didn't stop her wishing he was still there. There were moments when she missed him desperately.

She pulled the cork out of the bottle of wine and felt a sense of relief the minute she poured it into a glass. This was *her* time, her time to relax, even if it was on her own. Sometimes, it was lonely, like when there was nothing to watch on TV, or when she began to think too heavily about Matthew, but most of the time, she was asleep on the sofa before the loneliness had a chance to take hold. Tonight, all she could do was stare at the business card Hermione had given her while she set the microwave timer to two minutes and popped in a carbonara meal for one.

*Elite Escorts* it said in glittery letters. There was an address in the town centre, a telephone number, email address and a website. Kate took a swig of her wine and opened her laptop.

She typed in the web address and almost at once, the page flickered into life and music blared out. It was the theme from *Baywatch*. Kate hurried to turn the volume down before it woke Bethan, almost knocking her glass over in the process. She half expected to see a bare-chested David Hasselhoff pop up on screen. Not that it would have been a bad thing. She'd always had a soft spot for him since *Knight Rider*. Or maybe that had just been because of the cool car.

More glittery letters appeared and then flashing icons came up and an option to choose *Gentlemen* or *Ladies*. Kate clicked on *Gentlemen* and was given an entire gallery of men to look through. This was certainly a happy kind of shopping!

The first man she clicked on, *Barry*, looked very camp, like a younger, much shorter version of Dale Winton. The next one was *Keith*, who looked friendly enough, but according to his date of birth, he was forty-seven. She then looked at *Michael* (had little hair and reminded her of Harry Hill), *Finlay*, who said he liked Boyzone and *David*, who was six foot five inches tall. There was no way, even if she wore heels, that she would be able to talk to anything but his navel.

It was then she noticed the search section. In this, you could input all your likes and dislikes, just like building your own perfect man. Now halfway down the glass of wine, Kate actually smiled at the screen and began to type.

Less than six foot, but over five foot seven, dark hair, no preference on eye colour, athletic build, educated to at least O-level equivalent, likes films, music and dining out. It was like shopping online at Argos but much more entertaining. She half expected the computer to build her perfect man in front of her very eyes with the capacity to have him packed and shipped.

Kate pressed the search button and a large picture was displayed of *Stephen*.

Stephen said he was five foot ten, athletically built, dark hair, green eyes, with an A-level in economics. He liked action films and dining out. He was good-looking but not her usual type; he had a friendly smile and kind eyes. Kate stared at the photograph and took another sip of her wine. To book Stephen, you had to fill in another form with your details and the date and time you wanted to order him for. Even more like shopping online at Argos, but no delivery charge. Kate took a deep breath. This was insane. What was she doing?

She got up from the table to fetch the bottle of wine and suddenly remembered she had microwaved her dinner about half an hour ago. She set it to cook again and stared over at her computer, still displaying the smiling photo of Stephen. She put the glass of wine to her lips again and cursed the Lady Dragon for putting her in this position. The microwave beeped. She got a fork out of the drawer and, plastic container of overcooked carbonara in hand, walked back over to the table. Stephen didn't look like an escort – that was a good thing – but did he look ordinary enough for the Lady Dragon to believe Kate was dating him? Possibly, although he was better looking than Matthew. Kate swallowed. She didn't believe she had just thought that. She loved Matthew; she had thought he was handsome the minute she set eyes on him. She looked over at the photo of Bethan and Matthew on the sideboard. They were both smiling, father and daughter together. She had loved him but perhaps she hadn't really ever known him. The person she had been in love with wouldn't have left her and his daughter without a second thought.

Now feeling angry, Kate turned to the laptop and pressed a key to submit. She wanted to forget Matthew. Perhaps Hermione was right; maybe a night out *was* in order.

* * *

When the telephone rang, it woke Kate up. She had eaten the chewy pasta meal, finished the bottle of wine and attempted to watch a programme about overweight children at a fat camp. It had been such a good documentary, she had fallen asleep within the first five minutes, just after fifteen-stone Kylie from Stoke had admitted her partiality for ring doughnuts.

Half asleep, she grabbed the phone and put it to her ear.

'Hello.'

'Hello, is that Kate Baxter?' a male voice asked.

It was a nice voice. Soft and deep, strong yet not overpowering.

'Yes, it is,' Kate answered.

She was slightly concerned it could be her bank manager. It didn't sound like him but he had been known to make his assistants do the initial call before he came on the line and gave her an earful about her financial situation. Like she wasn't fully aware she was poor.

'Hi Kate, I'm from Elite Escorts. My name's Joel,' the lovely voice informed her.

'Joel?' Kate queried, rubbing her eyes and trying to wake herself up. She was glad he wasn't from the bank but concerned he wasn't called Stephen.

'Yes, I know you were expecting Stephen but I'm afraid he's booked up the whole weekend and I was your next best match,' Joel continued.

'Oh, well, I...' Kate began.

'I'm just ringing to check what time you want to meet up and where,' Joel spoke.

'Oh, I don't know, um, I haven't done this before,' Kate blurted out.

And very unlikely to do it again and in fact wouldn't be doing it at all if it wasn't for her interfering childminder.

'That's OK. Listen, I usually meet people at Fenton's, the wine bar in the town square. Do you know it?' Joel asked her.

'Erm – I'm not sure,' Kate began, looking around for a pen and paper in case she needed to make notes.

'It used to be the biker's pub,' Joel added.

'Oh yes, I know where that is – used to avoid it like the plague,' Kate spoke, overturning Bethan's drawings in an attempt to find a piece of paper that hadn't been drawn on.

'Good, so what time? Seven? Half past?'

'Erm, better make it seven; the meal's supposed to start at eight,' Kate replied, finally pulling out an A4 pad and reaching for a pen.

'And where are we going? In your email, you said it was a work function.'

'Yes, it's a dinner, banquet thingy, something posh like that. It's at the Grand,' Kate replied.

'Is it black tie?'

'No, at least I don't think so. Shall I check?' Kate asked, becoming flustered.

It would be posh but she didn't know the dress

code. The Lady Dragon was wearing an Oscar-worthy dress though so maybe it *was* black tie.

'That's OK; I'll dress smart and bring the dinner jacket in the car just in case,' Joel replied.

'Good,' Kate said, not knowing what else to say.

How could she find out the dress code without actually speaking to the Lady Dragon? Lynn! She would ask Lynn.

'Right, well I'll meet you at seven at Fenton's on Friday,' Joel spoke.

'Good, OK – wait – how will I recognise you?' Kate wanted to know, a hundred things going through her mind.

'I'll be wearing a tulip in my lapel,' the honeyed voice replied.

'A tulip, right, OK,' Kate responded, writing it down on her pad.

'I'm just kidding! You can have a look at my profile on the website; there's a photo,' Joel responded, a hint of amusement in his voice.

'Oh, yes, of course,' Kate answered, her cheeks flushing with embarrassment. She was so glad he couldn't see her or he would be running a mile in the other direction and changing his phone number.

'OK, well I'll see you on Friday.'

'Yes, good, Friday. I mean not as in Good Friday, as

in next Friday, sorry,' Kate babbled, her cheeks red-dening as she cursed herself.

'Bye,' Joel ended.

'Bye.'

Her heart was racing as she put the phone down. What had she done? She had engaged the services of a male escort to accompany her to a work function. If it backfired and people found out, she would never be able to hold her head up again. And it wasn't going to be Stephen! Smiling Stephen with the kind eyes and a hint of stubble that she thought had really suited him. She had almost got used to the idea of passing a few hours with Stephen. Kate raced back over to the lap-top. She didn't have a clue what this Joel looked like. What if he wasn't appropriate? God, had she really said that? What a snob! He had said he was a close match to the criteria she had entered. But what if that meant he had one eye instead of two or no hair when she had definitely asked for hair? She almost couldn't bear to look as she typed the name into the search en-gine and waited for something to appear. She didn't have to wait long. In a matter of milliseconds, Joel's profile appeared on her screen and looking through her fingers, she let out a horrified gasp. There was no way she could take him to the function, no way in the world.

# 3

Kate was still flustered the following morning when she dropped Bethan off at Hermione's. She had spent a fretful night wondering what she was going to wear and whether she could possibly attend on her own. She could say her date had gone down with swine flu or something equally contagious. Yes, her date could have been an important, influential member of the Mexican government who she had met at the embassy when she had been doing research for a client matter, Mr Gonzales' divorce, his new will and ownership of the taco business. That way, the Lady Dragon would be impressed at his status and she wouldn't have to go through the whole humiliating experience of employing an escort.

'Hello sweetie, Cyrus and Sky are just setting up a den in the living room. So you want to go and play? There we go,' Hermione spoke as she let the two females into her house and relieved Bethan of her coat.

'Give Mummy a big kiss, Bethy and I'll see you later. Have fun with Aunty Hermione,' Kate said, cuddling her daughter and kissing her lightly on the lips.

'Cyrus, Sky, play nicely with Bethan, please. No curtain pulling or climbing on the chairs,' Hermione ordered the older children.

'Yes, Mum,' Sky replied with a laugh.

Cyrus also let out a whisper of agreement.

'Have you time for tea? I sense there's something you want to get off your chest. Am I right?' Hermione asked Kate as she led the way towards the kitchen.

'I did as I was told, stupidly. I took your advice. I looked at the website, I inputted my criteria and I was matched with Stephen. He was good-looking but nothing too striking, perfect for my purposes. Then I get a phone call from someone called Joel telling me that Stephen's unavailable and that *he's* my closest match,' Kate blurted out, pacing up and down Hermione's kitchen.

'So you got someone. Well, that's good; I don't see the problem,' Hermione answered, watching Kate walking back and forth.

'*This! This* is the problem!' Kate exploded and she banged down Joel's profile and photograph on the table.

Hermione picked up the papers and began to smile, much to Kate's annoyance.

'Well, well, well,' Hermione remarked, shaking her head and putting her hand to her mouth to stifle her laughter.

'It isn't bloody funny! Look at him, for God's sake, just look at him! I cannot take him with me to a work function; I would be a laughing stock,' Kate said, tears welling up in her eyes.

'I think the Lady Dragon will have a hard job keeping her tongue in her mouth. He's absolutely gorgeous,' Hermione said, still staring at the photo.

'Exactly! He's gorgeous; he's one of the most gorgeous men I've ever set eyes on,' Kate remarked, snatching the paperwork back from her friend.

'Then I don't see the issue. And it would be one in the eye for Miranda; there's no way she'll be bringing a date that tops this Joel. Hmm, even that name is sexy, isn't it?' Hermione remarked, trying to get another look at the escort from over Kate's shoulder.

'The problem is, no one's going to believe that he's going out with *me!* Look at him, Mione and look at me!

He's – perfection personified and I'm – a mess,' Kate answered.

'That isn't true; you're just a busy mum who's neglected herself a bit, that's all. I thought we had this conversation yesterday; all you need is a little bit of "you" time and you'll soon have your sparkle back,' Hermione assured her.

'I could have a whole year of "me" time, Trevor Sorbie and Gok Wan at work twenty-four hours a day and I still wouldn't have enough sparkle to pull off pretending I was *his* girlfriend,' Kate replied.

'Nonsense!' Hermione responded with a snort of annoyance.

'It isn't going to work; I shouldn't have done such a mad, stupid thing in the first place. I mean *please*, a male escort! What was I thinking?' Kate asked.

'You're not going to cancel, are you?'

'Yes! Of course! That's exactly what I'm going to do. What other option do I have?' Kate said with a sigh.

'How about going to the function with a drop-dead gorgeous guy and enjoying yourself for once?'

'Oh Mione, you don't understand! I knew you wouldn't. Miranda's main enjoyment in life stems from seeing me struggle. She would take one look at this Joel and instantly know that he was a hired help,' Kate attempted to explain.

'I don't believe that; that's all in your mind. You think, for some daft reason, that this chap is too good for you. You haven't met him yet; he might stink and have a limp. Although looking at this sexy picture, I very much doubt it,' Hermione replied.

'I should have just had the courage to tell her I don't have a partner at the moment and I was going on my own,' Kate said, pausing in her pacing.

'So is that what you're going to do now?'

'No, it's too late now; I told her I was bringing someone. I've decided either to invent a swine-flu-ridden Carlos or go sick myself,' Kate said.

Hermione let out a squeal of laughter and put her hands to her mouth again.

'What?' Kate asked.

'Well that will be playing right into her hands,' Hermione told her.

'Well, what d'you suggest? I go, with this Joel, and have the entire firm knowing I use male escorts by first thing on Monday morning?'

'Male escort or not, believe me, you are going to have every woman at the dinner table wishing they had him sitting next to them.'

'Argh! This is mad! How did my life get like this?' Kate questioned, picking up Joel's profile from the table.

'You, sweetie need to lighten up. It's just a night out; take it for what it is and to hell with what Miranda thinks,' Hermione spoke.

Kate let out a heavy sigh. It was easy for Hermione to say; she was good at everything. She had a perfect life with a husband who adored her and three children who thought she was the best mother in the world, which of course she was. She had no idea what it was like to be abandoned and feel unwanted and useless.

'Enough of this talk of cancelling. Tomorrow, bring Bethan's overnight bag when you drop her off in the morning and I don't want to see you again until Saturday.'

'I'll probably need all that time to try and make myself look like I could have a boyfriend like this,' Kate said, staring at the picture of Joel.

'If the banquet's crap, you can always come round here; I wouldn't mind five minutes with him,' Hermione answered with a grin.

# 4

It was almost 6.00 p.m. before Kate left work on Friday evening. The Lady Dragon had given her two sets of accounts to finalise that apparently she wanted to review first thing on Monday. Kate knew she had done it deliberately but she had almost given up caring. She didn't have the energy for workplace games; it was all she could do to concentrate on the job. She dutifully did as she was told, not wanting to give Miranda any more reason to ridicule her. Of course the Lady Dragon had disappeared at 3.30 p.m. to what was down in her diary as an 'out of the office meeting'. Kate suspected it was a visit to the hairdresser or the beautician. Somewhere exclusive and expensive, somewhere that catered for the rich and famous and Oscar nominees.

Kate had managed to get her hair done in her lunch break. She had never been to the salon before but she hadn't had time to be picky. She had been quite scared when she arrived as the sign over the door had letters missing and instead of reading *Crimpers* it now read *Crap* where someone had added an 'A' with a black marker pen. She wondered how long it had been like that and whether anyone else knew or cared.

The inside wasn't much better; everything was vinyl and the sinks were avocado green. There was one woman having her hair tweaked with an afro comb. She had ended up with a dodgy perm like Deirdre Barlow in the early nineties and another woman, hair set in rollers, seemed unperturbed by smoke billowing out of the back of her dryer. No one else looked bothered about it either so she had taken a seat and leafed through a 1998 edition of *Woman's Weekly*. Thankfully, 'Natalie' had put her more at ease, making her a coffee and giving her a copy of the latest *Star Life* magazine.

She had a wet cut and it cost much more than expected. She almost choked when Natalie told her the price but she did like the finished result. Frankly, that was amazing given that she had seen two women with very dodgy feathering and another woman with purple highlights. Her usually untamed, dark-brown mop had been cut into a sleek, modern bob that seemed to instantly make her look younger. Anything that did that had to be worth the money. But the expensive do had meant there wasn't enough left for a new outfit or a manicure.

When she got home, she luxuriated in a bubble bath courtesy of Bethan's Mr Matey. She couldn't remember the last time she had had time for a bath. The water felt wonderful, soft and silky on her skin. She had opened wine as soon as she had got in (her favourite South African was back on the shelf, £2.99 and 14 per cent) and now she was halfway down the bottle. She wished she wasn't going to the stupid banquet. She wished she could have just stayed in the bath, relishing the fact she was completely on her own. There were no nappies that needed changing, no bottles to warm, no relentless, mind-numbing children's television programmes to endure. Her eyes closed. She was so tired; sleep would be nice: completely uninterrupted sleep. She imagined being asleep, being covered up in her duvet, her head on the pillow. And as she began to relax and let her mind wander, Matthew was next to her in the bed. Handsome, wavy-haired Matthew, the husband she loved. Then the image of him suddenly became distorted. He wasn't lovely Matthew any more; he was Matthew who had left her and left their daughter: the Matthew she hated. As that realisation came to the forefront of her thoughts, she snapped open her eyes and hurriedly sat up. She started to wheeze and cough, desperately trying to clear her lungs of the water that had seeped into her mouth while she had been fantasising about someone she loathed. She took another drink of wine to clear her throat and checked her watch. It was 6.45 p.m. and she wasn't even dressed.

\* \* \*

Half an hour later, she almost fell through the door of Fenton's wine bar. It was 7.15 p.m., the taxi had been late and she hadn't had a chance to take any time over getting ready at all. She had managed foundation and lipstick but that was it on the make-up front. In the end, it had been a case of throwing her one and only good dress over her head and hurrying out of the house, hoping she had managed to avoid white deodorant marks in her haste. Now she was being overwhelmed by atmospheric dim lighting (so dim, she could barely see) and hideous cocktail bar piano music.

She scrutinised the people stood at the bar. There was a group of men in dinner jackets sharing bottles of champagne and laughing loudly at every second word one of the older men in the group said, all on their way to being pissed. There were two women her age sat at the bar whispering to one another over cocktails and licking their lips over the barman. And finally, there was one man sat on his own, back to the door, picking at the bowl of nuts on the counter. He was dark-haired and Kate judged he was approximately six foot. It could be Joel, or maybe, given her late arrival, Joel had gone home. She didn't know whether she wanted him to be here or not. She could still invent Carlos. She knew a lot about swine flu; she had researched it on the internet in case Bethan developed symptoms.

'Excuse me, are you Kate?' a velvety voice asked from behind her.

She knew that voice. It sounded like it could wrap her up in silk and feed her caramel-centred chocolates.

Kate turned around and immediately looked into a face she also recognised. Despite the picture on the internet making him look like some sort of Adonis, somehow it hadn't really done him justice.

'I'm Joel,' the gorgeous vision in front of her pro-
claimed.

Kate couldn't stop herself from very obviously
looking him up and down. He was over six foot, athletically slim, with dark hair and the largest eyes she had
ever seen. He was impeccably dressed in a dark-blue
suit teamed with a white shirt.

'Are you Kate?' he repeated as she hadn't spoken.

'Yes, yes I am. Hello, I'm Kate, nice to meet you,'
she hurriedly spoke, offering her hand to him.

Joel ignored the offering, leant forward and kissed
her on the cheek.

'If we're supposed to be dating, I don't think we
should shake hands,' he said quietly to her.

'Oh no, I suppose not,' Kate answered, her cheeks
flushing.

'Can I get you a drink?' he offered.

'Oh no, I should pay. What would you like?' Kate
asked, fumbling in her handbag for her purse,
knowing that she only had about five pounds in cash
and that her credit card was on the verge of meltdown.

'I insist,' Joel said and he took her hand out of her
bag and smiled at her.

'Oh,' Kate responded in the meekest voice ever.

'What will it be?' Joel asked again.

'A white wine please, medium,' Kate responded.

'OK. Why don't you take a seat and I'll bring it over.'

Kate nervously nodded her agreement and moved to the nearest available table. She sat down and checked her appearance in the window. Her hair still looked good, although getting it wet in the bath and almost drowning hadn't been in her plans. She screwed up her eyes. She wished she'd brought her eye make-up with her because it would have drawn attention away from the bags she had been unable to conceal. She pursed her lips. She would need to reapply her lipstick when they got to the hotel; it was already making a break for freedom.

She was still making a face at the window like a ghoul when Joel appeared opposite her with the drinks.

'Medium white wine,' he announced, passing a glass to her and sitting down.

'Thank you. Aren't you drinking?'

'Maybe later. Is there a free bar at the hotel?' Joel asked her.

'I hope so,' Kate responded, burying her face in her glass and taking a large gulp.

'So what is it we're going to? You said a work function; is it dinner?' Joel asked.

'Yes, at least I think so. It was last year. Five courses

or something mad like that, then some boring slides and an awful disco, but we don't have to stay for that.'

'And what's our background?'

'Background?'

'Yes, how do we know each other? Where did we meet? What do you do for a living?' Joel asked.

'Sorry, you must think I'm stupid. I haven't done this before. I expect you hear that all the time too, but I really haven't done this before,' Kate answered, taking another big mouthful of wine.

She was sounding like a desperate single mother who had forgotten how to behave in the normal world. Any minute now, she would be telling him about a nice collage Bethan had done the other day with dried pasta. It was as if she had forgotten how to be an adult.

She looked at Joel with almost terrified eyes.

'That's OK,' he replied kindly, smiling at her with both his full mouth and his saucer-sized eyes.

'Um, I'm a legal executive in the Probate department of Randall's solicitors in town. The do tonight is being hosted by a client of ours and some of my work colleagues will be there, like the Lady Dragon – I mean Miranda. She's the head of my department and Colin, he's a partner and a bit of a goon if I'm honest – God, it's going to be terrible; I wish I wasn't going,' Kate spoke, downing the glass of wine in one go.

'So did I meet you through work?'

'No! God no! They would know. The Lady Dragon knows everyone I see and you wouldn't be the type of client I would see; I mean, you're about three times younger than any of my clients and three times more attract... I don't know, what do you usually say to people?' Kate said quickly, stopping herself hurriedly.

'How about we met at the gym? That's where I work when I'm not doing this. I'm a personal trainer; we could have met there, and we've been dating for what? A few weeks?' Joel suggested.

'The gym. No, I don't think so. I mean, do I look like I've been to the gym recently? I don't really do exercise; the spare time I get is very limited. I have a little girl,' Kate answered, wishing there was still some wine left in her glass.

'Oh really, how old?'

'She's two,' Kate responded, a smile spreading across her face as she thought about Bethan.

'Sounds like you have your work cut out with one that age,' Joel said, smiling at Kate.

'Yes, definitely. Look Joel, the thing is, the reason I have you here is because of my boss. She's evil. Well, perhaps evil is too strong a word. She's a dragon in high heels, hence the nickname. She loves to make people feel small – well, me anyway – and she's expecting me to have a date tonight. And I don't have a little black book, I don't have a book of any kind – you know – with men in it. You see, my husband left me a short while ago and I haven't really been out since,' Kate babbled, wishing her wine glass full with every ounce of energy she had.

'I see,' he replied with a nod.

'Sorry, you're probably not interested in me at all, or the fact I don't have a book of men,' Kate said and she stuck her hand in the bowl of nuts on the table, taking a palm full and putting them into her mouth.

'OK, how about we met at the pool when you were taking your daughter swimming. Does that sound more plausible?' Joel suggested.

'But we haven't been there yet and I'm not really very good in the water.'

'It doesn't matter, it's just pretend. I'll fill in the gaps, don't worry,' Joel told her and he took hold of her hand and gave it a reassuring squeeze.

She flinched, the shock of the physical contact jarring her. She couldn't remember the last time a man had touched her.

'So what did you say the dragon in high heels is called? Her real name,' Joel asked.

'Miranda. Be warned, she'll probably try to sleep

with you,' Kate answered, grabbing more nuts and tipping them into her mouth.

# 5

It was just after 8.00 p.m. when Kate and Joel arrived at the Grand. The banquet was being held in the Regency room and when they got to the door, Kate could see it was full to capacity and everyone was already seated. Thankfully, within seconds, Miranda let out one of her ear-splitting, over-the-top laughs and Kate was able to distinguish the Randall's table from all the others.

'Right, into the lion's den I guess,' she spoke, more to herself than to Joel.

As she prepared to head off into the room, Joel took hold of her hand again. It was soft and warm but also strong and supportive. Kate looked up at him, meeting the saucer-sized eyes again.

'I'm afraid, if you want people to think we're dating then we're going to have to get a little bit intimate,' Joel told her, giving her hand an encouraging squeeze.

'OK and we met at the swimming pool, about six weeks ago. Was it six weeks?' Kate asked, looking at him nervously.

'Six weeks is fine.'

There were approximately two hundred people in the huge hall, all sat at round tables with white and gold crockery set out before them. At the bottom of the room was a large stage with spotlights erected at both sides and men with television cameras. At the previous year's banquet, the president of the company, Frank Peterson, had bored everyone stupid with slides on their work in Africa, followed by a quiz about the slides and he had ended with a lecture about using less water. The cameras and lights probably meant a jazzed-up version of the same. Perhaps he had finally mastered PowerPoint. The good news was there was no sign of a disco.

Kate saw the two empty seats at the Randall's table and with her head down, she made a beeline for them in the hope she could sit down before Miranda noticed she had arrived.

It wasn't to be.

As she went to swing herself into her seat, she got

her foot caught on the chair next to Frank Peterson. She fell forward and ended up having to grab at Miranda's seat for support, narrowly avoiding whipping the tablecloth off like an amateur conjuror.

'Are you OK?' Joel asked her, steadying her and helping her remain upright.

'Hello Kate, we were beginning to wonder whether you were going to make it – oh hello, now we definitely haven't met before. I'm Miranda, Kate's boss,' Miranda spoke, spotting Joel and immediately standing up to give him the full effect of her horrendously short dress.

Kate was convinced Kate Winslet had never worn anything that short or crass to the Oscars.

'Hello, I'm Joel, pleased to meet you,' he spoke politely, smiling at Miranda and taking the hand she offered him.

'Likewise. Goodness, you *are* tall and so handsome. Where have you been hiding this one, Kate?' Miranda asked, holding onto Joel's hand and continuing to look him up and down.

'We met at the swimming pool; Bethan just loves going there,' Kate said hurriedly, fixing a smile on her face and sitting down next to Frank Peterson.

Frank was in his late fifties. He had made his money on the stock market, had a thriving financial advisory business with offices all across Europe and was also now involved in helping African communities set up small sustainable businesses. He was a happy-go-lucky character who loved nothing more than entertaining. He was one of Kate's favourite clients. In fact, he was her *only* favourite client.

'Hello Kate, how are you?' Frank asked, grinning jovially at her.

'I'm fine, thank you Frank. No Marion tonight?' Kate enquired, noticing his wife was absent from the table.

'No, she's laid up, my girl, had a little op on an in-grown toenail and it's got to stay up for a week,' he responded.

'Oh poor her, give her my best wishes for a speedy recovery,' Kate said, spotting the open bottle of white wine and willing it closer to her. She wished she had paid more attention to Paul McKenna shows although she wasn't sure even he could hypnotise inanimate objects.

'So this is your chap is it? Hello there, I'm Frank Peterson,' the president introduced himself.

'Joel Brown, pleased to meet you,' he replied, shaking the man's hand and sitting down next to Kate.

'I can't believe you've kept this one a secret, Kate; what a dark horse you are. Anyone would think you had him manufactured, he's so perfect,' Miranda carried on, her eyes out on stalks, unable to keep them from Kate's date.

'I'm flattered but to be honest, I'm the really lucky one,' Joel answered and he put his hand on top of Kate's and held it.

He was good. Half convincing. He obviously did this a lot. Perhaps this was going to work after all. It was a shame he wasn't drinking. If he got a bit drunk and dishevelled himself, he might look less good-looking.

'Can I get anyone some wine? Miranda? Perhaps a drink will distract you from ogling the poor fellow. I'm Colin, nice to meet you Joel,' Colin Sykes spoke, standing up and shaking Joel's hand before getting more wine.

'Nice to meet you,' Joel answered.

Colin was a partner in the Private Client department. He had started as a runner in the post room when he was sixteen, had been given a training contract at twenty and worked his way up. Now he was listed as a leader in his field in the Chambers guide. Unfortunately, although he was successful and loaded, he was also balding, skinny and had a nose the size of Luxembourg.

'Could I have some wine please, Colin?' Kate

asked, pushing her glass nearer to the bottle he was offering.

'Of course – so are you getting nervous?' Colin asked, smiling at Kate as he poured the liquid into her glass.

'Nervous?' Kate queried, picking up her drink and taking a much-needed sip.

'About the contest. Very good of you to volunteer; you're a braver person than I,' Colin continued.

'I'm sorry Colin, I'm not sure what you're talking about. What have I volunteered myself for? Frank, you don't need me to sell raffle tickets again, do you?' Kate asked with a smile at her client.

'No, my girl, the contest on stage. It's my treat for everyone here after I bored you all rigid with the slide show last year, or so Marion tells me,' Frank answered.

'Contest?' Kate spoke, none the wiser but a feeling of unease creeping over her.

'Oh Kate, don't tell me I forgot to mention it! Goodness! How remiss of me! That was why I was so keen for you to bring a date tonight. You and Joel are going to be Randall's representatives,' Miranda exclaimed excitedly.

'Representatives for what?' Kate asked, a lump of terror forming in her throat.

'I'm hosting the local heat of *Knowing Me Knowing*

*You*! It's a national competition and Peterson Finance is sponsoring it. The two highest scoring couples tonight go through to one of the regional heats and the first two couples from that go into the national finals. It's televised and everything – well, it's on one of those funny satellite channels,' Frank attempted to explain.

'Isn't it exciting?! You and Joel are our entry. There are five other couples I think so competition is fierce,' Miranda spoke.

'You must remember the old *Mr and Mrs* on TV; well, this is a bit like that but updated for the twenty-first century. Couples don't have to be married, or even straight – I believe we have a Bjorn and Michael entering – and according to Frank here, the questions are a little bit racier,' Colin continued.

'I had no idea about this! God, I couldn't possibly compete in something like that. If you want to win then you need your best people out there, don't you Joel,' Kate spoke hurriedly, looking at her date with pleading eyes.

'I think Joel is going to look perfect on camera. I can't wait to watch it back, in complete privacy,' Miranda interrupted, smiling widely at the escort and rolling tendrils of her blonde hair through her fingers.

'I've had a better idea; why don't you and Colin do

it? Yes, that would be a wonderful advertisement for the firm. A partner who has worked his way up to the top and the highly successful, vivacious head of the Probate team,' Kate said.

'But we're not a couple and actually Kate, it was Frank who suggested you,' Miranda told her, her voice stern.

'Oh was it? Oh Frank, that's very sweet, but I really think—' Kate began, determined she was not going to take part in any show.

'I won't hear another word; you're going to do brilliantly. This girl is a marvel, Joel; she's made my estate all tax efficient,' Frank interrupted.

Kate gulped back her wine, grabbed the bottle from the table and refilled her glass. She didn't do games of any sort and a relationship contest with someone she didn't know was most probably going to expose her as a fraud.

Anything anyone said flew over her head after that announcement. She drank as much wine as she could get her hands on and she barely ate. She picked at the asparagus spears, pushed the roast duck around her plate and took two mouthfuls of raspberry soufflé before declaring she was completely full. She couldn't think about anything else other than the fact that as soon as dinner was over, she had to get up on a stage in front of over two hundred people and answer questions, possibly risqué questions, about someone she had met at 7.15 p.m. that night.

Fortunately, Joel talked for the both of them. He chatted to Colin and Frank intently and was gracious to Miranda even though she kept leaning over the table flashing her cleavage at every opportunity. She also found any excuse she could to touch him, passing the salt, passing the wine, knocking her fork off the table.

As the waiters came round with the coffee, Kate made her escape to the hotel bar. She ordered a rum and Coke and knocked it back in one go. She put the glass back on the bar and ordered a second. She was halfway down the glass when someone took it out of her hands.

'I don't think you should have any more of those,' Joel spoke, putting the glass back down on the bar.

'I'm sorry, I didn't realise I was paying you to do impersonations of my mother,' Kate snapped.

'I just think it might be better if you didn't have too much more, that's all,' Joel replied, taking hold of the glass as Kate tried to reach for it.

'Give me my drink back,' Kate ordered, gritting her teeth and fixing Joel with a hard stare.

'No.'

'Give it to me!' Kate repeated and she made a lunge for the glass he was holding.

Joel dodged out of the way and Kate fell forward for the second time that night and bashed her elbow hard on the bar.

She hurriedly stood herself upright and straightened her dress, trying hard to hide any embarrassment.

'All we have to do is answer a few questions; it's no big deal. It'll keep your client sweet and it will backfire on Miranda, who obviously nominated you to make you feel uncomfortable,' Joel told her.

'She spends her life finding new ways to make me feel uncomfortable,' Kate mumbled in reply.

'So show her you don't mind stepping into the breach and entering the contest – rise above her.'

'There are bloody TV cameras out there!' Kate exclaimed, still looking longingly at the drink Joel was shielding.

'I don't see the problem. It's one little quiz; you must have done quizzes before,' Joel replied.

'Yes, in pubs, with friends, about music and films, not about someone I've only just met! We know

nothing about each other! How is that going to look?!'
Kate shrieked, making other patrons of the bar turn in
their direction.

'You're overreacting. Come on, we're going back in,'
Joel spoke, taking hold of Kate's arm and leading her
back towards the door of the function room.

'This is madness! And what sort of escort agency
do you work for? You're bullying me and you're
hurting my arm,' Kate hissed as Joel propelled her
through the doors and back towards their table.

'It will be over in an hour or so; we'll probably
only be on stage for ten minutes. Think how many
brownie points this will earn you with Frank,' Joel
whispered to her, smiling at Miranda as they approached.

'They said the questions were intimate. What side
of the bed do you sleep on? What underwear do you
prefer?' Kate asked.

'Kate, we don't have to win,' Joel replied.

'No, but they have to believe we're a couple,' Kate
responded, putting an 'everything's fine with me' smile
on her face and pulling out her chair to re-join the
others at the table.

If she got up on that stage and revealed to
everyone in the room that she knew nothing about
Joel, she would look a complete idiot. And what the

hell was a racy question anyway? Was it did she like it on top? Or maybe where does she buy her bras? Either way, Joel wouldn't have a clue and she didn't know the first thing about him either.

'There you are my girl; no time for sitting down, I'm afraid. The producer is looking for you two. Got to join the other couples backstage; it's curtain up in a few minutes,' Frank spoke, stopping Kate before she had a chance to sit down.

'Ooh Kate, I'm so excited for you; the limelight is beckoning and we'll all be watching. It's going to be perfect,' Miranda spoke, smiling falsely at her.

Kate faked a smile back, her face aching, as Joel took her hand and led her in the direction of 'backstage'.

Behind the scenes, there were couples chatting eagerly and excitedly amongst themselves and to each other. There were television crew wearing headphones and carrying clipboards, all walking around looking busy. There was also a very rotund man, obviously wearing a toupee, dressed in a silver suit. He was having powder put on his face by a woman wearing a make-up belt around her middle. There were lights and people shouting, 'Sound check' and holding their ear as they waved a hand in the air. And just in front of them was someone wandering around in a seven foot bird costume clutching a golden egg.

'This is a circus,' Kate commented, taken aback by what they had walked in to.

'It does look a little chaotic,' Joel admitted.

There was no time to consider the situation they had found themselves in as a loud, exaggerated scream had them turning round and coming face to face with a woman with bright-pink hair piled high on her head. She was wearing a black t-shirt with *Knowing Me Knowing You* embroidered on it in sequins.

'There you are! I take it you're Kate and you must be – is it Joe?'

'Joel,' he corrected.

'Joel, right. Brian! New name badge over here! It's Joel, not Joe. Hi, I'm Becky, but everyone calls me Becks. Gosh, aren't you tall,' the pink-haired girl spoke as Brian arrived with the altered name badge. She stuck one on each of them.

'Look, Becks, this is all a bit spontaneous for us. We really don't know what to expect, with the questions,' Kate babbled nervously.

'Oh you'll be fine. You're the second couple on; we drew names out of the hat. What will happen is that

Larry, the guy in the silver over there, he will call you onto stage. He'll ask you a little bit about yourselves and then you Joel will be put into a booth at the side of the stage. It's supposed to be glass but it's plastic; they're working on a glass one for the final. You'll have headphones on and be listening to music and Larry will be asking Kate some questions about you. Then when she's answered the questions, you'll come back onto centre stage and give your answers. We want as many correct matches as possible to get you in the top two couples and through to the regional heat,' Becky explained in double quick time.

'Can't I go into the booth? Joel's a little claustrophobic,' Kate spoke hurriedly, dreading stage time on her own.

'Oh, are you?' Becky asked, looking at him with concern.

'I'll be fine, especially if I have music to listen to,' Joel replied, putting an arm around Kate and making her feel even more uncomfortable.

'Did I mention the Love Dove?' Becky questioned.

'What?' Kate remarked.

'The Love Dove, he's over there. He'll lay three golden eggs during the course of the show and if he lays an egg when you two are on stage, you get to answer a bonus question that will win an instant cash prize and an additional Kissing Gate on the board,' Becky said with excitement in her eyes.

'Wow Kate, doesn't that sound great,' Joel answered.

'I'm egg-static.'

'Great, well I think I've covered everything. The show's going to start in a minute so if you just follow me round here, we'll get a bit of powder on you and give you some briefing notes,' Becky spoke and she swung her pink hair around and headed off at break-neck speed.

* * *

Within minutes, they had both been powdered and lip glossed and were waiting in the wings as the *Knowing Me Knowing You* show kicked off on the function room stage and aired to viewers at home.

'I just want you to know that this is probably the worst night of my life,' Kate whispered to Joel.

'If you're going to fill in a customer satisfaction sheet on my performance, can you maybe tone that sentiment down a bit?' Joel replied.

'I completely blame *you* for this.'

'What? How can you blame me for this? I didn't instigate it.'

'You've made me get up here and you took away my drink. I was going to slip away into the night, away from all this ridiculous behaviour. I never thought I'd actually say it but I would rather be watching the African slides again. I mean, what is Frank thinking of? This is so downmarket for him, so trashy, it's as bad as, I don't know, having to appear on an episode of *Jerry Springer*,' Kate continued to speak.

'It's fun,' Joel responded, looking through the briefing notes.

'You have got to be kidding me! Fun! This is your idea of fun! I knew there was something wrong with you. I can't believe you were the closest match to Stephen. If Stephen were here, he would have taken me away from all this.'

'Stephen doesn't really have an O-level and his picture is ten years out of date,' Joel answered.

'Oh, shame on you, sullying the reputation of one of your colleagues to get you out of a corner.'

'You employed me to come here with you. Your client and your boss have somehow between them set you up to do this. I just think that the easiest, most pain-free way to get through the evening, and probably the rest of your career, is to just do it. We don't know each other, we answer the questions, we get them all wrong, the end of the show, the end of the night, the end of the date,' Joel said.

'Fine, we'll do it, get it all over with,' Kate answered, crossing her arms in front of her chest.

It was only ten minutes and an advert break before Larry Rawlins was calling them to the stage.

# 6

'And please welcome our next couple, Kate Baxter and Joel Brown. Let's give them a big hand as they take to the stage.'

Kate and Joel stepped out from behind the curtain and were greeted by Larry, his bright-silver suit and an array of spotlights and cameras directed at them from just below the stage.

'Welcome Kate, welcome Joel, lovely to meet you. So Kate, you are looking lovely tonight, isn't she, ladies and gentlemen? I'm guessing you do modelling, right?' Larry questioned, sticking a microphone into Kate's face.

'Er, no,' she replied.

'No? I'm shocked. So tell everyone here and at home what it is you do for a living,' Larry ordered.

'I'm a legal executive at Randall's Solicitors.'

There, she'd got a plug in for the firm that would please Miranda if nothing else. There was loud whooping and shouting from the crowd which was unmistakably the Lady Dragon and one of the larger cameras swung around to get a close-up shot of the table. Kate cringed and willed the ordeal to be finished.

'Bit of advertising there, Kate and you've got some support in the audience, I hear; that's good. And Joel, what do you do? It looks like you work out if you don't mind me saying. Have you seen him, ladies and gentlemen? A virtual Adonis!'

'I'm a personal trainer at Highbridge Leisure Centre,' Joel responded.

'That is lovely. So how long have you two known each other and where did you meet? Was it lust at first sight? Did you see her, Joel and just know you had to have her?' Larry questioned, performing an elaborate wink to the audience.

'Most definitely,' Joel answered, smiling at Kate, knowing how much she was hating every second.

Kate cringed. He almost looked like he was enjoying this. She hated him. Why oh why had Stephen already been booked?

'We met at the swimming pool six weeks ago – well, approximately. It isn't like I'm counting or anything. Is it six weeks now?' Kate asked Joel with a nervous swallow.

'It certainly is, darling,' Joel replied, trying to keep a straight face.

'Only six weeks. In the first flush of romance, ladies and gentlemen, how lovely. Right, I've been told you've been explained the rules; what happens now is we pop Joel in the booth and once he's in there and I'm happy he's listening to some romantic tunes through the headset, we'll make a start. I will ask you three questions about Joel, you will answer and then we get Joel back and see if your answers match. Everybody happy? Good, right Joel, take yourself over to the booth, slip on the headphones and blindfold and when I'm sure you can't hear me, I'll begin interrogating your lovely Kate.'

Kate watched as Joel headed for the plastic booth, sat on the chair inside and put on the blindfold and large headphones. He still managed to look hot wearing game show paraphernalia.

'Ah Kate, look at your man now, oblivious to everything. Any secrets you want to tell, now is your op-portunity.'

'No.'

'Just kidding, right Kate, down to business. Are you ready?' Larry asked her.

'As I'll ever be,' Kate replied, gritting her teeth.

'Good, right, this first question then for one Kissing Gate on the board. So, if Joel were a member of the cat family, what would he be? Would he be A, a tiger, hot blooded and always ready for action? B, a panther, silky, sleek and perfectly aligned or would he be C, a pussy cat – cute, cuddly and romantic.'

Kate didn't know what to say. She just stood, al-most open-mouthed, staring at Larry's shiny suit that had started to make her eyes go funny. What sort of a question was that? It wasn't racy, it wasn't intimate and she was sure she would never have known the answer if she had been asked about any of her *real* boyfriends. What member of the cat family?!

'I'm going to have to hurry you for an answer, Kate. I know it's only been six weeks but surely you must have discussed which member of the cat family he would like to be,' Larry joked.

'You would think so, wouldn't you?' Kate said with the most false laugh she had ever performed.

Larry looked at her, wondering what noise was

going to escape her lips next. Her mouth suddenly felt very dry.

'Well, I don't know really, I'll have to guess, I suppose. I'll say A,' Kate blurted out.

'She said A, a tiger, hot blooded and always ready for action. I can just bet he is,' Larry said with a camp smile to camera.

The audience laughed and Kate could feel the palms of her hands starting to sweat.

'OK, question two. If Joel were planning a night out for you both, which of these nights would he be more inclined to organise? Would he choose A, a night out at the cinema, to watch a rom com or perhaps B, a night at the bowling, something fast paced to enjoy with friends or C, a night at the casino, something frivolous and exciting,' Larry continued.

All Kate could think of was how annoying Larry was and how impossible the questions were. She wasn't sure she would have been able to answer them even with Matthew as her fellow contestant. He had hated the cinema, they'd never been bowling or had the kind of money you needed to visit a casino. He'd liked the odd go on the slot machine at the pub but...

'I'm going to have to hurry you a little, Kate.'

'These questions are very hard,' Kate said, trying to wipe Matthew from her mind.

'I need an answer.'

'C,' Kate said determinedly.

'That's C, a night at the casino, something frivolous and exciting. Wow, a frivolous tiger is our Joel. OK and the final question is – Joel wants to try out a new position in the bedroom, and I don't mean moving the furniture around here, Kate. How does Joel "tackle" the issue? Does he A, sit you down and suggest spicing things up? Does he B, say nothing, things like that shouldn't be discussed or does he C, throw you into the new position during lovemaking and see what happens?'

Kate's cheeks were now on fire. All eyes, lights and lenses were on her and all she could look at was Joel in the booth with the shiny headphones on. What had her life come to? But more importantly, did he look like someone who would want a discussion about sexual positions or someone who would just go with the flow? She had no idea; she didn't *want* to have any idea. This was wrong on so many levels. And why was she even worrying about getting the answer right? Who cared?

'Kate, do you want me to repeat the options for you?' Larry enquired, bringing Kate back to the realisation that she was stood on a stage being scrutinised.

'No, no don't repeat them. Um C, I think, but well

we have only been together six weeks,' Kate answered, dreading the outcome and the frailty of her knowledge of Joel being revealed to Miranda.

'Well done, that's all done. Come and join us, Joel,' Larry spoke and he walked over to the booth, opened the door and let Joel out.

Joel followed Larry back towards centre stage and took hold of Kate's hand, smiling at her. God, he was so good-looking but the fact that he seemed to be revelling in this ridiculous game show was less than attractive.

'Welcome back, Joel. Did you enjoy the Booth of Tranquillity?' Larry asked him.

'Apart from the Chris De Burgh,' Joel answered.

'Good, good. Right, Joel, let's get straight down to business. The first question I asked Kate was – if Joel were a member of the cat family, what would he be? Would he be A, a tiger, hot blooded and always ready for action? B, a panther, silky, sleek and perfectly aligned or would he be C, a pussy cat, cute, cuddly and romantic,' Larry informed.

'God, that's a tough question. It's between two – um, I'll go for a tiger,' Joel spoke.

'THAT'S RIGHT!!!! Well done Kate, you have one Kissing Gate on the board. Let's see if we can make it two. I asked Kate, if Joel were planning a night out for you both, which of these nights would he be more inclined to organise? Would he choose A, a night out at the cinema, to watch something romantic, B, a night at the bowling, something fast paced to enjoy with friends or C, a night at the casino, something frivolous and exciting?'

Kate couldn't look anywhere. She didn't care about getting things right or wrong now; she just cared about getting off the stage and going home. Well, heading home and stopping at Threshers for some Cape White.

'Probably all three but if I had to choose it would be A, the cinema,' Joel answered.

'Oh Joel! That isn't a match – bad luck Kate. She said the casino – perhaps something to arrange in the future. It seems she's keen on spending your cash frivolously! OK, still only one Kissing Gate. Right, the final question – oh hang on, hang on, who is this? It's the Love Dove! Let's hear it for the Love Dove, people,' Larry shouted into the microphone.

Much to Kate's utter disbelief, the audience began singing and clapping to the tune of 'When The Saints Go Marching In'.

*Oh he's our dove, so filled with love*
*Oh he's our dove so filled with love*

*His golden eggs could win you prizes*
*Oh he's our dove so filled with love*

She wanted to know exactly how many of the audience had had their drinks spiked. Alcohol alone could not account for the ridiculous display of singing and arm-waving. It looked like they were all members of a pantomime chorus. She half expected thigh slapping and, 'He's behind you's.

'It's the Love Dove, everyone. Hey Lovey, does this mean that you're going to lay one of your golden eggs for Kate and Joel?' Larry asked.

The bird-suited individual nodded its head and then proceeded to simulate straining, like he was about to do a dump. He flapped his wings and screwed up his beak and then somehow, through the magic of camera work and a stagehand in black, a golden egg appeared on the floor under the Love Dove's backside. He picked it up, nestled it in his wing and took it over to Larry.

'The Love Dove, folks! Let's hear it for the Love Dove! Thanks Lovey, off you go now for a little lie down. Right, now the way the Golden Egg bonus round works is that I will ask Kate the question hidden in Lovey's egg which will be something about her and

Kate must write down her answer on this board,' Larry explained.

Still holding the egg, the presenter collected a clipboard and marker pen from stage left and handed it over to Kate.

'Then, when Kate is happy with her answer, I'll ask the question to Joel, he'll answer it and if it's a match, you'll get a hundred pounds and a bonus Kissing Gate on the board!' Larry spoke, encouraging the audience to get even more excited than they so obviously already were.

Kate could just make out Miranda behind the myriad of cameras and lights pointing her way. She was smiling up at her, a sickeningly sweet smile of satisfaction. Kate knew she was in no doubt she was loathing every moment of the game show and that would make her night – well, probably her weekend. But then Frank came into view as camera two moved to the left and he smiled so genuinely and gave her a thumbs up, it almost pulled at her heart strings. Lovely Frank who liked her, rich Frank who gave her champagne at Christmas, Frank with the ill wife and a son who sponged off him constantly. Kate smiled back at him and tried to swallow the knot of hopelessness that was caught in her throat. Then Colin Sykes got to his feet, clenched his fist into a ball and rolled his hand around in the air making gorilla noises. Kate kept the smile on her face, her cheeks aching. There was one thing she was certain of: they had definitely finished off the wine.

'OK, let's open the egg – here we go. There, right, Kate, the question is – and remember, don't say anything, just write the answer on the board – the question is – what is your middle name?' Larry spoke, making the question sound like rocket science.

Kate hurriedly wrote on the board and looked back to Larry.

'All done? Final answer? Don't need to ask the audience?'

'You said I wasn't allowed to say anything,' Kate reminded him, getting more and more annoyed with the presenter.

'OK then, Joel – what is Kate's middle name?' Larry boomed excitedly.

'She doesn't have one,' Joel responded almost confidently.

'And let's see the board!' Larry exclaimed, his eyes bulging in anticipation.

Kate turned the board around to show the audience and it said in large letters:

*Don't have one*

'YES!! A MATCH! Well done, Joel! That's two Kissing Gates on the board! And one hundred pounds. There you are Kate, you can keep hold of that cheque, maybe spend it at that casino Joel is going to take you to, that's lovely.'

'Lovely,' Kate repeated.

'So, back to the game. The final question I asked Kate was – Joel wants to try out a new position in the bedroom, how does he tackle the issue? Does he A, sit you down and suggest spicing things up? Does he B, say nothing, things like that shouldn't be discussed; or does he C, throw you into the new position during lovemaking and see what happens?'

Kate's cheeks flamed; she couldn't look at Joel. She wanted the stage to eat her up and quickly. She could almost feel Miranda's delight at her obvious embarrassment. She would be sniggering under her breath, whispering, 'Perfect' like a female Bond villain. All she needed was a cat to stroke and a monocle. She was poised, waiting with bated breath to see just how moronic Kate was going to look next.

She couldn't even remember what she had answered to the cringeworthy question. She didn't even care; she just wanted to get home. She didn't want to be out any more; being out was not the frivolous fun Hermione had spoken about at length. She wanted to be with Bethan, being a mother and watching repeats of *Peppa Pig*.

'Definitely C,' Joel answered.

'YES!! That's a match! Well done, Kate and Joel; together with your Golden Egg bonus, that means there are three Kissing Gates on the board and you are our current leaders! Congratulations! Although bear in mind, there are several other couples to come. OK, let's give Kate and Joel a big hand,' Larry announced and he held out his silver-sleeved arm, directing them stage right.

Kate practically ran for cover, her face glowing and her mouth dry. She needed to get to the bar; she almost felt sober and she did not want to be sober. She didn't want to be able to remember any part of this evening.

'Hey, we're the current leaders!' Joel said to her as they prepared to leave the backstage area and return to the tables.

'Fantastic! How the hell did that happen? How do you know I don't have a middle name?' Kate questioned, trying to squeeze herself past the Love Dove, who was blocking one of the exits.

'You didn't put a middle name on your profile for Elite Escorts so I presumed you didn't have one. How do you explain knowing I wouldn't want to waste time discussing a new sexual position?' Joel asked.

'I guessed you wouldn't be a talker, given the biceps,' Kate replied, pushing open the door.

'Hey! Wait, wait, wait! Where d'you think you're going? STOP!' a loud, high-pitched call screamed out.

Kate and Joel turned around to see Becky scurrying towards them, her cheeks as pink as her hair.

'You can't go yet; you're our current leaders. You have to wait here until we're sure you aren't going to finish in the top two couples. I have a manual leader board right here,' Becky spoke, pointing at a hand-drawn grid on her clipboard covered in squiggles, crossings out and bullet points.

'You are joking! I can't sit here all night; there are places I need to be – like the bar,' Kate replied, all sense of being polite leaving her.

'Oh you don't have to wait right here; we have a green room. It's this way – free drinks and nibbles,' Becky responded, starting off towards the other exit.

'Free drinks? As in alcoholic drinks?' Kate asked, her keenness to leave suddenly departing her.

'Yes, of course. This is television,' Becky answered with a grin.

'Lead on then, Becks; you've just become my new best friend,' Kate responded, hurrying after her.

# 7

'I'll have a rum and Coke – make it a double. Hang on, make it two – doubles, that is. Did you want anything?' Kate asked, turning to look at Joel.

'Just a water, thanks. Don't you think perhaps you should have water too?'

'Didn't you hear the girl with the pink hair? FREE DRINKS, she said. I can get water any time I like. Water for the fitness guru here, please; he needs to rehydrate after all that excitement with the golden egg,' Kate spoke to the barman.

'I think you drink too much,' Joel told her bluntly.

'I'm not paying you to have an opinion,' Kate retorted, eagerly waiting for her drink.

'Just an observation.'

'Well, I don't want you to have any of those either. We don't have to pretend we're a couple now. Miranda and Frank and anyone else it matters to are sat out there,' Kate reminded him.

'Why does it matter to you that they believe you have a boyfriend?' Joel wanted to know.

'Rum and Coke, my best friends! And a water for you. Cheers, bottoms up and all that,' Kate spoke as the drinks arrived and she immediately began to drink her glass dry.

'You shouldn't need someone on your arm to make you feel adequate, particularly if it's only for the benefit of other people,' Joel spoke, leaning on the bar.

'I don't need someone on my arm; the Lady Dragon set me a challenge. She insisted I brought someone to this function and I didn't want to stick out like a sore thumb by not bringing anyone so I *bought* you. Anyway, isn't it people feeling inadequate for being single that keeps you in business?' Kate asked.

'Not at all. Most of my clients are businesswomen who don't have time or the need to form a relationship; they just like a bit of male company every now and then. I don't think that's you.'

'Why not? I'm a businesswoman, I didn't have time to find a date for tonight and I don't need a relationship. I've just got rid of one piece of deadwood I don't need to look for any more. I have Bethan,' Kate reminded him.

'Fair enough,' Joel responded, sipping his water.

'What about you? Do you have time to form a relationship when you're taking desperate business-women out to dinner?' Kate asked, beginning to drink the second rum.

'No and I'm too busy perfecting my biceps in any spare time I get,' Joel answered quickly.

'That reeks of someone with a relationship hang up. Now do you have a wandering eye or do you just find it hard to trust?' Kate asked mockingly.

'Neither actually, it's just not every woman chooses a tiger as their favourite member of the cat family,' Joel replied.

'So you do escorting for your bit of female company.'

'Well, it's always entertaining and you never know quite what you're going to get.'

'So do you have "regulars" like Jonny?' Kate asked, drinking more alcohol and enjoying the burn on the back of her throat.

'Jonny?'

'Apparently, he's Libby's very special friend.'

'I see two women regularly, about twice a month; they've been clients for just over a year.'

'God, where do you go? What are they like?'

'I can't tell you details; it's confidential,' Joel replied.

'Come on, I don't want their names; I'm just intrigued. Do they wine and dine you? Do they take you to the opera? Do you have to take their coats on and off and open doors? Do you have to call them Hot Lips?' Kate rambled.

'One woman wanted me to call her Evita once. She had a bit of a musical theatre obsession. But her real name was Rita so trying to remember to call her Evita – well, it fell apart altogether when I ended up calling her Ryvita,' Joel informed her with a smile.

'No!' Kate exclaimed and laughed out loud, making other people in the green room look up from what they were doing.

Joel laughed with her. He had a nice laugh. It made his whole face crinkle up.

'I haven't been on a date since my husband left me,' Kate spoke heavily.

'You told me.'

'I don't want to, you know, because I don't think I should, with Bethan. But other people seem to think I should want to and *they* want me to. Hermione, she's Bethan's childminder, and my friend, she is so desperate for me to "move on". She keeps trying to push men in front of me at every opportunity and I don't think I'm ready for that. Besides, the men she lines up, well, they're either Morris dancers from one of the folk fairs she's done tarot readings at, or it's one of Philip's archaeological friends from the university and I don't do relics of any kind; I mean, I can't even stand *Time Team*,' Kate explained.

'I don't know anything about having children but I really don't think you should let go of who you are as an individual just because you have someone relying on you.'

'Goodness, those sound like wise words coming from a personal trainer.'

'Actually, besides the biceps, I have four A-levels and a degree.'

Kate looked at Joel, astounded. He couldn't be clever and that good-looking; it wasn't legal, was it? Perhaps in the pages of Mills and Boon but not in real life surely!

'Appearances can be deceptive. You shouldn't judge every book you meet by its cover. I'm a personal trainer because I enjoy it, not because I'm a fitness freak who's academically challenged,' Joel replied.

'Now I'm feeling very stupid,' Kate answered, draining the contents of her glass.

'It's fine. I know most people book me because of

how I look; that's all part and parcel of the job. And I'd be lying if I said it wasn't flattering.'

'But if you're so qualified, why do you do the escorting? You could work part-time doing personal training and part-time doing something that would use your skills and challenge you,' Kate suggested.

'Maybe I don't want that,' Joel responded coolly.

'Goodness, if I had four A-levels and a degree, I would be ruling the world by now.'

'You don't know that. Just because you have something doesn't mean using it is the right thing to do.'

'Are we having a debate? I don't think I've ever had a debate with anyone before,' Kate remarked.

'No, we definitely aren't. Conversation closed,' Joel replied, drinking some of his water.

'So am I the best date you've had this month? Don't think too hard about the answer; I need a confidence boost,' Kate spoke.

'You're probably the most bizarre date I've had since Ryvita,' Joel answered.

'What do you think I should do about dating then? To date or not to date? That is the question,' Kate spoke, picking up Joel's water glass and drinking from it.

'If you don't think you're ready to date again, don't

let anyone else make the decision for you, no matter how well-meaning they are,' Joel replied.

'Hermione is quite difficult to sidestep when she's fully loaded with good intention.'

'And as for Miranda, I think you need to stop worrying about what she thinks. She's one of those people who needs to be admired all the time. She has major confidence issues; she's not someone to be intimidated by. And as well as all that, I'm convinced she wears a wig,' Joel informed her.

Kate almost spat out the water she had in her mouth. She hurriedly managed to swallow and take a breath of air and then gasped out loud.

'What?'

'I'm sure that mane of blonde hair is a wig. A good wig mind you, well made and expensive, but I'm pretty sure it's fake,' Joel repeated.

'No, it can't be. I mean, you should see how much she flicks it around at work; it's her signature move: the Hair Toss. That's what she does; that's who she is,' Kate explained, picturing Miranda swishing and sweeping the blonde locks around.

'Well, as I said, not absolutely positive, but pretty sure. One of my regulars wears a wig, I would never have known if she hadn't told me, but now I can spot one a mile off, even a good one. It's all about the rise and fall,' Joel responded.

'No, it can't be. I mean...' Kate began, still re-running Miranda's hair flick in her mind.

'Ooooooooooo!'

The loud squeal was accompanied by Becky suddenly appearing and starting to jump up and down in front of them like an excited rabbit. Her pink hair swung about wildly and her hand clapped against her clipboard.

'I've just been told you're through!' she shrieked at the top of her voice and she threw her arms around Kate excitedly, almost bowling her over.

'What?' Kate questioned, a shiver running over her as she tried to detach the girl.

'You're through to the next round; you came second. Come on, quick, quick, we need you back on stage after the commercial break with Hayley and Anthony. Oh this is so exciting, didn't you do well?' Becks said happily, sounding more and more like Bruce Forsyth by the second.

'Jesus, I don't believe it. I don't want to go back on the stage. This whole thing is completely ridiculous,' Kate said and she picked up an abandoned glass of wine from the bar and downed it in one go.

'Even the Love Dove?' Joel asked.

'Especially the Love Dove, although he was in-finitely more skilled than the presenter with much better hair – well, feathers – well, you know,' Kate remarked.

'Kate! Joel! Come on, we need to be quick; you'll have to jog,' Becky shouted from the exit to the stage.

'Jog? Is she kidding? In *these* shoes?' Kate asked, picking up another abandoned drink and beginning to drink it.

'Come on. Let's see it through,' Joel suggested and he took the glass out of her hand and replaced it on the bar.

'I've never liked limelight and I'm not warming to it,' Kate responded, reluctantly following him towards the door.

'Do it for Frank; it looked like he was having a ball out in the audience and his wife *is* ill,' Joel reminded.

'It's an ingrown toenail, not a life-threatening disease.'

They arrived backstage and stood next to Hayley and Anthony. They were a tangerine-tanned couple who looked like they had spent the last ten years of their lives on a sun bed. They were dressed all in white, making them look all the more orange and both of them had an abundance of curly hair. Anthony's made him look like Graeme Souness and Hayley's was more like Barbra Streisand.

'Right, now in a second, Larry will announce you and you'll be back on stage for the final surprise!' Becky said, doing a mini-jump on the spot.

'Surprise? Oh, what is it? Oh Anthony, what do you think it is?' Hayley began to gabble in an Australian accent, her curly hair bobbing up and down.

'I don't know, sweetheart but it sounds exciting,' he responded in an equally thick drawl.

They sounded like they had just stepped off the tarmac of Ramsay Street.

'You won't be disappointed but I can't say any more; it's just seconds away!' Becky said, her eyes wide.

'I can hardly contain myself,' Kate muttered.

Her head was beginning to pound with both the stress and the alcohol she had consumed in such a short space of time.

'Ladies and gentlemen, we have our two winning couples; please welcome back to the stage, Hayley and Anthony and Kate and Joel!' Larry's voice boomed through the PA system.

Joel took hold of Kate's hand and they followed the

Australian couple onto the stage to again be blinded by the lights and Larry's silver suit.

From the audience, Miranda let out a loud shriek of almost genuine appreciation, Colin started bellowing and thumping his chest like an aroused baboon and Frank Peterson was clapping and yelling, 'Bravo' at every opportunity. Kate screwed up her eyes and tried to scrutinise Miranda's hair as she flicked it around in Colin's face, but the lights in the room were too bright and trying to stare over them was hurting her eyes.

The Love Dove came up behind Kate and tickled her side with its wing. She span around and glared at it. The bird feigned chuckling, its wing over its beak and moved along the stage to Larry where it collected two glittering envelopes.

'Couples, as our winners tonight, not only have you won yourselves passes through to the regional finals next month; you have also won the contents of one of these envelopes that Lovey is carrying. Both contain super prizes but one is a little bit extra special. So Lovey, do your little dance, spin yourself around and then we will give our winners Hayley and Anthony first choice,' Larry spoke.

Loud dance music began and the dove jigged up and down, shook its tail feathers and crossed and uncrossed its legs. It was all a bit pointless as the envelopes it was carrying under each wing never altered. Now really feeling the effects of all the alcohol she had consumed during the evening, Kate let out a laugh at the desperation of the whole event.

'So Hayley and Anthony, which wing?' Larry questioned in a serious voice, turning to the curly-haired duo.

'Oh Anthony, what do you think? Left has always been lucky for you and we live on the left-hand side of the street, don't we? What do you think?' Hayley questioned her partner seriously.

Kate couldn't help herself; she was overcome. She burst out laughing at the woman's stupidity and had to grab hold of Joel for support as she rocked on her high-heeled shoes.

'Are you OK?' he questioned, holding onto her hand.

'Is she insane? Left-hand side of the street?!' Kate said out loud, holding her sides as she laughed hysterically.

Hayley and Anthony gave Kate a short look of bemusement and then went back to concentrating their efforts on the Love Dove, who was flapping his wings in a frenzied fashion.

'Do you want to sit down?' Joel whispered.

'No I want to see what's in the envelope. Hurry up and choose, will you!' Kate ordered the other couple.

'We'll have the envelope under the left wing,' Anthony decided finally.

'Left wing Lovey, bring it here, lovely, thank you. OK, drum roll please – Hayley and Anthony, you have won – a voucher valid for twelve months for food from the Highbridge branch of Chunky Chicken. Yes, nuggets, strips, wings, chips and sides will all be yours on presentation of your voucher. Meals are limited to two main meals or one mega deal per week, other terms and conditions apply. Congratulations!' Larry exclaimed, passing the envelope to the Australians.

Hayley squealed excitedly and wrapped her arms around her partner, almost knocking him over.

'Give me the other envelope; what have we won? A twelve-month voucher for the off-licence would be good, no limitations,' Kate spoke loudly.

'Lovey, pass me the envelope under your right wing and let's see what Kate and Joel have won. Drum roll please,' Larry ordered as the lights dimmed.

Kate's mouth felt dry as she almost eagerly watched the host rip open the envelope and pull out what was inside.

'Kate and Joel, you have won – a weekend in the romance lodge when we take the competition to the next stage in Bournemouth. Yes, you will spend a weekend of luxury in your own log cabin complete with sauna and hot tub when we take over the Waterfield Country Park next month. This includes full use of all the facilities including pool, steam room, gymnasium, horse riding, archery, to name but a few. Relax in comfort and style, courtesy of Waterfield Country Park and our sponsors, Peterson Finance,' Larry announced to the room as everyone began applauding.

Larry handed the envelope to Kate and immediately, she began to laugh hysterically, unable to hold herself together any longer. She threw her arms around Joel and then felt the urge to be sick overwhelm her.

'I don't feel very well,' she admitted as her face drained of colour.

'Come on, let's get you home,' Joel said, holding her up and helping her to the side of the stage.

'I think there was something wrong with your water; I shouldn't have drunk it. Water on its own doesn't agree with me,' Kate informed him as they walked.

'I'm sure that must have been it,' Joel agreed.

## 8

It was midday on Saturday before Kate made it to Hermione's. She didn't remember getting home the night before. The last thing she remembered was being poked by a giant bird whilst she stood on a stage being stared at by her boss and one of her wealthiest clients. She had found the one hundred pounds and golden voucher when she had gone to make a cup of much-needed coffee. A weekend in a romance lodge... Suddenly, the whole sorry evening had come back to her. *Knowing Me Knowing You* – what had that all been about? She had drunk too much and she had probably made an arse of herself.

Hermione opened the door to her, fresh faced and full of life as usual. There was nothing worse than having competent, sober, happy-go-lucky people in your face when you felt like crap.

Hermione was wearing a flour-spattered apron and Kate immediately smelt the scent of freshly baked bread. It made her feel queasy.

'Hello Mrs TV Game Show Star!' Hermione announced far too loudly.

'What?' Kate replied, stepping into the house.

'I saw you last night on the telly! You kept that quiet, sweetie,' Hermione continued.

'I don't believe you saw it! It was on a satellite channel so far down the list, no one should have seen it, apart from maybe a tiny Asian village in the middle of nowhere,' Kate exclaimed in horror.

'I like alternative television. So, why didn't you tell me?' she repeated.

'Because I didn't know! The Lady Dragon set me up and it was awful,' Kate said as she led the way into the kitchen.

'I don't see how spending an evening with that hunk of a man could ever be awful. He looked amazing! That photo you had did not do him justice; he is to die for!' Hermione exclaimed.

'God, it was the worst night ever. Right before dinner, the Lady Dragon announces I've got to take part in this ridiculous quiz. Then the wine seemed to dry up, but then again, even that could never have been plentiful enough to drown the dreadfulness of everything,' Kate spoke, sitting down at the table.

'And Joel? I can't believe he was dreadful too,' Hermione said as she put the kettle on to boil.

'He was OK, nice enough, I guess; he did his job. Not sure the Lady Dragon believed we were a couple but then I told you that would happen the minute I saw his picture; he was too good-looking. I should have gone for someone less handsome, but it was late notice I guess and I couldn't have taken the one that looked like Dale Winton,' Kate replied with a heavy sigh.

'But you won! Well, you were second, you got one hundred pounds and a weekend in a romance lodge.'

'Hmm,' Kate answered.

'Well don't sound *too* excited! I wouldn't mind having a weekend in a romance lodge with him, I can tell you,' Hermione responded.

'Don't be stupid; we aren't going to go! Joel's an escort I paid to date me last night; he isn't my boyfriend,' Kate reminded, drumming her fingers on the table and trying to quell the sick feeling in her stomach.

'But you have to go; you're through to the next round.'

'Mione! I didn't want to enter the pathetic contest

in the first place. I only played along last night because the Lady Dragon and Frank Peterson were there. It was a one off, and there will be no repeat performance,' Kate stated definitely.

'But a weekend away would do you good,' Hermione spoke.

'Maybe, but I wouldn't choose to spend it standing on a stage holding hands with a stranger watching a huge fake dove lay golden eggs,' Kate answered.

'That bit was quite naff,' Hermione admitted.

'It was all *very* naff.'

'So what are you going to do with your golden voucher? Give it to the mad Australians who like to pretend they're sheep when they have sex?'

'Did they say that? How scary. No, I'm going to phone the production company. I'm going to tell them Joel and I have split up and it's up to them what they do with it. Perhaps they'll give it to the third placed couple,' Kate spoke.

'Oh no, not Mark and Sandra, I didn't like them at all. He kept winking at the camera and she had a moustache,' Hermione remarked.

'God, Mione, did you sit through it all?'

'Yes, with half a dozen cups of nettle tea and some carrot and parsnip crisps. Would you like some?'

'No thanks, they sound awful. I'd better take

Bethan off your hands and get home; I've got stuff to look at I've been putting off.'

'Well, Philip's taken all the children down the park so they can burn off some energy. Cyrus is here today and he's been driving me mad. He isn't just whispering now; he's stamping his feet as he does it which all but drowns out what he's trying to say completely,' Hermione informed.

'Hang on. I thought Philip was away. I wanted to borrow him, remember and you said no and made an excuse.'

'Change of plan, he's going relic hunting in a few weeks now. One of his team had an unexpected birth, two months early, baby boy, small but doing well. Anyway, it isn't as if the ancient treasures are going anywhere.'

'So was Bethan good? Didn't wake? Not up too early? Did she eat all her breakfast?'

'She was an absolute angel, as always.' Hermione reassured.

'Oh I'm so glad. Thanks so much for having her, Mione. Can I settle up with you next week – it's just it's not pay day until the twenty-fifth,' Kate spoke, a little embarrassed.

'Don't be silly, I don't want paying. Last night wasn't child-minding; last night was babysitting for a friend and I won't hear any more about it,' Hermione insisted.

'Thank you,' Kate replied.

'How are things financially if you don't mind me asking?'

'Fine. I won a hundred pounds, remember,' Kate answered, hiding her eyes.

'I'll read your tea leaves,' Hermione threatened.

'Things are tight but I'm managing. Must stop booking escorts, though; it isn't cheap,' Kate replied.

'Well, I have to say, I'm disappointed. I read the runes and I read the cards and they told me that last night was going to be the start of something for you,' Hermione said with a sigh.

'Oh, it was; it was the start of my investigation into whether or not the Lady Dragon wears a wig,' Kate said excitedly, a wicked smile crossing her face.

'What?! Oh tell all!' Hermione said, clapping her hands together in delight.

## 9
---

Kate's head was still thumping that evening when she put Bethan to bed. Although Philip had worn the children out at the park, Bethan had demanded game after game of hide and seek in the garden when they had got home. Trying not to die of boredom when her daughter hid in the same place was usually challenge enough, but it was infinitely worse when you felt like death.

'Mummy,' Bethan spoke, reaching up a hand and pulling at Kate's hair.

'Time for sleep now, Bethy. Give Mr Crisps a cuddle,' Kate spoke, handing her daughter her favourite bear.

Mr Crisps was so named because he was a limited-edition bear from a crisp manufacturer. Just three to-kens plus postage and packing. Bethan had been having a lot of bargain treats lately. Matthew had bought her a Steiff bear when she was born. It had been a show of wealth and he had told everybody and anybody about it. But the bear was sat on top of the wardrobe, still in its box, not played with. Kate thought it had an angry little face and she was terrified of Bethan swallowing the button from its ear.

'Teddy crisps,' Bethan said and hugged the bear into her.

'Night night, darling,' Kate said and stroked her daughter's hair, watching her eyes flicker closed.

Bethan laughed and smiled and Kate turned off the light and left the room. She closed her eyes and took a deep breath before descending the stairs. She knew what was waiting for her.

Her laptop was open on the table and next to it was a pile of urgent bills. There were almost a dozen. Electricity, water, gas, telephone, mobile phone, inter-net, council tax, etc. etc. There was a demand for al-most everything.

Kate bypassed the invoices, opened the fridge and took out a box. Tonight, it was chilli con carne, ready in three minutes. She slipped off the sleeve, pierced the container and put it in the microwave. She set it to cook, opened the fridge and took out the bottle of wine she had bought on the way back from Hermione's. Italian tonight, on a BOGOF, 12 per cent but as she had two for the price of one, she wouldn't feel too guilty if she had to open the second bottle.

She hurriedly opened it, poured herself a glass and drank half of it in one desperate gulp. The headache seemed to ease instantly.

She sat down at the laptop and began to go through the bills. She clicked onto the internet and logged into her bank's website to check her account. She knew she had saved two hundred pounds to cover the urgent bills plus there was the seventy-five pounds Matthew paid into her account every Friday for Bethan. Hopefully, it would be enough to pay everything that needed to be paid. If not, she would be back to a diet of tinned soup and Value bread for a week.

She clicked into her account information and the details came up. There was just the two hundred pounds in the account. Kate furrowed her brow and clicked into the statement of transactions. There had been nothing paid into her account from Matthew since the previous week. There was also a direct debit due to go out the next day.

The microwave beeped to inform her it had finished cooking the chilli. Kate looked at the account, totted up some figures on the calculator and stared at the screen. She couldn't afford to pay the bills. She could put some on her credit card but that was building up too, what with early-evening trips to the wine section of the supermarket and paying for Elite Escorts. But that apart, why hadn't Matthew's standing order gone through?

As she was reheating the chilli, she telephoned the bank, hoping against hope that there was some technical fault their end or that she had missed a bank holiday or something. But there was no explanation and there was no fault with her account. The money from Matthew hadn't been received and there was nothing stuck in the electronic system.

She didn't know what to do. She really needed the money, but that meant phoning Matthew. She couldn't phone him. She hadn't spoken to him since just after he left. He had phoned about a week after his departure, while she was still moping at home in front of CBeebies, cornflakes in her hair and an undressed Bethan on her lap. He'd given her his address and phone number and told her he had set up the standing order. He hadn't asked about Bethan; in fact, he hadn't even mentioned her name. The entire correspondence since had been through their solicitors and very quickly, the divorce had come through.

There had seemed little reason to interact at all after that.

Kate took out her address book from the drawer of the dresser, found the entry and stared at it. Matthew Baxter. Her husband's name in her address book in her handwriting, just like every other entry. It was just his details but seeing his name conjured up so many images. Maybe she was overreacting; it was obviously just an oversight. Maybe the money would be there tomorrow or in the week. She didn't want to phone him; she didn't want to hear his voice. She was afraid of what hearing it would do to her.

She picked up the phone. She put it down. She took a deep breath and composed herself. Why did thinking of him still do this to her? She was divorced from him; he had left her and Bethan. He was part of her past and nothing more. He had abandoned them.

She snatched up the phone and dialled in the number. It rang and she waited, holding her breath.

'Hello.'

The sound of a woman's voice shocked her and she didn't know what to do. Should she hang up? Who was this woman? Should she speak? What should she say? She cleared her throat and tried to compose herself.

'Oh hello is, er, Matthew there, please?'

'Who's calling?' the woman asked in secretarial tones.

'It's Kate.'

There was complete silence at the other end after she had said her name and she could tell the mood of the woman had changed. It was an almost hostile silence until she eventually spoke.

'Matt, it's *her*.'

*Her*?! Kate had never been referred to as a 'her' before. A 'her' was someone despised; 'her' was a reference you would use if you were speaking about someone playing the part of a mistress to your adulterous spouse. But she wasn't a mistress; she was an ex-wife and she was the injured party here. Kate cringed and felt angry and upset at the same time, tears pricking her eyes. She didn't want to be doing this but she had to, for Bethan.

'Hello,' Matthew spoke.

Kate's heart flipped just hearing him and she was mad at herself for feeling that way. He had a nice voice, soft and low, sultry even. And she used to love the way he laughed, a mellow, deep laugh like his vocal chords had been soaked in honey. She hadn't spoken and she needed to.

'Oh hello Matthew, I was just online checking my bank account and your standing order hasn't gone through this week,' Kate spoke hurriedly, pushing the words out as fast as she could.

'No,' Matthew replied, not sounding surprised.

'Oh, you knew? Was there a problem with your bank?' Kate enquired.

'No.'

'Oh, well what's happened? I mean...' Kate began, sensing a flatness in his voice that she barely recognised.

'I can't pay you any more, Kate; I don't have the money,' Matthew answered.

His voice definitely wasn't sultry now; it was matter-of-fact and cool.

Kate felt like she had been shot. What had he said? He couldn't pay her any more? No, he can't have said that; they had a long-standing agreement.

'I... I don't understand,' Kate replied meekly, her chest pounding.

'I can't afford it, what with bills and the car and my flat. I just can't afford to pay you any more,' Matthew repeated in a business-like tone.

'But Matthew, Bethan needs the money. She needs clothes and nappies and food and—' Kate began, trying hard not to cry.

'You've got a good job; ask for a pay rise. Anyway, I told you, I never wanted a kid in the first place. I don't see why I should pay for something I didn't want,' Matthew spoke.

The words cut at Kate like little arrows fired at her heart. This wasn't the man in their wedding pictures. This wasn't the man who waltzed her on the dance floor to Celine Dion and kindly held the best man's head over the toilet as he puked up before the cake-cutting. This was someone else; this was the man who had pre-packed his belongings and left her standing tearfully in the kitchen trying to ignore the depressing wails of Chris Martin.

'How can you say that, Matthew? She's your daughter. Why doesn't that mean anything to you?'

'I don't want to talk to you about this, Kate.'

'But we have to talk about it. I need some financial help from you; it's what was agreed in court. You have to help pay for her; it's the law.'

'Look, I can't afford it, it's as simple as that, sorry,' Matthew said, not sounding as if he was sorry at all.

'Matthew, I really think—' Kate started.

The phone went silent. He had hung up.

Kate looked at the phone, unable to believe what had just happened. He wasn't going to pay her any-thing. He didn't care about Bethan; he had a new flat, obviously a new girlfriend and a new life. Kate and Bethan were history, he had moved on and he wasn't looking back. He had hung up on her; put the phone down like she was a cold caller from Calcutta.

Suddenly, she was overcome with grief all over again. She burst into tears and waves of sobbing rode over her. She put the phone down, sat on the sofa and cried into her hands until they were saturated with tears. What was she going to do? Her beautiful little girl had a father who had disowned her and a mother who was struggling to make ends meet. She had wanted the best for her, a good, solid start in life with a mum and dad who adored her and could give her everything she needed. The reality was the complete opposite. It wasn't fair, she didn't deserve this and she didn't know how to get out of it.

But very quickly, aided by another glass of wine, the hostility Matthew had in his voice hit her like a train. It had been like he was talking to someone he hated, not the mother of his child, not someone he had shared a life and a marriage with. Kate hurriedly wiped the tears off her face and wiped her nose with the back of her hand. She picked up the photo frame that contained their wedding picture. Calmly, she opened the back and took out the image. She looked at it, her smile, her beautiful dress, Matthew next to her. The wavy hair and boyish looks. He had held her hand so tightly. It had all been a lie, all his declarations of love and vows of eternal devotion. Looking at the photo now just made her feel sick. She ripped it harshly, first in half and then into tiny little pieces until there was nothing visible left.

Then, almost controlled, she went back over to her laptop and typed *Child Support Agency* into the search engine. She would not let him ruin Bethan's start, and she was not going to be walked over any more.

# 10

'Morning,' Kate spoke cheerily as Hermione opened the door to her on Monday morning.

'Ooh, someone sounds happy. What did you get up to yesterday? Any more television shows I should know about? Hello, Bethan sweetie,' Hermione greeted, lifting up the little girl and giving her a kiss.

'God no, no I spoke to Matthew on Saturday night and briefly to his new girlfriend,' Kate stated in a matter-of-fact manner.

'Daddy,' Bethan suddenly announced at the mention of his name.

Kate swallowed and ruffled her daughter's hair, a pang of hurt tugging at her. If only she knew.

'I have a grapefruit tea infusing; come into the

kitchen. Brook! Can you take Bethan to do drawing with you for a minute, please?' Hermione asked her daughter as she appeared in the hallway.

Kate followed Hermione into the kitchen and sat down at the table.

'So what happened? Why did you phone Matthew? I thought you two hadn't spoken for months,' Hermione said as she prepared the tea.

'We haven't. He hadn't paid in Bethan's money this week; there was nothing from him in my bank. I thought it was an oversight or a mistake at his end but no, I phoned him and he told me he doesn't intend to pay anything towards Bethan's care. In fact, what he said was he didn't see why he had to pay for something he never wanted in the first place, or words to that effect,' Kate explained.

'Oh Kate!' Hermione exclaimed in shock.

'Nice thing to say about your daughter, isn't it? Well, I cried and I cried and then I ripped up one of our wedding photos and felt mildly better and then I thought, what a complete and utter bastard, how dare you. How dare you treat me and Bethan like that, like we don't matter. So I got on the internet and I made an online application to the Child Support Agency. I don't care if he can't make ends meet; I am having some of what he *does* have for my daughter,'

Kate spoke firmly, her eyes flashing with deter-mination.

'Good for you, it's only right,' Hermione agreed, putting a cup on the table in front of Kate.

'And I have been far too sentimental about him for far too long a time. There was nothing there from him; he couldn't care less about us now. And after what he said about Bethan...' Kate said, tears welling up.

'So what are you going to do about money in the meantime? If waiving my fee for a while will help then consider it done,' Hermione spoke.

'No, I won't hear of that; don't even think it. You do too much for me already giving Bethan a cooked meal every day and treats she can't have at home, no. I phoned my Aunt Jess yesterday, I told her the situa-tion, every sordid little detail, and I asked her for a loan. I didn't want to do it, I mean we don't really get on, but I have to think of Bethan and not my stupid pride. And, as I suspected she was more than happy to lend me the money and that should tide us over for a bit,' Kate explained.

'And the long-term plan?'

'Promise you won't laugh or say I told you so.'

'Would I ever?'

'I'm going to go to the next round of *Knowing Me Knowing You*, I'm going to get through to the finals and

I'm going to win. I am going to win that hundred thousand pounds if it kills me,' Kate announced.

Hermione let out a scream of laughter and put her hand to her mouth.

'I know I said I would rather die than do anything like that again, but I have a daughter, I have a shit for an ex-husband and I need the money. Think how much that would pay off my mortgage,' Kate explained, taking a sip of her tea.

'I think it's a marvellous idea and it sounds like you've thought it all through.'

'I've done nothing but think about it all night.'

'Now, I don't want to put a dampener on your good mood but doesn't *Knowing Me Knowing You* require a couple?'

'Yes of course, that's probably going to be the hardest bit. I'm going to have to call Elite Escorts, speak to Joel and try to persuade him to enter into this mad scam with me. I don't even remember getting home the last time we went out so I don't expect him to be pleased to hear from me,' Kate said.

'And will you be able to pay for his time? I mean, there'll be two weekends at least, plus other nights out to go over questions and things.'

'Hmm, that's another stumbling block I've got to get over. I have to get him to do it all for a cut of the prize money, a very small cut and no guarantee of us winning. How do you think that's going to go down?' Kate asked her friend.

'How about a different way to raise some cash? How about having some candle parties? Or becoming an Avon representative; lots of my ladies do that for a bit extra. I mean, game shows are...' Hermione began.

'You don't think he'll do it.'

'I think you might have to spend some time on your pitch,' Hermione told her.

*  *  *

When Kate arrived at Randall's, everyone she said hello to or passed in the corridor looked at her with a wry smile on their face. She checked her reflection in the lift mirror expecting to see Marmite on her cheek or felt pen on the collar of her shirt, but there was nothing odd about her appearance that she could immediately identify.

However, when she walked into the Probate room, she was greeted by all her colleagues stood around her desk, cheering and whooping. The desk itself was covered in heart-shaped confetti, balloons and streamers and there was a big banner on the wall proclaiming, *Well Done Kate.*

'God, what did I do? Don't tell me, we got the IHT refund on the Whitchurch case,' Kate said, putting her jacket on the back of her chair and admiring the decorations.

'Nothing to do with work, as you well know. I've been telling everyone who wasn't at the Peterson Finance dinner about your amazing performance on Friday night in *Knowing Me Knowing You*,' Miranda spoke, coming out of her office and standing with the group, toying with the ends of her hair.

'Oh, that, hmm,' Kate replied, not really liking all the attention.

'She was marvellous, and so was her partner, the lovely Joel. I have to say, I'm an incy bit jealous of you, Kate, having bagged a gorgeous hunk like that. Honestly girls, you will not see a more honed pin-up, not even on the cover of *Men's Health*, and he was such a gentleman too,' Miranda explained.

'He snores and he leaves the lid off the toothpaste,' Kate said hurriedly, smiling at her workmates.

'Anyway, we just wanted to say well done Kate for your success and for getting into the next round. If there's enough interest, we will arrange transport to the next show in Bournemouth and we just know you're going to do equally well there,' Miranda spoke in her well-practised head of department tones.

Everyone clapped, much to Kate's embarrassment.

'Right, perfect, back to work everyone. And Kate, when you've got a minute, could you come through,' Miranda asked in a serious tone.

'Yes, of course, I'll just clear some balloons,' Kate said, pulling out her chair and making confetti fall on the floor.

Miranda saying 'when you've got a minute, could you come through' always filled everyone with dread. She didn't tell you what it was about, and because she didn't tell you, it made you think of all the awful things it could be, like getting your P45, having her point out a mistake you had made on something that was too late to rectify, etc. And she knew this, which was why she didn't elaborate; it was all about power and control. Miranda loved nothing more than control.

Kate knocked on Miranda's office door and waited to be summonsed.

'Come in,' she called, like a high court judge directing barristers to enter Chambers.

Kate opened the door and offered her boss one of her 'yes I'm absolutely fine, thanks for asking' smiles.

'Would you like to sit?' Miranda offered, saying it like an order rather than a request.

Kate sat down and her eyes were immediately

drawn to the file on Miranda's desk which had red pen scrawled all over a set of accounts.

'I was just looking at the Prestwick file,' Miranda said and she ran her manicured fingers over the spreadsheet on top of the file.

'Oh yes,' Kate replied, racking her brain and trying to remember the details of the case.

'I have to say Kate, the accounts you supposedly finalised for me are very shoddy,' Miranda stated.

Kate didn't know how to respond. The words hung in the air. She was sure she had checked the Prestwick accounts thoroughly, even for space between columns, full stops in the right places, underlining. All of which were usually more important to Miranda than the numerical accuracy.

'They don't even balance,' Miranda added.

'They do,' Kate snapped back immediately and slightly unexpectedly.

If there was one thing she knew, it was that they would balance. She sweated blood over every set of accounts until they were right to the last penny. She'd never presented an unbalanced set to Miranda in her life.

'I'm afraid they don't; see for yourself,' Miranda spoke and she passed Kate the file for her to look at.

Kate could feel Miranda's eyes boring into her as

she checked her figure work. Miranda was right; the accounts didn't balance. She couldn't understand it. She had spent hours on them; everything had been perfect. She was certain they had been absolutely faultless the last time she looked at them. But maybe she was wrong. She had been distracted lately, not on top of her game; maybe she had missed something.

'Now I know things haven't been easy for you lately and I can't begin to imagine how hard it is to bring up Bethan without a father there, but you really have to start paying more attention to your work. Perhaps, now your personal life is on the up, we can expect a little more dedication?' Miranda said mockingly.

Bitch.

'Miranda, I don't know how these accounts got like this. They were finalised, they balanced, I did the memo and put them in your tray,' Kate tried to explain, feeling desperately inadequate.

'Yes, I have the memo; it was attached to these haphazard, unbalanced accounts,' Miranda replied.

'Well, I just don't know what to say.'

'There's no need to apologise, I've called the client and explained the delay. Perhaps you could prioritise them for today, together with the Lawrence papers, I need those by lunch time,' Miranda said with a smile that could advertise Max Factor.

Kate looked at her boss, not knowing how to respond. And then Miranda tossed her hair backwards and for a brief second, all Kate could think of was whether or not the blonde mass of hair really was a wig. She knew she was staring but she couldn't help herself. She didn't know whether it was her turn to talk; she was too focused on the follicles.

'I'll leave it with you then,' Miranda said, making it clear their conversation was over.

'Yes, OK, fine,' Kate replied, getting to her feet and turning to the door.

'Perfect,' Miranda ended, turning her back on Kate.

Kate stepped back into the main room and let out a deep breath as she hugged the Prestwick file to her chest. She wasn't relishing looking at the accounts again; they had taken her long enough to sort through in the first place. Plus she hadn't started on the Lawrence papers yet. Since when had they become urgent?

'Everything OK?' Lynn Charles asked, stopping opposite Kate as she took another deep breath, hoping to force in oxygen and force out the realisation she was going to be looking at figures for the rest of the day.

Lynn was Kate's secretary. She was a young, slight blonde who was extremely efficient in everything she did. It was Lynn's organisational skills that had got Kate through the trying time when Matthew first left. She had screened all Kate's phone calls, arranged only the most urgent appointments and taken on anything else she could to help. Despite being an excellent secretary and a reliable friend, Lynn did tend to talk the back limb off a mule, usually around the water cooler where the whole world could hear. Discretion was an unknown entity to her.

'Yes, fine – well, actually no,' Kate admitted, turning to head back to her desk.

'What's the Lady Dragon said now?' Lynn questioned in a loud whisper, following Kate.

'Shh! Don't call her that; someone else will hear you and you'll get in trouble and then *I'll* get in trouble and then we'll *both* be in big trouble,' Kate spoke, her eyes wide as she looked around to check no one had heard.

'Sorry.'

'Do you remember the Prestwick accounts? You did the memo for me?' Kate asked, showing Lynn the file as she put it down on her desk and splattered more confetti on the floor.

'Yes, I remember, they were thirty-seven pages long

– took me ages to photocopy because the Lady Dragon can't have even a hint of a paper crease on them,' Lynn responded.

'Yes, well, these thirty-seven pages weren't the thirty-seven pages I finalised, I'm sure of it,' Kate told her, passing the information over.

'I can easily check; I save a copy of everything I do in a separate directory. So even if the main directory has been changed, I'll be able to compare the two,' Lynn said.

'Oh Lynn, you're a life-saver; could you have a look? I mean, it could be that I'm imagining I ever finalised them but I'm sure I spent at least three hours of my life staring at these figures.'

'I'll have a look. The Lawrence file is there, by the way; the Lady Dragon said you'd need it,' Lynn spoke.

'Great,' Kate answered sarcastically.

'So, I hear you have a new boyfriend,' Lynn commented.

'Shh!' Kate exclaimed, looking over her shoulder at her colleagues in the hope they were all too busy working to pay any attention to Lynn's loud voice.

'I think the Lady Dragon is bristling about it. Word in the office is that Colin Sykes is dating one of the trainees,' Lynn spoke in slightly more hushed tones.

'Really! Now that will have got her back up for certain. She's been sniffing around him since he became a partner.'

'Mm, so expect a foul mood for a few weeks, until she sets her sights on another victim. My money's on Andrew Kent,' Lynn said, speaking of one of the other partners in Randall's and touching her nose with her finger.

'Isn't he married?' Kate enquired.

'Wife left him last summer. Watch this space.'

# 11

Highbridge Leisure Centre was only five years old, built between the Princess Diana, Queen of Hearts memorial garden and the BMX ramps. It had a leisure pool, a twenty-five metre pool, a large sports hall and, as Kate was finding out, it had state of the art gym facilities with giant flatscreen TVs all across the walls, some showing European football matches, others blaring out the latest hits on MTV.

Getting a message to Joel through Elite Escorts had proved to be a fruitless task. The receptionist insisted that she couldn't give out any personal information and in fact, the only thing she *could* do was book an appointment, which required immediate payment. So here Kate was, in her lunch hour, in the middle of a gym, somewhere she hadn't ever set foot in, feeling awkward and out of place amongst the fit individuals around her.

It was so noisy, she could hardly hear herself think and she couldn't see Joel anywhere. This was definitely where he worked; he'd told her. She couldn't find anyone else to ask; they were all busy running or stepping or cycling ridiculously fast, especially the twenty or so people pedalling and being yelled at by a psychotic woman wearing a headset. She was just about to give up when she saw him at the side of the room, doing sit-ups with a pretty, dark-haired girl.

She took a deep breath, trying to run over in her mind what she was going to say to convince him to help her. But as she moved closer, seeing how fantastic he looked in a very tight top and shorts, all her carefully thought-out plans went out of the window. He was never going to agree to this – why would he? It was a mad plan.

Before she got too close, she turned abruptly and found herself walking into a luckily unoccupied rowing machine. She banged her shin; the pull bar unfastened and made a loud clank as it hit the metal frame.

Joel and the woman he was working out with both sat up and Joel quickly came to her assistance.

'Are you OK?' he asked, arriving at her side.

'Fine, thank you. Hello, again,' she greeted, her cheeks reddening as she turned to face him.

'Kate,' he replied, surprised to see her.

'Don't worry, I haven't come to join the gym or to stalk you or anything. I just wondered if I could talk to you, for a minute, in private. I have – a proposition for you – it's nothing illegal or dirty or anything like you think, I don't think. But if I could just ask you, I...' Kate began.

'Sure, I'm intrigued to know what it is. Susie, do another twenty and I'll be back with you in a minute,' Joel called to his training companion.

He led the way to the end of the room where the water cooler was positioned. The electrical hum of the equipment lessened. He filled a plastic cup with water and offered it to Kate. She shook her head and Joel took a sip.

'I should have remembered, all but allergic to water, aren't you?' he spoke with a smile.

'Hmm, look, about Friday night – first of all, I want to apologise for whatever happened then. I don't really remember all of it – well, the getting home part mostly; that's very blurry – and I want to say sorry if I did anything or said anything that was insulting or rude or in any way inappropriate,' Kate began, sweeping her hair behind her ears and trying to avoid Joel's huge eyes.

'I think it's the taxi driver that needs the apology, not me,' Joel responded with a smile.

'God, really? I don't want to know any more. Anyway, I'm sure he's had much worse on a Friday night. At least I wasn't sick in his cab. I wasn't, was I?'

'Well...'

'Stop! Enough! OK, right, the thing is, I have a bit of a financial problem at the moment and things with my husband – my ex-husband – are a little bit difficult. Basically, I really need to find a whole lot of money so that I don't have to rely on him any more,' Kate started, shifting from foot to foot as she tried to say what she wanted to say. This was so difficult!

'I see,' Joel replied.

'OK, good. Right, well, I know Friday night was a disaster and I know I wasn't the easiest of dates, but when I thought about how to get a lot of money easily and quickly without robbing a bank, I thought about *Knowing Me Knowing You*. I know, it's crazy, it was the most terrible thing I've had to endure but I just thought I, that is, *we*, shouldn't throw away the chance of winning that money,' Kate blurted out as best as she was able.

'I'm sensing there's a "but" coming on,' Joel spoke, drinking more of his water.

'No, well, yes, maybe. The thing is, I can't do it without you, can I? I mean, it was us who got through to the next round, Kate and Joel – I can't really do it alone. I'm sure they don't allow for break-ups in the rules and answering questions on your own wouldn't really work with the format, would it?'

'No.'

'Look, I'll just say it. I can't do it without you but I can't afford to pay you for your time – you know – like dates and stuff. So I thought maybe we could strike a deal with the winnings. If we win, which we probably won't and then neither of us will have got anything out of it, but I thought an eighty/twenty split in my favour – seeing as it was my connections with Frank Peterson that got us into the game show in the first place.'

Joel didn't reply.

'Look, I know you don't really know me at all and I know that there's absolutely no reason why you should give your services free of charge to someone you barely know, but I'm not asking for me – I'm asking for my daughter. This is all for her and I'm just being a mum and trying to do all I can to give her the best I can,' Kate spoke, her eyes welling up with tears.

'Sixty/forty in your favour and I'll do it,' Joel replied.

'You'll do it?! Sixty/forty? Well – how about seventy/thirty in my favour. I mean...' Kate began, trying not to sound too elated as she bargained.

'Sixty/forty is my only offer; there's no guarantee we'll win and remember, you can't do it without me,' Joel reminded.

Kate hesitated, mulling the idea over in her mind. She hadn't expected him to agree to do it; sixty thousand pounds would go a long way to lightening her current financial burden and Joel could end up not getting anything out of it at all. There was only one answer she could give.

'OK,' Kate agreed and she put out her hand to him.

Joel leaned forward and kissed her on the cheek, which immediately made Kate blush. She still had her coat on and the gym suddenly felt very warm.

'We're supposed to be dating. If this is really going to work, you're going to have to stop trying to shake hands with me,' Joel told her with a smile.

'Sorry, it just feels a bit strange – but I can work on it,' Kate insisted with a determined nod.

'Good. I'd better get back to Susie or she'll be completely crunched out,' Joel said, reminding her he had a client waiting.

'Oh OK, yes. Um, do you want to come round for dinner or something? I'll cook – well, I'll try to cook – and we can talk about a strategy,' Kate suggested awkwardly.

'Sure. When?'

'Um, I don't know. Are you free tomorrow night?' Kate asked.

'Tomorrow's fine,' Joel said, heading away from her.

'Good, right, well, about eight? Wait! Don't you need my address? It's—' Kate began, trying not to shout too loudly.

'Thirty-one Waverley Road. You really don't remember the taxi ride home, do you?' Joel commented, smiling at her.

'Apparently not,' Kate answered.

'I'll be there, eight o'clock,' Joel replied. He joined Susie and encouraged her off the floor and onto a treadmill.

'OK, good,' Kate said to herself.

She watched him as he spoke to his client and got onto the treadmill next to her. And then she turned away and headed for the door, smiling gleefully to herself. He had agreed to her plan – things were looking up.

## 12

'He said yes,' Kate announced to Hermione that evening.

'Who said yes?' Hermione asked as she tried to loosen a stamping Cyrus from her skirt.

'Joel,' Kate said, picking Bethan up and swinging her around.

'God! No! He said yes?! For no fee? Cyrus sweetie, could you stop doing that? Mummy will be here in a minute to pick you up. Would you like a breadstick or some raisins?' Hermione offered the boy.

'Chocolate,' Cyrus whispered so quietly, it was barely audible over his loud, drumming feet.

'No chocolate sweetie; we don't have chocolate

here, do we? You could have an apple, how about that?' Hermione bargained.

'Chocolate,' Cyrus whispered again, his large, black eyes glaring at Hermione.

'Chocolate isn't very good for you, Cyrus; it'll give you spots and make your teeth fall out,' Kate offered helpfully.

Cyrus let out a high-pitched screeching noise and fell to the floor. He rolled up into a ball and began to sob.

'There there, come on now, come and see what we've got in Hermione's cupboard. How about an organic flapjack?' Hermione offered.

Cyrus got up off the floor and sniffed, as if deciding what to do next.

'They eat these at Hogwarts,' Hermione said, holding the flapjack out to him.

'Hogwarts,' Cyrus whispered, his face turning up into a smile.

The doorbell rang not a moment too soon.

'That will be your mummy, Cyrus. Let's get your coat,' Hermione said, giving the boy the treat, gathering up his things and leading the way down the hall to the door.

When Hermione came back into the room, she slumped down at the table and let out a heavy sigh.

'That child is going to be the death of me; he's been an absolute horror all day. Whispering darkly, like he's something out of *The Exorcist*, drumming his feet on the floor, wanting things he isn't supposed to have. He has numerous intolerances but I'm getting intolerant to him,' Hermione said, putting her head in her hands.

'Where are the others?' Kate asked, referring to Hermione's children, Heather, Sky and Brook.

'My mother's taken them to the big Asda. She does that every so often, rings up after school without warning, whisks them off and when they come back, they've been spoiled rotten, had cheap, all-day break-fasts for tea and have a whole new wardrobe of clothes each. I shouldn't complain really, should I? Oh Bethan, at least I had you here to look after me,' Hermione said, smiling at the little girl.

'Joel said yes,' Kate repeated her announcement from earlier.

'Ah! Joel said yes. Yes, how exciting. So what's the strategy? What plans do you have to ensure you take the title of winners of *Knowing Me Knowing You* 2011?' Hermione asked her.

'Well, I haven't actually thought too much about that yet. I had been working on my case to argue should he say no. But I thought that we probably need to know a bit more about each other at the very least – so I've invited him to dinner tomorrow night,' Kate informed.

Hermione exploded into a fit of laughter that vibrated the table and almost had Kate reaching for her ears.

'You can't cook!' Hermione announced, laughing hard.

'I can.'

'Microwaving things doesn't count,' Hermione replied.

'I don't microwave everything,' Kate answered, offended.

'Well granted no, not salad. What's on your menu for tonight then?'

'I haven't decided yet.'

'Bet it comes in a little plastic tray with film to pierce.'

'Those meals are quick, easy and nutritious.'

'Those meals are full of hidden fats, salts and sugars.'

'And they taste delicious when complemented with lots of white wine.'

'Oh Bethan, what are we going to do with your mummy? What are you planning to cook Joel then? I mean, he isn't going to want to go through all this for a piping hot on the outside, lukewarm in the middle cannelloni,' Hermione spoke.

'I don't know. I have all day tomorrow to think about it.'

'But you'll need to go shopping to buy the ingredients – you need to decide on a recipe.'

'Well I don't know, maybe I shouldn't have said dinner. But I thought it would be better to be at home, not seen in public so we don't have to do any of the pretend kissing he does and I won't try and shake hands with him which apparently is what I do.'

'He kisses you – yum.'

'Well come on, you've insulted my cooking abilities; what am I going to cook him for dinner? I so obviously need help.'

'Toast,' Bethan piped up, bouncing up and down on Kate's knee excitedly.

Hermione let out another laugh and Kate couldn't help but smile at her happy daughter.

'She might have hit the nail on the head there; toast might be your safest bet. Well done, Bethan,' Hermione responded, clapping her hands.

'I'm not talking to you about it any more,' Kate answered.

'Oh come on, let me help you. Now, I'm sure I have a really simple recipe for chicken here. That wasn't meant to sound patronising by the way but it is fool-proof,' Hermione insisted and she began to rifle through a pile of papers on her sideboard.

'I can cook, I have recipe books, I just haven't used them for a while, that's all,' Kate replied grumpily.

'Ah, here we are: chicken in a chasseur-style sauce. All you need is chicken, mushrooms, onions, a red pepper, a small amount of wine, some flour and some stock. Here you go,' Hermione said, passing Kate a piece of paper.

'Thanks,' Kate answered, glancing at the before and after photos with little interest.

'And if you need any help during the cooking process, you can always call me,' Hermione offered kindly.

'I'll be fine,' Kate assured her with a smile.

* * *

As soon as she left Hermione's house, Kate rushed to the supermarket to pick up the ingredients for the chicken chasseur recipe.

Bethan got distracted by the children's magazines and started to scream every time Kate moved the trolley away from the section. Peace only reigned when *Charlie and Lola* was handed over to her.

Screwed-up recipe in hand, Kate rushed around the shop, Bethan ripping the magazine to pieces. She picked up the ingredients as quickly as she could before it started to get too close to bed time. Then she got distracted by the wine section. Australian was a third off and there was a three for ten pounds offer on a selection of reds. Red wine wasn't a favourite of hers but she didn't know what Joel preferred. She should ask him; they might need to know for the contest and the more she knew about him, the better.

She grabbed three reds and three whites, ran back to the veg section for an onion and headed for the checkout. Bethan had almost succeeded in ripping the magazine into tiny pieces and was now content poking bits of paper into her mouth.

'Beth! Don't do that, darling; you mustn't eat it,' Kate ordered, trying to manhandle the paper from her hands and poking a finger in her daughter's mouth to get rid of anything inside.

Bethan began to scream and kick her feet against the trolley in temper. She made a grab for what was left of the magazine and screamed again as Kate quickly moved it out of her reach.

'Do you want some help with your packing?' Kirsty, the very young-looking cashier asked.

Kate was very familiar with Kirsty because she

always seemed to be on the checkout Kate chose. She had eight earrings in her left ear, bitten fingernails and was without a doubt having some sort of relationship with Wayne who worked behind the deli and always seemed to find an excuse to come over.

'Oh no thanks, we'll be fine. Stop it, Bethan!' Kate ordered, looking sternly at her daughter as she put her items on the conveyor belt.

Bethan held her breath, waited until she had turned purple and then let out the scream of all screams. It was like the cry of someone who had just had their entire body deep-fried. Everyone turned to stare. Other mothers in the queue with seemingly angelic children in their trolleys waited with bated breath to see what she was going to do. OAPs with slightly more sympathy on their faces gave her a hopeful smile and two young men carrying four-packs of lager just smirked her way, looking youthful and smug.

'That will be thirty-five forty-eight please,' Kirsty announced as Bethan continued to scream and Kate bagged her shopping up.

Kate handed Kirsty her debit card and shook a packet of pasta up and down to calm Bethan.

'When we get home, Bethy, we'll get you in your

pyjamas, get you some lovely warm milk and watch *Ben and Holly's Little Kingdom,'* Kate spoke softly.

'Could you enter your pin number?'

'And when we've watched *Ben and Holly*, Mummy will take you and Mr Crisps up to bed and we'll read all about Tiger,' Kate said, tickling Bethan's tummy as the scream turned into a meek whimper.

'Er, have you got another card? This one's been refused,' Kirsty piped up in the loudest voice imaginable.

She could only have said it louder if she had yelled it into a loud hailer. Or she had morphed into Lynn.

Kate looked at Kirsty. She was holding her card out to her and chewing her gum up and down, flashing her tongue stud.

'What?' Kate asked, not believing what she had heard.

'Card's been declined – insufficient funds. Have you got another method of payment or shall I get someone to put the stuff back?' Kirsty boomed like Brian Blessed.

'No, no, of course not – um, here,' Kate said as she hurriedly dived into her purse and pulled out her credit card.

The humiliation! She had two hundred pounds in the bank last night; what had gone out since then? She thought she had got the timings of direct debits sorted out now. She entered the pin and held her breath, waiting for confirmation of the transaction and the sound of Kirsty's voice clarifying that all was well.

'That's fine – remove your card now,' Kirsty told her in almost a whisper.

Kate swiftly took the card out of the chip and pin machine and put it back in her purse. It felt as though everyone was looking at her. Her, the useless single mother with no money in her bank account and a kid that screams blue murder. A few months before, she would have looked and tutted and thought herself superior. Not any more.

When she got outside, it was raining. She hurriedly pushed the trolley to the car, struggled to get Bethan's legs untangled from the seat and literally threw her daughter into her car seat before she got too wet.

Bethan grinned up at her, wet faced with a happy smile, still holding the remnants of the *Charlie and Lola* magazine.

Kate felt a shiver run over her. The magazine – she hadn't paid for it.

She undid Bethan, put her over her shoulder and sprinted back into the shop as heavy rain began to soak them both. She ran up to Kirsty's checkout, dripping water all over the conveyor belt and butting into the queue.

'I'm so sorry, I forgot to pay for the magazine. Don't worry, I have cash and I've still got the barcode,' Kate announced and she offered Kirsty the smallest strip of paper from the front of the magazine containing the magic numbers.

'D'you want a bag for that?' Kirsty enquired.

## 13

The next night, Kate stared at her cooker. She knew how to work the hob but she wasn't really up to speed with the oven. She obviously knew how to turn it on and set the temperature but she wasn't at all au fait with the timer or the various other settings she was sure Hermione probably used on an hourly basis.

It didn't matter for the chasseur but she had bought garlic bread and it was frozen and she hadn't known whether to defrost it or not before cooking. Garlic bread she had decided went with everything and even if Joel didn't like it, she could always polish it off herself.

And you couldn't go wrong with a Sarah Lee

chocolate gateau for pudding. Who didn't like stuff made by Sarah Lee?

She had already started to sample the Australian white, some of which was destined for the dinner. She looked at the recipe. *Cut the chicken into chunks of approximately two centimetres in diameter, heat oil in a pan, fry chicken until sealed* (what did that mean?), *roughly chop the onion and the mushrooms.*

The phone rang and Kate put down the recipe and picked up the handset.

'Hello.'

'I can't believe you've done this,' Matthew's voice spoke angrily.

'Hello,' Kate repeated, not knowing what else to say.

She thought perhaps if she pretended she didn't recognise who it was, he would say something else and not sound so mad. She knew what this was about.

'I've had a phone call from the Child Support Agency. Do you know how much they want me to pay?! Almost five hundred pounds a month! Five hundred!' Matthew continued.

'Oh,' Kate responded, trying to keep the delight out of her voice.

Almost five hundred pounds! That was a lot. She could buy something frivolous like Heinz baked beans instead of supermarket own brand with a sum like that.

'It's crazy! I can't afford to pay that sort of money. I have a flat and bills and Amanda has—' Matthew ranted.

'Amanda. Who's Amanda?' Kate questioned, anger burning her throat as a name was put to the horrible voice that had called her a 'her'.

'I can't afford five hundred a month Kate; you know how much I earn,' Matthew replied, deliberately avoiding the question.

'You should have thought about that before you stopped the standing order. Anyway, exactly what does Amanda have that you need to pay for ahead of paying for your daughter?' Kate questioned, rage building up.

'It doesn't matter, I can't pay it and I've told them that. Look, can we try and be grown up about this? Let's not involve the CSA. Let's arrange something between us,' Matthew suggested to her, the tone of his voice changing immediately. It was like an actor switching roles halfway through a performance.

'What, like you reinstating the standing order?' Kate asked, picking up her wine and taking a long swig from it.

She had the upper hand here now; she was dictating proceedings for once.

'Well, yes, but not for as much – maybe fifty pounds a week or something?'

'No,' Kate replied immediately.

'Come on Kate, it would be something. I really can't afford to pay the CSA what they want,' Matthew spoke.

'That isn't my problem and I think, if you don't pay, they just take it out of your wages,' Kate responded coldly.

'Kate, don't do this. Please, I mean, I wouldn't be able to live,' Matthew said in a small and pitiful voice she had never heard before.

'Goodbye,' Kate said and she put the phone down, feeling in control for the first time in a long time.

She was glad he would struggle. Wasn't she struggling just to maintain herself and Bethan? Him having a new girlfriend with expensive tastes wasn't really an unavoidable expense as far as she was concerned and she was certain the CSA would take the same view.

Unfortunately, the feeling of control didn't last more than five minutes. She prepared the chicken as best she could and then Bethan started screaming loudly, lying on the floor and kicking her legs in the air. Having placated her with *Teletubbies* and a rowdy rendition of 'Polly Put The Kettle On', the chicken was now sticking to the bottom of the pan. Desperate, Kate phoned Hermione.

'The chicken's sticking to the pan, it doesn't say how much flour to add to this stock stuff and what does "roughly chop" mean? Does it just mean I go at it like a woodcutter?' Kate blurted down the phone as soon as Hermione picked up.

'More oil in the pan but you only need to fry it until it's sealed. That means just until the outside of the chicken turns white, then add the other in-gredients.'

'And the stock and the flour? Bethan, don't put that in your mouth, it's dirty,' Kate spoke as Bethan picked up a stray mushroom from the kitchen floor.

'Just add enough flour to make the stock thicken – so it turns into a sauce rather than a soup,' Hermione instructed.

'Joel's going to be here in ten minutes, Bethan won't settle in bed, I've got flour in my hair and down my clothes and the dinner looks like shit,' Kate ad-mitted with a heavy sigh.

'Well it's a good job it's only business then and not a date,' Hermione answered sceptically.

'I still want the dinner to taste nice. I mean, he's helping me out for no fee and we might not even get any money from the competition – the least I can do is feed him,' Kate replied.

'Stop panicking, take a deep breath and relax; it will all be fine. I read your tea leaves again and good things are coming your way,' Hermione admitted.

'I thought I told you to stop doing that without asking me.'

'I just wanted to put your mind at rest, that's all.'

'Did the leaves tell you that my dinner is going to be a success?'

'They're never that specific so just keep it simmering until the vegetables are cooked, add the sauce and leave it on a low heat until you're ready to eat,' Hermione advised.

The doorbell rang and Kate almost dropped the telephone.

'Oh God, he's here, he's early. Bethan's still up, the dinner isn't cooked – I've got to go,' Kate spoke hurriedly.

She ended the call and wiped her hands on the tea towel.

She hurried down the hallway, Bethan hot on her heels, and opened the door.

On the doorstep stood a tall, red-haired woman aged about twenty-five. Kate didn't recognise her.

'Are you Kate Baxter?' the woman asked.

God, maybe she was from the bank? Maybe they were going to talk to her about her lack of funds. This could be the perfect opportunity to ask for the overdraft she'd been putting off. She didn't look too scary.

'Yes, I am. Are you from the bank?' Kate enquired hopefully.

Before she could do or say anything more, the woman struck out, punching Kate hard in the face. Shocked and bewildered, she put a hand up to her bloody nose as Bethan screamed and began to cry, pulling at her legs.

'Just leave Matthew alone, you vicious witch,' the woman spat.

'I...' Kate began, trying to speak as blood trickled down the back of her throat.

Without saying another word, the woman turned her back on Kate and hurried down the path, almost bowling into Joel, who was on his approach.

# 14

---

'Christ, what happened? Are you OK?' Joel asked, immediately noticing Kate's face and hurrying up the path to her.

'I'm fine. Mummy's fine, Bethy. Could you pick up Bethan while I find something to wipe my face with?' Kate spoke, putting her hands under her nose to collect the blood.

'Sure,' Joel said, putting down the bag he was carrying and scooping the child up into his arms.

Kate hurriedly grabbed the tea towel and held it to her nose.

'Who was that woman? Did she do this?' Joel questioned, sitting down on the sofa and bouncing Bethan up and down on his knee.

'I think I just met Matthew's new girlfriend,' Kate told him.

'Should I call the police?' Joel suggested.

'No! No, I'm fine, honestly. Oh shit! The dinner! I need to add the sauce and it needs to simmer,' Kate exclaimed, hurrying to the pan where everything was beginning to stick.

'Here, let me,' Joel spoke, putting a happy Bethan on the floor and moving into the open-plan kitchen area.

'Sorry about this. It was supposed to be ready, Bethan was supposed to be in bed and I was supposed to have finished writing the list of questions to ask you. I haven't succeeded on any count,' Kate moaned.

'Well, I could finish the dinner while you take Bethan up to bed if you like,' Joel spoke, taking the spoon from Kate's hand and stirring the meal.

'It's supposed to be chicken chasseur but I'm so hungry, I really don't mind how it turns out – as long as you're happy with that,' Kate answered.

'That's fine, go on,' Joel insisted, looking at the sauce Kate had made.

'OK. Come on Bethy, time for bed. Pick up Mr Crisps and say goodnight to Mummy's friend Joel,' Kate spoke, picking up her daughter, who was hugging her bear to her.

'Goodnight Bethan and goodnight Mr Crisps,' Joel said, smiling widely at the child.

'Night, night,' Bethan answered, waving her hand in the air.

'I won't be long,' Kate spoke.

'It's fine,' Joel told her.

'If you want a drink, there's wine already open in the fridge. Sorry, started earlier when I couldn't cut my chicken the right size.'

Excitable though Bethan was, she was also very tired. Kate read her two of her favourite stories and very shortly afterwards, she was fast asleep.

Kate quickly changed out of the flour-covered top and inspected her nose in the bathroom mirror. It was swollen, bruised and sore. So, that was the new woman in Matthew's life. She was young though, younger than her, and pretty in a pale sort of way. It was no surprise she was red-haired; Matthew had always liked red-haired women. Drew Barrymore in her red phase had been much lusted after. So had her cousin Sophie at their wedding. Perhaps that was why he'd left her. She hoped not; she could have been persuaded to dye it.

By the time she got downstairs, Joel was serving up the food and her kitchen looked like it had been given a spring clean. All her dishes had been washed up and everything was neat and tidy. The chaos had completely evaporated.

'Are you gay?' Kate blurted out, watching Joel spooning out the food onto plates.

'What?'

'Sorry, I mean you always seem to look immaculate, you enjoy female company but you don't have a girlfriend, you've finished cooking the dinner without any of the problems I encountered and now you've tidied my kitchen for me. I just wondered, that's all. That isn't straight male behaviour.'

'And I do love *Glee*,' Joel added with a grin.

'You do?' Kate queried.

'Hell no! And I'm not gay,' Joel answered with a laugh.

'Not that it would matter, because I mean...'

'Dinner's ready,' Joel said, carrying the plates to the dining area where he had also set up the table.

'Great,' Kate said and hurried over to sit down.

'I take it you don't cook all that often,' Joel spoke as he sat down opposite her and began to eat.

'What makes you say that? Have you tasted it? Is it bad?' Kate asked, drinking some wine.

'No, it was the year's supply of microwave meals in the cupboard, the complete lack of fresh food in the fridge and the absence of a spice rack.'

'I don't get the time and I'm not really that good at it,' Kate admitted, taking a bite of her food.

'This is good, though,' Joel told her as he ate.

'This is Hermione's foolproof recipe and I almost cocked that up – well, not that the punching thing was my fault, but I'm not sure I added enough flour to the stock anyway.'

'Well, I think it's pretty good. So, do you want to tell me why Matthew's girlfriend would be attacking you on your own doorstep?' Joel asked, looking over at her.

Kate hurriedly explained.

'And I guess she hasn't taken the maintenance increase too well.'

'No, so it seems. Look, Joel, thank you for agreeing to do *Knowing Me Knowing You* with me. I mean, it means a lot to me to try and not be dependent on Matthew and—' Kate started, taking another drink of her wine.

'You don't have to keep thanking me; if we win, I'll be taking my cut of the proceeds,' Joel asked.

'Of course,' Kate agreed.

'So, where do we start?' Joel enquired.

'Well, I've got some questions right here,' Kate said, reaching over to the sideboard and picking up a piece of paper.

'Cool.'

'OK, I've written down to ask about family background, siblings, parents, where you used to live, etc. and then I've moved into the realms of what car do you drive, what aftershave do you wear and what do you find most attractive in a woman. I thought that sounded like a question that would roll off Larry Rawlins' tongue.'

'You're probably right,' Joel agreed with a laugh.

'Do you want to start?' Kate suggested nervously.

'Sure. Well, first off, I'm adopted. So, as far as I know, I don't have any brothers or sisters. My adoptive parents live in Kent and that's where I was brought up. I did A-levels, I went to university, did my degree, did some highly embarrassing underwear modelling and then I joined the Army. After that, I got the job at the gym here in Highbridge. I've got a Honda Civic, I wear Davidoff Cool Water and the most attractive thing for me in a woman is a sense of humour. I think everyone should stop taking themselves so seriously.'

'God, you sound like you've done this sort of thing before; all that tripped right off the tongue,' Kate remarked, eating a forkful of food and drinking some more wine.

'So, how about you? Or maybe I should guess.

Right, let's see, I'm thinking always lived in Highbridge, worked hard to qualify as a lawyer, drives a Ford Fiesta because I've seen one parked outside with a *Baby on Board* sign. I know you wear a perfume by Yves St Laurent because believe me, I've got to know my perfumes over the last eighteen months, but I have no idea what you would find most attractive in a man. Intelligence? Maybe – warmth?' Joel spoke, smiling at Kate.

'Not bad, I suppose. My parents, they died, five years ago, in a car accident. I don't have any siblings either, the Ford Fiesta is mine and I do wear Yves St Laurent, it's called Opium by the way, but I'm on the absolutely last dregs of it so don't wear it often. Most days it's eau de porridge for me,' Kate answered with a sigh.

'I'm sorry about your parents,' Joel said.

'That's OK; it was one of those things, a stupid twist of fate: wrong place, wrong time. And they left me with a pile of debt to sort out that I didn't have a clue about, which is partly why I'm in the mess I'm in now – no savings to speak of. There we are, that's my life in a nutshell. More wine?' Kate offered.

She didn't like to talk about her past; it was still painful and with Matthew gone, it just made her realise how alone she really was now.

She filled up Joel's glass before he had a chance to decline.

'And what's most attractive for you in a man?' Joel asked her.

'Well, er, I don't know, really – honesty, maybe. Honesty might be appropriate at the moment because I haven't had a lot of it lately,' Kate said.

'Is that Matthew there?' Joel asked, indicating the picture of Matthew and Bethan on the sideboard.

'Yes, that's Matthew,' Kate replied with a heavy sigh.

She'd removed most of the pictures: the wedding one she ripped up, the one at the lovely little fish restaurant on their honeymoon, the one she took of Matthew wearing a nun's habit on his thirtieth birthday. She couldn't eradicate him from her life completely though; he was Bethan's father and although he didn't want to see her, she didn't want her daughter to completely forget what he looked like, especially if one day, she turned round and blamed Kate for her not knowing who he was. It happened; she watched *Jeremy Kyle*.

Later, after a bowl of Sarah Lee's finest and two bottles of wine, they sat on the sofa and attempted to re-enact the game show. Kate, glowing from her sixth glass of wine, was determined to impersonate Larry Rawlins.

'Just concentrate hard and pretend I'm wearing a ridiculous toupee and a flashy, silver jacket. OK Joel, we asked Kate, if she could be any brand of chocolate bar, which one would it be? Would it be A, a Kit-Kat, simple yet satisfying; would it be B, a Mars bar, hunky and chunky; or would it be C, a Crunchie, plain on the outside but mouth-wateringly exciting inside?' Kate spoke, camping up her voice to sound like the host of *Knowing Me Knowing You.*

'I think you should be writing the questions,' Joel responded with a laugh as he watched her.

'Come on Joel, I need an answer from you. Don't make me repeat the options and keep the lovely Kate in that rather poor excuse for a glass booth over there.'

'OK, OK, I think C, a Crunchie.'

'CORRECT! That's another Kissing Gate on the board!' Kate announced, dancing from one foot to the other and picking up her glass of wine to down the contents.

'You're crazy,' Joel said with a shake of his head.

'It's your turn, come on. Get some more wine, get into character, feel yourself actually becoming Larry Rawlins,' Kate said, sitting down on the sofa and making Joel stand up.

'I didn't sign up for role playing.'

'No? Didn't I mention that? Now, I want to hear an authentic voice and see some winking at camera one, which is over there, by the way,' Kate spoke.

She was definitely halfway to drunk – things were becoming fuzzy round the edges – but it wasn't such a bad feeling, especially when she had someone like Joel to look at. She was going to give him 40 per cent of the money if they won the contest; she may as well ogle him while she had the opportunity.

'OK, ladies and gentlemen, we asked Joel, if you and Kate have a disagreement, what is it usually about? Is it A, money, Kate spends too much on hiring escorts; is it B, food, all Kate eats is microwave meals; or is it C, Larry Rawlins – who does the best impersonation of him?' Joel spoke.

Kate laughed out loud and then threw a cushion across the room at him.

'You aren't taking this seriously! That isn't the sort of question he would ask. Ask me another,' Kate ordered.

'OK, OK, sorry. We asked Joel what sort of underwear he preferred his women to wear.'

'OK, maybe I would have preferred the other question.'

'Would it be A, a thong – after all, less is more; or

would it be B, Bridget Jones pants – because a lady should have curves in all the right places; or is it C, plain, white, cotton, bikini briefs – because we all remember our first time?'

'I think I've had enough now; I feel sick,' Kate said, sitting down on the sofa with a sigh.

'Don't know what type of underwear I prefer?' Joel asked with a smile.

'I couldn't care less,' Kate answered, holding her arms across her chest, annoyed he was predictably interested in lingerie.

'Neither could I,' Joel said with a laugh.

'What?'

'I don't have underwear preferences, I just thought it was the sort of lame question they would ask,' Joel told her.

'We haven't asked each other a dilemma question yet,' Kate said as she poured more wine into her glass.

'Well go on, let's try one,' Joel suggested.

'You want me to think one up?'

'You suggested it.'

'OK, well Joel, we asked Kate – if you thought that Joel was cheating on you what would you do? Would you A, ignore it, it will burn out soon enough and your relationship can survive any crisis; B, confront Joel about it, no one treats you like that and you need to get to the bottom of it; or C, dump him, any sniff of a rumour is enough for you.'

Joel looked at Kate as if hoping to find the answer in her face. His eyes were so large, like saucers filled with dark coffee. His gaze was so intense, she had to look away and clutch hold of the wine bottle to distract herself.

'I would like to think it was B, because I would want things out in the open and I don't really do cheating by the way.'

'Well you'd be completely without a Kissing Gate there because the correct answer would be A,' Kate replied.

'You'd ignore it? Why?'

'I hate confrontation, of any sort. I wouldn't know what to do or say and I'd be scared what you would do or say. Speaking hypothetically, obviously.'

'I'm surprised; I didn't have you down as that sort of person,' Joel admitted.

'Oh I'm a doormat, always have been,' Kate replied with half a smile.

'Is that what happened with Matthew? He cheated on you?' Joel asked.

'No. No, at least, I don't think so. I don't know, maybe he did. I guess he might have; I didn't think about that. God, how stupid,' Kate exclaimed, her brow furrowing as she considered what Joel was suggesting.

'Sorry, I didn't mean to pry, I just thought, because of the question you asked...'

'God, you're probably right, he was probably seeing this Amanda all along. That's why she came round here and thumped me. I expect it isn't just the money thing; I expect I've been a thorn in her side for ages.'

'Forget I said anything. Let's talk about something else,' Joel suggested quickly.

'Good idea. Tell me about the Army. What did you do? Where did you go?' Kate asked quickly, shaking her head as if to remove Matthew from her thoughts.

'A lot of different places,' Joel said, shifting in his seat.

'Well where? I'm interested.'

'Well I went to Germany for a while, Northern Ireland and then – Afghanistan,' Joel replied with hesitation.

'God, really? Was it awful? Did you have to kill people? I mean, I know that's what you have to do ordinarily but some people in the Army don't do that, do they; they just play in the Army band or cook or something. Ah, you were a chef! That's why you're so good at cooking and tidying up and making things shiny.

They do that in the Army, don't they – scour pans until you can see your face in the bottom,' Kate gabbled drunkenly.

'I wasn't a chef,' Joel replied with an absent look on his face.

'Bugler? I could definitely see you bugling.'

'No, I—' Joel began.

'Drummer? No hang on, paramedic-type person – you must know first aid for your job at the gym. Yes, I could definitely see you carrying people over your shoulder under heavy gunfire.'

'I'd rather not talk about it to be honest; it was a while ago now and—'

'Lynn at work, her husband's in the Army and he went to Afghanistan. He got blown up by a mine or something. Well, he didn't personally, but he was close to the person who did get blown up and he got injured – lost one of his hands. I don't think he's allowed to do too much now,' Kate continued, not noticing Joel's reluctance to discuss the topic.

'Shall we do another question because they won't be asking about the Army in the show, will they? Not exactly light-hearted entertainment, is it? They'll be asking about who snores more loudly and who gets up in the night to pee the most,' Joel spoke, putting a smile back on his face and trying to direct the conversation.

'Is that why you left the Army? Did you get injured or something?' Kate asked, not hearing his desperation to move on.

'No, I didn't get injured. Listen, I really don't want to talk about the Army any more,' Joel told her in serious tones.

'Oh, sorry,' Kate said, finally ending her questioning and seeing the unease in Joel's expression.

'I'd better get going. I didn't realise it was so late,' Joel said, checking his watch and immediately rising to his feet.

'Oh are you sure? I mean, there's plenty of wine, at least I think there is. I know there's some gateau left,' Kate offered, also standing up.

'I'm fine, thank you and thank you for dinner; it was really nice,' Joel spoke, his heart-stopping smile back on his mouth.

'Well thank you for coming and for answering all the stupid questions. I think we did quite well, didn't we? Whoops, now I'm sounding like Bruce Forsyth,' Kate said as she showed Joel to the door.

'We did well,' Joel agreed.

'So, shall I call you? Do you think we should do this again?' Kate spoke.

'Give me a call, maybe next week,' Joel replied, opening the door.

'Oh OK, well, see you then, bye,' Kate said and she let Joel out and watched him walk down the path.

She let out a sigh as she closed the door. Although Bethan was asleep upstairs, the house seemed so quiet and empty, like the fun and laughter had just left along with Joel. She was sorry he was gone. She had enjoyed his company and playing the silly game and her mouth actually ached from full-on belly laughs she thought she had forgotten how to perform. She closed her eyes as she leant against the door. She hadn't laughed enough with Matthew. Maybe that was why he left her. She hadn't laughed enough with him and her hair wasn't red.

# 15

'So? How did the chicken chasseur go down? Goodness sweetie, what happened to your nose?' Hermione asked as she brought a cup of blueberry tea over to Kate the following day.

'Oh it's not as bad as it looks. I think I had a visit from Matthew's girlfriend last night. At least I hope it was her because otherwise, I have no idea who it was. Can't remember giving out my home address to any irate clients just lately,' Kate spoke, taking a sip of her drink.

'God Kate, she thumped you? What did you do?'

'I stood there with a nose bleed and Bethan winding around my legs, not knowing what to do. Luckily, Joel turned up.'

'And how did the dinner go? Learn lots about each other?' Hermione asked excitedly.

'It was quite good fun. Actually, I haven't laughed so much in ages,' Kate admitted, smiling as she remembered the role play.

'That's great! So, what next?'

'I don't know, it all went a bit weird. It was my fault; I was a bit tipsy, and I kept asking him about the Army and it was obviously a sore point and I think he got fed up with me going on about it. I do go on about things when I'm drunk, don't I?' Kate spoke.

'Mm, just a bit. I remember the time you had one glass of Philip's home-made wine and didn't shut up about George Clooney.'

'Well that stuff was very strong.'

'So he's been in the Army.'

'Yeah, Ireland and Afghanistan. Oh and he's been an underwear model but I didn't get round to asking details,' Kate spoke.

'Sloppy! I'd like to hear much more about that! Goodness, Afghanistan, that can't have been nice. I wouldn't have had him down as a soldier, though – far too charming, not at all like the squaddies I used to go out with. Their idea of romance was nine pints of lager and a kebab,' Hermione said.

'And he's adopted. I didn't like to ask too much

about that. I mean, you never know quite how people feel about that situation, do you?'

'But you have to ask; that's what getting to know the ins and outs of someone is all about. And that's the knowledge you need to win the contest.'

'I know but I didn't want to pry too much straight away. I mean, we've only just met.'

'So when are you meeting up again?'

'I don't know, he said I should call him next week but I don't know what to suggest doing. I mean, we had to make up our own questions last night and it didn't work properly. What we need is someone to set some for us; that would really be a test,' Kate informed, drinking more of her tea.

'Well, that would have to be someone who was familiar with the format of the show and the sort of questions they ask,' Hermione said.

'Mm, yeah,' Kate responded.

'And someone who knows you quite well obviously, to play along with the ruse,' Hermione continued.

'Yeah,' Kate replied and she suddenly put down her tea and looked at her friend.

'Look no further! I would love to set the questions! I can't think of anything more fun! Philip would love it too. Phone Joel, you can both come to dinner next week and we'll re-enact *Knowing Me Knowing You* right here in my kitchen,' Hermione spoke excitedly.

'Are you sure? I mean, I don't want to keep taking up so much of your time and—' Kate began.

'It's being offered, sweetie and I won't take no for an answer,' Hermione said firmly.

'CHOCOLATE!' Cyrus whispered loudly, walking into the kitchen and drumming his feet on the floor.

'Mum, I can't find my school tie,' Heather called, appearing at the door as Cyrus started to march around and around in a circle.

'Sorry Kate, I'd better go and sort my tribe out or no one's going to get to school today,' Hermione spoke, getting to her feet.

'That's OK, I've got to head off anyway. Thanks for the tea. Bye, Bethan,' Kate called into the living room as she passed.

She looked in on her daughter and saw she and Sky were making the beginnings of a den using the chairs and a sheet.

'See you later. Stop that, Cyrus!' Hermione said firmly.

\* \* \*

When Kate arrived in the Probate department at Randall's, she could barely see her desk for the second time that week. This time, it wasn't covered with streamers and balloons; it was covered in files. Probate files were always large and bulky due to the nature of the work but the files piled high on her workspace looked fit to burst and eerily old. Some even had cobwebs on them.

'Morning,' Lynn greeted, entering the room and approaching Kate.

'Morning, what happened here? Did someone clear out archives and leave it all on my desk?' Kate asked her secretary, staring at the files in horror.

'Afraid not, Kate,' the Lady Dragon's voice boomed as she materialised before them like something out of *Quantum Leap*.

'I'd like you to look at these for me. They've all got money on client account – small amounts mainly and I don't remember who gets what. Could you go through and sort them out for me?' Miranda finished, batting her eyelashes and flicking her blonde hair back.

'Well, actually, I've got quite a lot on today and—' Kate began, deciding she didn't want to be walked over.

'What do you have outstanding?' Miranda asked,

her mouth thinning as she looked at Kate disapprovingly.

'Well, I need to finish the accounts on Carruthers and start the IHT papers on Watson and—'

'That shouldn't take you too long though, should it? If you could sort these by tomorrow, that would be perfect,' Miranda spoke, the smile returning as she sensed triumph.

Kate just smiled back, not knowing what else she could really do or say. And then before she knew it, she was studying Miranda's hair again. Was it a wig? If it was then it wasn't obvious. It looked like real hair, it moved like real hair, it had to be real hair.

'And I'll have a coffee when you have a minute, Lynn,' Miranda said, facing the secretary and flicking back her hair again.

Lynn met her boss' eyes and then cracked a false smile that resembled an over-enthusiastic clown.

Appearing satisfied with her show of power, Miranda tip-tapped back across the room and returned to her lair.

'I'm going to have to move these or I won't be able to get on with any work,' Kate spoke as she began to lift the files down from her desk.

'Here, let me help you,' Lynn offered.

'Stupid bloody Dragon. I don't know why she's got

it in for me,' Kate said, putting the files onto the floor next to her desk.

'I might. Rumour has it Colin Sykes wants you to take that exam thingy – you know, the one that turns you from a legal executive into a solicitor. I think she's terrified of that happening because once you're a solicitor, you could become a partner,' Lynn explained.

'Where do you get these rumours from? You spend far too much time chatting by the water cooler in my opinion,' Kate joked.

'Actually, I got it from Colin's secretary, Sophia. She told me in the strictest confidence. He's been looking at the exams: timescales and stuff.'

'For me?'

'Yep, but don't tell anyone I told you because it's not common knowledge. The only people that know are Colin, Sophia and me – and the water cooler, obviously. Expect a memo, though.'

'Why would he want me to do that? Miranda is ripe for becoming a partner; it's virtually a done deal,' Kate spoke, dumping the last file on the floor and sending up a cloud of dust from the carpet.

'I think she's putting noses out of joint. Rumour has it a few clients have complained about her,' Lynn informed as quietly as she could manage, which was about two decibels below a Boeing engine.

'Really? But I thought she was always good with clients. I thought she was everyone's golden girl.'

'Good with the chat, less good with the knowledge, allegedly. You didn't hear that from me either.'

'God, I would never have thought that; she always seems so capable.'

'Things aren't always what they seem. By the way, she *did* change those accounts you did. I checked my copy. Yours were perfect; she's taken bits out and put bits in, and I know it was her because she left her log-in name on the system. Not very clever to forget to cover your tracks. Two sandwiches short in the deception department if you ask me,' Lynn informed.

'But why would she—'

'Duh! Colin thinks you're partner material, she's under scrutiny because clients have complained; she'll be looking to discredit you.'

'But at the expense of sending incorrect papers to the clients?' Kate asked, horrified.

'She's a ruthless bunny; that won't matter to her. They'll be *your* mistakes and she can take the credit for sorting them out. Come on, Kate – stop being so nice all the time,' Lynn boomed.

'God, is this what they call warfare in the workplace?'

'Yes! Good! Nice to hear you're awake now! I've

sorted the accounts; I've sent a copy to your email and saved them in triplicate.'

'Well, what do I do? If she's determined to make me look like an idiot? She's the boss, she has all the means.'

'Give me the Carruthers case for a start; they only need a tidy up. You can get on with Watson, I can help you with these balances later, and then, at lunchtime, when she's out having her talons manicured or whatever today's beauty treatment is, we can strategize and plan our attack,' Lynn spoke almost excitedly.

'God, Lynn, I'm not sure I have the enthusiasm for it. Playing games isn't really my thing.'

'No? Four little words: *Knowing Me Knowing You*.'

'That's not fair.'

'You can't let her get away with it.'

'You really think Colin's earmarked me for the solicitors' exam?'

'Sophia never lies when I've plied her with Hob Nobs,' Lynn insisted.

\* \* \*

At 1.00 p.m., just as Lynn and Kate were about to gather around a desk with sandwiches and strategy, Kate's telephone rang.

'Hello, Kate Baxter.'

'Hello Kate, I have a Joel Brown in reception for you,' the switchboard operator announced.

'Oh, OK, I'll come down – Lynn, Joel's in reception for me. I won't be long. Shall I make some tea when I come back up?' Kate suggested.

'Sure, I'll just log in to the Lady Dragon's emails and see what she's been plotting,' Lynn replied, tapping away on the keyboard and concentrating on the screen.

Kate hurried from the room and went down the two flights of stairs to reception. When she got there, Joel was sat in one of the really uncomfortable yet classy-looking, leather chairs, flicking through a magazine. He was smartly dressed in a plain, white shirt and dark trousers looking as gorgeous as ever. He raised his head and she caught sight of the charcoal-coloured eyes.

'Hello,' Kate greeted rather stiffly.

'Hi,' Joel replied and he hurriedly stood up and kissed her on the cheek.

'Shall we go outside?' Kate suggested quickly as she blushed from head to foot.

She knew they were supposed to be giving the impression they were madly in love but every time he did something as simple as pecking her on the cheek, she was taken aback and embarrassed. Plus, she didn't want either of the receptionists to be privy to anything she was going to say. Ruby was terribly nosey and she was related to Miranda in some bizarre way, Miranda's aunt's boyfriend's mother or something. And the less Miranda knew about her relationship with Joel, the better.

'Sure,' Joel agreed and he opened the door for her.

Once outside, Kate realised just how cold it was and wished she hadn't made the suggestion. Privacy wasn't worth freezing to death for. She hugged her jacket to her and tried not to shiver.

'Sorry to bother you at work. I just wanted to apologise for leaving so abruptly last night. It was really rude of me and I didn't thank you properly for the dinner,' Joel spoke, looking a little ashamed.

'Oh, well that's OK. I think I drank a bit too much and I was going on and on about the Army and—'

'No, you weren't, you were fine – it was me,' Joel insisted.

'Oh good, I'm glad I didn't do anything stupid. I had a vague recollection that I was doing really bad impressions of Larry Rawlins. Tell me I'm wrong.'

'Ah, well, I hate to be the bearer of bad news but...'

'I guess it could have been worse; I could have been pretending to be the Love Dove.'

'Maybe you can try that the next time,' Joel suggested.

'I was going to call you about the next time, actually. If you still want to do it that is, I mean, I promise, no more interrogation, just gentle questioning,' Kate spoke, concerned.

She didn't want him deciding it was all too much hassle and back out of the whole thing.

'Gentle questioning, huh?'

'You haven't changed your mind, have you?'

'No,' Joel told her.

'Phew! Thank God for that. I thought I might have blown it last night with the crap dinner and the SAS inquisition.'

'I've got a strong constitution, on both counts.'

'Great. Well Hermione – you know, my mad friend who does the tea leaf reading – she's invited us to dinner and offered to make up some questions for us. She knows everything, you know, that we aren't really a couple and you're an escort. In fact, she was the one who gave me the card. And she watched the show. Actually, I'm starting to worry about her because she seems to know everything there is to know about it. I'm afraid she has it on Sky+ and is watching it on a loop,' Kate gabbled.

Joel laughed and smiled at her.

'What do you think?' Kate asked.

'It sounds like it would be very entertaining and good timing seeing as there's only two weeks until the next show.'

'Is it only two weeks? I don't even know whether you're a wet or dry shave man. I'm thinking wet.'

'Then you have a Kissing Gate on the board,' Joel answered.

'Really? How excellent!'

'Listen, I was thinking – would you like to go bowling?' Joel asked suddenly.

Kate looked at him blankly. It sounded like he was asking her out on a date. Was that possible?

'Oh,' Kate said, not committing, leaving it open for him to clarify his motives.

'If you don't want to, that's fine; it was just an idea. I thought we could throw a few balls, practise looking like a couple.'

'No, it sounds good; I mean, we could try some questions over a few strikes – strikes of mine, of course. When?'

'Tomorrow night? I could pick you up, about seven-thirty?' Joel suggested.

'I'll have to check if Hermione can babysit. Shall I call you?' Kate asked.

'Sure.'

'Great, well I'll—' Kate began.

Suddenly, there was a loud bang and a car kangarooed up the road. Kate jumped at the noise but Joel reacted in a more extreme manner. He grabbed hold of Kate, bundled her to the floor and covered her head with his arm as the car let out another horrendous clap of noise which sounded like a cannon going off.

Kate's face was pressed against the wet pavement and she had banged her elbow on the ground. She could feel his body tight up to hers. His heart was racing and he was breathing heavily.

Rapidly realising what the noise had been, Joel hurriedly got to his feet, red faced and embarrassed. He helped Kate up and began rubbing down his jacket.

'I'm so sorry, I didn't know what that was, I...' Joel began not able to look Kate in the eye.

'People shouldn't be allowed to drive cars that aren't roadworthy,' Kate found herself replying, trying to ignore her pavement-stained suit.

'I'd better go,' Joel said quickly.

'And I'd better get back to Lynn; she's devising some scheme to oust the Lady Dragon,' Kate spoke, pushing open the door to Randall's and feeling awkward.

'Sounds intriguing,' Joel managed to say.

'I'll tell you all about it tomorrow. Bye,' Kate spoke, stepping back into the offices and waving a hand at Joel.

'Bye,' he ended as he watched her go.

Kate ignored the quizzical look from Ruby on reception and raced up the stairs. She suspected the nosey old bag had seen everything anyway on the security camera.

'How are you getting on?' Kate asked as she rejoined Lynn at her desk.

'What the hell happened to you? You're covered in muck,' Lynn remarked as Kate tried to brush down her jacket.

'Oh, nothing. What have you found?'

'You won't believe it. She's been altering more than your accounts; she's been writing letters to some of your clients. Look,' Lynn spoke, showing Kate the evidence.

'That was Joel, in reception,' Kate spoke, not really looking at what Lynn was showing her.

'Yes, you said. So he's the new boyfriend, is he?'

'I guess he sort of is.'

'Well either he is or he isn't.'

'It's a little bit of both, actually,' Kate replied.

'I don't understand at all, but take a look at this: the Lady Dragon's been sending memos to the managing partner about your incompetence,' Lynn announced loudly.

'What? You're joking? What does it say?' Kate exclaimed in horror, moving closer to the screen to get a look.

'It's in draft and she's listing all the files with errors on. This is cool!' Lynn announced excitedly, tapping on the keyboard.

'What? Cool? How can it be cool? She's putting mistakes on my files and trying to discredit me!' Kate said furiously.

'Yes but she's listed all the files so we can go in and put the errors right and then she'll look a complete idiot,' Lynn told her.

'Maybe I should just confront her about it. I mean, I know I don't like confrontation, even Joel knows that, but I haven't really got the time or energy for any of this,' Kate answered with a sigh.

'Leave it to me. I love little challenges like this and believe me, with an opponent like the Lady Dragon, you need to be underhand and devious. I can do underhand and devious. I watch all the right TV programmes; I can do Ray Winstone or any of the culprits in *Trial and Retribution*. It's all about keeping one step ahead of the game,' Lynn assured her, narrowing her eyes and grinning like a distant relative of the Kray twins.

'Why does she hate me so much?' Kate asked out loud.

'You're better than she is and she can't cope with that. People kill for less, you know. Did you see the latest *Rebus*?' Lynn asked.

'No,' Kate replied with a sigh.

'Or any of the *Cracker* series?'

'No.'

'Well, not to worry, I've seen enough for the both of us. One thing's for certain, though: you're going to have to toughen up. No mercy, as they say in all the best films!' Lynn told her seriously, looking at Kate like she was now a member of a crack SAS unit.

'You're scaring me,' Kate admitted.

Lynn let out a laugh and then trained her eyes on the computer screen like she was looking through the sight of a sniper's rifle.

'She's as good as body bagged,' Lynn said.

# 16

---

'Thanks for this, Mione. I know I'm taking advantage of you at the moment and—' Kate began as she raced around the living room and then the kitchen looking for a missing earring, one shoe on her foot.

'How many more times, sweetie? I love spending time with Bethan and believe me, once she's gone to bed, your house is going to be my little sanctuary. I've bought a book, I have fennel pastries and Philip is taking care of my noisy tribe.'

'Well I won't be late. I mean, I expect we'll just play one round and then head back and there's only so much questioning you can do in one evening. Unless he throws me to the floor again and won't let me go,' Kate said, finding her earring and putting it in her ear.

'You're making that sound like it would be a bad thing.'

'I suppose the floor of the bowling alley would be kinder on my clothes.'

'Are you going to speak to him about it? I mean, it isn't quite normal behaviour, is it?'

'It was when the car backfired; I'm presuming it has something to do with him serving in a war zone and that topic of conversation is off limits. I don't want to piss him off and have him pull out on me,' Kate spoke.

'Well, you take as long as you like, we'll be just fine here, won't we, Bethy,' Hermione responded, bouncing Bethan up and down on her knee.

The doorbell rang and Kate squealed, scanning the room for her other shoe.

'I'll get that for you; I have to see him in person. I've heard so much about him I almost feel like I've met him already,' Hermione spoke, leaping off the sofa and practically running down the corridor in a bid to reach the door before Kate.

She opened it and smiled widely at Joel.

'You must be Joel,' she purred, extending her free hand for him to take.

'And you must be Hermione; Kate's always talking

about you. I feel like I've met you already,' Joel answered, taking her hand and kissing it lightly.

'Oh my God, you have a psychic mind; I just said the very same thing to Kate,' Hermione answered excitedly.

'Let the poor guy in will you and stop drooling over him,' Kate called from the living room.

'Hmm, I do hope she's only told you the good bits about me or her childminding fee will be going up,' Hermione said, tickling Bethan's tummy and making her giggle.

'Joel, Joel,' Bethan shouted, waving a hand at Joel.

'She's remembered your name! Clever girl, Bethy!' Kate exclaimed as she joined them all in the hallway, now wearing both shoes and putting on a coat.

'Hello, Bethan,' Joel greeted, taking hold of the little girl's chubby hand and giving it a squeeze.

'OK, shall we go? Mr Crisps is in her cot, her milk's in the fridge and help yourself to anything, although not the microwavable faggots because I'm having those tomorrow,' Kate instructed Hermione.

'They sound so disgusting, there's no way I would even touch them, let alone put them near my mouth. Have a good time both of you and no need to hurry back,' Hermione insisted, opening the door for them and almost shooing them out.

'God, sorry about that. Did she take hold of your hand? She does that to get a look at your life and love lines on your palm. She will have you half sussed out by now,' Kate spoke, leading the way down the path and stopping at the gate.

'I was more distraught at the thought of microwavable faggots,' Joel admitted.

'I highly recommend them.'

'Well, I hope you like steak too. I couldn't get a lane until nine so I booked a table at the Ranch House. Have you been there before?' Joel enquired, opening the car door for her.

'Is that the place where you cook your own food?'

'Yes, it is. It'll be fun,' Joel replied, shutting her door for her.

'But you know I'm no good with cooking,' Kate told him.

'I'll help and if we get into real difficulties, there's always KFC,' Joel said with a smile.

Half an hour later, they were sat at a table cooking steak and sausages on a grill set into their table. They were wearing cowboy hats and neckerchiefs and had been served by a waitress called Darlene. Kate was convinced it couldn't be her real name.

'Do you think they're done yet?' she asked with a sigh.

The novelty of cooking your own food had worn off twenty minutes ago. The grills seemed to take forever to cook the meat and there were a set of triplets sat at the table next to them who had screamed ever since they got there. Kate had slight sympathy for the parents because she was a mother and she knew how hard it was to look after children, particularly in a public place where they were liable to be on their worst behaviour. But when they started to bang their knives and forks on the table and the parents seemed completely oblivious to the din, all sympathy quickly evaporated.

'A few minutes more, unless you want yours rare. See how easy it is to make steak and salad?'

'Is this my nutrition lesson? I feel like an experiment or one of those sad cases on *Freaky Eaters*,' Kate replied, leaning on her elbow and looking glum.

'It's just a misconception that ready meals are quicker to make. You can steam vegetables in a few minutes, you know.'

'How fascinating. It's a good job we're not on a real date; you would have bored me rigid by now.'

'Bethan would have great fun helping you prepare a salad. Kids love anything with colour in and they're more likely to eat things they've helped prepare,' Joel carried on.

'That's very good information, Jamie Oliver, but is the meat on this grill cooked? If not, I'm tempted to suggest a self-service spit roast to the management, starting with one of those kids,' Kate told him, indicating the badly behaved trio who were now shaking condiments all over the table and flicking salt and pepper at each other.

'Let's see. Yep, I think that's fine. Here you go,' Joel said and he put a piece of steak and a sausage on Kate's plate.

'So, d'you come here often?' Kate asked, adding salad to her plate and dousing it all with dressing.

'Cheesy line,' Joel remarked.

'Well?'

'No, I haven't been here before – well, not to this particular one. They have one of these near where I lived with my parents. They used to take me and I loved it. I thought cooking food at your own table was so cool! I still do. I guess that makes me about twelve,' Joel admitted with a smile.

'It is quite cool, I suppose, if you have all night and aren't sat next to the Devil's offspring,' Kate admitted.

'Kids will be kids,' Joel replied, unfazed by the un-ruly behaviour as the three boys started to stamp their feet on the floor.

'Not at a restaurant. I would die if Bethan behaved like that.'

'People spend a lot of time these days worrying what other people think of them. We should just be who we are and people can take us or leave us,' Joel told her.

'God, that was profound for a steak house in Highbridge.'

'Well I just think you should be genuine, not pre-tend to be something you aren't. What's the point of that?'

'Speaks the man who's pretending to be my boyfriend to win a relationship contest,' Kate spoke with a laugh.

'There are extenuating circumstances for that situ-ation and it's only temporary,' Joel reminded.

Kate smiled and desperately tried to ignore the three boys who had now mounted the backs of their chairs and were pretending to wave lassoes in the air and shoot each other, their fingers stuck out like pistols.

'So what sort of stuff did you do with your par-ents?' Joel asked.

'We weren't the going to the restaurant sort of family, if that's what you mean,' Kate replied.

'Then what stuff did you do? Any great family holidays?' Joel asked.

'I only remember going on one family holiday, to Bognor Regis. I had one perfect day on the beach building sandcastles and chasing my dad with seaweed. The next day, my mother said she was ill and we had to go home. She said she was ill a lot so Dad would take me off somewhere.'

'So if I was Larry Rawlins, would you be a sun seeker or a snow lover?'

'Oh sun, definitely, you won't get me on skis, ever. The salopettes look hideous and having two planks of wood attached to your feet is just unnatural,' Kate replied, trying desperately not to let salad dressing drizzle down her chin.

'So have you travelled?' Joel asked.

'I went to Spain with some girlfriends once – Torremolinos. It's all a bit hazy – well, it was a hen weekend and they're supposed to be hazy, aren't they? I came back with food poisoning and a straw donkey. And then I went to Cuba on honeymoon. Matthew didn't like it; he said it was too hot and he got diarrhoea on the third day – I was pretty much on my own after that. I saw the sites, though. I did Havana and smoked cigars – well, one and it made me sick but I had to do it; it was Cuba,' Kate informed him with a grin.

'I would love to go there; it's such a one-off place and so full of history.'

'Well, where have you been? Apart from touring all the major war zones which we definitely aren't going to mention again.'

'I am so sorry about yesterday: the whole throwing you to the ground thing, I thought—' Joel began, his face flushing.

'That it was a bomb going off?' Kate offered.

'Yeah, something like that,' Joel admitted.

'Did scare me a bit too.'

'But you didn't take cover,' Joel responded.

'I might have done, if you weren't there coming to my aid and putting me to the pavement in double quick time.'

'Now you're being too kind,' Joel responded with half a smile.

'So where have you been? Tell me about the nice places.'

'I lived in Germany for a while, great sausages and excellent beer.'

'But what about the sites and the history? The Rhine and the Danube?'

'They were good too but the beer and sausages were more spectacular in my opinion.'

'Philistine.'

'After Germany, there was Croatia, Czech Republic, Netherlands...'

'Now you're just showing off.'

'But I fell in love with France. The country and the scenery, the cafés, the food, the slow pace of life.'

'The cheese, the onion sellers, the Eiffel Tower, Gerard Depardieu...'

'Don't mock it; it's a fantastic country. I try and go at least once a year to this little village in the south. I stay at this ancient farmhouse surrounded by the greenest fields you can imagine and I spend my time letting the peace and quiet soak into me,' Joel spoke.

Kate watched his expression, saw tranquillity washing over him as he conjured up obviously very happy memories.

'Sorry, you must think I'm crazy. It's just I can't seem to find that feeling here. When I'm in Marchette, there just seems to be so much space and time. Everything seems so stripped back and simple and that's what I like.'

'It sounds lovely but I can't afford to even think about a foreign trip anywhere at the moment. I want Bethan to see everything and do everything but when you're a single mum, you have to concentrate on the essentials; luxuries have to take a back seat.'

'But when we win the competition and the money, the world will be your oyster,' Joel reminded her.

'That money will be going on the mortgage; I don't want repossession knocking on my door.'

'Bethan would love Euro Disney. I did and I was twenty-three when I went,' Joel said.

'You don't look like a Disney kind of guy.'

'And what does a Disney kind of guy look like?'

'Goofy.'

'That's lame.'

'Who did you go with?'

'My girlfriend at the time and no, before you ask, she didn't look like Minnie Mouse.'

'Why did you break up?' Kate asked directly.

'She wanted to wear costumes in the bedroom.'

'No!'

'No,' Joel confirmed with a laugh.

'So why?' Kate asked him seriously.

'I don't know really. It just wasn't right,' Joel told her thoughtfully.

'Obviously, that's how Matthew felt about me. I just wish he'd concluded that before we exchanged rings and had a baby,' Kate said with a sigh.

'More salad?' Joel offered.

'Oh no thanks, I'm saving myself for pudding. Is that chargrilled too? Because if it is, I can't wait to see what they come out with.'

\* \* \*

'I'd better warn you,' Kate said later, when they were preparing to start their game at the bowling alley, 'we had an outing at school once and out of my whole year, I won.'

'I feel threatened and, if I was competitive, I would care – but I'm not and I don't,' Joel replied, picking up a ball.

'I don't believe you aren't competitive; I saw you at *Knowing Me Knowing You*. you were desperate for us to do well.'

'I was making sure everyone believed we were a couple; I wasn't concentrating on anything else.'

'Yeah sure. OK, here goes,' Kate spoke and she approached her lane.

She lined up her ball, looked down the alley and with one forceful flick of her wrist, she threw it.

It smashed against the pins and knocked eight of them down. Kate screeched excitedly and jumped up and down like a child, throwing her arms in the air as she celebrated.

'See! Still got the touch,' she spoke, blowing on her fingers and picking up another ball.

'You won't get the other two down – too spread out,' Joel told her.

'Watch and learn,' Kate replied, approaching the line.

She took a deep breath, looked up and prepared to throw the ball. She swung her arm back and was about to deliver a shot down the alley when her attention was distracted by action on another lane. She had to look twice. It couldn't be. The person she was looking at turned around and seemed to look straight at her. Kate dropped the ball on the wooden floor, narrowly missing her foot.

Two lanes across from where Kate stood were Matthew and the woman who had punched her. She was definitely Amanda, the new girlfriend. He was wearing the navy jeans she had bought him last Christmas and her favourite shirt of his: blue with a thin stripe. Seeing him made her heart lurch.

The ball made a loud crash and everyone in the centre looked in her direction.

'Kate,' Joel called to her.

Kate stood, unmoving, unable to keep her eyes off the couple. Because of the noise of the ball smashing on the floor, both of them were now looking over at her.

'Do you want to go?' Joel asked, recognising who it was.

'He never took me bowling,' Kate spoke quietly, still staring at them.

'Come on, let's go and get a drink,' Joel suggested.

Kate didn't reply and stood her ground as Matthew and Amanda left their game and started to approach them.

'So this is how you're going to spend my money, is it? Nights out bowling with your new boyfriend?' Matthew asked, standing in front of Kate.

'I don't think that's necessary,' Joel spoke, moving closer to Kate protectively.

'Oh you don't, do you?' Matthew retaliated.

'No,' Joel replied, standing his ground.

'I'd take some advice from me if I was you. Ditch her now while you have the chance because if you're not careful, she'll be knocked up and after you for maintenance before your six-month anniversary,' Matthew snarled.

Kate didn't say anything. She couldn't bring herself to; it was like there was a bowling ball stuck in her throat. All she could do was look at Matthew, narrowing his eyes and looking at her with hatred. She wondered whether he had ever been the person she thought he'd been.

'Stop hounding Matt, ringing up and begging for money; it's pathetic,' Amanda joined in, glaring at Kate.

'I won't be paying the CSA more than I can afford. I never wanted a kid and I don't want one now,' Matthew spat, moving his face closer to Kate's.

Kate looked up at him, her eyes stinging with tears at the cruelty in his tone and manner. She was back to being a doormat again, taking the comments, soaking them up and not having the guts to fight back.

The very next thing she knew, there was a yell, a loud crash and Matthew was on the floor of the bowling alley, Joel's knee in the back of his neck.

'Get off him! You're hurting him!' Amanda shrieked, pulling fruitlessly at Joel's sleeve.

'I suggest you go back to your own lane and stop harassing Kate before I talk her into pressing assault charges against you for the other night,' Joel spoke, looking up at Amanda.

'Let him go. Please, you're hurting him!' Amanda said as Matthew yelped, his face pressed into the ground.

'Joel, let him go,' Kate spoke, clearing her throat and hurriedly wiping the tears away from her eyes.

Joel got up and stood next to Kate as Matthew dragged himself up off the floor and glared at them both.

'You're a maniac! And *you* – I don't know what I ever saw in you. You're nothing but a money grabbing —' Matthew yelled, pointing his finger.

'Do you want to go back on the floor?' Joel questioned, taking a step towards Matthew.

'Matt, let's just go,' Amanda spoke, taking hold of her boyfriend's hand and pulling him away.

'He's a psycho! What did he do to me? Did you see?' Matthew muttered as Amanda coaxed him from the scene.

'Just forget them, babe; she's nothing to you, remember? Just some girl who forced you to marry her and then got pregnant to try and keep you,' Amanda told him.

Kate watched them leave, arms linked together, heads close. The tears were stinging her eyes now.

'Are you OK?' Joel asked Kate.

'You didn't have to do that. In fact, why *did* you do that? It's nothing to do with you,' Kate spoke, trying to regain some of her composure.

'What he said about Bethan, that was uncalled for and—' Joel began.

'But it isn't your battle; it's mine. Anyway, he's said

all he can say now; nothing else can hurt me,' Kate answered.

'It didn't look that way to me,' Joel responded.

'He doesn't mean anything to me. You saw him; you heard what he said. How could he mean anything to me any more?' Kate asked.

'We don't choose the people we have feelings for; it just happens,' Joel told her.

'I don't have feelings for him. I don't,' Kate replied determinedly.

She knew she was less than convincing and she didn't really know why.

'Shall we go? Do something else?' Joel suggested.

'No, I don't want to go. Why should I go just because he's here?'

'If you're sure,' Joel replied.

'Yes. I mean, I've still got these two skittles to get down,' Kate reminded, indicating the alley.

'You have,' Joel agreed.

'You shouldn't have done what you did to Matthew, roughing him up like that,' Kate spoke sternly.

'No,' Joel answered.

'But can you teach it to me? Was it an Army trick?' Kate enquired, picking up a ball.

'If I told you where I learnt it, I would have to kill you,' Joel said with a smile.

* * *

'Well, here we are,' Joel announced later as he pulled up outside Kate's home.

'Yes, here we are. Thanks for the meal and every-thing. Are you sure you don't want me to pay?'

'I'm sure. It was my idea and you did win at bowl-ing; call it the prize.'

'I did win, didn't I? Haven't lost it on the bowling alley.'

'Glad to hear it,' Joel answered with a grin.

'Oh God, I didn't realise quite how that sounded!' Kate shrieked, putting her hands to her mouth and laughing.

'I wouldn't go round saying it to everyone, just in case they get the wrong idea.'

'Look, do you want to come in? I could make coffee – well, instant coffee anyway; I don't have one of those fancy machines or anything but it's nice stuff, nothing from Aldi, I promise,' Kate suggested.

'That's OK, I'd better go; I've got a client first thing,' Joel told her.

'Escorting in the daylight? Is that allowed?'

'It's not escorting; it's the gym.'

'Oh, OK. Well, I guess I'll see you next week for the

dinner at Hermione's,' Kate reminded him as she opened the door to get out.

'Do you want to share a cab there? I could come here; it sounds like the type of evening where alcohol needs to be consumed.'

'Yes, it will definitely be that sort of evening.'

'Well, I'll call you, we'll fix a time.'

'OK,' Kate agreed, getting out of the car.

'See you,' Joel ended.

'Bye.'

She watched Joel drive away up the street and let out a sigh as she turned towards the front door. Joel was beginning to get to know her too well already. After all Matthew had put her through, why did she still have feelings for him?

# 17

The memo was on her desk when she arrived at work the following Wednesday.

*Kate*

*I wondered if you had considered the possibility of taking the exam to convert from legal executive to solicitor. As a firm, we will be looking to change our management structure over the next five years and this qualification may be of benefit to you when the plans are implemented.*

*Let me know your thoughts.*

*Colin*

'Told you, didn't I? Told you you'd get a memo,' Lynn spoke, leaning over Kate's chair and reading it again.

'I still don't believe it. I mean, why me? Jenny's been here longer and what Carol doesn't know about Probate isn't worth knowing,' Kate spoke, staring at the piece of paper.

'Duh! Because you're the best at your job: all the fiddly, technical stuff and everything, all the clients like you – need I go on?'

'You're making me sound like Wonder Woman – I like it,' Kate answered with a smile.

'So did you want me to draft a reply?'

'No! I mean, I don't know what I'm going to say yet. I don't know if I'm going to do it.'

'What?! You *have* to do it! Think of the wonga! If you get made a partner, you'll be on megabucks,' Lynn exclaimed.

'D'you think? I mean, I have no idea how much they earn.'

'Try at least sixty k a year, company car and profit share.'

'How do you know all this?'

'I talk to all the right people; you'd be amazed how much us secretaries know. Mere typists we are not,' Lynn answered with a smug smile.

'You're frightening me again,' Kate replied.

'I'm always doing that with Darren. I know more about his regiment than he does. The wives are really the ones with their fingers on the pulse.'

'How is Darren now? I mean, I know he isn't OK but, is he – you know – OK-ish?' Kate enquired, turning to face her colleague.

'You mean, has he got used to having half an arm? No, not really, but then it hasn't been that long: just over six months. His doctor says they can try and fit a state of the art hand thing in a few weeks but Darren's as pessimistic as ever,' Lynn told her.

'Does he ever talk to you about the Army – you know, what went on over there?'

'Goodness, no! He doesn't talk to me about anything like that, never has. It's a job to get out of him what he wants for tea, let alone anything about roadside bombs. He saw a counsellor a couple of times after it happened but that just seemed to make him angry.'

'Oh.'

'Why d'you ask?'

'No reason really. Well, it's just Joel was in the Army, in Afghanistan. He doesn't like talking about it and I just wondered if it was the same with Darren.'

'Yep, the same, although I'm not sure it has anything to do with the Army or getting blown up; I think it's just a bloke thing,' Lynn spoke, carrying on tapping on Kate's computer.

'Yes, right, of course, probably.'

'So, you tell me which company car you're going to have – apparently, there's a choice of three. Me, I'd plump for the Audi,' Lynn replied with a smile.

'Oh Lynn, I don't know,' Kate responded, picking up the memo and looking at it again.

'What's there to think about? They want you to do it, they think you're more than capable and it would be loads more dosh than you're on now. Think of what you could buy for Bethan; no more shopping at Mothercare, it would be Laura Ashley all the way,' Lynn remarked.

'Yes, I guess it would and believe me, I need the money. I just don't know whether I'm really capable of doing it,' Kate replied with a sigh.

'Of course you are! No self-belief, that's your trouble.'

\* \* \*

'I have to warn you, Hermione doesn't ever do things by halves. She will probably have laid on a *Knowing Me Knowing You* style banquet with heart shaped tofu cutlets or something,' Kate spoke as she and Joel approached the front door of the Wyatt's home.

'Great, I love tofu.'

'This from the man who took me to the Ranch House, I don't believe it. But then again, you are health conscious and tofu is low in fat, so I've heard.'

'I like a lot of different things.'

'I'll remember that,' Kate spoke and she rang on the doorbell.

There was the sound of giggling coming from inside the house and then heavy padding down the hallway. The door swung open and Kate gasped out loud as she was greeted by a seven foot chicken.

'Oh my God,' she remarked, putting her hands to her mouth as the chicken began to flap its wings and strut around the hallway, making pecking motions with its head.

'You were right about them not doing things by halves,' Joel remarked, stifling a laugh as the chicken began to shake his tail feathers at them.

'Ah, Kate and Joel, our lovely contestants, everything is arranged. First, we eat, then we play,' Hermione spoke, appearing from the kitchen dressed in a silver, sequined jacket and black trousers, her hair gelled back flat to her head.

'I'm taking it that's supposed to be the Love Dove?'

Kate queried as Philip, the wearer of the chicken suit, shook a wing in her direction.

'Yes, sweetie. Do you know how hard it is to get hold of a dove outfit? Come on, come in, come and sit down, before the heart-shaped steak and kidney puddings are overcooked,' Hermione spoke, her voice leaving the realms of Larry Rawlins and returning to normal.

'Told you,' Kate said to Joel.

'Er no, you definitely said tofu.'

'Can I take the head off now? Just for a bit, it's hot in here,' Philip called from beneath the feathers.

* * *

Hermione had made steak and kidney pudding, mange tout and dauphinoise potatoes with a beetroot sauce.

'This is wonderful food, Hermione,' Joel remarked as he poured Kate another glass of wine and then added to his own.

'Thank you. I wasn't quite sure how the sauce would turn out, but it was red and we were going for a red hearts and flowers theme.'

'It's very nice,' Kate agreed.

'Much better than a microwave meal,' Joel added.

'Ah but have you tasted the Asda mushroom risotto?'

'Thankfully, no.'

'That's enough sparring at my dinner table; aren't you two supposed to be madly in love?' Hermione ticked off.

'Oh yes, almost forgot that,' Kate answered.

'So Joel, what do you do? For a living, I mean?' Philip asked, having no idea and receiving a kick under the table from his wife.

'Oh let me tell him, see if I can get through the timeline,' Kate spoke hurriedly.

'By all means, the floor's all yours,' Joel agreed.

'OK. Joel works at Highbridge Leisure Centre, he's been there for eighteen months or so and he has a qualification in sports science, amongst other things. He's been in the Army, he's done underwear modelling and he was the face of Francois, which was a French aftershave, now discontinued,' Kate reeled off.

'How do you know that? I never admitted to the aftershave advertising,' Joel exclaimed.

'It's amazing what turns up when you Google. So how did I do?' Kate asked, eating more food.

'I'm impressed,' Joel admitted.

'Where did you meet?' Hermione suddenly barked across the table, like an officer from the Gestapo.

'At the leisure centre, when I took Bethan swimming,' Kate replied quickly, feeling the scrutiny in her friend's eyes.

'What size shirt does he wear?' Another question was fired.

'Oh, erm, a fifteen?'

'Shoe size?'

'Erm, I don't know, nine?'

'Side of bed he sleeps on?'

'Mione! I have no idea!' Kate shrieked.

'Joel, what dress size is Kate?' Hermione continued.

'Mione, they don't ask questions like that! You saw the show; it's mostly scenario based,' Kate screeched.

'Size twelve,' Joel answered confidently.

'Shoe?'

'Hello! Is anyone listening to me? I said they don't ask—'

'Five.'

'Side of bed?'

'Nearest the door.'

'Stop! How do you know all this? The side of the bed I sleep on! Jesus!' Kate exclaimed.

'You really don't remember anything that happened after the first show, do you?' Joel said with a smile.

'Don't go making things up.'

'I put you to bed,' Joel informed her.

'Rubbish! I don't believe you; Mione has put you up to this. Ha, ha, very amusing!'

'Not guilty! Hmm, put her to bed. Kate, you should have stayed conscious for that. Shame on you!' Hermione spoke with a grin.

'I'm not speaking to any of you any more,' Kate replied, folding her arms across her chest.

'Come on, that's not the spirit of the night. I've got heart-shaped cheesecake for dessert,' Hermione spoke, helping herself to more wine.

'I put you down on one side of the bed; you groaned, moved over to the other side and hugged your pillow. It was all perfectly innocent,' Joel assured her.

'This is getting very embarrassing; I don't want to hear any more,' Kate said, putting her hands over her ears.

'You've got too many inhibitions, sweetie. Have some more wine; there's plenty more where this came from and there's Philip's wheat and raisin to try later.'

'You have to try some of that, Joel; it warms you right down to the soles of your feet,' Philip announced.

'Which are a size eleven, just for the record,' Joel added.

*  *  *

After the cheesecake, Hermione recommenced her role as Larry Rawlins in the sequined jacket and stood at the end of the room with Philip clucking around her, minus the head which had brought him out in a rash.

'Now Kate, if you would like to leave the room – no booth tonight, I'm afraid. We are going to ask Joel some questions, then we'll ask you back and if your answers are a match then that's a Kissing Gate on the board,' Hermione announced, putting an excited hand out towards the imaginary audience.

'I've got to leave? Can't I just listen to my iPod or something?'

'Larry has spoken, out with you and no eavesdropping at the door.'

'Can I take the wine?' Kate asked, picking up the bottle and hugging it to her.

'I don't think so; that share is mine,' Joel spoke, grabbing it out of her hands.

'I hope the questions make you squirm,' Kate retorted as she headed out towards the hallway.

She closed the door behind her and checked her watch. It was just after 9.00 p.m. She took her mobile phone out of her pocket and dialled her home number.

'Hello,' Lynn's voice spoke.

'Oh hi Lynn, it's me. Is everything OK? Did Bethan go down OK?'

'Mainly OK, yes.'

'What does that mean?' Kate asked, immediately concerned.

'She's fine, we had a few tears and a bit of screaming when we had a little misunderstanding. She kept saying, "Crisps, crisps" and I thought she was hungry but of course she meant Mr Crisps the bear, which I'd completely forgotten about, even though you told me about five times. Duh!' Lynn explained.

'So she's asleep now?'

'Fast asleep, has been for ages. Oh and I've eaten one of your mushroom risottos, hope that was OK; there was about six of them in the cupboard.'

'That's fine,' Kate replied.

'Kate! You can return to the stage now!' Hermione called loudly.

'Who's that shouting? Are you at a club?' Lynn questioned.

'No, sorry, I've got to go, I'll see you later,' Kate said and she ended the call and put the phone back in her pocket.

'Have you been listening at the door?' Hermione barked as Kate re-entered the kitchen.

'No, of course not, I've been checking on Bethan. Why are you all smiling?'

'You haven't heard the questions I just had to answer,' Joel remarked, grinning.

'You wouldn't say that on stage, Joel. Let's please get back into character. Kate, please re-join Joel and we'll see how many Kissing Gates we can get on the board,' Hermione spoke, resuming her role as Larry Rawlins and winking to her imaginary camera.

Kate did as she was told, picking up a glass of wine on the way and drinking it back as hurriedly as she could.

'Right, Kate, we said to Joel – there is a clash of televisual treats. You want to watch one thing; Kate wants to watch another. How do you resolve this? Did Joel say A, he's going to watch his programme; there's no way he's going to miss this. Or did he say B, he would let you watch your programme; if you're happy, he's happy. Or did he say C, the television gets turned off and you do something else together,' Hermione questioned, looking quizzically at Kate.

'Hmm, well, I don't think Joel's really a television person and he is a gentleman so I'm going to say B, he would let me watch my programme.'

'CORRECT! A Kissing Gate on the board, well done Kate and Joel,' Hermione announced as Philip began to cluck loudly and dance around in a circle.

'Don't get too confident; that was the easiest question,' Joel said.

'Oh and here I was thinking we were going to breeze this.'

'Question two. We said to Joel, Kate's Auntie Jess comes to stay and is all expensive perfume and pearls. When Kate is out of the room, Auntie Jess makes a pass at Joel. What does he do? Does he A, completely rebuke her and immediately tell you what has happened? Does he B, try and turn the obvious advance into a platonic hug to save Auntie Jess and himself some embarrassment or would he C, rebuke the advance but not tell you about it because he knows how much it would upset you?'

'Oh,' Kate spoke with a swallow.

'It was a hard one for me; I don't even know what Auntie Jess looks like,' Joel piped up.

'And that would alter your answer, would it? If she was hot, you might kiss her back?'

'No, I just meant that you obviously all know what she looks like and I don't. I was imagining Barbara Windsor for some reason.'

'Well, she doesn't look like Barbara Windsor, she looks like Lulu,' Kate announced, a little annoyed.

'I'm going to have to press you for an answer, Kate,' Hermione broke in.

'Well now I don't know what you would do. Obviously if you found her attractive, you wouldn't be rebuking her at all. Was there a D option? Joel advances on Auntie Jess and forgets all about Kate?' Kate questioned, the alcohol loosening her tongue.

'I need an answer, please.'

'Oh, I don't know, B, the platonic hug – at least in that option, he got to have his hands on her,' Kate replied with a sigh.

'WRONG. I'm afraid Joel said A, he would rebuke her advances and tell you immediately. No Kissing Gate for you,' Hermione answered.

'You said trust was important to you and it's important to me too. I couldn't keep something like that quiet; I would have to tell you,' Joel spoke to her.

'Whatever,' Kate said and drank more of her wine.

'And the final question: Joel has noticed that you are putting on a little weight. What does he do about it? Does he A, say nothing; he loves you just the way you are. Does he B, mention it to you kindly and suggest both of you ought to cut down on the takeaway meals or does he C, not say anything but try and make you get more active.'

'Oh, definitely C. Look at him: gym obsessed. He would have me on a treadmill eating lettuce as soon as he could,' Kate answered confidently.

'I'm afraid that's the wrong answer. Joel said A, he loves you just the way you are. Hypothetically, of course,' Hermione announced as Philip scratched fiercely at the rash on his face.

'Are you OK?' Joel asked, taking hold of Kate's hand.

'Yes, fine. Can we go? I don't feel very well,' Kate spoke, her face feeling flush as the wine took hold.

'Of course but we're only halfway through the questions, I thought—' Joel began.

'I want to go home; I've had enough of all this,' Kate insisted.

'I'll call a taxi,' Joel said, getting out his mobile.

'Can we walk? I can't wait.'

'Sure, OK.'

'Are you OK, sweetie?' Hermione asked, becoming herself again.

'I'm just really tired and I don't want to keep Lynn too late. Sorry Mione, thank you for all the effort you've gone to and you, Philip, you've been an excellent chicken – I mean dove,' Kate spoke as she picked up her bag and coat.

'It's been a real pleasure and it was lovely to see you again, Joel,' Hermione spoke, grabbing hold of the tall man and squeezing him into an embrace.

'Thank you both for the wonderful food and for the questions. It was a really good evening,' Joel spoke as Philip led them to the door.

'We had such fun preparing it all, didn't we, Phil?' Hermione said.

'We did. We'll have to do it again, maybe minus the bird costume next time,' Philip answered.

'I'll see you tomorrow; we'll have a good chat,' Hermione spoke quietly to Kate as Joel stepped outside.

'Bye,' Kate responded with a sigh.

'See you and thanks again,' Joel called as they walked down the path and joined the street.

Kate gave Hermione and Philip a lacklustre wave and headed down the road towards home.

'Are you sure you're OK?' Joel asked.

'I'm fine, I just want to get home and go to bed. The last few days at work have been a complete nightmare. The Lady Dragon is trying to discredit me and Colin Sykes wants to promote me. I don't know which one is worse,' Kate admitted.

'Do you want to talk about it?' Joel offered.

'The question about Auntie Jess tipped me over the edge.'

'I did pick up on that.'

'It's stupid. I shouldn't let it still get to me; it's in the past.'

'Auntie Jess made a pass at one of your boyfriends?' Joel exclaimed.

'No, at Matthew – or the other way round, probably. It was the one and only time she came to stay. I caught them in the kitchen in an embrace, red-faced and trying to distract my attention by picking up scattered pretzels. But I knew what had happened; I knew how the pretzels got scattered.'

'I see.'

'She's my only relative. I asked her for a loan recently and she was more than happy to oblige. She still feels guilty for exchanging tongues with my husband – never thought that situation would work to my advantage.'

'I see.'

'Mione doesn't know; it's not something I've ever broadcast.'

'I see.'

'Stop saying that, you don't see, you must think I have "mug" printed on my forehead. I forgave him so many things, so many and in the end, it was all for nothing,' Kate exclaimed loudly.

'It wasn't all for nothing; you have Bethan,' Joel reminded.

'I hope Mione didn't think I was rude; she'd gone to so much trouble tonight.'

'I think Mione would be mortified if she thought one of her questions had made you feel like this,' Joel replied.

'I'm an idiot; it was just a game, a silly question we were practising for an even sillier TV show. It isn't real.'

'My answers were real; there's no point pretending if we want to win.'

'Even the question about me having put on weight?'

'Yes, although if there had been an option suggesting cutting down on the microwave meals, I might have chosen that.'

'Oh Joel, you must wonder how on earth you got involved in all this. Another Friday night and it might have been Stephen in your place,' Kate said with half a smile.

'I wouldn't change things now, especially not when Hermione has promised to read my runes,' Joel informed her.

'Oh God, we're truly doomed; she won't stop at that. She'll be plotting your astrological chart and getting her crystal ball out.'

'Perhaps she'll see us taking the title of *Knowing Me Knowing You*.'

'Or failing at the next round.'

'We're not going to fail; I think someone needs to work their negativity out of them.'

'Well, I'll have to work on that before next week. Next week! I can't believe we're going on stage again next week!' Kate exclaimed.

'And how's your talent shaping up? Have you had much chance to practise?'

'Talent?'

'Yeah, it said about it in the rules you gave me a copy of: couples in the next stage need to have a talent to show the audience.'

'I didn't read that! I can't do that! I don't have a talent, what sort of talent? Like juggling or something? This is insane; I had no idea, why didn't you mention it before?' Kate spoke wildly.

'I just presumed you knew.'

'Well what's your talent?'

'I play guitar a bit. I was going to do that.'

'Oh great, yeah, you're going to just whip up a song and play the guitar, while I what? Shake a tambourine in the background? That will impress people.'

'Do you sing?'

'Only when I'm drunk and then it's really bad. Like someone's reaction to having boiling water poured over them.'

'Well, you have a week to think of something.'

'Think of something, practise it and perfect it while trying to maintain my child/life/work balance.'

'I could bring a tambourine along just in case,' Joel suggested.

'Don't you dare.'

# 18

---

'Think of a talent,' Kate spoke as she passed Lynn by the filing cabinet and hurried over to her desk.

'What?' Lynn queried.

'Shh, come here,' Kate beckoned as she turned on her computer and started to go through her in tray.

'What's all the whispering for?' Lynn asked in a whisper.

'I don't want Lady Dragon to hear. I've got a client in ten minutes and I should be reviewing the file but this is important. I need a talent by the end of today. Something I can learn, something I can perform on stage at this *Knowing Me Knowing You* thing,' Kate continued, opening a file and sitting down.

'Like fire eating? Or sword swallowing? Now that would be really cool,' Lynn remarked with a grin.

'I was hoping for something that wouldn't kill me and something I can learn quickly,' Kate replied.

'Ooh, I know just the thing. Burlesque!' Lynn exclaimed excitedly.

'What?'

'Burlesque, you must have heard of it.'

'I have no idea what you're talking about.'

'Well basically, you dress up in a raunchy yet tasteful costume, like a corset and gloves and those dresses with the ruffles at the back and it's kind of a striptease but in good taste,' Lynn attempted to explain.

'A striptease in good taste. Is that possible?' Kate asked.

'Yes, it's more about suggestion rather than anything sleazy. My friend Melanie does it. I can ask her for a costume. Yes, that's definitely what you should do. It would be great. We're coming, by the way – to the show – me and Darren,' Lynn added.

'Oh you don't have to do that.'

'I can't wait; we haven't had a proper night out in ages. Right, well I'll phone Melanie about the costume and you can look up burlesque on the internet. Google

Dita Von Teese or Christina Aguilera; she's got some film coming out.'

'You're talking in riddles,' Kate exclaimed as Lynn disappeared towards the door.

'Mr Watkins will be here in seconds,' Lynn called.

'Kate, do you have a moment?'

Kate hadn't noticed Miranda arrive at her shoulder. She looked sombre faced and was in the little black suit she usually reserved for funerals and meeting the bereaved for the initial meeting. If she was wearing it for any other reason, it usually meant bad news.

'Well, Mr Watkins is due in any minute and—' Kate started.

'I hear Colin has suggested you take the legal practice course to gain your solicitor's qualification,' Miranda continued.

'Yes,' Kate answered with a swallow.

'And how do you feel about that?'

'Well, I haven't really had a chance to think about it.'

'No, I suppose not, what with a child and everything to worry about. It's a big decision and an enormous responsibility taking on more studying, isn't it?'

'Yes, it is,' Kate responded.

She knew exactly what Miranda's game was. She

had to be really floundering to launch a one-on-one attack.

'Reading through all those text books until the small hours, burning the midnight oil, no time for anything else,' Miranda continued.

She sounded so desperate.

'As I said, I haven't had time to think about it yet.'

It might be fun to keep her hanging, not give any clue as to her feelings about the offer one way or the other. Seeing as she'd been trying to discredit her in the office and to her clients, the cow deserved to sweat.

'No, of course. Well, I wasn't trying to put you off. I just thought you should know that it isn't all pass an exam and get a fancy title; there's a lot of hard work that has to go into it,' Miranda responded quickly, flicking her mane of hair back.

'I realise that,' Kate spoke, staring at her hairline and squinting her eyes to try and study it more closely.

'Perfect, good. Well, don't keep Mr Watkins waiting,' Miranda spoke, preparing to depart back to her office.

'I won't. And thanks Miranda for your advice; it's really appreciated. I hope you're coming to *Knowing Me Knowing You*. I know Joel was looking forward to seeing you again,' Kate spoke with a 'life is wonderful, I'm getting on without him' smile.

'Of course I'll be there. In fact, Andrew Kent is taking me,' Miranda said a smug smile spreading over her perfectly made-up face.

'Perfect,' Kate replied, clutching the Watkins file to her chest.

Miranda tossed her blonde hair high over her shoulder and teetered back to her room, closing the door behind her.

Kate let out a sigh. The silly tart was obviously pissed off Colin had made the offer. She didn't know what she wanted to do. It would mean a lot of study, attention away from Bethan, but it would also mean more money and more status within the firm. She would be on an equal footing with Miranda. And then, if she was offered partnership, she would be stepping over the Lady Dragon entirely. She didn't know how that would work though, what with Miranda being the head of department, perhaps she would have to move departments. Did she want to do that? And it was more responsibility; there would be no margin for error, she would have to be on top of her game. Was that what she wanted? Sometimes, her head felt like it was going to explode when she was getting into the technicalities of inheritance tax. Did she really want that feeling every day?

Her phone rang and Ruby announced the arrival

of Mr Watkins. From what Kate remembered from the last time she met him, he had a full-length beard and breath that smelt of pickled onions. If it was the same case today, he would have to be over and done within five chargeable units.

\* \* \*

'Do you know anything about burlesque?' Kate asked Hermione as her friend put a cup of green tea down on the table in front of her.

'Ooh la la! Burlesque! Why do you ask, sweetie?'

'Oh I have to have a stupid talent to show off at the show and I had no idea what to do. I didn't even know about it until Joel told me it was on the show information sheet, which I didn't read properly. So then Lynn suggests burlesque and gets all excited and phones her mental friend Melanie who turns up with this, this and this and I haven't a clue what to do with any of it,' Kate explained, pulling a corset, a fan and a feather boa out of her bag.

'Ooh I say! Va va voom!' Hermione spoke excitedly.

'Am I totally mad? What am I doing? It was bad enough standing on stage just answering questions; now I am going to have to prance around like some sort of nineteenth-century hooker,' Kate exclaimed, drinking some tea.

'What does Joel say?'

'I can't tell him; he would be so embarrassed, he would probably pull out of the show.'

'What's his talent? Apart from obviously being a perfect gentleman and the most gorgeous guy on the planet.'

'Apparently, he plays the guitar. He's probably had lessons from James Blunt. He's going to be great and I'm going to be terrible.'

'Well, my suggestion to you would be to think "role play". When you dress up in costume, give yourself a whole new identity. I don't know, make yourself Maria De Cruz, the Spanish countess, not Kate Baxter, the legal executive. You are mysterious, exciting, sultry and alluring, lose yourself in your music, be at one with the fan, use your props like they are part of you,' Hermione spoke and she picked up the fan, flicked it out with force and hid her face so only her eyes were showing, attempting to bat her eyelashes seductively.

'Have you heard yourself?'

'You want to win the show, don't you?'

'Well yes, but I also don't want to make an idiot of myself in front of the Lady Dragon and the partners of Randall's.'

'It will look worse if you don't commit to the performance. Don't you watch *X Factor*? How many contestants get accused of lacking emotion and not committing? Simon Cowell practically says it every week.'

'How many of them attempt burlesque?' Kate queried.

'That would be novel, wouldn't it? But more *Britain's Got Talent* I'd say.'

'I've got to look on YouTube later, see exactly how much dancing and seductiveness is required. Are you still OK to have Bethan overnight that night?'

'Of course, I'm looking forward to it. We're going to go swimming and make apple tarts.'

'Want to swap? You do the burlesque routine and I'll bake and swim?'

'You know I would in a flash but it isn't *my* name on the entry form, more's the pity. And besides that, I'm not sure I would let you use my oven unsupervised.'

'Mummy, Mummy!' Bethan called as she toddled into the kitchen and held her arms out to Kate.

'Hello darling! Come and give Mummy a cuddle,' Kate spoke, scooping Bethan up in her arms and savouring the feeling of the daughter.

'She's looking more like you every day. And when I

say something she doesn't like the sound of, like "come and have your face wiped" she wrinkles her nose up just like you do,' Hermione said.

'You've never offered to wipe my face and I don't wrinkle my nose,' Kate answered, immediately wrinkling her nose.

'Oh Bethan, Mummy is funny, isn't she?' Hermione said with a laugh.

\* \* \*

When Kate got home, there was a pile of post waiting on the doormat. There was a new menu from a Chinese takeaway with an offer on sweet and sour chicken and prawn crackers, another leaflet about losing half your body weight at Joel's gym and the rest were bills. She picked them up and deposited them on the table. She couldn't face looking at them just yet.

She bathed Bethan, put her to bed and spent the next hour looking at burlesque dancers on the internet. It made her shudder. The women all looked so confident in themselves and their bodies. They looked submissive, yet powerful, prim, yet flirtatious, playful, yet controlled. She had no idea where to begin. In the end, watching the dancers being everything she wasn't was getting her down so she turned the computer off and set her Fisherman's pie to cook. She had a litre of German Hock to wash it down with and she had started that already.

There was a council tax bill, a credit card statement and a car insurance renewal. When she opened the fourth envelope, her heart almost stopped. It was from the Child Support Agency. She read the words, trying to take them in, but as she read, a chill crept over her. Matthew was questioning Bethan's paternity; he wanted a DNA test.

Kate's heart began to pound as she re-read the letter, trying to take it all in. Why would he do this? *How* could he do this? She wanted to cry but the tears wouldn't come; a ball of emotion was lodged in her chest, unmoving.

She picked up the phone and dialled in Hermione's number. It rang and rang and no one picked it up. The microwave beeped and Kate's breathing quickened as she ended the call and dialled a different number. Her mind was working overtime. How dare he? How did they take DNA tests these days? Was it a blood test or a mouth swab? She should ask Lynn; she was up to speed with detective shows.

'Hello.'

'Oh, er hello Joel, it's Kate. I, erm, I'm sorry to call, Hermione isn't in and I just need...' Kate began, trying hard to swallow the tears that were beginning to leak out.

Why had she phoned him?

'Is everything OK?' Joel asked.

'No, I... I'm sorry, I'll call someone else. I shouldn't have called you. I'll try Lynn,' Kate spoke as she began to cry out loud, the thought of subjecting Bethan to any procedure making her feel sick.

'Don't do that. I'm coming over; I'll be there as soon as I can,' Joel replied and he ended the call.

Kate slumped down onto the sofa, the letter in her hand, the words swimming in front of her eyes. He was getting back at her; he was using his own daughter to get back at her for involving the CSA, for making him pay what he should towards her care. She was only two; she was just a little girl.

When she opened the door to Joel, her face was awash with tears and her eyes were red and sore.

'Sorry I called you, I'm fine now. I just couldn't get hold of Hermione and—' Kate began, feeling embarrassed.

'It's OK, are you all right? What happened?'

'Matthew's told the CSA there's doubt over Bethan's paternity. He wants a DNA test,' Kate blurted out and then burst into tears all over again.

Just saying the words brought the raw emotion

back. It didn't seem real or fair; it was like someone
was punishing her. Just when she thought things
couldn't get any worse, Matthew trumped his last action all over again.

Joel put his arms around her and drew her towards
him, holding her tightly. Kate began to cry loudly and
Joel hugged her to him consolingly. She felt so hurt
and betrayed by the man she had loved and she
couldn't believe he was willing to put a little girl
through an unnecessary ordeal because he didn't want
to acknowledge her or pay to support her.

'She's just a little girl; she's his daughter,' Kate
spoke.

'I know,' Joel replied.

'Why would he do this? It's so horrible. He's so
cold.'

'He's doing it because he doesn't want to pay; it's as
simple as that. It's a delaying tactic, that's all, and that's
how you should look at it,' Joel answered.

'Do I have to do it? I don't want her to have a blood
test or whatever for no reason.'

'I think it's a mouth swab now.'

'Do you watch *Waking the Dead*?' Kate queried.

'No. Why?'

'It doesn't matter. Whatever it is, I don't want to do
it. I shouldn't have to – it's wrong.'

'I know,' Joel agreed.

'Sorry, I shouldn't be burdening you with this, it just got to me and I didn't know who to call.'

'It's OK.'

'I don't know, the minute I think I'm on top of things and I'm doing OK, something else happens. Would you like a drink? Sorry, I should have offered – come through. There's wine – oh, well there was,' Kate spoke, picking up the large bottle of wine and finding it was empty.

'I'll just have a coffee or something; I've got the car. What can I smell?' Joel suddenly asked.

'Probably Fisherman's pie.'

'It smells disgusting. Were you going to eat it?'

'Yes, of course.'

'Did you know that they make those meals out of the crappiest off-cuts they can find?'

'No. Perhaps I suspected, but I never dwelt on it.'

'Do you want me to make you something?' Joel offered.

'No! I'm fine, honestly.'

'Do you have eggs?'

'Maybe.'

'Cheese?'

'Possibly.'

'Onion?'

'It's probably past its best.'

'Introduce me to your frying pan,' Joel instructed.

'You don't have to cook for me; I'm really not the helpless damsel in distress. I just had a weak moment, that's all. Everyone has weak moments; even *you* must have weak moments,' Kate insisted, feeling foolish.

'I'm not cooking for you; I'm cooking for me. I stayed late at work and haven't eaten yet. And as for weak moments, yes, a car backfiring usually does it for me. Frying pan?'

\* \* \*

Joel made omelettes with the contents of Kate's fridge plus some tinned mushrooms and new potatoes he found at the back of the cupboard.

'They taste better with fresher ingredients,' he admitted as they ate.

'It's nice,' Kate replied, eating hungrily.

'And you saw how easy it was.'

'Yes, yes, I'm a lazy working mother, whose idea of cooking is ripping the lid off a Pot Noodle, I know, I know.'

'So, have you found a talent yet?'

'Yes, I have,' Kate answered with a smile.

'Really? I'm impressed; that's quick work. So what is it?'

'I'm not telling you.'

'Oh come on, I told you mine.'

'No, my lips are sealed. Besides, if I say the words out loud, I will probably realise how crazy the idea is and change my mind about the whole thing.'

'Am I allowed to guess?'

'Absolutely not.'

'Contortion?'

'Joel!'

'Escapology?'

'No.'

'Plate spinning?'

'I'm not saying.'

Joel laughed and finished his omelette.

'I can't wait to hear you play the guitar. What style do you play in? Are you more Jimi Hendrix or The Gipsy Kings?'

'Somewhere in between, I hope.'

'The Lady Dragon doesn't think I have what it takes to be a solicitor. She cornered me today, tried to put the thumbscrews on. Told me how much hard work it would be and how I couldn't possibly cope, especially as I have a child,' Kate spoke suddenly, changing the conversation.

'You mean she's frightened you might have *just* what it takes,' Joel replied.

'Maybe.'

'Do you want to be a solicitor?'

'I don't know what I want to be.'

'What did you want to be before Matthew left?'

'Just a wife and a mother with a decent job that paid reasonably well – that's what I was, that was all I wanted to be. I didn't need to think any more about it.'

'Then apart from the marital status, nothing's changed. You're a mother with a decent job; you don't need to be a wife to feel complete. Haven't we had this conversation once before?'

'I don't need a man to make me feel complete but I miss the feeling of security. I wasn't on my own, I had someone to share the responsibilities with, share the decision making with. It's very lonely at 3 a.m. when you're tired and your daughter's vomited every half an hour for the whole night and you're the only person she can rely on.'

'There are plenty of single mothers out there doing a fantastic job and you have Hermione.'

'I don't want to be a single mother. In fact, that was the last thing I ever wanted to be. I wanted to be married before I had children, I wanted to do things right, the old-fashioned way. I thought I was doing things right and now what I have isn't what I wanted.'

'Plans go awry; some things are just out of your control.'

'You think I'm stupid,' Kate said with a sigh.

'No, of course I don't. I just think you put too much pressure on yourself. From what I can see, apart from not looking after yourself very well, you do a terrific job looking after Bethan and working and trying to do everything you can to keep things on an even keel,' Joel told her.

'Like entering a relationship contest in a bid to win some money off my mortgage?'

'That is dedication of the highest order,' Joel agreed with a smile.

'You think I should get the DNA test done.'

'I think you should get it done and not give Matthew any reason to hold back paying for his daughter.'

'You're right, he's done this because he knows it will upset me and I shouldn't still let him do that.'

'That's the spirit. Now, tell me about this talent.'

'No, but I will give you a clue. It involves a lot of ruffles and some feathers.'

'You're going to do an impersonation of the Love Dove?' Joel guessed.

'No!' Kate answered with a laugh.

# 19

'Ooh, it has a fountain at the entrance!' Kate exclaimed excitedly as Joel pulled the car up to the reception of Waterfield Country Park.

The day of the next show had arrived and they had travelled for an hour and a half to the outskirts of Bournemouth. Kate was both nervous and excited. She had drunk a litre of water and eaten a family-sized bag of crisps, two Kit Kats and an orange that Joel had insisted she ate when they stopped at the services for smoothies.

'A fountain is surely a good sign; I read somewhere that fountains are a symbol of success,' Joel said, turning off the engine.

'Stop teasing me; you sound like Mione! Let's get the keys! Let's go and see our lodge,' Kate spoke excitedly, leaping out of the car and hurrying to the reception office.

'I see someone's got excited, having spent the first half an hour of the journey worrying whether she'd left enough clothes for Bethan for one night and wondering if she's going to need more than the two bags of toys you packed,' Joel said as he followed her.

'I can't remember the last time I stayed away. OK, having to stand on stage with a giant bird and Larry Rawlins is a major downside, but let's hope the luxurious lodge compensates for it. Come on!' Kate ordered, leading the way.

Before she even got through the door, Kate caught sight of a shock of pink hair.

Becky pulled open the door and unleashed a party popper straight in Kate's face.

'Hello guys, come in, come in!' Becky spoke, ushering the two of them into reception.

'I think I've got a bit of coloured string in my eye,' Kate remarked, trying to pull the papery coils from her face.

'Right, let me take you through the itinerary. You've got about an hour to settle in. Everything should be set up for you in the romance lodge; if not, just give reception a call and they will sort everything out. At three, we have a photo call on the piazza followed by drinks and canapés and at five, we have poolside games where you get to relax and let your hair down with the other contestants. We then need you dressed and ready for the show at seven in the green room before we go live at eight,' Becky announced and she handed Joel and Kate a piece of A4 paper.

'Then we better have our keys because it doesn't seem like we have long to unpack,' Kate remarked, looking at the itinerary.

'Here we are, RL forty-two, here's your park map and your club and fitness suite passes. It's just past reception, second turning on the left,' Becky spoke, handing the information to Joel.

'Thanks. Come on,' Kate spoke, tugging at Joel's arm and moving towards the door.

'Enjoy! See you later!' Becky called as the couple left reception.

'Poolside games? Photo call and canapés! This accommodation better be good,' Kate announced as she got into the car.

* * *

The romance lodge was pink. It was a pine-clad, New England style cabin with a hot tub on the veranda.

'Ooh, a hot tub! Do we have to go to a photo call? Can't we just stay here?' Kate asked excitedly.

'Do you want to upset the girl with pink hair?'

'Ooh, there's a flatscreen TV with surround sound, a remote-control fire, lovely dining table crying out for a ready meal, ooh, a big bath and a double shower and a television set right into the wall of the bathroom, and a sauna, goodness! Oh – oh dear,' Kate suddenly remarked as she looked into the bedroom.

'What's the matter? It was all sounding so good,' Joel spoke, moving into the lodge to join her.

'There's, er, only one bed. Only one bedroom,' Kate remarked, her cheeks going red.

'Oh, well that's OK; I can sleep on the sofa,' Joel responded immediately.

'No, that's not fair. We'll toss a coin for it; the loser sleeps on the sofa,' Kate suggested.

'I don't mind honestly and you said you can't remember the last time you stayed away; you should have the bed,' Joel insisted.

'I know it's romance and everything but I did stupidly think there would be more than one bedroom.'

'It's fine. I'll go and get the bags,' Joel said.

As soon as Joel left the lodge, Kate got out her phone and dialled Hermione's number.

'Hello.'

'I'll have to be quick. There's a problem: there's only one bedroom!'

'So there should be, it *is* a romance lodge. What are you going to do? Bunk up and see what happens?'

'No! Of course not! Joel's offered to sleep on the sofa but that's very small and he's really tall and I feel bad about it.'

'Then bunk up! Look at him, sweetie – what's not to like?'

'Mione, stop it! Yes, yes, we're fine, got here in good time, is Bethan OK?' Kate spoke hurriedly as Joel re-entered the lodge.

'Have a few drinks, play your quiz game and then jump on him as soon as you get back there,' Hermione spoke.

'That's good, I'm glad she's fine. You have got Lynn's mobile number, haven't you? Just in case you need to call during the show. She's going to keep her phone on and pass me any urgent messages by semaphore.'

'Yes I have it, now get off the phone and go and have fun! Proper fun! Not the half-hearted, I don't know whether I should sort of fun you usually have,' Hermione ordered.

'Bye,' Kate ended.

'And is Bethan still OK?' Joel asked with a wry smile.

'I didn't phone her, honestly; she phoned me,' Kate lied, taking her bags out of Joel's hands.

'So, what do you want to do?' Joel asked, putting his bag and guitar down on the bed.

'What?' Kate asked, looking at the bed, her heart thumping.

'Do you want to check out the park or do you want to try the hot tub?'

'Oh, sorry, er, why don't we check out the bar facilities? I might need a drink or two before the photo call,' Kate admitted.

'Good idea,' Joel agreed.

It was a good white wine and it came in a large glass with ice and a straw. Kate closed her eyes and sipped the drink as she and Joel sat on the terrace over-looking the sea. It was a beautiful afternoon, it was warm, there was a light breeze and it felt good to be outside with a little less responsibility than usual.

'Wine always tastes so much nicer in the sun,' Kate remarked, sipping some more.

'Everything seems better in the sun,' Joel replied.

'Am I losing you lots of income taking up your evenings and weekends? How many escorting dates do you usually have booked in?' Kate asked.

'I actually haven't taken any bookings for a while,' Joel replied, taking a swig from his bottle of beer.

'Oh? Don't tell me Elite Escorts are having a downturn.'

'No, at least I don't think so. I asked not to take any bookings for a while.'

'Oh. Why not?'

'I don't know really, spur of the moment decision, thought I would give escorting a rest for a while.'

'Oh,' Kate replied.

'And I don't really have time, what with the competition and everything,' Joel admitted.

'Oh no, it's my fault, I knew it. You don't have time because you're doing this for me. Now I feel awful and even more under pressure. What if we don't win? What if we don't get through tonight?' Kate gabbled.

'It isn't your fault and we're not under pressure; it doesn't matter if we lose. I'm not going to hold anything against you – whoa, I think that came out wrong,' Joel answered with a grin.

'Do you think people really believe we're a couple?' Kate whispered, stirring her wine with the straw.

'Of course. Why wouldn't they? Apart from when you still try and shake my hand.'

'That's not fair; I haven't done that for ages.'

'What made you ask?'

'Well, if I was looking at us, I wouldn't think we were a couple.'

'Why not?'

'Why not?! Because you look like something off the cover of *Men's Health* and I look like...'

'You look like what?'

'Like someone who has seen better days,' Kate answered with a heavy sigh.

'That's in your mind,' Joel told her.

'No, it's definitely in the mirror; I see it, every day.'

'I'm not listening to this; you're just fishing for compliments and I'm not that sort of guy,' Joel told her.

'I'm not, I—' Kate began.

'You need to work on your self-esteem as well as your addiction to wine and microwave dinners,' Joel commented.

'But, I—' Kate started again.

'No one will believe we're a couple if you aren't at least trying to believe it,' Joel told her.

'I am trying, I just...' Kate said, unable to finish her sentence.

'Hold my hand.'

'What?'

'Hold my hand, like you would if I was your guy,' Joel told her.

'What now?'

'Yeah.'

'Well, I...' Kate started, becoming flustered.

Joel took hold of her hand and held it in his. Kate's fingers tensed immediately. It was warm and very nice but it also felt strange. She hadn't held hands with anyone since Matthew, back in Greece, after they'd eaten at the lovely fish restaurant. She couldn't remember doing it since, though she must have – Greece was years ago.

'Didn't Matthew ever hold your hand?' Joel enquired as if reading her mind.

'Of course he did. Well, sometimes. He wasn't really like that; *we* weren't really like that,' Kate admitted with another sigh.

'Perhaps that's where you went wrong. I don't understand why people are so scared to touch one another. I mean, you can say a thousand words with just one touch,' Joel spoke as he gently stroked her fingers.

Kate felt a shiver run up her back. God, he was so

attractive. What would she do if he was someone she had met under normal circumstances? What would she do if he wasn't being bribed into being here?

'I'm not scared of it,' she responded, not sounding particularly convincing.

'Good, then we're going to breeze through into the final.'

He let her hand go as rapidly as he had taken it and Kate grabbed at her wine to hide her shaking fingers. She was just doing this for Bethan, after all.

\* \* \*

'Kate, Joel, look this way please?' the photographer called as they stood in front of a large, garish love heart bearing the *Knowing Me Knowing You* logo.

'Have you seen the Australians? It has to be fake tan, doesn't it?' Kate remarked as she looked at Hayley and Anthony, the couple who had beaten them in the first heat.

'I would say sun beds,' Joel answered, smiling at the camera professionally.

'I forgot you were used to all this camera work, but isn't it usually top off and trousers down?' Kate remarked with a giggle.

'It can be arranged,' Joel responded and he started to unbutton his shirt.

'Shit, I wasn't serious! It was a joke. Please, don't take it off!' Kate exclaimed in panic.

Joel laughed at her.

'Stop winding me up and go and get some of those chicken tikka vol-au-vents,' Kate ordered, wrinkling up her nose.

'Thank you everyone for cooperating with the photographer. Could I ask you all now to change into your swimwear for the pool games which will commence in fifteen minutes,' Becky called through a loud-hailer to everyone on the piazza.

'Looks like the tops are off now anyway,' Joel remarked.

'I cannot wait to see what Hayley and Anthony are going to wear. I think the smallest bikini ever made for her and a thong for him,' Kate spoke, taking a vol-au-vent from the tray on the table.

'And what about Gloria and Mark? She's sixty if she's a day and he's definitely younger than me,' Joel commented.

'They are completely scary,' Kate agreed with a nod as she took another canapé.

'Well, I'll go and get changed. See you in the pool,'

Joel spoke and he leant forward and kissed Kate lightly on the lips.

'OK,' she replied, thinking nothing of it.

She watched him go inside towards the changing rooms and then as she prepared to eat the canapé, she let out a squeal and touched her lips. A few people looked over at her and she smiled and grabbed another nibble, stuffing it quickly into her mouth. She still wasn't used to him kissing her but at least she hadn't tried to shake his hand.

* * *

Kate walked out to the pool with her towel wrapped around her. She had seen all the other contestants slipping into their revealing bikinis and suddenly her plain black swimsuit seemed to be shouting 'frump'.

She saw Joel at the far end of the pool and hurried along the edge towards him. She sat down on the side, whisked her towel away and jumped down into the water before anyone got a chance to look at her attire. It was freezing and she took a sharp breath inwards and tried not to look down at her nipples, which she knew would be poking out like walnuts.

'We're just about to start water polo,' Joel informed her.

'Great,' she replied in unconvincing tones.

'Come on, it will be fun,' Joel spoke, standing up in the water and giving Kate the benefit of seeing just how toned his physique was in trunks reminiscent of Daniel Craig in *Casino Royale*.

Her gaze was only redirected from Joel's torso by the arrival of someone else. Walking towards them, along the edge of the pool, strutting as if she were a catwalk model was someone she recognised.

The Lady Dragon Miranda, clad in a tiny, gold bikini and high, gold sandals, tip-tapped across the concrete. She was wearing huge sunglasses and carrying a glass of fluorescent pink liquid. Inside the glass were two umbrellas and a cardboard parrot.

'God, what is she doing here already?' Kate remarked to Joel, turning away from the arriving party.

'Who?'

'The Lady Dragon – don't look, I don't want her to see us,' Kate said, ducking down into the water despite the sub-zero temperatures.

'Kate! Joel! What a surprise! I didn't expect to see you in the pool. Thought you might be making use of that romance lodge you're staying in,' Miranda remarked, lowering her sunglasses to look at Joel.

'Oh we made plenty of use of that earlier,' Joel

replied and he slipped his arms around Kate's waist as he stood behind her.

'I just bet you did, you naughty boy. So, how are preparations going for the show tonight? I have to say Joel, you look in perfect physical condition. If I were hosting the show, I wouldn't care what your answers to the questions were. Full marks from me. Perfect.'

'Have you come with anyone? I hear Colin is bringing Dawn, the trainee from the Family department,' Kate said, looking for Miranda's reaction.

'Yes, apparently so. I've come with Andrew Kent. He's just at the bar ordering some snacks; he'll be here any minute,' Miranda replied, unfazed.

'We'd better join the others for the water polo,' Joel said, steering Kate away from Miranda.

'Ooh, water polo, all that splashing and leaping about chasing a ball. I can't wait to watch you in action,' Miranda said, smiling at Joel.

'Ah, here's Andrew now. My word, I could never have envisaged how he would look in trunks,' Kate commented as the rotund, fifty-year-old partner appeared from the main building wearing Oakley sunglasses and carrying a large, silver tray on which was a bottle of champagne, two glasses and what looked like two bags of pork scratchings.

Miranda ignored Kate's comment, put her sunglasses back on and carefully lowered herself down onto a lounger.

'You're cruel,' Joel remarked as they moved to join their fellow contestants.

'It was the least she deserved for eyeing up my boyfriend,' Kate joked and she splashed Joel in the chest with the water.

'Hey!' he called, chasing after her.

# 20

'This is crazy, what was I thinking? I can't do this!' Kate remarked, downing a rum and Coke.

She and Joel were sat in the green room waiting for the show to begin. A draw had been made to settle the order and they were on first.

Each couple had to answer two questions and then it was the talent round which was to be judged by a specialist panel consisting of a previous *X Factor* contestant, a theatre arts drama coach and Judith Chalmers. After those results were in, there would be a final question to determine the winners.

'We're going to be fine; we've probably practised more than any couple here,' Joel reassured her.

'Because we don't know each other!' Kate reminded him.

'And how much do you think real couples know about each other?'

'Everything.'

'Like you and Matthew?'

'That's below the belt.'

'I'm just trying to get your confidence up. We can do this; we've practised and we know each other. We couldn't have done much more if we tried,' Joel spoke.

'I'm dreading the talent round,' Kate said, finishing her drink.

'I can't wait. I have absolutely no idea what you are going to come out and do.'

'Neither do I.'

'You're going to be fantastic,' a familiar voice spoke.

Kate turned around to see Lynn and her husband Darren stood behind them.

'Oh Lynn, you're here! Hello, Darren,' Kate greeted as she enveloped her secretary in a hug.

'Excuse me if I don't shake hands,' Darren joked, waving his stump at Kate.

'Stop doing that, Darren; everyone thinks it's really freaky,' Lynn told him.

'Joel, this is Lynn and her husband Darren. Lynn's

my saviour at work; she does far more than she should,' Kate introduced.

'Hello. Nice to meet you both,' Joel greeted shyly, trying not to look at Darren and his injury.

'Has Hermione rung? Is Bethan OK?' Kate asked.

'I phoned her just before we slipped past the security man on the door. Bethan's in bed, fast asleep with Mr Crisps. Hermione, Philip and the older kids, I forget their names, are sat in front of the telly waiting for the show to start,' Lynn informed her.

'God, I wish you hadn't told me that,' Kate replied.

'So, are you nervous?' Lynn enquired.

'Yes! I've already had three drinks on top of the drinks I had with the canapés earlier,' Kate said.

'You'll be fine. Just focus on the Lady Dragon. You have got to see what she's wearing. Think Liz Hurley in *that* dress, you know, the one with the safety pins, and then mix that image with something Lady Gaga might turn up in,' Lynn explained.

'God, I'd better not look. The bikini at lunchtime was almost enough to make the chicken satays reappear.'

'And Andrew Kent is wearing leather trousers.'

'Stop! I don't want to hear any more,' Kate shouted.

'Kate! Joel! We need you backstage! Chop, chop!'

Becky suddenly yelled as she bounced towards them with her clipboard.

'Oh good luck! We'd better go back to our seats. See you later,' Lynn spoke, waving a hand at the couple.

'Bye,' Darren added, directing the response at Joel.

Joel hurriedly took hold of Kate's hand and led her towards Becky, who was rushing to the stage door.

'You're shaking,' Kate remarked, feeling Joel's hand.

'Nerves,' Joel replied with a smile.

'But you don't get nervous, ever. You told me,' Kate spoke, looking up at him.

'First time for everything,' he replied.

The music began. Larry Rawlins introduced himself and ran through the rules of the show for the audience and the viewers at home. Kate and Joel were introduced to the crowd and then it was time for the questions to start.

Kate could see Miranda in the audience. She was wearing a white dress, tied down the sides with thin crisscross strings and Andrew Kent was next to her, dressed in black, leather trousers teamed with a bright-red shirt and a thin, eighties-style leather tie. His hair was slicked back and he was chewing gum.

He didn't look like a partner in a successful law firm; he looked like a pimp.

Colin Sykes and Dawn the trainee were sat at the same table, all over each other. She was almost sat on his lap and his shirt was half undone.

'So Kate, it's you to go into the Booth of Tranquillity while we ask Joel two questions,' Larry spoke as the Love Dove, now sporting a sequined waistcoat, grabbed Kate's arm and hauled her towards the booth.

'Right, Joel, as soon as Kate has her blindfold and headphones on, I will ask the first question – OK, I'm assured she can't hear us now. Right Joel, Kate has been invited to a party organised by her very best friend but she has a cold and doesn't really feel like going. What does she do? Does she A, go to the party, she hates to let people down; does she B, not go to the party, she feels too unwell and her friend will understand; or C, does she tell her friend she's too ill to go but offer to bake something for the party to make up for it,' Larry spoke.

The audience let out a trickle of completely unnecessary laughter.

'Well, Kate definitely doesn't bake so it won't be C. I will have to say A, she would go to the party and not let her friend down,' Joel answered.

'Ah! Kate's a good friend, ladies and gentlemen,

isn't that nice. OK, question two. Kate finds out that her best friend's chap is cheating on her. What does she do? Does she A, tell her friend straight away, honesty is the best policy; does she B, tell the guy she knows exactly what he's up to and order him to come clean; or C, does she do nothing at all, after all, it's none of her business?'

'That's a tough one – but I think she would say A, she would tell her friend straight away,' Joel spoke.

'Right, well, without further ado, let's get Kate back and see if we can get some matches and some Kissing Gates on the board,' Larry spoke theatrically.

Joel took hold of Kate's hand as she re-joined them and he gave it a reassuring squeeze.

It was hard to adjust to the bright lights when you had been blindfolded in a plastic tube but as Kate's eyes regained their focus, it seemed like there were hundreds of people in the audience, all looking at her. It was completely unnerving now, but what was it going to be like when she was dressed up in a skimpy burlesque outfit?

'OK, Kate, we said to Joel – Kate has been invited to a party organised by her best friend but she has a cold and doesn't really feel like going. What does she do? Does she not go to the party, she feels too unwell and her friend will understand or does she tell her friend she is too ill to go but offer to bake something for the party to make up for it, or does she go to the party, she hates to let people down,' Larry asked.

Kate looked at Joel as if to gauge from his expression what he had answered.

'Well, I don't like to let anyone down so I would go to the party,' Kate said, tentatively.

'YES! A match and an all-important Kissing Gate on the board!' Larry yelled, prompting the Love Dove to start flapping its wings and running over to the scoreboard.

Kate smiled at Joel and he squeezed her hand again.

'OK, let's not get carried away. The next question, we said to Joel – Kate finds out her best friend's chap is cheating on her. What does she do? Does she tell the guy she knows exactly what he is up to and order him to come clean? Does she tell her friend straight away, honesty is the best policy? Or does she do nothing at all, after all, it's none of her business,' Larry enquired.

'I would tell my friend straight away because honesty is always the best policy,' Kate answered confidently, looking at Joel.

'YES! A match! And a second Kissing Gate on the board! Kate and Joel, full marks, you can't get any better than that! Let's give them a big hand, ladies and gentlemen and we will see them a little later in the talent round. Kate and Joel, everyone!' Larry spoke, directing them offstage.

Kate was beaming when they arrived backstage. It was the best start they could ever have imagined.

'I can't believe we got full marks; we couldn't have done any better!' Kate exclaimed happily.

'No,' Joel replied with a nod.

'What's the matter? We're completely on course for the finals and the money!' Kate screamed excitedly.

'Yeah, I know.'

'Can you believe we got both the questions right? Let's have a drink. Lager?' Kate offered, bouncing towards the free bar.

'Sure,' Joel replied with a half-hearted smile.

'Dreading the next bit, though. Wish I'd had time to think of a proper talent; my effort is going to get our marks down for sure. Judith Chalmers is going to absolutely hate it. I mean, she's been places, she's seen exotic dancers in every corner of the globe, I am just going to look like some sort of untrained, old-fashioned stripper,' Kate babbled as the barman gave her the drinks.

'If it's any consolation, my song isn't the best either,' Joel spoke.

'No, it's no consolation! I was relying on you to be a

hit with the judges! Where's your guitar? Did you want to have a little practise?' Kate suggested.

'No.'

'But if you're worried – do you want to play it to me?' Kate asked.

'No, it's fine, I'll be fine,' Joel insisted with a sigh.

'Are you OK?' Kate questioned.

'Yes, fine.'

'You don't look fine; you look a bit peaky. Are you ill or something? You should have said if you needed painkillers or something, I always carry Calpol and Ibuprofen.'

'I'm all right, honestly. It's a bit warm in here, that's all,' Joel replied, taking a swig of his drink.

'Do you want to go outside?'

'No.'

'OK.'

'I'm just overcome that we did so well,' Joel joked with a smile.

'Me too,' Kate replied with a happy grin.

\* \* \*

'Now ladies and gentlemen, we are in for an entertainment extravaganza next when our competing couples retake the stage to perform their talent for us. Remember, after the first round, we have Kate and Joel, Hayley and Anthony and Brian and Martha all in joint first place with two Kissing Gates each. But the couple winning this round gets five Kissing Gates and the runners up get three Kissing Gates, so there is a lot to play for in this section of the competition. So then, without further ado, let's welcome back onto the stage Joel, who is performing a James Morrison number on the guitar,' Larry Rawlins introduced.

'Good luck,' Kate spoke as she waited in the wings, her coat covering her burlesque outfit.

Joel smiled at her and went onto the stage where a stool and microphone had been set up. The audience applauded his entrance and then waited for him to begin.

He took a moment to compose himself and then he started to play.

As soon as his fingers hit the strings, a hush descended over the room and everyone seemed mesmerised by every note. When he began to sing, Kate could see the jaws of every female fall open as they admired this gorgeous former model with the fantastic voice. Joel sang powerfully and with emotion. The audience didn't seem to faze him at all. He played beautifully, he sang well and when he came to the end of the

performance, the crowd clapped and cheered appre-
ciatively.

He accepted his applause and then left the stage to
re-join Kate.

'You were brilliant. I had no idea you could play
and sing like that,' Kate remarked, smiling at Joel as he
took the guitar off.

'It was a bit rough around the edges, especially on
the second verse,' Joel replied with a sigh.

'Rubbish! James Morrison himself couldn't have
performed it better and Judith was smiling the whole
way through, tapping her fingers on the desk in time.
She loved it,' Kate informed him.

'...please welcome onto the stage, Kate Baxter!'
Larry announced.

'God, it's my turn. Here, hold my coat,' Kate ordered and she whipped it off to reveal the vintage
cream and gold dress with a corset-style top.

Kate took a deep breath, thought about the reason
she was doing this and closed her eyes. She had to get
into character if this was going to work. She walked
onto the stage and tried her best to look demure and
in control.

Who was she trying to kid? She looked like
someone out of Readers Wives or the 'before' look of
someone from *Extreme Makeover*.

Some male members of the crowd whooped and cheered and Kate, although focussed, could see Colin Sykes sit a little further forward on his chair. Miranda had a face that looked like it had been sucking lemons and Andrew Kent was starting to perspire heavily due to the combination of spotlights, an ill-fitting shirt and the leather trousers.

The music, reminiscent of a funked-up Glenn Miller, began and Kate tried to remember everything she had learnt from a few evenings on YouTube, a phone conversation with Mental Melanie and a couple of practise runs in front of the mirror. She moved lightly, yet confidently, pulling at her elbow length gloves and removing them as slowly and demurely as she could, much to the crowd's enjoyment. She used her prop, a chair, swooshing her leg over it, sitting astride it, front to the audience, back to the audience, removing clothing as she went along. She smiled and looked in control, she held her arms high in the air and as the music reached a crescendo she whipped off the front of her dress so she was stood only in the corset and stockings.

The men wolf-whistled and cheered and the whole crowd applauded as Kate felt her cheeks redden. She bowed politely, collected her discarded clothes and then hurried off the stage, grabbing her coat from Joel and putting it on as quickly as she could.

'Wow,' Joel spoke, smiling at her broadly.

'What?' Kate asked, hugging her coat to her.

'I've never seen anything quite like it before,' Joel told her.

'And I doubt you ever will. Was it that terrible? I don't think any of the judges were particularly impressed. I'm sure I saw Judith purse her lips at one point.'

'Are you kidding? It wasn't terrible, it was terrific. I had no idea you did that,' Joel spoke.

'I don't do that and I won't be doing it, ever again. It was Lynn's stupid idea and I couldn't come up with anything else at short notice. So there we go! We're doomed!' Kate spoke.

'After that performance, I'd say we had it in the bag,' Joel told her.

'Really? Was I good? It was completely out of character really and I didn't have a clue what I was doing,' Kate exclaimed excitedly.

'It didn't come across like that,' Joel assured her.

'Well, good. I was focussed, I was thinking about Bethan and the reason I am doing this whole insane competition and then I thought about the solicitor's exam and I realised that without Matthew, the world is my oyster. I can do whatever I want to do and I can be whoever I want to be. If I want to be a burlesque dancer then I will be,' Kate spoke, beaming.

'And is that what you want to be?'

'I don't know yet. I think I need to try pole dancing too, just to compare,' Kate admitted with a smile.

'Now that I would like to see,' Joel said.

\* \* \*

'Come on, come on, all back on stage for the results of the talent round, chop, chop Madeline and Michael. Have I got Brian and Martha and Hayley and Anthony?' Becky questioned as she flapped about in the green room, collecting everyone together.

'I guess that means us as well,' Kate said, downing her drink and preparing to join the group.

'I guess it does. I hope we don't have to perform again if the judges can't decide,' Joel remarked.

'That won't happen; they're on a tight schedule. They have to finish on time for ad breaks and things,' Kate replied.

'Thank God for ad breaks.'

'Right, let's welcome them all back on stage please, our wonderful *Knowing Me Knowing You* contestants,'

Larry Rawlins introduced, holding out a sequined arm.

The contestants filed back onto the stage as the audience and judges applauded them.

'Right, without further ado, the two couples, winners and runners-up in the talent round are...'

Kate held her breath and took hold of Joel's hand. She squeezed her eyes shut and willed Larry Rawlins to say their names.

'Gloria and Mark!'

Kate squeezed her eyes shut even tighter and felt her chest contract. She also sensed Joel's grip tighten on her hand.

'And Kate and Joel!' Larry announced finally.

Kate snapped her eyes open and grinned gleefully.

'And out of those two couples, the judges were unanimous, the winners, with five Kissing Gates to add to their board are – Gloria and Mark with their wonderful acts, the juggling and the aerobics,' Larry spoke, clapping his hands together as the sixty-year-old Gloria French-kissed her partner for all to see.

'Oh God, please tell me *he* did the aerobics,' Kate remarked.

'So well done Gloria and Mark, five Kissing Gates and Kate and Joel, three Kissing Gates, which means you are our front runners with one round left to go,' Larry announced.

'Don't be disappointed,' Joel said.

'I'm not. Well, perhaps a bit. I'd like to see what fantastic juggling and aerobics they did,' Kate said.

'We're second; we only need to come second to be in the final. We just need to do our best in the last round,' Joel encouraged.

'Yes, I know,' Kate replied, looking out into the audience.

Lynn was waving wildly and whistling, Colin was necking Dawn and Miranda was laughing ridiculously loudly and touching Andrew Kent's knee. All looked the worse for booze.

The next half an hour didn't really matter to them, but it was absolutely crucial to Kate. She had to make the final; she needed that prize money. She wanted to get her life back on track. She wanted to give Bethan everything she needed without having to struggle. But most of all, she needed to shake herself free of Matthew. If she could do that financially, then her emotions should surely follow suit.

# 21

'You're doing so well! The Lady Dragon hates it! And have you seen Colin and Dawn? They've hardly come up for air!' Lynn exclaimed, pouncing on Kate as she waited with Joel.

'You shouldn't be in here; you'll get us disqualified. Plus, I want to know all about the other couples. You can't report back if you're in here with me and missing the action,' Kate spoke.

'Darren's keeping an eye on things while downing all the wine. Still, whatever keeps him in a good mood,' Lynn replied.

'My dancing was terrible, I was so embarrassed,' Kate remarked.

'It was great! And isn't Joel a terrific singer? There's

no way that wrinkly Sylvia doing star jumps and all that thrusting was better,' Lynn said with a nod.

'Joel's getting some drinks, do you want one?' Kate offered.

'No thanks, just popping in to give moral support.'

'Well just hang there a second. I'm desperate for the loo but I'll be back. I want to know all the gossip from the table. Joel, give Lynn my drink,' Kate spoke as Joel returned and she made a mad dash towards the exit.

'Hello again,' Joel greeted, passing Lynn Kate's drink.

'Hello. I was just saying to Kate, I thought your song was really good,' Lynn told him.

'Thanks – listen Lynn, don't say anything to Kate, will you? I want to tell her myself,' Joel spoke, a serious expression on his face.

'OK, am I supposed to know what you're talking about? Don't tell Kate what?' Lynn asked, confused.

'Darren didn't tell you?'

'Darren didn't tell me what?'

'It doesn't matter. I just thought – it doesn't matter – it's nothing, honestly,' Joel answered with a smile.

'Hmm, now you're worrying me. Is he keeping secrets from me? Have you two met before or something?' Lynn questioned, staring at Joel suspiciously.

*  *  *

Kate washed her hands and looked at herself in the mirror. Her face was glowing and for the first time in ages, she felt like her. This was how she used to feel when things had been uncomplicated, with no pressure at work, marital strife or single motherhood. She smiled at her reflection and was just about to walk towards the door when someone walked through it, tossing their blonde hair back.

'Oh Kate, hello,' Miranda greeted.

'Hello.'

'Aren't you and Joel doing well? Who would have thought it? I expect you're glad you selected him – handsome, intelligent, such a fabulous singer.'

'Yes,' Kate replied, not really knowing what to say.

'But then he is the best choice on the Elite Escorts website, isn't he? I didn't think much of any of the others,' Miranda remarked.

Kate froze, Miranda's words hitting her like a bulldozer. Her heart leapt up into her throat.

'I admire you really; an escort agency isn't something I would ever consider using. But I know it must be hard being divorced and being a single mother. All those lonely nights in front of the television wondering how your life came to this,' Miranda continued.

'I don't know what you're talking about,' Kate muttered stupidly, knowing her shocked expression had all but given her away.

'No, of course not. You met Joel at the swimming pool, didn't you?' Miranda spoke smugly.

'Yes,' Kate replied unconvincingly.

'I doubt the organisers of this competition would be very pleased to hear that one of the current leading couples were nothing more than fakes. And I just can't imagine what it would do to Frank Peterson – his solicitor cheating, his integrity questionable,' Miranda continued.

Kate couldn't say anything; tears were welling up in her eyes already.

'But then no one need find out. If you, say, turned down Colin's offer, told him you didn't want to take the solicitor's exam. I'm sure your little secret could stay a secret,' Miranda spoke, a smile crossing her face.

'I don't know what you're talking about. Joel and I are a couple.'

'Oh Kate, in your dreams! Look at him! Look at *you*!' Miranda exclaimed, laughing out loud.

'Not everyone judges everything on face value,' Kate replied as hurt built up in her chest.

'I would think very carefully about what your next move is going to be. I mean, all you have to do is turn down the offer of the exam and then you can carry on with the contest and carry on as a legal executive. Nothing has to change.'

Kate just looked at Miranda. The Lady Dragon was sneering at her, smiling smugly, pulling at a tendril of blonde hair.

'You're in shock; you didn't think I'd find out. Well, why don't you have a little think about it over the weekend and let me know on Monday how you wish to proceed,' Miranda suggested, speaking to Kate as if she were a client she was going to report for money laundering.

'Joel and I are a couple,' Kate stated again as if saying it a dozen times was going to make it real.

Miranda laughed out loud and then turned on her heel and left the toilets like a pantomime bad fairy.

Kate put a hand to her chest the second Miranda had closed the door in an attempt to quell the panic. The Lady Dragon knew and now she was going to try and blackmail her. She couldn't let her jeopardise the contest; she and Joel had worked too hard to let that happen.

She looked at her reflection in the mirror again. The smile had gone and the worry lines had reappeared. It was back to normality.

\* \* \*

'The final round, the round that will decide which two couples go through to the grand finals, to be held in London, is called "Bitter or Sweet". This will be a quick-fire round where the couples will be given two words and they will have to pick the word they think best reflects their partner's preference. For example, "savoury" or "sweet". Is everyone clear?' Larry Rawlins asked the contestants and the audience.

All Kate could do was stare into the audience at Miranda. She was perched on Andrew Kent's knee, sipping champagne and licking her lips. Kate had never wished death on anyone before but she wished it now. She looked at the sparkling chandeliers hanging from the ceiling and wondered how she could arrange for the one over the Randall's table to be loosened. A loosened screw and it could fall, land on Miranda's head. Shards of glass would scratch into her face, one large sharp piece would pierce her heart and she would lay across Andrew Kent's leather trousers, bloodstained and lifeless.

'Are you OK?' Joel asked, taking hold of her hand.

'Yes, yes, I'm fine,' Kate insisted, hurriedly putting a smile on her face.

'I'm a savoury, by the way, not a sweet, just in case they do ask that one,' Joel spoke quietly.

'Oh,' Kate replied.

'Are you sure you're OK?' Joel asked again.

'Yes, fine, nothing another drink won't cure,' Kate said as she prepared to leave the stage.

'Listen, when we get back to the lodge, there's something I have to tell you,' Joel spoke seriously.

'Oh, you know! Did she speak to you too?' Kate exclaimed, half horrified but half delighted that she didn't have to keep Miranda's knowledge to herself.

'What?'

'Miranda.'

'Kate, what are you talking about?'

'She knows you're an escort,' Kate said nervously.

'What?!'

'You didn't know.'

'No, when did this happen?'

'She confronted me, in the toilets. She knows and she's going to tell everyone we're frauds if I don't turn down the solicitor's exam,' Kate informed as they followed Becky down the corridor towards the green room.

'She can't do that,' Joel replied, opening the door for her.

'She can and she will. I've told you, she's evil, she

hates me and for some reason, she feels threatened by me and – what are we going to do? I don't want to lose our chance,' Kate said, looking at Joel, wide-eyed.

'I'm not going to let her do this,' Joel spoke.

'I don't think I have a choice; she's given me the weekend to think about it but I'm going to have to turn down the offer of the exam. I'm not sure I wanted to do it anyway.'

'No.'

'What else can we do? We could pull out of the competition or deliberately lose but I don't want to do that. Hermione and Lynn and you have put so much into this it isn't just about the money any more,' Kate spoke, picking up a stray drink from the bar and swallowing it.

'We're not pulling out or throwing the competition; leave it with me,' Joel said confidently.

'I'm sorry, I don't know how she found out. Perhaps it was me, not looking like your girlfriend and trying to shake hands with you...' Kate began, feeling guilty.

'It's OK, don't worry about it; it's not important. You just worry about getting the questions right in the "Bitter or Sweet" round,' Joel spoke with a smile.

'But...'

'Come on, let's get another drink,' Joel urged her, taking hold of her hand.

* * *

'They got nine out of ten,' Kate announced, downing the drink in her hand.

'Who?'

'Sodding Gloria and Mark. We can't win now; the best we can do is come second.'

'Then that's what we'll do. Come on, don't be so defeatist,' Joel informed her.

'We don't know each other well enough.'

'We do. How many of the other couples will have been practising questions together most nights?'

'Anthony and Hayley will have been; the rest of them don't need to because they're...'

'Sleeping together?'

'Well, yes, I suppose so, although—'

'You don't get to know someone by sleeping with them.'

'No, I guess not.'

'So what's the problem? We know each other, we've spent the last few weeks getting to know each other, we know enough.'

'Come on, come on! Chop, chop, you're next!' Becky announced, her pink hair hitting Kate in the face as she swung around and led the way to the stage.

'And here they are, ladies and gentlemen, our current second-place couple – Kate and Joel,' Larry announced to the cameras.

'You know me, Kate,' Joel said seriously, squeezing her hand.

'Hello guys, are you ready for the "Bitter or Sweet" round? Joel, it's your turn to go in the booth so if you would like to trot over there, slip on the blindfold and the headphones, we'll get underway.'

Kate watched Joel as he went into the booth and covered his eyes and ears with the pink, velvet accessories.

'Don't look so nervous, my love; I'm sure you're going to do very well. OK, a quick recap. I am going to say two words, for example, "savoury" or "sweet", and you are going to answer how you think Joel will answer, taking into account his preferences. Everything clear?'

'Yes, I think so,' Kate told him with a nervous swallow.

'OK, can I have thirty seconds on the clock please?'

Kate looked out at the Randall's table. Lynn was biting her nails but when she saw Kate looking, she gave a thumbs up. Colin was unbuttoning Dawn's blouse and paying little attention to what was happening on stage and Miranda had taken off her shoes and was having her feet massaged by Andrew Kent.

'OK Kate, ready? And start the clock – savoury or sweet?'

'Savoury.'

'Action or relaxation?'

'Relaxation.'

'Up or down?'

'Up.'

'Tea or coffee?'

'Coffee.'

'Nightclub or wine bar?'

'Wine bar.'

'Ferrari or Porsche?'

'Porsche.'

'Truth or dare?'

'Truth.'

'Gym or bed?'

'Gym.'

'Flower or tree?'

'Tree.'

'Hot or cold?'

'Hot.'

'That's great; you managed all ten, well done,' Larry spoke as he came to the end of the time.

Kate could feel herself sweating. She really didn't know whether she had given the right answers or not. She had just said the first thing that had come into her head; there hadn't been any time for consideration.

'OK, let's get Joel out of the booth and I will pose the same questions to him and see how many matches we get and how many Kissing Gates we can add to your board,' Larry announced.

Joel re-joined Kate and took hold of her shaking hand.

'OK, Joel, we asked Kate, and remember, these answers relate to you, so answer them honestly. Savoury or sweet?'

'Savoury.'

'Action or relaxation?'

'Relaxation.'

'Up or down?'

'Up.'

'Tea or coffee?'

'Coffee.'

'Nightclub or wine bar?'

'Wine bar.'

'Ferrari or Porsche?'

'Porsche.'

'Truth or dare?'

'Truth.'

'Gym or bed?'

'Bed.'

'Flower or tree?'

'Tree.'

'Hot or cold?'

'Hot.'

As the questioning came to an end, Kate had no idea how they had done. She had been too nervous to remember the answers she had given.

'Right, well, I think you have done pretty well, just waiting for confirmation through my earpiece. Yes, yes, Kate and Joel you scored nine matches out of ten. It seems Joel prefers bed to gym, you lucky, lucky girl. Congratulations! That means you cannot be caught and we have our winning couples, winning *Knowing Me Knowing You* here in Bournemouth are Gloria and Mark and our runners-up, also through to the national finals are Kate and Joel!' Larry announced.

With that announcement made, the Love Dove bounded onto the stage with two giant golden eggs and gave one to the ecstatic pensioner Gloria and one to Kate.

'And your prize for this evening is five thousand pounds plus a night in an executive suite at the Metropole Hotel in London when we take the game show the whole country is talking about to the capital,' Larry announced.

A mixture of fear and excitement swept over Kate

and she didn't really know what to do. Lynn was on her feet screaming at the top of her voice and Darren had mounted a chair and was waving his stump in the air, a bottle of red wine in his good hand.

And then suddenly, the golden egg fell out of her hands and hit the floor as Joel picked her up and swung her around. Kate screamed and held on to him until he eventually put her down.

'Come on, let's go and celebrate,' Joel spoke excitedly.

'I thought there was something you had to tell me,' Kate replied, picking the egg up from the floor.

'It can wait. Come on, let's have champagne,' Joel encouraged, taking Kate by the hand and leading her back towards the green room.

## 22

'I've definitely had too much to drink, I'm sure there weren't two hot tubs here earlier,' Kate spoke as she staggered up the steps towards the door of the romance lodge.

'I did warn you against a third cocktail,' Joel replied, getting the key out of his pocket and opening the door for them both.

'Of course you did, it was like having a virtuous voice of conscience in my ear.'

'Are you calling me boring?'

'No, I couldn't call you that, it would be rude after you bought the champagne for everyone on the Randall's table. You shouldn't have done that, by the way, it was too much.'

'It's just money.'

'God! Listen to you! It's just money! We may have five thousand pounds to divide up, sixty/forty in my favour, but there's no need to go throwing it away.'

'OK, point taken. Do you want a coffee?' Joel asked her.

'Does the virtuous voice in my ear think I should have one?'

'Most definitely.'

'Then I will have one,' Kate agreed and she sat down on the sofa, kicked off her shoes and wrapped her legs underneath her.

'Shall I put the fire on?' Joel asked as he filled the kettle.

'Ooh now you sound like my butler, yes please, Jeeves,' Kate joked, taking off her earrings and putting them on the coffee table.

'So how did Hermione take the news of our progression into the grand finals?' Joel asked, switching on the fire and coming to sit down next to Kate.

'She screamed, loudly, like only she can and then kept saying "I told you so" to Philip, who was clucking like an overexcited Love Dove in the background. Apparently, she did a rune reading that afternoon that told her there was no way we weren't going to make it through. I wish she had told me that.'

'No you don't. You don't really believe in any of that stuff,' Joel answered.

'Well it can't be true, can it?'

'Why not?'

'Because it's fortune-telling, fairground mumbo jumbo that people make up to suit themselves.'

'You think Hermione lies to people?'

'No. Well, not intentionally. I don't know, I don't really know what she does or why she does it but I can't believe in something that has no logical explanation,' Kate said determinedly.

'Like love?'

'What?'

'Love, romance. That doesn't have any logical explanation, or are you of the belief that love happens because of a chemical reaction between two people?'

'No, of course not,' Kate scoffed.

'So if you believe in love, something that has no set course, no logic to it, why can't you believe that Hermione can read the runes?'

'I don't know,' Kate answered stupidly, looking at Joel and swallowing. Why was he making her nervous?

'I'll make the coffee; it's probably too deep a conversation to have when we're both worse for wear,' Joel said, getting to his feet.

'I hope Lynn's OK with Darren. He could hardly stand up when they left, which is bad enough for someone with two good arms, let alone someone with only one.'

'She seems really nice,' Joel replied as he made coffee.

'She is, she's so nice. In fact, she is the nicest person in the whole office and a fantastic secretary.'

'Kate, I'd already met Darren – before tonight,' Joel stated nervously.

'Oh?'

'Yeah, that's what I wanted to tell you before.'

'Oh.'

'Well, there was more to it than that. I wanted to tell you about the Army: about why I didn't want to talk about it.'

'You don't need to tell me anything,' Kate said immediately.

'I want to,' Joel said firmly.

'You're shaking,' Kate remarked, looking at his hands.

He was nervously playing with them, cupping them together then almost wringing them out.

'I'm OK,' he insisted.

'Come and sit down,' Kate ordered, making room for him on the sofa.

Joel did as he was told and continued to hold one shaking hand with another.

'When I was in Afghanistan, something really bad happened and I'm still struggling to come to terms with it,' Joel began.

'You don't have to explain anything to me Joel, I—' Kate started.

'It was OK out there to begin with – well, not OK, but bearable – and at the end of the day, it was just a job: an important job that needed to be done,' Joel continued as if not hearing her.

Kate just watched him, seeing the tension enter his whole body as he spoke.

'Well, one day, we were pushing deep into enemy territory, looking to take ground and clear an area that was one of the enemy strongholds. We were engaged, unexpectedly, by far more enemy than anticipated and it turned from something routine into – well, a bloodbath.'

Kate swallowed, hearing the pain in his voice.

'All of them were killed, every one of my troop, except me. I ran, I called in air support and I spent the next few minutes hiding in the smallest niche you can imagine, praying the strike would miss me,' Joel explained, his voice faltering as he concluded.

'Oh Joel,' Kate said not knowing what else to say.

'I just can't get over it. It happened almost three years ago and it's always on my mind. They were my friends, they were like family to me and all of them died. I feel so guilty because I'm here and they're not and not a day goes by without me thinking about it. Why didn't I die? Why was I the only lucky one?' Joel questioned, tears brimming in his eyes.

'Oh goodness, you can't think like that,' Kate said, sitting forward and taking his hands in hers.

'I know I have to try and move on but I just can't. I've had counselling, I've had tablets to try and help but it doesn't get any better. I can't forget and I can't sleep. I get nightmares and flashbacks and they're so real, it's like I'm there all over again. That day when the car backfired, I thought I was back there, you know I heard that sound every day and it still terrifies me,' Joel continued, the tears finally spilling from his eyes.

'Oh Joel, don't cry, please.'

'Sorry, it's just I had to tell you in case Darren told Lynn and she told you and I needed you to hear it from me. Darren was there, you see – not there when it happened, but in Afghanistan at the same time, part of my regiment. After that day, I couldn't carry on, I couldn't even bear to hold my gun any more and the smell of the uniform just made me wretch. And afterwards, I know some of the others felt differently to-wards me and I couldn't bear them looking at me, knowing they resented the fact I was alive and their mates weren't. It wasn't my fault they all got killed but it has to be my fault that I survived. Why wasn't I up front that day? I was always up front; what made me hang back?'

'I'm so sorry I pried and asked you about it; it's none of my business and I apologise if I made things worse,' Kate said, putting her arms around him and holding him tightly.

'No, don't be sorry. It isn't your fault and it wasn't just seeing Darren that made me need to tell you about it,' Joel spoke, wiping his eyes with the back of his hand and looking at Kate.

'I don't understand.'

'I haven't been able to talk about it before. Not to anyone. I had counselling session after counselling session and I still couldn't talk about that actual day.'

'I still don't understand.'

'You said honesty was important to you and that's why I had to tell you about Afghanistan, about what it did to me and how it still affects me.'

'I appreciate that,' Kate answered.

'I'm not making myself clear, am I?'

'No.'

Joel leant forward and kissed her on the mouth, softly and tenderly. Kate was taken aback but she didn't move. She let him kiss her and she touched his cheek with her hand as he drew away again.

'I'm trying to tell you that I'm falling for you,' Joel blurted out.

His words almost took Kate's breath away. She took a deep breath inwards and just touched her lips with her fingers and looked at him, unable to speak.

'I know what you're thinking. You think I don't know what I'm saying, you think that spending all this time together pretending to be a couple has clouded my judgement – well, it hasn't. I haven't escorted since you asked me to help you win the money. I don't know why, it just didn't feel right. I felt something for you then and I wanted to find out what it was. I still want to find out,' Joel continued.

'I don't know what to say. Is this because of what Miranda said? Because you don't have to pretend any-thing because of that,' Kate admitted.

'I'm not pretending anything. Look, I know things are difficult for you right now, with Matthew, but I want to be much more than an escort to you, Kate.'

Kate swallowed as Joel took hold of her hand.

'Have I just made a complete fool of myself?' he asked her.

'No, no of course not. I just had no idea you felt like that, no idea at all. I mean, Miranda's right, look at you, look at me,' Kate spoke.

'Why do you keep saying that? I'm nothing special, and you've just heard it, I'm damaged, on the inside. I don't know whether that can ever be repaired. You, you are amazing. You're strong and you're beautiful and you have this big, honest heart and you make me laugh. No one's ever made me feel quite like you do. These past weeks learning about each other has been the best time I've had for such a long time.'

Kate couldn't say anything; the words were battering her heart, trying to fight their way in but for some reason, she couldn't open the door to them.

'I shouldn't have said anything; you don't feel anything like the same way, do you?' Joel spoke, standing up and running his hands through his hair.

'No. I mean, I don't know, it's complicated. I'm complicated and all this has come right out of the blue.'

'And you're still in love with Matthew. It's OK; I think I already knew that.'

'No, no, I'm not and Joel, you are so nice and if things were different then maybe...'

'You'd consider it?'

'Yes, but at the moment, only in the "God, he's so

hot, I wonder what he would be like in bed" kind of way and that's not really fair because there is so much more to you than that. I'm just not sure I'm ready for anything else yet,' Kate responded, blushing as she spoke.

'Thinking I'm hot is a start,' Joel replied.

'Of course you're hot; I was the envy of every woman in that room tonight.'

Joel smiled at her.

'But you know that, right?'

'It's just superficial. It isn't important.'

'No but—'

'I thought your burlesque routine was the most sensual thing I've ever seen,' Joel admitted, looking at Kate with his saucer-sized eyes.

Kate swallowed and gazed back at him.

'I couldn't keep my eyes off you,' he whispered.

She could see his breathing was rapid and her own heart was banging an intense rhythm on her ribcage. A ripple of desire surged through her, heating up parts of her that had been cold for so long.

'I really don't want to sleep on this very small sofa,' Joel admitted, coming back over to her.

'I don't want you to either,' Kate found herself replying, shaking as he sat down next to her again.

'Let's just be honest with each other. I want you,

Kate. I want to hold you and kiss you and—' Joel started, brushing her hair with his hand.

'I want you too,' Kate interrupted quickly, desire overriding her mind.

Joel kissed her, intensely this time, and she clung to him, enjoying the sensation of his firmness against her. Effortlessly, he picked her up and carried her into the bedroom.

## 23

When Kate woke up, it was to the sound of an annoyingly cheerful song on the radio and crockery being moved about. She opened her heavy eyes and looked around the room, for a moment unable to re-member where she was. And then she looked at the pillow next to hers and recalled the previous night. She pulled the duvet up around her and closed her eyes again. It had been almost surreal, Joel kissing her and touching her every part. It had felt intense and unstoppable, new and exciting; however, there had also been a sense of complete familiarity. She had given in to him so much more than she ever had with Matthew. It had been fantastic and she had felt like a woman again, not the porridge-splattered mother of a two-year-old.

Though now morning was here, she was scared. She didn't know what this meant, if it meant anything. She hadn't had time to think about herself at all since Matthew left. At the beginning, she had wanted him back, no matter what he had said and done and in moments of weakness, she did still think of him and how the plans she had for their future would now never be. But what she had never considered was her future without him. It had all been about Bethan; there hadn't been a moment to think about Kate Baxter, the young woman.

She got out of bed and put on her robe. When she entered the kitchen, Joel was stood at the hob tending to something he was cooking. He looked gorgeous, as always. His hair was wet and tousled from the shower and he was wearing jeans and a pale-blue shirt.

'Hi,' Kate greeted.

'Hi. Now listen, I know your idea of food heaven is Admiral's pie done in three minutes but I've made some fruit salad and salmon and scrambled eggs are almost ready,' Joel informed, turning to look at her.

'Oh, well it sounds great. Not quite Admiral's pie but I suppose it will do,' Kate remarked, swallowing the 'morning after the night before' awkwardness as best as she could.

'Have a seat. I've made coffee too,' Joel said, indicating the pot on the table.

'You seem to have thought of everything.'

'Well, I've been awake since four. I went for a run, I went in the hot tub, I went to the on-site shop as soon as it was open; breakfast was the next thing.'

'You didn't sleep,' Kate remarked.

'About an hour, but that's good, really,' Joel admitted with a smile.

'Maybe you should go back to the doctor, tell him you're still suffering,' Kate suggested, trying her best to talk normally even though she couldn't look at him without remembering the way he tasted.

'I would if I thought it would do any good. I haven't heard that they've developed any miracle cures so I don't think there's anything else they can offer me. Apparently, I'm meant to give it time. I'm hoping they don't mean waiting until I'm drawing my pension,' Joel replied as he dished up a plate of scrambled eggs and salmon and put it in front of Kate.

'I could come with you,' Kate suggested.

'It's OK, honestly.'

Joel brought his plate to the table and sat down opposite her.

'It smells delicious,' Kate spoke, picking up her knife and fork.

'I probably made too much. I like cooking and I like eating – bad, bad combination,' Joel answered, grinning.

Kate watched him eat. Last night, he had undressed her so slowly, she had been trembling by the time he so much as kissed the tip of her shoulder. She had held him close to her, run her hands down his back and across his thighs.

'About last night...' Kate said, suddenly breaking her own daydream.

'You want to forget it ever happened?'

'No, I don't want to forget it; I just want to know what I should be doing, that's all,' Kate answered, flushing with embarrassment.

'What you should be doing?' Joel queried.

'Yes, I don't know, what do you think? I mean, we —' Kate started.

'I feel the same way this morning as I did last night,' Joel spoke bluntly, looking at her with his huge, slate eyes.

'Joel, I have to put Bethan first and I don't know how I feel about relationships in general at the moment, let alone embarking on one myself. There's so much at stake, there's Bethan and the competition and the Lady Dragon and this solicitor's exam offer. I haven't got time to breathe just now, let alone make a considered decision about something,' Kate attempted to explain.

'Then don't,' Joel answered.

'Don't what?'

'Don't make a considered decision about it.'

'What d'you mean?'

'You think about absolutely everything you do; why not stop thinking for once and just see what happens?' Joel suggested.

'Would you be happy with that? Because I do really like you, I just can't quantify my feelings at the moment. That sounds really tragic and unromantic, doesn't it?'

'It certainly does,' Joel agreed.

'What I'm trying to say is, I don't know when I'm going to be ready to make a relationship commitment; I don't even know if I'm ever going to be ready. I don't want to string you along and then—' Kate began.

'Last night, we said no promises, just honesty. You're being honest with me; I can't ask for more than that. But just to warn you, I'm not one for giving up easily,' Joel told her.

'Noted,' she answered.

\* \* \*

'Come here the future *Knowing Me Knowing You* champions 2011, come in, come in. Philip! Kate and Joel are here!' Hermione announced as she grabbed Kate and enveloped her in a bear hug.

Kate managed to escape the clinch and Joel was next for the embrace as Bethan toddled down the hallway to greet the arrivals.

'Mummy!' Bethan exclaimed excitedly, bouncing up and down and tugging at Kate's jeans.

'Hello darling, have you had a lovely time with Aunty Mione?' Kate asked as she picked up her daughter and cuddled her tightly.

'We have had a lovely time and so have you two by the looks of things. Look at you both, you are practically glowing! It must be that sea air. Come into the kitchen; Philip and Cyrus have been baking,' Hermione announced, leading the way.

'Where are your three?' Kate asked, carrying Bethan.

'Helping, or rather hindering, at my mother's WI fete. I've had Cyrus since eight; his mother had some urgent business meeting or something. Now, who's for cranberry tea?' Hermione offered.

'Let me help. Hi, Philip,' Joel greeted as they all entered the kitchen.

'Hey Joel, what a dark horse you are, playing the guitar and singing like that. I play the accordion, very badly according to Mione, but maybe we could have a jam session one time,' Philip suggested.

'That sounds like it would be a lot of fun,' Joel agreed with a smile.

'JUICE!' Cyrus whispered satanically, drumming his feet on the floor.

'Cyrus, ask nicely please. We don't get things if we ask like that,' Hermione spoke to the little boy.

'JUICE!' Cyrus repeated the drumming getting faster.

'Cyrus, you ask nicely and you say please,' Hermione told him.

'Juice, juice,' Bethan mimicked, waving her arm up and down.

'JUICE!' Cyrus said again, banging his feet even harder on the floor.

'Hey Cyrus, how about this: "can-I-have-some-juice-please?",' Joel spoke, tapping his feet on the floor in rhythm with the syllables of the words.

Cyrus just stared at Joel, transfixed.

'Come on, you try it: "can-I-have-some-juice-please?",' Joel repeated.

'I'm afraid Cyrus has communication problems. He only whispers and stamps and talks in one word sentences,' Hermione whispered to the adults.

'Can-I-have-some-juice-please?' Cyrus spoke audibly, tapping his feet in time to the words.

'Oh my God,' Hermione said out loud, putting her hands to her mouth in shock.

'Can-I-have-some-juice-please?' Cyrus repeated, a broad smile on his face.

'How did you do that? He hasn't spoken a proper sentence in all the time I've been minding him,' Hermione spoke, astounded.

'I did some work with children in Germany. Sometimes, music or rhythm provides a focus for kids who find it hard to communicate,' Joel answered, ruffling Cyrus' hair.

'Well I don't know what to say. You're nothing short of a miracle worker. Wait until I tell his mother,' Hermione said, pouring some juice for Cyrus and handing it to him.

'How did you know about that?' Kate wanted to know.

'I studied a bit of child psychology at university, along with the sports science,' Joel told her.

'Thank-you,' Cyrus said to Hermione, banging his feet on the floor twice.

'You're-welcome,' Hermione answered, copying him.

'So he sings, he plays guitar and he knows all about children. I would snap him up, Kate if I was you,' Philip remarked with a wink.

'Joel, Joel,' Bethan shrieked, reaching out at Joel.

Joel took hold of the little girl's hand and squeezed it.

* * *

'Are you sure you can't stay for lunch? I could make a stew, it wouldn't take long,' Hermione spoke as Kate looked out of the kitchen window into the garden. Philip, Joel, Cyrus and Bethan were running around, kicking a football.

Kate smiled as Joel picked up Cyrus and put him onto his shoulders, running around with him and making the boy squeal with delight.

'Kate Baxter, I'm talking to you,' Hermione said, turning to see why her friend hadn't replied.

'Sorry, what did you say?'

'Hmm, I think I want to hear all about what happened in that romance lodge,' Hermione spoke, eyeing her friend with suspicion.

'Nothing happened,' Kate replied, her cheeks already flushing.

'Oh my God, sweetie, what happened? Are you and Joel...'

'No, well, yes – I don't know,' Kate admitted.

'Sit down and tell me everything!' Hermione demanded, pulling a chair out for her.

Kate sat down and let out a sigh, turning to look out of the window again at Joel.

'We slept together,' she admitted.

'Ooooooooooo! I knew it! I saw it in the tea leaves and the runes. I knew this was the start of something, I told you, didn't I tell you!' Hermione gabbled excitedly, tapping her hands on the table in appreciation of the news.

'It isn't like that,' Kate replied.

'What d'you mean, it isn't like that? Like what? You've been pretending to be a couple for weeks; now you *are* a couple. Simple.'

'We aren't a couple.'

'Now you've lost me, sweetie. I thought you said you had—'

'Slept together, yes. But it isn't as simple as that; things are difficult for me at the moment,' Kate told her.

'Don't tell me he was no good in bed because I simply won't believe it.'

'It isn't him, it's me.'

'*You're* no good in bed?'

'No! Well, I don't think so. It isn't anything to do with the physical stuff; it's me. I don't know how I feel about Joel and I don't know how I feel about starting a relationship. This is the same dating dilemma I was having before all this mad *Knowing Me Knowing You* stuff started.'

'I don't see the problem. He's gorgeous. From what I've seen, he's kind and considerate, he's intelligent and funny and he's great with kids. Look at him out there playing with Cyrus and Bethan,' Hermione spoke, indicating what was going on in the garden.

'Matthew hurt me; I can't go through that again,' Kate admitted.

'He isn't Matthew. I'm not sure there are any other men out there who are like that piece of worthless—' Hermione began.

'Don't, Mione, he's Bethan's father.'

'But he doesn't want to be. Stop defending him. What he's doing to you two is despicable,' Hermione stated.

'I know and I'm not defending him. I know what he is, but he wasn't that person when we got together.

He was kind and considerate just like Joel and he made me laugh. What if—'

'What if Joel turns out the same way?'

Kate nodded her head.

'Love is all about putting your faith in someone and learning to trust them. There are no guarantees, but if you don't take a chance, you never get to learn how wonderful things are when they actually work,' Hermione told her.

'I wouldn't want to bring someone into Bethan's life and have them walk out on her again.'

'Look out there; he's *already* in her life,' Hermione told her.

Kate looked out in the garden and saw Joel holding hands with Bethan and running towards the swing. He lifted her into it and pushed her high into the air as she laughed and giggled.

'He says he's falling in love with me.'

'Could you fall in love with him if you let yourself?'

'Very easily,' Kate admitted.

'Want me to read your leaves again?'

'No, it's something I've got to work out for myself.'

'Well, if I was you, I wouldn't leave it too long. You could miss out on the best thing that's ever happened to you,' Hermione spoke seriously.

\* \* \*

'Bethan's asleep,' Kate remarked as Joel pulled his car up outside her home.

'All that running around the garden and two hundred goes on the slide would make me need a sleep. In fact, watching her do it has the same effect,' Joel replied.

'Could you help me with my bag and I'll carry Bethan?' Kate asked him.

'Sure.'

Kate carefully undid Bethan's car seat belt and lifted the sleeping child out and into her arms. As she walked up the path and approached the door, something felt wrong. She looked up and noticed one of the windows upstairs was open.

'Joel,' Kate spoke cautiously.

'Yeah.'

'I think someone's been in the house; the window's open.'

Joel joined her on the path and put her bag down.

'Maybe you just forgot to close it,' he suggested.

'I didn't, I'm sure of it. Would you go in first?' Kate asked, handing Joel the key.

'Sure, wait here.'

Kate held Bethan to her as she watched Joel open the front door and enter the house.

'You'd better come in,' Joel called a minute or two later as he returned to the front door.

Kate hurried in and was greeted by the sight of Matthew, sat on her sofa, a cup of coffee in his hand, his feet up on the table and the television blaring out a football match.

'Hello, Kate,' he greeted softly, hurriedly putting the cup down and removing his feet from the table.

'How did you get in? What are you doing here?' Kate blurted out, her heart thumping in her chest as she looked at him.

'Hello Bethan. Aw, she's asleep. She looks so much like me when she's peaceful like that, doesn't she?' Matthew spoke, standing up and moving towards Kate to look at Bethan.

'Get away from her. Joel, could you take Bethan up to her room?' Kate asked, transferring Bethan to him.

'Why don't *I* do that? She always liked it when I put her to bed,' Matthew said, attempting to take his daughter.

'Don't you touch her!' Kate exclaimed immediately, hurriedly passing Bethan to Joel.

'She's my daughter.'

'Last week, you didn't believe she *was* your daughter; you said you wanted a DNA test. Joel, please take her upstairs. How did you get in here?' Kate demanded to know as Joel took Bethan away from the situation.

'I still have a key. Look Kate, there's no easy way to say this so I'm just going to come right out and say it. I want to try again,' Matthew told her.

'What?' Kate exclaimed, thinking she was hearing things.

'I want us to try again, be a family,' Matthew repeated.

'You have got to be joking,' Kate said.

'No, I've never been more serious in my life. I know I've been a bastard to you and to Bethan. I don't know why; call it a midlife crisis if you like. I felt trapped, I felt overwhelmed by the responsibility of having a child, I didn't take to it like you did.'

'I didn't have a choice. She arrived and someone had to get on with it,' Kate spat.

'And you were amazing; you *are* amazing, Kate. I know I've walked out on the best thing that's ever happened to me and I need to try and put things right. I need to make it up to you and I need to make it up to Bethan,' Matthew spoke.

'Yes, you do. But not like this and it's gone way past making things up to me. We're divorced,' Kate reminded him.

'It isn't irrevocable.'

'It is as far as I'm concerned. And what's happened to that rabid Amanda?'

'I don't know what I was thinking; she was a passing fancy, nothing in comparison to you,' Matthew spoke, reaching out for Kate's hands.

'I'll go,' Joel said, re-entering the room to see the couple holding hands.

Kate snatched her hands away from Matthew and turned to face Joel.

'No, don't go,' Kate said, looking at him pleadingly.

'I think you two have a lot to talk about, that's all,' Joel answered coolly.

'I've got nothing left to say to him. I told you that,' Kate whispered.

'You need to sort things out for Bethan,' Joel told her.

'But that's all.'

'Give me a call,' Joel said, backing towards the door.

'Joel,' Kate said, tears welling up in her eyes.

'It's OK, honestly. I understand,' Joel told her, giving her an encouraging smile.

Kate watched him leave and a lump formed in her throat as she couldn't help but recall the way he had touched her the night before and whispered her name as she clung to him.

'Who is that thug anyway?' Matthew questioned as he appeared in the hallway and brought Kate back to reality.

'He isn't a thug,' Kate snapped back.

'I still have bruises on my neck from what he did at the bowling alley. Where did you meet someone like that?'

'I want you to go,' Kate said and she opened the front door.

'Come on Kate, please. I've got so much I want to say to you. I told you, I want to make things right between us. I want to try again and be a proper family. I want to be the husband you deserve,' Matthew spoke.

'No.'

'Why not?'

'Because I can't forgive you – the things you said, what you did, it's all completely unforgivable.'

'People deserve second chances, don't they?'

'Sometimes, but Matthew, this has come so out of the blue. You stopped paying for Bethan, you had a new girlfriend who came round here and thumped me, you refused to pay the CSA, then there was the

DNA, now you want to try again. I just don't believe you,' Kate spoke with a sigh.

'I saw you, on the TV last night, in that ridiculous game show – with him,' Matthew admitted through gritted teeth.

Kate didn't reply but just looked at her ex-husband, seeing his angry expression. It was then that realisation hit her.

'Oh my God!' she exclaimed, putting her hands to her mouth.

'What? I saw you with him, I saw you smiling and laughing with him and I was jealous – there, I admit it – I wanted it to be us together again.'

'This isn't about me or Bethan; this is about the money! Oh my God, how stupid am I? You want to get back in my affections because you think I might get my hands on a hundred thousand pounds,' Kate spoke hysterically.

'What?'

'Oh, very good – act surprised when I mention the prize money, nice touch. And this is typical of you; you always were selfish and self-centred. I just ignored it before, tried to pretend it was endearing. But it wasn't; it isn't. All you've ever been interested in is things. It was you who wanted the John Lewis wedding list, not me, you wanted the Caribbean honeymoon, I would

## 24

---

'Can I borrow your phone?' Kate asked, handing Bethan to Hermione and entering her house the next morning.

'Morning Kate, hello Hermione, did you enjoy the stew you made yesterday? Yes, thank you, I did,' Hermione spoke as Kate brushed past her and headed to the kitchen.

'Joel isn't answering his phone. I thought if I rang from here, he might think it was you and he'd pick up,' Kate attempted to explain as she picked up Hermione's phone and tapped in the number.

'What's happened?' Hermione asked, bringing Bethan into the kitchen.

'Matthew happened.'

'Daddy, Daddy,' Bethan spoke on cue.

'What d'you mean?'

'He turned up, let himself in to my house, was there when we got back from here. Said he was sorry, said he wanted me back, wanted to try and be a family again,' Kate explained quickly.

'Oh good God, you're kidding,' Hermione exclaimed.

'And Joel just left. I asked him to stay but he said Matthew and I needed to talk, which we didn't really. Joel was just being nice and staying out of it and he went and told me to call him but he isn't answering and I just need to hear his voice,' Kate said, tears forming in her eyes.

'Is it ringing yet?'

'Yes that's all it does do and then it goes to voicemail and I've left at least five messages. I don't know where he lives, Mione.'

'No, but you know where he works,' she reminded.

'But I can't go there until lunchtime; I've got a stack of work to do this morning. And what with all the confusion with sleeping together, I didn't tell you the other bit of news from the show on Saturday.'

'Go on,' Hermione urged, handing Bethan a saucepan and wooden spoon to play with.

'The Lady Dragon has somehow found out that

Joel's an escort and is threatening to blow our cover unless I turn down Colin Sykes' offer to do the solicitor's exam,' Kate babbled.

'Oh God.'

'What am I going to do?' Kate asked.

'My advice would be to sit down and have a cup of peppermint tea before you go anywhere or do anything and put the phone down,' Hermione ordered.

'I care for him, Mione; I care for Joel. Maybe I'm not ready for a relationship but I care for him and I don't want to lose him yet. Why did Matthew have to do that? I was coping with him being a bastard, I had almost got used to it and now he's thrown a spanner in the works,' Kate said, emotion threatening to bubble over.

'I don't want you wasting another second of thought on Matthew.'

'And the Lady Dragon?'

'I would like five minutes in a room with her. I could always make a voodoo doll! Haven't made one for a while but the results can be really effective,' Hermione responded.

'I'm not sure I can do the whole solicitor thing anyway. Look at me, I'm a wreck and if I'm honest, I'm finding the work totally boring. Maybe I should just leave Randall's and take up something else that doesn't numb my brain.'

'Any ideas?'

'I don't know, burlesque? It seemed to go down well at the contest.'

'Dance, dance,' Bethan said, twirling around with Mr Crisps.

'Can-I-play-with-jigsaw?' Cyrus spoke, tapping his feet to the syllables of the words.

'Of-course-you-can-Cyrus, in-the-bottom-drawer,' Hermione spoke, copying the pattern in her steps.

'Joel taught him to do that,' Kate said, her eyes misting over.

'Yes, he's a marvel; Cyrus' mother just broke down when he greeted her with, "Hello-Mummy-I've-had-fun".'

'And he's funny and clever and gorgeous and kind and—'

'Perhaps he's just giving you a bit of space; I mean, the weekend must have been an intense experience: all that time together doing the show and whatever happened in the romance lodge. Perhaps he's just giving you a wide berth to think about things.'

'We talked through things, though; we agreed we would be honest with each other and he said he would give me time – *time*, not space. I don't want space,' Kate explained.

'Maybe that's what you need to tell him.'

'And I will but he isn't answering the phone. Shit, is that the time? I've got to get to work; I don't want to give the Lady Dragon another excuse to give me a black mark. Bye, bye Bethan, have fun with Auntie Mione. Mummy will see you later,' Kate spoke, kissing Bethan on the cheek and standing up.

'Joel, Joel,' Bethan said excitedly, turning around and around in circles.

* * *

When she got into the car park, she dragged a brush through her hair. She hadn't had the time or energy to put make-up on even though she knew she looked terrible. She hadn't slept properly the night before; all she had done was dream: about Matthew, about Joel, about Larry Rawlins and the stupid Love Dove. She had a five thousand pound cheque in her handbag and she hadn't even given that a second thought.

She took the lift to her floor and when she got into the Probate room, she couldn't see her desk for the bouquets of flowers all over it.

'Morning Kate, I take it the romance lodge worked

its magic then! I've never seen so many flowers,' Lynn remarked as she put down the contents of Kate's filing tray and turned to greet her.

'Oh, they're lovely, aren't they?' Kate remarked, looking at a bunch of roses and taking out the card.

'You don't need to look to see who they're from do you? Duh!' Lynn said.

Kate read the card.

*I'll never give up until we're a family again. All my love Matthew x*

'Apparently I do. Could you get rid of them please, Lynn – every bouquet. Get one of the runners to arrange to distribute them at the hospital,' Kate said, starting to push the flowers to one side.

'Oh, OK, I take it they're not from Joel,' Lynn stated.

'No, they're not from Joel, they're from Matthew and I don't want to look at them a second longer,' Kate stated, switching on her computer.

'Well, that's funny,' Lynn remarked as she began to gather up the flowers.

'Funny?'

'Yes, because Joel's in the Lady Dragon's office. He's been in there for the last ten minutes and I just presumed he'd brought in the flowers, seeing as he was here,' Lynn informed.

'What?' Kate exclaimed.

'Joel's in Miranda's office,' Lynn repeated.

'Are you sure?'

'Duh! Of course I'm sure, he said, "Hello Lynn" and then he went into her office and closed the door.'

'Well, what's he doing?'

'I don't know, the door's closed. Why don't you go in?'

'No, I can't. I mean, I don't know what they're doing in there.'

'He looked hot, though. He's got jeans on and a t-shirt, a white one. She'll like that; she had a thing about one of the workmen that did the room alterations. Wore a white t-shirt every day, he did, covered in sweat by midday but somehow, it just made him look even hotter,' Lynn informed.

'I've got to go in there; I can't sit here and—' Kate began, standing up from her chair.

The door to Miranda's office opened and Joel walked into the Probate department. He smiled at Kate and came over to her desk.

'Hi,' he greeted.

'Hello,' Kate responded.

'I'll just do this filing then,' Lynn remarked, leaving rapidly.

'I've being trying to ring you; you didn't answer,' Kate stated.

'No, that's because my mobile's in the romance lodge. They're sending it by courier; I should have it this afternoon. I did try and call you about nine last night but it was constantly engaged,' Joel spoke.

'I was trying to call you, every ten minutes or so,' Kate admitted with a blush.

'How did it go with Matthew? I saw the flowers.'

'He left, just after you.'

'Did you manage to sort anything out?'

'He said he wanted to give our marriage another chance; he said he wanted to be a proper dad to Bethan. He apologised for everything he'd done.'

'I see. Well, that's good.'

'He didn't mean it. He saw us on TV; he knows about the prize – he saw pound signs.'

'Are you sure he wasn't being sincere?'

'I didn't care either way,' Kate replied.

'I don't want to complicate things for you,' Joel told her.

'You haven't. I want to see you; I want to carry on seeing you, like we were – just to see – what happens,' Kate spoke quietly.

'I'm glad,' Joel replied.

'So do you want to tell me why you were here seeing Miranda?'

'I went to see her to ensure our survival in the competition. She won't be telling anyone I was an escort,' Joel replied with a wink.

'What did you say to her?'

'I can't possibly say but if you want to do that solicitor's exam, the way is clear, and she'll support you every step,' Joel informed her.

'I don't understand,' Kate said.

'I'd better go or I'll be late for sixteen-stone Geoffrey. See you,' Joel replied and he leant forward and kissed her cheek.

Kate felt her face redden but she caught hold of his hand and gave it a squeeze before he could leave her.

'See you,' Kate spoke, enjoying touching him again.

'Bye,' Joel replied with a smile.

No sooner had he left then Miranda's office door opened and she emerged. Kate braced herself for another pile of work coming her way but Miranda looked uneasy. Her eyes looked watery and her trademark swagger of superiority was fundamentally diminished. She flicked her hair back and then rushed like a scared rabbit towards the ladies toilets.

## 25

'Oh my God!' Kate exclaimed out loud at her desk the following morning.

For the first time in a long time, she had caught the postman before she left for Hermione's. She had taken the letters to work and as Miranda was out of the office for the morning, she took the chance to open them before she looked at her files. A large, brown envelope had a familiar look to it and she ripped that open first.

'What's the matter?' Lynn asked, hurrying over to Kate's desk, as she recognised the panic in her voice.

'The *Knowing Me Knowing You* contest just got even more bizarre. You won't believe what they want us to do now,' Kate remarked, holding the letter out to Lynn.

Lynn took the letter and began to read it. Her eyes started to bulge after reading a few sentences.

'I told you it was bizarre,' Kate said, letting Lynn continue reading.

'Create a wedding dress to wear for a wedding fashion catwalk, decorating a wedding cake in two minutes and writing your own personal vows to act out in the final "Showdown of Sincerity". Oh my good God,' Lynn commented.

'How can I do any of that? It also says the men have to create an outfit for themselves as well. What does "create" mean? Could that involve buying?' Kate wanted to know.

'I think they want you to make it.'

'I know that but I could say I used to be a seamstress or something and just get a not too elaborate little number from BHS.'

'Think they might notice.'

'Great, so now I have to turn into a Blue Peter presenter and whip up a wedding frock and a morning suit in less than two weeks.'

'Don't you have your old dress you could alter and spruce up?' Lynn suggested.

'Oh, I couldn't wear that,' Kate said immediately.

'Might save a bit of time.'

'No,' Kate said firmly.

'Well, if I was you, I wouldn't have Joel in a morning suit, I would have him in swimming trunks – very short swimming trunks. In fact, why not forget about clothes altogether,' Lynn told her.

'Lynn!'

'Sorry but duh! Covering it up is a complete waste.'

'Sorry to interrupt, ladies but Kate, could I have a word?'

Neither of them had noticed Colin Sykes entering the room.

'Yes, of course,' Kate agreed.

'I'll go and get started on that dictation,' Lynn replied, backing away from the desk and putting the *Knowing Me Knowing You* letter down.

'Thanks, Lynn.'

Colin waited until Lynn had disappeared before speaking.

'I just wanted to see if you had made any decision about the Legal Practice Course,' he began.

'Well, no, not yet. I haven't had a chance to really think about it properly – I mean, it sounds like it would be a good opportunity but I need to make sure it's the right thing for me,' Kate answered hurriedly, feeling uncomfortable.

'Of course and I expect this competition has somewhat taken over your life, hasn't it? It's a bit of a roller coaster of an experience, isn't it? Very enjoyable, though – I'm looking forward to the final,' Colin remarked with a smile.

'Well, I think the final is really going to be something special,' Kate said.

'I like your chap, Joel; he seems to have a good head on his shoulders,' Colin said.

'Yes, he does,' Kate agreed.

'And how are things with Miranda? I had thought that perhaps my offer to you might have ruffled a few of her feathers,' Colin spoke.

'I don't think so – feathers look pretty intact,' Kate replied quickly.

'Very diplomatically put. Right, well I won't hold you up. I see you have my client Dean on your desk so I'll let you get started,' Colin said, preparing to leave.

'I will let you know as soon as I know – about the exam,' Kate added before he departed.

'I know you will,' Colin replied with a smile.

Kate let out a sigh as he went and picked up the letter again. She couldn't make a wedding dress but she knew a woman who could.

She picked up the phone and dialled. Her call went to voicemail.

'Joel, it's me. Could you meet me at Hermione's tonight, about six? Prepare to be measured.'

She put the phone down and turned back to her computer.

'Sorry to be back again but Frances on reception just gave these to me,' Lynn spoke, handing Kate a large bunch of pink gerberas.

'The hospital again please, Lynn. In fact, more aptly, take them to the hospice,' Kate ordered, passing them back to her secretary.

'Er, sorry, I took the liberty of reading the card – just to make sure because you freaked out before. They're not from Matthew; they're from Joel,' Lynn told her.

'In that case, could you get me a vase, please?' Kate asked, smiling at the bouquet.

\* \* \*

The morning had passed quickly and as she hadn't had Miranda breathing down her neck and passing her more files than she could handle, it had been very productive.

She had just stopped what she was doing and sunk her teeth into a large ham and salad sandwich when her phone rang.

Kate cursed but picked it up.

'Hello, Kate Baxter,' she answered.

'Oh Kate, it's Ruby on reception. There's a gentleman down here for you.'

'Is it Joel?'

'No, it's a Mr Bruce Carmichael.'

'Oh, does he look like a potential new client?'

'I'm not sure but he asked for you by name.'

'Oh OK, I'll be down.'

Kate put down her sandwich and picked up her executive folder and a pen. She checked her appearance in the glass door and hurried down the stairs.

'Mr Carmichael?' Kate greeted the suited individual who was sat in reception, his head bowed.

The person raised their head to greet her with a smile. It was Matthew.

'Kate, don't be angry. I knew if I said it was me, you wouldn't see me, so I lied,' Matthew spoke, getting to his feet.

'I don't want to see you. No matter what you're calling yourself,' Kate said, turning around and heading back towards the stairs.

'Please Kate, I mean it when I say I'm sorry. I would do anything to have another chance. I know I've messed up with you and with Bethan. I was a fool, I felt claustrophobic and I know that was stupid but—'

'You said all this on Sunday; I don't need to hear it again, especially not here,' Kate exclaimed, looking at

Ruby and fearing her business was going to be all over Randall's by tea time.

'I think you do. I don't think you believe I mean it.'

'I don't care if you mean it; it's too late,' Kate responded.

'You've moved on with this Joel?'

'No, I've moved on with Bethan. Joel and I are... Joel and I are...'

Ruby on reception was visibly pricking her ears up, waiting for the juicy bit of gossip to fall from Kate's lips.

'Are what?'

'It's none of your business.'

The door to reception swung open and Miranda entered dressed in a fur-trimmed jacket, a boutique bag in each hand.

'Oh hello, it's Matthew isn't it? Yes, I remember you from the last office Christmas party – you were a wonderful dancer,' Miranda remarked.

'Hello,' Matthew greeted immediately, smiling at the sight of an attractive blonde.

'We haven't seen you around here for a while. What brings you back? Business?' Miranda asked.

'Pleasure actually,' Matthew answered, looking at Kate.

'Excuse me,' Kate spoke and she left the two of them in reception and hurried up the stairs.

* * *

'Hello, hello, come in, come in. Joel, get your clothes off; I'm ready for your inside leg,' Hermione exclaimed as she opened the door to Kate and Joel that evening.

'What's going on? What's all this about measuring and stuff?' Joel asked as he stepped inside.

'You haven't told him? Oh dear, I'll let you explain while I get the tape, the material and the pins,' Hermione spoke.

'Hello-Joel,' Cyrus greeted, tapping his foot in time.

'Hello-Cyrus, how-are-you?' Joel asked, tapping back.

'Fine-thank-you,' Cyrus replied.

'Come on,' Kate said, ushering Joel forwards.

'Hang on, you don't get away that easily. What's going on? What's all this about measurements?' Joel asked.

'You don't really want to know, do you?'

'Yes.'

'It's mad.'

'I still need to know.'

'Hermione has wedding dress material.'

'What?'

'I told you you wouldn't want to know,' Kate replied, rushing into the kitchen and scooping up Bethan, who was playing with the plastic tea set.

'Wedding dress material?' Joel said to Hermione.

'Yes, I have a choice of two. Traditional white or contemporary navy.'

'Oh I don't know about navy; it reminds me of my school uniform and that never suited me,' Kate spoke, bouncing Bethan up and down.

'Traditional white it is then.'

'What did you get for Joel?'

'Again, a choice. We have charcoal grey or we have a midnight blue,' Hermione informed, holding up the materials.

'Ooh, I like the midnight blue, hold it up against him,' Kate ordered, becoming excited.

'What is going on here? I mean, I don't think I proposed but you know, sometimes after a few drinks, I might say something a bit crazy but—'

'Yes, we're getting married! On TV,' Kate explained.

Joel just looked at Kate, none the wiser.

'Don't panic, it's for *Knowing Me Knowing You*. We have to perform some dumb catwalk fashion thing, then decorate a cake, make up some vows and then pretend we're actually getting married and gaze into each other's eyes and say them like we mean them. But we aren't allowed to buy outfits; we have to make them – so Hermione's doing just that,' Kate told him.

'Come to me, big boy and let me put my tape around you,' Hermione beckoned, shaking out her measure.

'God, what a lot of trouble to go to,' Joel remarked, stretching out his arms for Hermione to measure.

'The last hurdle though and then it will all be over and we won't have to go through any of it again,' Kate spoke with a sigh.

'Hmm, like you haven't enjoyed any of it. All that free food and drink and a night in a romance lodge,' Hermione commented.

Kate's face reddened and she couldn't look at Joel. She was still having dreams about what had happened in the romance lodge – erotic, sexy dreams she never wanted to wake up from.

'Joel, Joel,' Bethan exclaimed, waving her hand at him.

'Free food and drink – good. Sitting in a plastic booth with a blindfold on, not knowing where the Love Dove is going to strike next – not so good,' Joel answered hurriedly.

'And open your legs a tad, sweetie,' Hermione said, a big grin on her face.

'Could you make a waistcoat with this too? I'm thinking white shirt, blue suit with waistcoat and a blue tie.'

'Oh yes, I think that would look wonderful on you, Joel – striking yet understated,' Hermione agreed.

'And what style is the bride going for?' Joel asked.

'Obviously something high fashion that covers all my lumpy bits,' Kate responded.

'Lumpy bits! You want to compare lumpy bits? I'll show you lumpy bits! I've had three kids and a hysterectomy,' Hermione spoke, about to lift up her top.

'No! No, that's fine, I believe you,' Kate replied with a laugh.

\* \* \*

'Do you want to come in?' Kate asked as she and Joel stood outside her house.

'Do you want me to come in?'

'Yes, I have two cheese and bacon pasta meals ready to be microwaved and a bottle of German wine in my handbag,' Kate informed him, putting Bethan down and letting her toddle up the hallway.

'How can I refuse an offer like that?' Joel asked her.

'I also have a takeaway menu if you would prefer that,' Kate replied.

'I think I might,' Joel answered.

'OK, well you have a look at it and I'll get Bethan ready for bed,' Kate spoke.

'Well, I could have a go at that, if you didn't mind.'

'Oh, well I—'

'It can't be so hard that I won't be able to do it,' Joel remarked.

'No, of course not, that's fine. Her pyjamas are in the top drawer in her bedroom and nappies are on the side. Mr Crisps is up there and I'll come up and read her a story in a minute. Bethan, shall Joel take you up to bed?' Kate asked her daughter.

'Yes please, Joel, Joel,' Bethan exclaimed, excitedly jumping up and down as best as she could.

'Well, it sounds like I'm redundant. I'll have a look at the takeaway menu then,' Kate said, getting the wine out of her bag and taking it into the kitchen.

'Come on then Bethan, let's get you ready for bed,' Joel spoke, picking the little girl up.

Kate smiled and watched Joel take Bethan up the stairs, tickling her tummy and making her laugh.

She opened the wine and poured two large glasses. It had been strange being measured for a wedding dress. She remembered it vividly the first time round.

She had trawled every wedding dress shop in a fifty-mile radius looking for something perfect. She had tried off the shoulder, round neck, square neck, halterneck, sleeveless, short sleeves, long sleeves and backless. Nothing had felt right. Perhaps she should have taken that as an indication that the marriage wasn't right. In the end, she had left it so late, she had to settle for the only thing the Highbridge Wedding Apparel shop had in her size. It had been nice, though: slim-fitting ivory with a long train trimmed with fur. But she hadn't felt a thrill of excitement when she'd put it on and she certainly hadn't had the tingle running down her back the way she had tonight when Hermione draped the wedding dress material around her. And it wasn't even going to be a real wedding dress; it was just a costume.

She finished the glass of wine and was just about to pour another when Joel came back downstairs.

'Oh, is she OK? Does she want me? I'll go and read her a story,' Kate said, getting up from the sofa.

'No need, she's asleep. She was asleep before I got to the end of *The Princess and the Pea*,' Joel told her.

'Bless her, she does love that story. OK, I think I'll have a chicken tawa with garlic rice and a plain naan. Oh and poppadoms – an Indian isn't an Indian without poppadoms. What would you like?' Kate asked, passing Joel the menu.

'I'll have a lamb bhuna and pilau rice.'

'Right, I'll order and it's my treat. Oh and I have a cheque for you, for your share of the five thousand we won,' Kate said, picking up the phone and preparing to dial the number for the takeaway.

'I don't want any of the five thousand,' Joel stated once Kate was off the phone.

'What?'

'I don't want any of it. We didn't know about it at the beginning so I don't want any of it,' Joel spoke.

'Don't be silly, we had an agreement.'

'About the hundred thousand, not this. Buy something with it, trade your car in for a four door. Think how much easier that would be to get Bethan in and out of,' Joel suggested.

'But, that wouldn't be fair and—'

'OK, I'll have my share and I'll buy the car for you,' Joel told her.

'You're so stubborn. Which one of your parents do you get that from?' Kate asked.

The second the words had passed her lips, she wanted to draw them back in again.

'Oh God, I'm sorry, I didn't think before I opened

my stupid mouth. Forget I said that,' Kate spoke hurriedly.

'It's OK, don't worry,' Joel said.

'Do you ever wonder about your birth parents? Have you ever thought about tracking them down?'

'I tried to once; I found out their names and the area they lived. Social services contacted them, told them I wanted to make contact and that was that,' Joel explained.

'What d'you mean?'

'They didn't want to see me,' Joel answered.

'Oh Joel, I'm so sorry.'

'Don't be, it's fine. I didn't really need them; I was just curious. I suppose I just wanted to meet them to see if I looked like either of them, or to find out if I had any brothers or sisters.'

'I don't understand why they weren't curious about you? How can someone have a child, give them away and then never wonder how they turned out?'

'There are all sorts of different reasons why people give up their children. My parents were young: my mother was only sixteen when she had me; my father was eighteen. They had no money, their parents had nothing either. I think it was the right thing for them to do. My adoptive parents gave me everything and believe me, no one could have loved me more.'

'They would have been so proud of you, Joel.'

'Maybe.'

'So if you did all these qualifications, your degree and everything, why did you join the Army? Was it something you always wanted to do?'

'Well, I left university with all the qualifications and I didn't really know what to do with them. My parents have friends in high places, I had job offers coming from every which way but I just needed to be my own person and to find out who that person was. I needed to see where I fitted into the world. The Army offered travel and excitement, opportunities to learn skills you can't learn outside of it. It was always just going to be a stepping stone to something else.'

'And is that what you got? Was it good before, well you know, before Afghanistan?'

'Yes, it was. I made so many friends, good friends, friends who would put themselves on the line for you. We had great times and we laughed so much. But the job changed, it got more intense, it got more dangerous. The laughter dried up and we all had to turn into people we didn't want to be,' Joel tried to explain.

'Sorry.'

'No, it's OK. Before all my friends were lost that day, I was going to leave anyway. It wasn't what I signed up for, the risks were increasing all the time, and I started to think about my parents and what it would do to them if I was killed. All that time, raising me, all that effort, bringing up someone else's child... I couldn't do that to them,' Joel explained.

'Well I'm glad you came back. I can't see us having met in the darkest regions of Afghanistan. I'd be like a fish out of water if there wasn't an Asda within five miles,' Kate answered.

'But you would have liked the packet meals,' Joel told her with a grin.

The telephone rang.

'Hello, oh hello – he's what? Well, he can't mean it – he's doing what? Oh I don't know, I don't know if that's a good thing – yes, I know but it's difficult – are you sure he's serious? All right, calm down, don't cry – well, where is he? All right, I'll come, yes, OK, OK, bye.'

Kate put the phone down and looked at Joel.

'What's wrong?' Joel asked.

'That was Helen, Matthew's sister. Apparently, he's threatening to commit suicide,' Kate informed.

'What?'

'I don't believe it for a minute but he keeps asking for me. Helen's round there but he won't open the front door. I tried to tell her that things were difficult but he's her brother and she's worried about him and —' Kate began.

'Sure, you have to go,' Joel answered.

'I don't want to go but—'

'Kate its fine, he's Bethan's dad – you need to check it out,' Joel responded.

'Do you mind?'

'Go, I'll stay and mind Bethan. I can't guarantee there'll be any takeaway left when you get back, though,' Joel replied.

'Keep a bit for me; I'm good at reheating things,' Kate replied, finding her coat and putting it on.

'Call me, though; let me know what's going on,' Joel responded.

'I will,' she promised.

* * *

'Hello,' Hermione greeted as she picked up the phone.

'Hello. I'm at the hospital,' Kate spoke, breathing in the outside air as she left the entrance of the accident and emergency unit.

'Oh sweetie, what's the matter? What's happened? It's not Bethan, is it?'

'No, no Bethan's fine, it's Matthew. He was threatening to commit suicide and he was really drunk and passing out so we called an ambulance,' Kate answered.

'Is he OK?'

'I think so. Helen's with him,' Kate informed.

'And what are you doing there?'

'Well, Helen called me and asked me to come. He wouldn't let her in and he said he'd taken a load of tablets and he kept asking for me,' Kate answered.

'I see,' Hermione responded stiffly.

'What does *that* mean? You said it in a funny voice; I sense disapproval.'

'Very perceptive. I'm just worried you're sending out mixed messages here, Kate. You're telling him it's over one minute and then racing to his bedside the next,' Hermione told her.

'It wasn't like that; his sister called me.'

'And you dropped everything and went to him. What were you doing? Were you with Joel?' Hermione asked.

'Well, yes, but it was only takeaway.'

'You were having dinner with Joel and you left to be with your ex-husband, the man who no more than a week or so ago wanted a DNA test on your daughter.'

'Why are you being horrible to me? I phoned you

for support. I'm tired and it's cold and the bloke in the bed next to him has spent the last half an hour on the bedpan.'

'I'm not being horrible; I'm just pointing a few things out. What sort of message do you think that will have sent out to Joel?'

'Joel and I are complicated.'

'I don't know why. I think that's a convenient excuse you use so you have all of the dating and none of the commitment. Because you're scared to move on, away from Matthew.'

'That isn't true.'

'Isn't it? You don't seem to know what you want. One minute, it's over with Matthew, the next, you're nursing him back to health. And what am I doing at this moment in time? Making you a wedding dress so you can compete in a relationship game show with someone you're treating very badly.'

'Mione, I—'

'I think you need to sit down and really think about what you're doing,' Hermione spoke severely.

'It's compli—'

'I'll see you in the morning,' Hermione interrupted and she ended the call.

Kate took the phone away from her ear and just

looked at it. Hermione's harsh words had hurt her. She had never spoken to her like that before. She had been the voice of reason on many an occasion but she had never sounded quite so angry. Matthew had looked weak and vulnerable, pale and inconsolable; he looked like he was quite capable of suicide. And Helen had been distraught, concerned for her brother. She hadn't had an option, had she?

*  *  *

It was almost 11.00 p.m. when Kate got back home. She entered the living room to see Joel asleep on the sofa. She looked at him, so handsome, so genuine, so honest, such fun. He said he was falling in love with her.

She was still looking at him when his eyes flicked open and he immediately sat up as if sensing her scrutiny.

'Hey,' he greeted, rubbing his eyes.

'You were asleep,' Kate remarked.

'Yeah, I do manage an hour or two here and there. Bethan's fine. She woke just after you left but I tucked her in and found her dummy and she went straight back to sleep,' Joel replied.

'Good, thanks for doing that,' Kate answered.

'How's Matthew?'

'He's OK, he hadn't taken anything. He's in the hospital though because he drank almost a whole bottle of scotch. Stomach's been pumped as a precaution,' Kate responded.

'Well, at least he's OK. I saved you some takeaway; it's in the microwave, ready to go,' Joel spoke, standing up and putting on his jacket.

'You're going?'

'Yeah, I've got an early start in the morning – sixteen-stone Geoffrey again.'

'But you don't sleep.'

'I need to try though, otherwise my body would completely get out of the whole sleeping routine and I may never sleep again,' Joel replied.

'Oh OK. Well, thanks for looking after Bethan and I'm sorry about dinner,' Kate apologised.

'That's OK. Look, I'm quite busy for the rest of this week; shall we meet up next week for a practice before the final? Hermione said she was going to bake a three-tier cake for us to decorate, didn't she?' Joel asked.

'Yes, but we'll need more fittings for the outfits and —' Kate began.

'I'll give you a call,' Joel spoke as he headed down the hallway towards the door.

'Joel, wait,' Kate called.

He turned back around and looked at her, waiting for her to speak.

Kate swallowed a lump in her throat but couldn't bring herself to say anything.

'Bye,' Joel said finally and he left, closing the door quietly behind him.

# 26

'Morning,' Hermione greeted as she let Kate and Bethan into the house the next day.

'Morning. I can't stop today; I have a tonne of paperwork to get through and two clients. Bye, bye Bethan, I'll see you later,' Kate spoke, kissing her daughter on the cheek and ushering her into Hermione's home.

'Ah, I see. We have a disagreement on the phone and suddenly, you can't stop,' Hermione remarked.

'No, of course not, I'm just busy, that's all,' Kate answered with a blush, not admitting to feeling awkward.

'Well I saw you parking up and I've made tea and I'll be cross if you waste it,' Hermione spoke.

Kate let out a sigh and walked reluctantly into the house.

'Bethan, why don't you go and find Cyrus. He's building a tent in the garden,' Hermione said, opening up the back door and letting the little girl go through.

Kate sat down at the kitchen table, her arms crossed defensively.

'I can't believe you went to Matthew last night? What were you thinking of?' Hermione blasted, putting a mug of tea in front of Kate.

'I wasn't thinking of anything. Helen phoned and asked me to go; she was going out of her mind with worry and he was asking for me. I had to go.'

'No you didn't, you wanted to. You needed to feel needed by him.'

'That is so untrue, Mione.'

'Is it?'

'Yes.'

'I don't believe you.'

Kate didn't respond but took a sip of the scalding hot tea and had to spit it back in.

'That man is a snake. All those things he said to you. All the nasty, vindictive things he did when you split up. The way he left, the new girlfriend, the total neglect of his daughter – do you need me to carry on?'

'I'm not stupid,' Kate answered.

'No, I know that. Which is why I can't understand what you're doing wasting another second on this man.'

'He's Bethan's father.'

'Which means he should be there for Bethan. It doesn't mean you have to have a lifelong devotion to him no matter how badly he treats you.'

'Everything is compli—'

'I swear, if you say the word "complicated" to me once more, I will slap you.'

'Everything's confusing. I feel so much for Joel but I don't know whether I love him and I'm scared of leading him on. I mean, he's so attractive and so kind and we have fun, but we've kind of been forced together through this show. I don't know whether anything would have ever happened between us if we had met under normal circumstances.'

'Of course nothing would have happened under normal circumstances because you wouldn't have let it. You were never going to date again because you couldn't let Matthew go. I thought that finally, when you had let Joel in, it would be Matthew's last, long overdue farewell,' Hermione spoke.

'I can't make myself hate him, no matter how hard I try. And worse than that, when he tells me he wants to try again, my heart flips over. I don't believe what he says necessarily, but I want to,' Kate replied.

'Oh Kate, I don't believe I'm hearing this.'

'I can't help the way I feel. I was so in love with him, I married him forever. *He* left, not me – my feelings didn't stop the day he walked out of the door.'

'So what if he means what he says? What if he does want to try again?'

'I don't know. I don't know if I could trust him again. I don't really know whether I want to.'

'And what about Joel?'

'He told me he's busy for the rest of the week, wants to meet up again for cake decorating. So I guess I've burnt my bridges there too.'

'Oh Kate,' Hermione spoke with a sigh.

'It's no more than I deserve,' Kate responded.

'I think you need to be honest with yourself. What do you really want? No matter what I think, or whatever anyone else thinks, what do you want?'

'I have absolutely no idea,' Kate replied.

\* \* \*

'Colin's been in already; I told him you were at a client's,' Lynn spoke as Kate sat down at her desk.

'Thanks, Lynn,' Kate replied, switching on her computer and putting down her handbag.

'So?' Lynn questioned.

'So what?'

'Duh! So have you decided yet?'

'About what?' Kate asked.

'About the solicitor's exam? That's what Colin wants to know. That's why he's stalking round here, looking for you,' Lynn spoke.

'I haven't decided yet,' Kate answered, tapping at her keyboard and trying to bring her programs to life.

'But it's a no-brainer, isn't it? Company car, bigger pay packet, boozy trips to Colin's villa in La Manga. You could take me, we could sip cocktails on the veranda underneath a perfect sunset, a flamenco guitar playing softly in the background...'

'Shut up, Lynn! I said I hadn't decided yet – it means I haven't decided. I can't think, I don't get time to think any more. *You're* getting on at me, *Hermione's* getting on at me, Miranda's out to destroy me and Joel – Joel's going to give up on me,' Kate shrieked, much to the surprise of her colleagues, who raised their heads briefly and then thought better of it.

'Whoa. OK, do you want to tell me what's happened? Because now I'm thinking this isn't just indecision over an exam,' Lynn said, wheeling a spare chair over to Kate's desk and sitting down.

Kate wiped at her tear-filled eyes and let out another sigh.

'I'm drowning, Lynn. I'm drowning in every sodding area of my life.'

'OK, so treat me as a life raft. Let me try and help.'

'You can't help, no one can, that's the problem. I need to make all these decisions and I can't do it.'

'Well, it would help if I knew the whole picture. I mean, what's the deal with Joel? Why would you think he's giving up on you? Did you pick him a really dodgy wedding suit? Because if you did, I can help you rectify that. Darren's cousin Ray has a market stall, knows all the suppliers, he could get you some material dead cheap. As long as you don't mind not asking any questions,' Lynn said.

'It's nothing Joel's done; he's amazing. It's me, I can't get my act together,' Kate told her.

'I'll make a cup of tea and I'll get a couple of cakes; there's some in the kitchen. Apparently, Kay on the third floor has passed her driving theory test,' Lynn spoke, standing up and heading towards the kitchen.

'No, I don't want a cup of tea, I don't want any cakes, I don't want anything. In fact, I don't want to be here at all. I've had enough. I can't concentrate. I'm going home. If anyone asks, tell them I'm sick,' Kate said, standing up and picking up her handbag from the floor.

'But, wait a second, you've got Mrs Briggs in half an hour,' Lynn remarked as Kate put on her coat and headed for the door.

'Phone her and cancel or if she's already left, get someone else to see her,' Kate ordered.

'Well, I—' Lynn began.

'Bye Lynn,' Kate responded hurriedly and she left the Probate room and headed for the exit.

When Kate got into the car, she burst into tears. She was done holding it together; now she couldn't even go into work and just get on with things like she had done before. Now she was living in fear of Colin Sykes creeping up on her, wanting a decision about her future plans for her career at Randall's. She didn't know. She didn't know if she would ever know.

All she could think about at the moment was Joel and Matthew. She thought about Joel all the time lately: driving to work, at work, at home, in the bath, in bed. But every time she thought about him, it was quickly followed by thinking about Matthew like she was comparing them. She seemed to flit from one to another so quickly. If she felt true affection for either of them, she shouldn't be comparing them, should she?

Yet she found herself at Highbridge Leisure Centre, wanting to see Joel, *needing* to see him. She didn't know where he was, she wasn't even sure if he worked every day, but she got a coffee from the café and sat at a table overlooking the leisure pool.

Why was it she needed someone in her life? She was capable, she had kept her and Bethan afloat so far, but all the time, it felt like there was something missing. Did she really need a partner to make her feel whole? The very thought made her shudder. Women burned their bras and threw themselves in front of racehorses for equality. Did she really need a man in her life to make her happy and if she did, was it Matthew? Was it Joel? Or was the truth that either one of them would do?

'Kate.'

She heard his voice and looked up from her coffee to see Joel stood at her table, looking at her. His hair was wet and he was wearing a black tracksuit. He had never looked better.

'What are you doing here? Aren't you working?' he

asked, sitting down opposite her and immediately noticing the watery eyes and pale complexion.

'Supposed to be, supposed to be seeing Mrs Briggs to talk about a Lasting Power of Attorney. She wants to appoint her granddaughter which is bound to put her son's nose out of joint but it's up to her at the end of the day. She's not gaga as far as I can make out – knew who David Cameron was, called him a silly arse,' Kate spoke with a sniff.

'Sounds like she knows exactly what's what then,' Joel responded.

'She always wears a fur coat though and has an endless supply of extra-strong mints in her handbag.'

'Maybe she feels the cold and has bad breath,' Joel suggested.

'Maybe.'

'Are you OK?' he asked.

'Are you?' Kate asked, looking up at him.

'I thought about you a lot last night, after I left,' Joel admitted with a sigh.

'About what an absolute cow I've been to you since the minute we met?' Kate asked.

'No, nothing like that. I just think it's all got a bit intense. I mean, we've been in a pressure cooker of a situation since *Knowing Me Knowing You* started and I think it's just got a bit too much,' Joel explained.

Kate didn't respond. She had a knot in her throat and her eyes were brimming with tears as she looked at him looking at her with his beautiful, moon-sized eyes.

'You've got so much to think about what with your job and Bethan and the contest. I was wrong to try and add more to your already full plate,' Joel spoke.

'What do you mean?' Kate asked, suddenly feeling terrified.

'I just think we need some space.'

'No, we don't, that's the last thing we need. I mean, we have a contest to try and win and we need to practise and—' Kate started frantically.

'I've got some time off here; I'm going to stay with my parents for a while,' Joel told her.

'In Kent?' Kate clarified.

'Yes, just for a week or so. I'll be back in plenty of time for the final, I promise,' Joel said, taking hold of her hand.

'Were you going to tell me?'

'What?'

'If I hadn't come here, were you going to tell me? Or were you just going to leave, perhaps while I was listening to Coldplay?' Kate questioned.

'Of course I was going to tell you,' Joel insisted.

'When are you going?' Kate asked.

'Tonight.'

Kate nodded and took a large swig of her coffee.

'I just think we need some—' Joel began.

'Distance, space, yeah you said,' Kate replied.

'I just think it would be easier for you if I wasn't here, just for a bit,' Joel added.

'You know you'll be consigning me to a week of ready meals and cut-price wine,' Kate spoke bravely.

'I'll write out the omelette recipe if you like,' Joel suggested with a smile.

'Don't give up on me,' Kate said suddenly.

'I won't,' Joel told her seriously and he gave her hand a squeeze.

'Well, I'd better go. The coffee here is terrible and I've got some dry cleaning to pick up. Not sure whether Giuseppe will have been able to get out the indelible pigeon shit but I'm keeping everything crossed,' Kate said as she got to her feet.

Joel smiled at her.

'Well, have a great time in Kent. Be sure to call in on the Ranch House and see how it compares to Darlene's service at the Highbridge branch.'

'I will,' Joel said.

'Look, could you text me? You know, when you get there. I worry about long drives and car accidents –

hazard of having your parents killed in one,' Kate said nervously.

'Sure,' Joel agreed.

'Well, I guess I'd better go. See you,' Kate said and before she could stop herself, she had held out her hand.

Joel ignored it, put his hand to her face and pulled her towards him, kissing her deeply on the mouth before she could do anything about it.

She looked at him, her breathing rushed, her eyes watery, and then she fled, running out of the gym as fast as she could.

## 27

Kate looked at her phone again. There were no messages. It was almost 11.00 p.m. She didn't know what time Joel was leaving for Kent but she was thinking that parents of at least age fifty plus would be going to bed before midnight. But then again, it was his family home; he probably had a key.

She had eaten spaghetti bolognese (six minutes to cook, two minutes to stand) and drunk a whole bottle of white wine while watching a documentary about Gulf War syndrome. She now knew that flashbacks and nightmares were part and parcel of some of the returning soldiers' lives.

She was just about to consider opening another bottle of wine when the phone rang.

She leapt on it hurriedly before the ringing woke Bethan.

'Hello,' Kate spoke quietly.

'Kate, it's Hermione.'

'Hi.'

'Kate, I've just had a call from the hospital. It's Joel,' Hermione spoke seriously.

Kate felt her blood run cold.

'What's happened?' Kate exclaimed.

'They wouldn't give me any details; they got my number from a message I left him about a suit fitting. They're trying to contact his parents. He's on Marlborough Ward.'

'Is... is he OK?'

'I'm sorry sweetie, I really don't know,' Hermione replied.

'Oh God, I have to see him, I have to go there,' Kate spoke, panic-stricken.

'Give me ten minutes, sweetie and I'll come and mind Bethan for you,' Hermione said.

'Did it sound serious? Was it a car accident? I told him to text me when he got there and he hadn't. I knew something was wrong,' Kate gabbled, close to tears.

'I'm coming over.'

'Mione, I've been drinking, I can't drive there,' Kate

exclaimed as she caught sight of the large empty wine bottle.

'Call a cab, tell them ten minutes – putting my shoes on now,' Hermione told her and she ended the call.

\* \* \*

By the time the cab dropped her off outside the entrance of the hospital, she was a bundle of panic and her heart was bursting with fear. What had happened? How bad was he? What if it was critical? There was so much she wanted to say to him. So much she should have said before.

She walked onto the ward and took a deep breath. She was terrified. She looked at some of the patients in the nearest beds and put a hand to her chest, frightened at their injuries. None of them were pretty.

A nurse hastened towards her, carrying some files, and Kate cleared her throat to speak.

'Excuse me, could you tell me which bed Joel Brown is in?' Kate asked.

'It's very late – are you family?' the nurse enquired, looking at Kate suspiciously.

'Yes, I, er, I'm his sister, Kate Brown. The hospital

called me, told me to come,' Kate lied, hoping she was convincing enough.

'He's in bay two, just across there. He's had an MRI and a CAT scan and we'll have the results in the morning. He's very lucky someone found him when they did. The doctor will be able to tell you more in the morning,' the nurse told her.

She pointed to a bay Kate had already glanced at without recognising the occupant. Looking a second time, she saw it was Joel. His face was swollen to almost twice its usual size and his lip was stitched up. She put her hands to her mouth, unable to hide her shock.

'Are you OK?' the nurse asked, seeing Kate's reaction.

'Is he conscious?' Kate questioned.

'Oh yes, he's just resting. So don't stay too long please and keep your voice down,' the nurse said quietly.

Kate took a deep breath and then propelled herself over to the bed, swallowing her concern and horror as best she could.

She sat down on a chair next to his bed and studied his horrific injuries. His handsome face was now a patchwork of red and maroon bruises and cuts. He looked like someone who had done ten rounds with David Haye without a gum guard or a referee.

'Joel,' she whispered.

His large eyes flickered open and he looked at her.

'Kate,' he said, sounding uncomfortable.

'Well, now, isn't this a fine way to get my attention? I mean, if you wanted attention, you just had to say. And what have you done to your face? That nice make-up lady at *Knowing Me Knowing You* isn't going to be happy with you,' Kate attempted to joke as she squeezed his hand.

Joel attempted a smile and then winced in pain.

'What happened? I told you to drive carefully. Why didn't you listen?'

'I wasn't in the car,' Joel replied.

'Then what happened?'

'I got jumped on the way home, by three or four guys,' Joel said, stifling a cough.

'Attacked? What, you mean mugged?'

'Yeah, they took my wallet,' Joel responded.

'Well, have you told the police?'

'Not yet. I will, they're coming in the morning, I think.'

'How could someone do this? And why did you make them fight you for your wallet? You should have just given it to them,' Kate said crossly.

Joel didn't answer.

'Are you hurt anywhere else, apart from your face?' Kate asked with a swallow.

'It hurts pretty much everywhere,' Joel informed her.

She squeezed her eyes tight and tried to stop the tears escaping.

'Hey, don't cry. Looks are superficial, remember and I've been told the inside is going to be just fine,' Joel told her.

'You have Hermione to thank for me being here. She left a message about a fitting for your wedding suit and the hospital called her to try and find your next of kin. Shall I ring your mum and dad?' Kate offered.

'No. No, I don't want to worry them,' Joel said.

'But, they'll be expecting you.'

'No, they won't.'

'But you were going to stay with them,' Kate reminded him.

This time, it was Joel's turn to sigh.

'You told me you were going to stay with them,' Kate repeated.

'I know.'

'You lied to me,' Kate said, taken aback.

'Because I didn't want to make things difficult for

you. I thought if you thought I was going away, it would just make it easier. I know you're still in love with Matthew,' Joel spoke, unable to keep the sadness out of his voice.

'I'm not,' Kate replied automatically.

'Kate, we agreed to be honest with each other, didn't we?' Joel said with a cough.

'Yes, and now you've lied about visiting your parents. So much for you always telling the truth.'

'I know I shouldn't have done that but I did it for the right reasons.'

'I don't know how I feel about anything at the moment,' Kate admitted.

'It's OK.'

'No, it isn't; it's not right. I mean, I'm not that sort of person. I mean, we've kissed and we've...' Kate began.

'Slept together,' Joel spoke.

'Yes. We shouldn't have done that.'

'Shouldn't we?'

'I don't know.'

'For the record, it didn't feel wrong to me.'

Kate shook her head.

'I don't want to let you go, Kate, not if there's the slightest chance you could feel the same way about me as you do about him,' Joel spoke.

'He hurt me and he threw me away.'

'I would never do that – ever.'

'I know.'

Joel coughed and tried to sit up to reach his glass of water. Kate reached for it and helped him drink it. He spilt some out of the corner of his mouth and Kate hurriedly reached for a tissue to mop it up.

'Thanks. I'm making more mess than Bethan, aren't I?' he replied with a half-hearted smile.

'Joel, when you get out of here, I want you to come and stay with me until you're better,' Kate said determinedly.

'But, you don't have a spare room,' Joel stated.

'I know. Just don't tell the nurse; she thinks I'm your sister,' Kate replied.

## 28

---

'Take it slowly, there's no rush. Tell him there's no rush, Philip,' Kate said as she and Philip helped Joel out of the car and towards her house.

'There's no rush, Joel,' Philip repeated, feeling he had to.

'Thanks, Philip,' Joel replied, taking no notice.

'Mione, you tell him, he isn't resting. The doctor said to rest and we've got the final in two days,' Kate exclaimed as Hermione opened the door to them.

'Come in and sit down on the sofa, Joel. You have at least half an hour before the cakes will be ready for decorating. Want a herbal tea?' Hermione offered.

'A coffee would be good.'

'No, tea is better for you. Have you got some

camomile with you?' Kate asked, rushing to put the kettle on.

'Look, will you all just stop for a minute,' Joel ordered.

'Joel, Joel,' Bethan spoke, running in from the garden and jumping up onto Joel's lap.

'I appreciate all the help and the trouble you're going to but I'm fine. I can do things for myself; I'm feeling a lot better,' Joel replied, giving Bethan a hug.

'Good, then you'll be able to tell me what Kate's favourite film is,' Hermione asked.

'That would be *Pretty Woman*,' Joel replied confidently.

'Very impressive and which toothpaste does she use?'

'Some sort of whitening stuff, probably Asda.'

'Ooh, you're scaring me,' Kate responded.

'And last one before I make the coffee. Is she a Ladyshave lady or a Bic razor woman?'

'Bic razor, definitely. Seen those in the bathroom,' Joel responded.

'Good lad, three out of three, Kate – can't do better than that,' Hermione remarked with a satisfied nod.

'No, it's very impressive, seeing as he's had several blows to the head.'

'Some things you never forget,' Joel replied with a smile.

'Right then, I'll put the kettle on. I've baked some apple tarts,' Hermione said.

'Mione's recorded the last *Knowing Me, Knowing You* show to DVD and brought it round; I thought we might watch it later for a laugh,' Kate said.

'Yeah, OK. Look Kate, you didn't have to go to all this trouble you know, I wasn't expecting any of this and—'

'Sorry about that – this is how we welcome people out of hospital around here. And I hope you're hungry because I have two Swedish meatball dinners all ready to microwave.'

'Please no, the hospital food was positively great compared to that. Don't you have eggs for omelettes?'

'Yes, but you're not cooking and I don't think my culinary skills are up to making omelettes. I think the meatballs might be the safer option.'

'You're probably right.'

'But we've got tarts and wedding cake to eat first so you might not need any more.'

'Here's hoping,' Joel answered.

'Are you warm enough?' Kate asked him.

'Are you turning into my mother? I'm fine; I don't need a blanket or anything else except a coffee.'

'Tea.'

'Come on! One coffee isn't going to halt my recovery.'

'One camomile tea and an arnica tablet. It's excellent, helps with the bruising,' Hermione said, bringing a cup and pill over to Joel.

'Thanks,' Joel replied.

'Apple tart?' Hermione offered.

'Maybe in a bit,' Joel said.

'Are we crowding you? Say if we're crowding you and we can leave the cake decorating for another time, can't we Mione,' Kate spoke.

'It's fine, everything's fine, honestly and I'm not an invalid,' Joel insisted.

'I'd just suck it up Joel; women never listen to a word you say,' Philip said, passing Joel an apple tart and sinking his teeth into one.

'Philip, that isn't true!' Hermione exclaimed.

'Are you too ill for the pub?' Philip asked him.

'Yes, he is,' Kate responded immediately.

'No, I'm definitely not,' Joel replied, easing himself off the sofa and standing up.

'Well then, we'll leave the ladies to cluck around baking and doing woman things and we'll go down the pub until the cakes are ready,' Philip said, putting on his jacket.

'But Joel, you shouldn't—'

'We won't be long and I haven't had a drink in a week,' Joel replied.

'Let them go, let them make their little stand,' Hermione suggested to Kate.

'We won't be long, love – just long enough for a couple of pints and a game of dominoes,' Philip assured.

'As long as that's all. No bar snacks – I've got stuffed mushrooms ready for tonight,' Hermione responded.

'I promise,' Philip replied.

The two men left as quickly as they could and Kate picked up Bethan and hugged her to her.

'Are you OK?' Hermione asked.

'Yes, why?'

'Well, do you think it's a good idea having Joel move in here with you?'

'It's only until he gets better. I didn't want him going back to his flat on his own and having no one there to look after him.'

'And that's the only reason?'

Kate didn't reply, but buried her face in Bethan's mop of brown hair.

'Have you made a decision yet?'

'Yes, I've made a decision not to make any decisions at the moment.'

'What does that mean?'

'I don't know. Don't go on, Mione – I don't know what I'm supposed to do.'

'Have you heard anything from Matthew lately?' Hermione asked.

'No,' Kate replied.

'And how does that make you feel?'

'I haven't thought about him; I've been too busy going to the hospital to visit Joel and getting things ready here.'

'You don't think he had anything to do with Joel's mugging, do you?' Hermione enquired.

'What?'

'Well, it all sounds a bit suspicious to me – four men attacking him on the way home from work.'

'They took his wallet, it was a mugging and anyway, Matthew wouldn't do anything like that.'

'I just think the timing's a little bit suspicious, that's all.'

'Has Joel said something to you? Is that what he thinks too?'

'He hasn't said anything to me; it was just something that crossed my mind.'

'Well, he wouldn't do that. I know he's capable of a lot of things but not harming someone. I mean, Joel could have been seriously injured,' Kate said, shaking her head.

'No, you're right, stupid thing to say. I've been watching too many gangster films,' Hermione said.

'I hope they're not going to be too long; Joel's not supposed to be doing too much.'

'Philip will look after him.'

'That's what I'm worried about.'

* * *

'We're not late, are we? Are the cakes ready for decorating?' Philip called as he and Joel re-entered the house.

'Shh, Bethan's in bed,' Hermione called as the two men came into the living room.

'Are you feeling OK? Do you want to sit down?' Kate asked, fussing as Joel took off his coat.

'Joel is absolutely fine, although his mouth might need a rest. He's been chatting away to Marina for the last hour,' Philip informed.

'Philip, it wasn't that long,' Joel protested.

'I think you'll find it was. Lovely girl, though – she had very nice opinions,' Philip replied.

'Oh yes, well who is she then? The barmaid?' Hermione wanted to know.

'Oh no, she wasn't the barmaid; she's a model, isn't she Joel,' Philip spoke, sitting down on the sofa.

'It was really bizarre, I worked with her when I first started modelling. She still models for the same agency. She's got family here apparently and she's visiting them. I told her all about *Knowing Me Knowing You* and she's back in London then so she's going to try and come along and watch,' Joel informed.

'Oh, well that's nice, isn't it – more supporters,' Hermione spoke, looking at Kate.

'Yes, that's nice,' Kate replied.

'OK, wedding cake. Here it is in all its three-tier glory!' Hermione announced, producing the cake and carrying it to the coffee table.

'What a coincidence, though, her being in the pub. She was lovely and she—' Philip continued.

'Blonde was she?' Hermione asked.

'Oh yes, blonde and tanned too. Just come back from an assignment in Brazil, hadn't she Joel?' Philip spoke.

'Shall we decorate these cakes?' Kate suggested, not wanting to hear any more.

'Yes, the cakes. Now, I have it on good authority that you are going to be given three cakes, rolls of icing, a piping bag and the stands to put the cakes on. So you have two minutes to make the cake look as good as possible and there are no Kissing Gates at all if you don't get the cakes on the stands and complete the three tiers,' Hermione informed.

'That's impossible; they want it to look nice in two minutes? It can't be done,' Kate exclaimed.

'Well, we're just about to find out. On your marks, get set, GO!' Hermione screeched and she pressed the stopwatch button.

'I'll roll the icing out and put it on the cakes and you can do the decorative bits,' Joel said, grabbing the rolling pin and trying to roll the icing out as smoothly as possible to fit over the cakes.

'But I'm not good with decoration. Come on, hurry up, get that layer on the bottom cake or we won't have any time,' Kate snapped, grabbing the roll of icing and plonking it on the cake.

'Well you get decorating that layer and I'll roll the next bit out.'

'Aren't you loving the teamwork here, Philip?' Hermione said, looking at her stopwatch.

'I am indeed, very methodical,' Philip mocked.

'This piping bag doesn't work; it won't come out. Oi! Don't do that, you're wrecking the icing,' Kate exclaimed as Joel nudged her arm.

'Oh dear, you'd better think about moving on to the next tier. Stick some of those little baubles around the edge and pipe if you have time left,' Hermione directed.

'It's easy for you to say; I haven't ever decorated a cake before,' Kate snapped.

'Running out of time, better start stacking the cakes. I'm going to count down from ten.'

'It can't be two minutes already. Joel, what are you doing? Just throw the icing on the last cake and help me stack them up!'

'Ten, nine, eight...'

'Oh bugger! Shit!' Kate exclaimed as she tried to get the cakes onto the stands.

'Six, five, you need the kissing couple on top, four, three, two, one and STOP!' Hermione ordered as her countdown ended.

'Damn it,' Kate said as her wedding couple toppled off the top of the cake and fell onto the table.

'Oh dear Philip, what do you think? Doesn't look very professional, does it? Silver balls aren't in any sort of pattern and the decorative roses don't look right to me,' Hermione said as she surveyed the cake.

'No but they did get all three tiers stacked up,' Philip said.

'Yes we did, come on; it was a decent first effort,' Joel insisted.

'But one effort is all you will get on the night and it needs to be better. Right, let's go again, take the stuff off the cakes and we'll take it from the top,' Hermione ordered.

'Oh God, do we have to?' Kate asked with a sigh.

'You want to win, don't you?'

'Yes, of course.'

'Then we go again, from the top in five,' Hermione instructed.

It was almost 9.00 p.m. before Hermione and Philip left. The cake decorating had been attempted four times and now it was nothing but a mound of icing and sponge with no clearly definable shape.

'I don't think I can bear to eat any of it; I've touched it too much,' Kate remarked, looking at it.

'Me neither and those silver ball things look like they would catch in your throat for sure,' Joel replied.

'Do you want a coffee?' Kate asked him.

'No, I'm fine, thanks.'

'So, do the police have any leads about the gang that attacked you?' Kate asked.

'No, I gave as good a description as I could but it was dark and they all had hoodies on,' Joel replied.

'Do you think Matthew arranged it?' Kate asked suddenly.

Joel didn't reply but he just looked back at her, his expression showing no emotion.

'He wouldn't do that, you know,' Kate stated, reading Joel's thoughts.

'You asked the question, Kate.'

'Only because Mione asked me and I told her it was a stupid suggestion but...'

'But what?'

'I'm not sure I know him very well at all any more.'

He didn't reply but leant forward to pick up his drink from the table.

'But I know he isn't a monster.'

'He loves you; he wants you back,' Joel finally spoke.

'But that isn't the way; he would know that isn't the way.'

'Is there a way?'

'I'm going to make another coffee. Are you sure you don't want one?' Kate offered, getting to her feet and going into the kitchen.

'I'm meeting Marina for lunch tomorrow,' Joel called.

'Oh,' Kate answered.

'I just thought I would tell you.'

'Well, that's good; it's nice to catch up with old friends, especially ones you haven't seen for ages. Where are you going?'

'Just to Piccolo's Pizza. She loved pizza when we dated,' Joel explained.

'Oh,' Kate replied, a knot forming in her stomach.

'You don't mind, do you?'

'No, of course not, don't be silly,' Kate said.

'Good. Well, I might go up to bed; it's been a tiring day,' Joel spoke, getting up from the sofa.

'Yes, OK.'

'Are you still comfortable with me sharing your bed, because if you're not, I can sleep on the sofa – or go home,' Joel asked as he paused at the door to the hallway.

'It's fine, I've just got some bills to pay online and then I'll come up. I mean, we're practically married, aren't we? And it isn't like we haven't shared a bed before,' Kate joked and then she had to look away.

'OK, if you're sure,' Joel replied and he left the room.

As soon as he had gone, Kate began to bite her nails. She didn't want him going to lunch with a blonde supermodel he used to date. Who was this woman? And why had she come to town now?

Her eyes caught on the photo of Bethan and Matthew on the dresser. She had loved him so much but he had almost destroyed her. Was there ever going to be a way back from that?

\* \* \*

Joel was asleep when she entered the bedroom. His face, chest and arms were still covered in scars from his attack but he looked as hot as ever. She took off her clothes and pulled a nightshirt over her head. She may have shared a bed with him in the romance lodge but it was the first time anyone had been in her bed at home since Matthew. She got in, pulled the covers up around her and turned to face Joel. A multitude of feelings rushed through her as she looked at him. She wanted to touch him but she was afraid to. She desired him more than she had ever desired anyone but it didn't just stop there. She felt she knew more about him than she had ever known about Matthew. She knew his deepest thoughts, his fears, his hopes and dreams. She reached out to touch his face and his eyes flicked open and he cowered away from her, gasping for breath.

Kate screamed and sat up, pulling the duvet cover to her and clinging to it.

'Oh Kate, I'm sorry, I'm so sorry,' Joel spoke, quickly moving towards her and reaching out to touch her.

'No, I'm sorry, I didn't mean to wake you. I—' Kate began, tears welling up in her eyes before she could stop them.

'It's OK, it's my fault.'

'No, it isn't,' Kate replied, bursting into a sob.

'Hey, come here, don't cry. What's wrong?' Joel asked, putting his arms around her and bringing her close to him.

'I'm terrified about the final,' Kate spoke through her sobs.

'What? The wedding catwalk and the cake decorating? Come on, we're going to smash it. Who else will have had someone like Hermione in their corner?' Joel asked her.

'It isn't that. I'm scared of it all being over, because when it's all over, I'll have to start thinking about other things in my life, things I've been putting off because of the stupid contest,' Kate explained.

'Like the solicitor's exam?'

'Like you and Matthew and my whole future. I don't know what I want to do with my life. Sometimes,

I can see myself being a solicitor and becoming a partner and drowning in money and status and then other days, I can see myself tending to chickens and eating baguettes and cheese in a small French village called Marchette,' Kate told him.

'And which one of those situations makes you feel happiest?' Joel asked her.

'Both of them could, in different ways. If I took the exam and made it to partner, Bethan and I would never have to worry about money. But it would be hard work and longer hours and more dedication than I've been giving to Randall's lately. But with the chickens, it would be a simple life; it would be more time with each other, less things but more quality.'

'OK, well, on Saturday night, you might be standing on stage in London holding a hundred thousand pound cheque. Gut instinct, what would you do with it? Buy into Randall's or buy a French farm with a garden full of poultry?'

'I really don't know,' Kate answered, her voice trembling.

Joel stroked her hair back away from her face and kissed her softly on the lips.

'Will you hold me until I fall asleep?' Kate asked him, burying her head in his chest.

'Come here,' he spoke, drawing her into him and enfolding her in his arms.

## 29

'Oh why won't this bloody computer do what it's told?' Kate screamed as she punched the keys in front of her, trying to get the system back into life.

'There, there, calm down. We need to have you focused and controlled for the big show tomorrow,' Lynn spoke, putting some letters in Kate's in-tray.

'I can't keep calm. Joel's meeting some bimbo for lunch,' Kate spoke, looking at her watch.

'What? I thought he'd moved in? I was expecting lots of gushing over how wonderful he is to look at over a bowl of cornflakes.'

'He's only staying temporarily, until he's better.'

'Recovered from the beating Matthew so obviously organised. I mean, it would take four men to get the better of Joel, wouldn't it? He's six foot and pure muscle, isn't he?' Lynn carried on.

'You don't think that too, do you? What is it with everyone? Matthew had nothing to do with it. And we know you watch too much *CSI* and stuff.'

'Have you asked him?'

'I haven't seen him. I don't want to see him.'

'Bet you a pricey cocktail at the bar tomorrow night that he did.'

'Lynn!'

'Sorry. So what's all this about a bimbo? Who is she?'

'I don't know, someone called Marina that he used to go out with when he was with the modelling agency.'

'Ooh, the agency in charge of finding models for those underwear commercials, yum; he should go back to modelling.'

'Lynn, he isn't a piece of meat, you know,' Kate remarked, not enjoying Lynn's unashamed drooling over Joel.

'No, sorry, getting a bit carried away. You were saying, the bimbo...'

'He's meeting her for lunch at one at Piccolo's Pizza.'

'Ooh, pizza, lucky her. All Darren bought me on our first date was a packet of crisps and a pickled egg.'

'It isn't a first date; it isn't any date. It's just two old friends meeting up to catch up.'

'And she's a model and he's gorgeous.'

'I need to see her, don't I? I need to see what she looks like,' Kate spoke.

'Duh! No! *We* need to see her. Get your coat because it's almost one,' Lynn said, tapping at her watch.

'No, I can't. It's nothing; she's just a friend,' Kate replied.

'Yeah, a friend, who's blonde and thin and probably has a face full of Botox.'

'We're not going to make it into town by one,' Kate said as she hurried to put her coat on.

'No and let's hope they aren't sat right at the back of the restaurant,' Lynn answered.

\* \* \*

'This is mad; we shouldn't be here,' Kate spoke as she and Lynn approached the pizzeria.

'I want to see what she looks like even if you don't.'

'I'm not sure I do. She's a model; she's going to be—'

'Oh my God, they're in there; they're sat near the

bar. What the hell is she wearing?' Lynn asked as she pressed her nose up against the window.

'Out the way! Let me see!' Kate demanded, pulling at Lynn's arm and looking in through the window herself.

'Now that is what I call a spray-on dress! If she didn't have the figure for it, that would be nothing short of desperate.'

Kate swallowed as she saw Joel sat with a tall, blonde-haired woman in her twenties wearing a very short, tight, red dress. He raised his head and looked over in the direction of the entrance and Kate hurriedly backed away from the window and pulled Lynn with her.

'Well, now you know what she looks like,' Lynn said.

'Yes, I do and I wish I didn't,' Kate responded with a sigh.

'It probably *is* just two friends meeting up over lunch but she was doing that thing the Lady Dragon does when she's about to leap on her prey.'

'What thing?'

'The licking the top lip thing. Haven't you ever noticed her doing that?'

'Maybe once or twice.'

'When she's been talking to Joel, I bet.'

'Why didn't he invite me to lunch to meet her?' Kate enquired, looking back into the window.

'Duh! Because he used to date her and you can't make your mind up who you want. It's a Joel day today, is it? Because yesterday, I was sure you were leaning towards Matthew,' Lynn spoke.

'That's not fair,' Kate remarked.

'It's no wonder he's taking someone else to lunch; the poor guy probably doesn't know whether he's coming or going.'

'He does, we—'

'I just wonder what's going to happen when this *Knowing Me Knowing You* show has finished. No weekends away, no limelight – back to reality,' Lynn carried on.

'I don't enjoy the limelight.'

'Speaks the woman who paraded on stage in nothing more than her underwear and a feather boa.'

'What are you trying to say, Lynn?'

'Look at him! In there, with Elle Macpherson! You said it yourself, why isn't he having lunch with you?'

'It's complicated.'

'A pound, please?'

'What?'

'We agreed, I get a pound every time you say those words.'

'We did not.'

'Well, we should.'

'Don't *you* start; I've got Hermione on my back enough as it is.'

'Probably because we can't see the problem. He likes you, you like him, what's complicated about that?'

'You don't understand.'

'No I don't – God, quick, hide!'

'What?'

'Joel's coming out. Do something!' Lynn hissed.

Kate turned around and faced the menu board, hiding her face as best as she could and hoping that Joel didn't notice her.

Lynn had pulled a notebook from her bag and had her head buried in it, pretending to be highly interested in the contents.

'Hi, Lynn,' Joel greeted, immediately seeing her.

'Oh hi Joel, didn't see you there. I was just—'

'Kate, fancy you being here,' Joel said.

'Oh, yes, well, Lynn has to organise a partners' lunch and she er, wanted to get some menu ideas for catering and I was coming to town anyway to post some letters and, here we are,' Kate spoke, hurriedly turning to face him, red from the neck up.

'Well, I could have picked up a menu from here for you. You should have called me,' Joel said.

'Oh well, I didn't think and Lynn, you didn't think of that either, did you?'

'No, I didn't.'

'So, are you having a nice lunch?' Kate continued.

'Well, we've only just ordered, but everything that's come out of the kitchen smells great. I just left my phone in the car,' Joel said and he opened the door and reached in for it.

'Oh well, we won't keep you. We have to go to the deli next,' Kate said, backing away up the street and pulling Lynn with her.

'OK, well I'll see you later,' Joel called.

'OK, bye,' Kate replied, waving her hand and smiling a 'life is wonderful, I'm getting on without him' smile.

As soon as he was out of earshot, Kate let out an exasperated breath.

'How stupid do I feel? Do you think he knew we were spying on him?' Kate enquired.

'Er, I would say – yes, definitely,' Lynn spoke with a nod.

'Great.'

Joel smiled as he watched Lynn and Kate walk up

the street in the direction of Randall's. He dialled a number on his phone and made a call.

'Mione, it's Joel. Yes, she was here.'

\* \* \*

That evening, Kate was still reeling from the embarrassment of being caught in the act of snooping. She had busied herself bathing Bethan and getting her ready for bed while Joel made dinner. But now they were on their own there was no avoiding it.

'So, what did you have for lunch?' Kate asked bravely.

'I had pasta, carbonara sauce,' Joel informed.

'Was it nice?'

'Yes, very nice.'

'And what did Marina have?'

'She had salad.'

'Should have guessed,' Kate muttered under her breath.

Salad! And she probably only ate a third of it.

'So, did you and Lynn get all the menus together?' Joel continued.

'What?'

'For the catering for the partners' lunch.'

'Oh yes, yes, she has four or five to look at now,' Kate answered.

She silently cursed herself for being so dim but smiled at Joel, trying to maintain face.

'Good.'

'Yes, good. So are you seeing Marina again?'

'Yes, she's going to come to *Knowing Me Knowing You*. She doesn't actually live far from the hotel,' Joel informed.

'Oh, that's nice,' Kate replied.

No it wasn't, it was shit.

'So how was your day? Is Miranda behaving herself?'

'She hasn't spoken to me since you came to see her. Well, just a vague good morning and a one-line sentence about client matters. It seems all the files of mine she altered have been corrected, so Lynn says. She's installed some alert system which tells her when Miranda is logging in to my client matters. Lynn's wasted as a secretary really; she would be an asset to MI5.'

'That's good.'

'So what did you say to Miranda to make her have a change of heart?'

'I can't possibly say.'

'Come on Joel, you have to tell me.'

'I don't.'

'You want this?' Kate asked, grabbing Joel's plate of Thai curry and holding it away from him.

'That's not fair. Give me the food.'

'Tell me what you said to her.'

'All right, all right, put the plate down.'

She waited for an explanation.

'I told her I knew she wore a wig. I rang my old client, the one I told you about and she gave me the name of her wig maker. You should have seen Miranda's face when I mentioned the company name; she went white. I thought she was going to be sick. I told her if she kept hassling you at work or if she told anyone at the contest that I was an escort, I would let every one of her colleagues and every one of her clients know her little secret,' Joel told her.

'Oh my God! She really wears a wig? I can't believe it! She's so proud of her hair; she flaunts it so much,' Kate exclaimed in shock.

'Well there you go. So hopefully, our secret is safe and you can get on with your work without her trying to sabotage it.'

'Thank you.'

'You don't have to thank me; I did it for my own

benefit as well: that 40 per cent of the prize money,' Joel answered.

'Do you really think we can win?'

'Yes, don't you?'

'It started out being something I was pushed into and now I can't imagine my life without the show,' Kate said with a sigh.

'You're going to miss being blindfolded and being asked what you would do if my mother-in-law's brother was cheating on me?' Joel asked.

Kate thought for a moment.

'That would be so gross.'

'Decided what to do with the money yet?'

'Pay back Aunt Jess the money she lent me, get her out of my life for good, clear my credit cards and throw the rest at the mortgage, I guess.'

'You could sell the house and buy your farm in France.'

'How many chickens do you think I'd get?'

'Enough to keep you in omelettes for the rest of your life.'

'Ah, but I would need someone to cook them for me.'

'That could be arranged.'

Kate smiled at him.

'Eurostar is getting cheaper all the time, especially for weekend breaks,' Joel replied, starting to eat again.

Kate swallowed, sensing the meaning in his reply. He didn't want her.

## 30

'Mione, it isn't a real wedding, you know. I don't need a bouquet or a lucky horseshoe,' Kate spoke as she and Hermione walked around Highbridge mall.

'Of course you need a bouquet, all the other brides will have one and anyway, that's already arranged. It's being delivered to the hotel tomorrow afternoon.'

'Good God,' Kate exclaimed.

'Right, we need to find earrings and something for your hair, maybe a fascinator,' Hermione said, diving into a jewellery shop.

'What on earth is a fascinator?' Kate shrieked, following her friend.

'Something pretty to wear in your hair to spruce it up a bit, sweetie.'

'Spruce it up?'

'Well, it's a bit plain, isn't it? We need something floral, perhaps an orchid or how about a gerbera? Aren't they your favourite flowers?'

'Yes, they are,' Kate answered.

'I never knew; Joel told me.'

'Hmm, it seems he knows almost everything about me,' Kate replied.

'Which is a good thing, seeing as you have a relationship contest to win tomorrow. So, how's it been having Joel in your bed? Not that it's for the first time,' Hermione asked as she looked at earrings on the counter.

'At first, it was strange, but now it just feels normal – which is really weird,' Kate said, admiring the bracelets.

'Nice weird?'

'Well, it's nice to have someone to hold when he isn't writhing around and having nightmares, but – he hasn't – you know – tried to, you know – at all.'

'And that's what you expected, did you? With him being injured and everything and having been kept at arm's length while you still hold a torch for your ex-husband.'

'No, of course not, but it's like he doesn't feel that

way any more. Like it's just platonic again and the night we had together never happened.'

'Maybe he's just keeping his distance until you decide what you want. You can't possibly blame him for that,' Hermione said, beckoning a sales assistant.

'No, I know, maybe,' Kate answered with a nod.

'So how was his lunch with Marina? She sounded a bit full-on from what Philip told me.'

'He didn't say much about it but she's coming to the show tomorrow. Probably going to be dressed up to the nines and covered in make-up and fake tan,' Kate moaned.

'Philip said Joel used to date her.'

'He told me. I like those earrings,' Kate said, pointing at some small silver and diamanté ones and changing the subject.

'Too small. They would never show up on camera. Can we have a look at these and these?' Hermione told the shop assistant, pointing at the ones she was interested in.

'I hope none of this is going to cost too much; I *am* on a budget,' Kate reminded.

'She's single,' Hermione said, looking at her watch.

'Who?'

'Marina. Philip says she's single and apparently, she's thinking of turning down the overseas jobs and staying in England. She might even be buying a flat in Highbridge; her mother isn't very well and she wants to be close,' Hermione informed.

'It sounds like Philip spent more time talking to her than Joel.'

'I think Philip was eavesdropping, actually. They were supposed to be playing darts but Marina just wouldn't stop talking.'

'Here we are, madam,' the sales assistant spoke as she got the earrings out for Hermione.

'So, which do you think, sweetie? The gold or the silver?'

'What colour's my bouquet?'

'Yellow and white.'

'Gold then I think.'

'We'll take these and that bangle,' Hermione said, pointing at something else on display.

'That will be forty-nine, ninety-nine, please.'

'Fifty quid!' Kate exclaimed.

'It *is* for your wedding.'

'Oh! Is it really? When is it?' the sales assistant asked, getting gooey eyed.

'Tomorrow,' Kate answered.

'God, tomorrow! You must have so much to organise.'

'Not really, it's all been taken out of her hands.

We've got the dress, the flowers and a seven-foot dove as a bridesmaid,' Hermione informed her.

'Don't ask,' Kate spoke, seeing the lack of understanding written all over the cashier's face.

Hermione smiled and picked up the bag from the counter.

'Come on, let's go and eat, I'm starving,' Hermione said, linking arms with Kate and hastening her out of the shop.

'Eat? You didn't say anything about eating? It's lasagne tonight, Joel's cooking, with garlic bread and everything.'

'Oh come on, just a small Chinese. I can't remember the last time I had a meal out and we've done so well with the jewellery. We'll manage a hairpiece in no time, come on,' Hermione begged, pulling at Kate's arm.

'A Chinese? Oh I don't know, I—'

'Call it a pre-wedding treat from me. I can't believe you don't fancy some prawn crackers and a bit of foo yung at least.'

'It doesn't sound like I have much choice,' Kate answered.

'Good, come on then, we'll go to that new place, that's nearest,' Hermione said, hurrying along the mall.

'I've heard it's really expensive.'

'Ah, who cares, like I said, my treat,' Hermione said.

Within a few minutes, they had reached the new Oriental Palace restaurant.

'Right then, here we are,' Hermione spoke, looking at Kate.

'Yes, here we are. It looks busy, maybe they don't have a free table,' Kate said as she looked inside.

'Well, let's go in and ask,' Hermione said and she pushed open the large, glass door, leading the way.

They entered the restaurant and stood by the bar, surveying the other tables and waiting for someone to come to their assistance. It wasn't long before Kate noticed a familiar diner.

'Oh, God, it's Matthew – with her, Amanda,' Kate stated, swallowing the shock and disappointment.

'What? Where?' Hermione questioned.

'There, just over there,' Kate said, tears beginning to fill her eyes.

'I thought he was so in love with you, he had left her.'

'That's what he told me at the hospital, in between unconsciousness. He said he had never loved anyone like he loved me.'

'Well, he was drunk and apparently suicidal,' Hermione replied.

'But he's with her, look at him, laughing and holding her hand. He sent me flowers, he came to my work and he said he wanted to start again,' Kate said tears spilling out of her eyes.

'Lying bastard. I'm going to tell him just what I think of him,' Hermione said, preparing to approach the table.

'No, no don't,' Kate said, wiping at her eyes with her fingers.

'Why? After everything he's done?'

'*I'm* going to tell him what I think of him,' Kate said, sniffing her tears away.

'Maybe we should just leave,' Hermione suggested.

'No, I won't be a minute,' Kate spoke and she took a deep breath and strode towards the table where Matthew and Amanda were sitting.

Amanda looked up first and then Matthew paled as he saw Kate stood in front of him.

'Oh great, what do *you* want? Shouldn't you be elbow deep in nappy changing or something?' Amanda questioned with a frustrated sigh.

'I can't believe you're still together actually because Matthew told me you had split up,' Kate spoke calmly, her eyes not leaving her ex-husband.

'Kate...' Matthew began.

'What's she talking about, Matt?'

'He told me you were over when he was begging me to give him another chance. What was it you said? "Amanda means nothing to me",' Kate continued.

'I didn't say that. Amanda, I did not say that.'

'He said he still loved me and he wanted to be a proper family. And he sent me flowers, dozens of bouquets of flowers and he tried to see me at work, called himself Bruce Carmichael so I wouldn't know it was him,' Kate carried on.

'That's my dad's name,' Amanda stated, going pale.

'Amanda, this isn't true. I was just trying to make amends a little bit for being a bit harsh over Bethan. I mean she *is* mine; I shouldn't have denied it, she even looks like me. You got the wrong end of the stick, Kate. I'm sorry if there was any misinterpretation,' Matthew spoke.

'You said you wanted nothing to do with the brat,' Amanda said, her tone wild.

'Amanda, this is all nonsense; she's making it up. Nothing's changed, you're the one I want to be with,' Matthew insisted.

'If I were you, I would get out while you can. He's a compulsive liar and an accomplished one. The only person he cares about is himself,' Kate said sternly.

'How could you? You sent her flowers and used my dad's name as an alias!' Amanda said, close to tears as she stood up.

'Amanda, don't go. Come on, don't listen to her, you know what she's like. Amanda!' Matthew called as Amanda threw down her napkin and rushed for the door of the restaurant.

Matthew reached into his pocket for his wallet.

'Well thank you, thank you very much,' he said, throwing his napkin down in frustration.

'That's Joel's,' Kate stated, wide-eyed, staring at the wallet in her ex-husband's hand.

'What?' Matthew said.

'That's Joel's wallet! That's his wallet, the one that was taken when he was mugged. It was you!' Kate exclaimed in horror, snatching it from Matthew's hands.

'I don't know what you're talking about. Give me the wallet; I need to pay for all this extortionate food,' Matthew blasted, indicating the meals on the tables.

'You arranged for a group of thugs to beat him up! You could have killed him!' Kate screamed as Hermione hurried to her side.

'You're mistaken; give me the wallet back,' Matthew demanded.

'No,' Kate said and she opened it up and tipped the

contents right into the middle of the shredded beef and hoisin sauce.

'Stay away from me Matthew and stay away from Bethan,' Kate spoke, shaking.

'I'll be speaking to my solicitor about proper access.'

'You do whatever you think you have to do.'

'She's my daughter.'

'Yes, she is. But I'm not your wife, not any more,' Kate answered, swallowing a lump in her throat.

She took one last look at him and then turned and bolted for the door.

'You come near Kate again and you'll have me to deal with,' Hermione threatened, narrowing her eyes at Matthew as he desperately tried to wipe sauce off his credit cards.

'I know all about you. What are you going to do? Put a hex on me?' Matthew asked with a chuckle.

Hermione picked up one of his cards and held it out to him.

'Yours, I believe,' she remarked, making him look up.

Matthew went to reach for it and as he did, Hermione jerked her knee up and landed a direct hit in his nether regions, making him audibly yelp in pain.

'That's the thing about the mystics – they can help but sometimes, brute force is the only real remedy,' Hermione ended, straightening her coat.

\* \* \*

Outside, the tears were falling from Kate's face as she looked at the leather wallet in her hands. She ran her fingers over the smooth front and felt like a complete fool. Why had she let Matthew take her in again?

'Are you OK?' Hermione asked, arriving at her side.

'He got people to attack Joel. This is his wallet,' Kate spoke, holding it up for Hermione to see.

'I know.'

'He told me he wanted to start again, he told me he loved me and he loved Bethan and he wanted to be a family again.'

'I know, sweetie,' Hermione said, feeling her friend's pain.

'He's made an idiot out of me,' Kate continued.

'No! You are not an idiot, Kate because you didn't fall for it,' Hermione insisted.

'Maybe not externally but perhaps I had – in here,' Kate admitted, touching her chest.

'Leopards can't change their spots sweetie, no matter how hard they try. Matthew hasn't changed. He never wanted to start again; he was just concerned about his finances and he saw a way to stop you getting ruthless about it. He was your Achilles heel and he exploited that. He's a liar and a cheat and a self-centred excuse for a man. He was that person when he left you and he's still that person now,' Hermione stated.

'I know.'

'Sometimes, things don't turn out the way we want them to but that isn't your fault.'

'I know.'

'Then why do you feel so much responsibility for what he did to you?'

'I don't know.'

'You're a wonderful person, Kate. A good friend, an exceptional mother and a bright, intelligent, young woman with her whole life in front of her. You need to move on from Matthew and do it with a fresh outlook and no turning back. What's done is done,' Hermione spoke, making Kate look at her.

'I've been so stupid, hanging on to some ridiculous idea that we could be a happy family again – even when he said all those horrid things about Bethan. Still I thought he would change his mind and come back.'

'You deserve so much better.'

'Like Joel, you mean?'

'Well, he wouldn't be a bad start.'

'I've not been entirely honest with him about how I feel,' Kate answered, rubbing at her eyes.

'What did I say about letting go and having a fresh outlook? Give him a chance; after all, you already know he's good in bed.'

'Mione! I never said that!'

'You didn't need to, sweetie.'

## 31

'Hey, you OK? I was getting worried; it's late,' Joel remarked as Kate struggled through the front door, three shopping bags on each arm.

'Have you any idea how long it takes to find the perfect accessories for a fake wedding?' Kate asked, dumping the bags on the floor and slumping down onto the sofa next to him.

'No idea.'

'Well let me tell you, it takes *forever*! But a bangle, a pair of earrings, a fascinator, a garter would you believe, two pairs of pearlescent stockings and a pair of shoes later and Hermione is happy we're ready,' Kate explained.

'It sounds like it was painful,' Joel remarked with a smile.

'Yeah, it was. But not as painful as something else,' Kate spoke and she reached inside her handbag and brought out Joel's wallet. She handed it to him.

'It is yours, isn't it,' Kate said, needing it to be clarified.

'Yes, but where did you get it? I mean—' Joel exclaimed.

'Matthew. You were right; everyone was right. You weren't just mugged, he arranged it and he had the nerve to use your wallet, flaunt it like some sort of trophy. I am so sorry, Joel,' Kate said, looking at him.

'I knew,' Joel replied, putting the wallet on the coffee table.

'I know and Hermione suggested it and I wouldn't listen and—'

'No, I mean I knew, for certain,' Joel told her.

'What?'

'When they'd finished kicking me, they pressed his business card into my hand,' Joel explained.

Tears pricked Kate's eyes and for a moment, she couldn't respond.

'But I couldn't tell you that. You still loved him and I wasn't sure you'd believe me. And he's Bethan's dad at the end of the day. I couldn't tell the police and be responsible for her father being on the end of an assault charge,' Joel spoke.

'You should have told me,' Kate said, wiping her eyes with the back of her hand.

'What good would it have done? I wasn't playing games like him. If you wanted to be with me, you had to decide that for yourself, not because of anything I'd told you or anything he'd done.'

'He hurt you because of me; it's my fault,' Kate spoke, trying hard not to sob.

'Now that's one of the most stupid things you've ever said and I don't want to talk about it any more,' Joel told her seriously.

'But what he did—'

'He did because he loves you,' Joel reminded her.

'No,' Kate said with a shake of her head.

'I think he does. I think he knows he made the biggest mistake of his life when he left you and he's desperate to make up for that,' Joel continued.

'No. He's still with Amanda. We saw them tonight, together – like he'd never made me any of those promises,' Kate told him.

'I'm sorry,' Joel said, looking at her.

'No, don't be. I needed to see it; it opened my eyes. There he was, looking at Amanda the way he used to look at me and I saw him and I didn't feel angry that he was looking at her like that; I felt sad because I didn't know if it was real. I mean, did he ever love me? Does he really love her?' Kate asked.

'I think he's a fool for letting you go,' Joel told her.

'He didn't just let me go; he walked away without a second thought,' Kate told him.

Joel took hold of her hand and held it tightly.

Kate looked up at him and felt a wave of feeling wash over her. Here she was, sat next to the most gorgeous man she had ever met, someone who had entered a relationship contest with her to help her and Bethan crawl away from near bankruptcy and she had wasted so much time pining for someone who didn't want her and perhaps never had wanted her.

She reached up to touch his face and Joel sprung from the sofa like she was about to poke him with a live wire.

'I saved you some lasagne. I'll warm it up,' he spoke quickly.

'Great, thanks,' Kate replied, not knowing what else to say.

She had left it too late.

## 32

'Hi, Joel Brown and Kate Baxter, we're here for the competition: *Knowing Me Knowing You,*' Joel spoke to the hotel receptionist.

It was the day of the final and Kate and Joel had arrived in London ahead of that night's show.

'Of course sir, let me just find your details.'

'I'm starving,' Kate remarked, looking about the foyer of the hotel in search of something food related.

'Me too. Let's get checked in and find somewhere to eat,' Joel agreed.

'OK, you are in Executive Suite Four which is on the third floor with a lovely view of the London Eye. Here is your key card. The lifts are just over there.

Would you like some help with your luggage?' the receptionist asked.

'No thanks, we're fine,' Joel answered, about to leave the desk.

'A three-course lunch will be served in the dining room at one for all the contestants and it is requested that you participate in short mat bowls afterwards,' she continued.

'Short mat bowls,' Kate stated, looking at the hotel employee quizzically.

'Yes, madam.'

'You're good at bowling,' Joel remarked to Kate.

'That's skittles, not short mat bowls. Could we have someone to help with our bags? You shouldn't be lifting anything,' Kate said, taking the bags away from Joel.

'Apart from the one hundred thousand pound cheque.'

'If anyone's getting the first lift of that then it's me,' Kate answered, leading the way towards the lifts.

'Wait! Wait!' Lynn screeched as she and Darren arrived in the hotel reception area.

Kate stopped and smiled at her friend as she hurried towards her.

'Where's the bar? We've been on that bloody coach for over two hours and I've had to listen to all Dorothy from accounts hospital stories,' Lynn exclaimed with a sigh.

'I think it's that way but we've only just got here ourselves and we have to have lunch with the other contestants at one, followed by a game of short mat bowls,' Kate informed her.

'Darren and I will be in the bar. He has a new hand, look,' Lynn spoke, pointing over at where her husband was talking to the receptionist.

'I'll go and see him. It's time we had a proper chat and it will give you two a chance to find the bar,' Joel said.

'It's weird them knowing each other, isn't it? Darren told me what happened, had to drag it out of him as usual but he told me,' Lynn said as Joel joined Darren at the reception desk.

'Joel has terrible post-traumatic stress; he blames himself for everything,' Kate informed her.

'Darren had nightmares to begin with but he seems to be dealing with it now. He sees a counsellor. Well, that's what he tells me – could be at the pub for all I know.'

'Perhaps if they start talking to each other, it might help them both,' Kate remarked, watching as Darren and Joel joked with each other and between them picked up the luggage.

'Oh here she comes, wearing some sort of bizarre jumpsuit. Oh and she has two suitcases! For one night!' Lynn remarked as Miranda entered the hotel, Andrew Kent following her like a lapdog.

'Gold sandals and Gucci sunglasses,' Kate said as the two women watched Miranda make her entrance.

'And a thong.'

'Enough information,' Kate told her.

'So have you got a great room?'

'We have a view of the London Eye, apparently.'

'Cool! Good God, who is that? Skin-tight jeans or what? And a smaller top than any of the Lady Dragon's. Oh! Oh! I recognise her, that's—' Lynn remarked as a tall, blonde-haired woman entered the foyer.

'Marina,' Kate remarked as she watched the woman walk up to the reception desk and enthusiastically greet Joel.

'She's going to kiss him. Bet she goes for the mouth,' Lynn commented as Kate watched the scene, unable to keep her eyes away.

Both the women watched as Marina threw her arms around Joel and kissed his lips.

Kate felt her chest tighten and she tried to swallow the feeling away. She had no right to feel jealous. She had spent the past couple of months sending out mixed messages and wishing she was back with her cheating ex-husband. She couldn't stop looking, though and didn't like the way Joel's arm had circled Marina's tiny waist.

'Hussy! She can't stop touching him. Maybe we should go and join them, make her realise who they belong to. She touches Darren and I'll swing for her,' Lynn remarked, eyeing Marina with suspicion.

Kate continued to survey the scene as Marina and Joel spoke to one another. There was no denying they made an extremely good-looking couple. Marina touched Joel's arm and he smiled and let out a laugh. Darren then began showing off his new hand and started trying to tickle Marina with the plastic fingers and she giggled loudly, flicking back her blonde hair. Now who did that remind her of?

'Right, that's it, she's going down,' Lynn announced and she began to stride over to the reception desk.

'No! Don't Lynn, please. Just ignore her. She's not interested in Darren; she's interested in Joel – just leave her,' Kate insisted, grabbing Lynn by the arm and dragging her back towards her.

'Are you going to just let her stand there and crawl all over your man?' Lynn asked, staring at Kate with wide eyes.

'I'm no competition for her. Look at her, she's perfect. I'm a wreck, I have split ends, stretch marks and

Bethan. Anyway, Joel deserves so much better than me,' Kate stated, still looking over at him.

'Kate...' Lynn began in serious tones.

'Hello ladies, it's a perfect day for the final, isn't it?' Miranda's voice announced as she arrived at Kate's side, still wearing her sunglasses.

'I think the sun beds are that way,' Lynn remarked before she could stop herself.

'It's a relief to be off that wretched coach, I can tell you. One cup of coffee and one toilet stop. Still, back to luxury here. Andrew and I are in an executive suite with a view of the London Eye, apparently,' Miranda continued.

'So are Kate and Joel,' Lynn commented.

'That's nice. I see Joel has a new friend over there,' Miranda remarked, indicating Marina.

'That's his sister,' Lynn said quickly.

'Oh really, come to support you both, that's perfect,' Miranda responded.

'We'd better find the bar, hadn't we, Lynn? Haven't had a drink since Fleet,' Kate spoke, taking Lynn's arm.

'Well, I'm sure I will see you both around the pool later, supposed to really hot up this afternoon,' Miranda said, smiling and flicking her hair back.

'Maybe, after short mat bowls,' Kate responded with a sigh.

'Come on, let's get you that drink,' Lynn said, leading the way across the foyer.

\* \* \*

'Two large rum and Cokes, please,' Lynn ordered as she and Kate sat down on a bar stool.

'Why is she here now? I mean, I know he said she was coming to the show tonight but it's not even lunchtime. What is she doing here? Is she going to be here all day?' Kate questioned.

'So you *are* bothered about Marina.'

'Of course I'm bothered by her. She's all over Joel, all *over* him, kissing him and touching him, and who can blame her? I've been such an idiot; I've pushed him away and now it's too late.'

'Duh! How can it be too late? She's been around two minutes; you've been doing this show with him for two months. You're in the final with him tonight. You're sharing an executive suite.'

'He doesn't care about me any more, not like he used to. And that's my fault because I've spent too much time hankering after Matthew.'

'The minger,' Lynn added.

'Yeah, the minger,' Kate agreed.

'I see, bad news Joel mate, they're on the rum already,' Darren spoke as he and Joel arrived at the bar.

'We haven't paid yet, what do you want?' Lynn offered.

'Two lagers will be the order of the day I think, don't you, Joel?' Darren said with a grin.

'Sounds good,' Joel replied.

Kate picked up her drink and drank a huge gulp.

'Where's Marina?' she questioned, trying to keep the bitterness out of her voice.

'Oh you saw her, why didn't you come over? I would have introduced you.'

'We were talking to the Lady Dragon. So where is she? Getting ready for short mat bowls?' Kate asked, jealousy leaking out.

'She's gone shopping. She just came in to check what time it started tonight.'

'She's a looker that Marina, isn't she?' Darren commented.

'Oh she is, is she?' Lynn remarked, glaring at her husband.

'Well, obviously nothing in comparison to you love, but you know, not bad,' Darren said quickly.

'She takes an hour to put her make-up on in the morning and even longer to take it off at night,' Joel informed him.

'Oh aye aye! Knows her early-morning routines, eh?'

'I'll have another one of these, please,' Kate spoke, passing her glass over the bar to the barman.

'Yeah, and me,' Lynn added, passing her glass too.

'Have I done something to upset you?' Joel asked, sensing Kate's mood.

'You? No, of course not, I'm just dreading the contestant lunch, that's all. Can't we skip it and go for a swim?'

'As much as I would love to, I think we ought to check out the other contestants, see what we're up against. We can always sneak out before the bowls starts.'

'Is that a promise?'

'Sure.'

'So, you and Darren have talked?' Kate asked as she saw Darren disappear towards the gents.

'Not properly, not about that day, but he's the same old Darren and we're good.'

'I'm glad.'

'Yeah, me too. It's a step in the right direction.'

'HELLO! If I could have your attention! Could all the *Knowing Me Knowing You* contestants meet in the dining room at one, that's in twenty-five minutes time. There will be a three-course meal followed by a photo shoot and a game of short mat bowls. Is Kate Baxter here?' Becky, the TV company assistant shouted loudly.

Kate froze as her name was called out and everyone started scanning the room, waiting to see what was about to happen.

'She's here!' Lynn shouted, pointing at Kate.

'Oh Kate, good. This arrived for you, very beautiful,' Becky spoke and she handed Kate a yellow and white bouquet of gerberas.

'Oh, thank you,' Kate spoke, her face flushing with embarrassment as all eyes were trained on her.

'Wow! That's gorgeous,' Lynn said, admiring the flowers.

'It was Hermione's idea, not mine; she said everyone would have one,' Kate responded, still flushed.

'It's your wedding day; you should have whatever you want,' Lynn told her.

Kate smiled and looked up at Joel. If only.

## 33

Kate slipped on her gold, strappy sandals and then turned to look at herself in the full-length mirror. The reflection took her back; memories filled her head and tears sprung to her eyes. She felt like she had spent the whole of the last year crying.

The dress Hermione had made was gorgeous. Any bride would have been proud to wear it on their special day. It was full-length, tight at the bust, in at the waist and then it flowed down in a straight, pleated style, finishing at the floor.

'It's almost five,' Joel called from the living area of their suite.

'OK, I'm just coming,' Kate hurriedly called back,

swallowing the ball of emotion in her throat and pre-paring to leave the bedroom.

She opened the door and there was Joel in the midnight-blue wedding suit she had chosen the mate-rial for. At the sight of him, her heart jolted. Despite the scars from his attack, he looked amazing and the way he smiled at her as she entered the room made her insides tighten.

'Kate, you look – stunning,' Joel spoke, his voice faltering.

'It's the dress, not me. I like your suit; Hermione is a genius.'

'No, it's definitely you.'

'Midnight blue was so the right choice for you,' Kate replied hurriedly, not wanting to acknowledge the charge in the room.

'You like it?' Joel asked, stretching out his arms to display the suit.

'Yes,' Kate answered, looking at him intently.

'It feels strange, being dressed up for my wedding.'

'Yes,' Kate agreed.

'I've never done it before.'

Kate nodded and tried to ignore the urge to cry. She had to hold it together; in a few hours, the contest would be over and things could get back to normal. He would be better off with Marina. They had more in common; they could work the camera together and eat healthily.

'Sorry, that wasn't meant to sound like it came out,' Joel said quickly.

'It's OK, honestly,' Kate answered, giving a small cough and getting rid of the knot in her throat.

'I'm just getting carried away with the occasion; one look at the Love Dove will have me back to reality – well, televisual reality anyway. Got to have steady nerves and a steady hand for the cake decorating,' Joel said, smiling at her.

'Yes and you mustn't get so heavy-handed with the silver balls. They need to be in nice groups, not large clumps,' Kate told him.

'Speaks the woman who knocked the head off the porcelain groom the other day.'

'We'd better go or Lynn will be banging the door down,' Kate said, looking at her watch.

'OK, oh, here, don't forget your bouquet,' Joel said, picking the flowers up from the table and handing them to her.

Their fingers brushed against each other and Kate grabbed onto the flowers as tightly as she could and headed for the door. She didn't want to touch him any more; it was agony knowing how close they had come to something special and how she had pushed it away.

'Come on, we don't want to be late.' Kate called to him.

\* \* \*

'One lager, one rum and Coke,' Darren spoke as Joel and Kate joined him and Lynn at the bar.

'Have you seen the mutton dressed as lamb over there?' Lynn asked, pointing in the direction of Kate and Joel's rivals for the *Knowing Me Knowing You* crown.

'God, is that Sylvia?' Kate asked, craning her neck to see.

'Yes, in black with a horrendously low-cut top that someone of her age just shouldn't be allowed to own. She does look every inch the bride, though – Frankenstein's.'

'The others look nice, though,' Kate said, admiring the other contestants' dresses.

'And so do you, and as for Joel! I have to hand it to Hermione; she got his measurements spot on. That suit fits him like a glove.'

'She spent long enough measuring him, I can tell you. Oh great,' Kate spoke, her voice dropping.

'What's the matter?'

'It's Marina, barely dressed, heading this way,' Kate

said and she downed her drink in one and put the glass back down on the bar.

'Hi Joel, hello Darren, lovely to meet you again,' Marina spoke and she began kissing the two men on both cheeks, much to Lynn and Kate's irritation.

'Hey Marina, I didn't think you could make it until later,' Joel said, smiling at the blonde-haired woman.

'Well the shoot finished early so I got ready and headed on down here. You look amazing in that suit,' Marina said, gazing intently at Joel.

'He does, doesn't he! He's getting married to Kate; this is Kate, his bride,' Lynn introduced, giving her a shove towards the pair.

'Oh Kate, I'm sorry, I haven't introduced you to Marina, have I? Marina, this is Kate, my co-contestant for the show. Kate, this is Marina.'

'Hello,' Kate said through tight lips.

Co-contestant! Was that all she was now? Yes, of course that was all she was because she had been stupid and she had passed up her chance of having the sexiest man alive. She was an idiot!

'Pleased to meet you,' Marina answered.

'Wow! Look at you Kate, and Joel, what a smashing couple you make,' Colin Sykes spoke as he and Dawn appeared at the edge of the bar.

'Wow to you too, Colin – nice shirt. I would never

have thought canary yellow for your skin tone, but it really does complement it,' Lynn remarked.

'Thank you, I think. Kate, could I have a quick word, before we all get too drunk and caught up in the occasion to be able to say anything sensible?' Colin asked with a smile.

Kate felt her heart sink. She knew exactly what he was going to ask her and it was the moment she had been dreading for the past few weeks.

'I won't keep you from your groom for long, I promise,' Colin said.

'Sure,' Kate replied and she handed her bouquet to Lynn and went to the corner of the room with the Randall's partner.

'You know what I'm going to ask you, don't you? I know I said no pressure but there's a course starting next month and I thought it would be good if you wanted to do it, we could—'

'I've decided not to do the exam,' Kate said bluntly.

'Oh,' Colin said in a tone that was both surprised and disappointed.

'It isn't what I want. It probably should be, but it isn't, not right now.'

'Has this got anything to do with Miranda?' Colin asked seriously.

'No, it hasn't,' Kate answered truthfully.

'Well, I can't pretend I'm not disappointed. I like you Kate, the other partners like you, your work is efficient and accurate and the clients have nothing but praise for you.'

'That's very kind of you to say but...' Kate began, looking back nervously at Marina, who had now linked her arm through Joel's.

'It's the truth, Kate; you're a very valued member of the team, highly regarded by all,' Colin assured her.

'And I regard you higher than anyone, love,' a familiar, loud, booming voice spoke from behind them.

Kate turned around to see Frank Peterson beaming at her. He was wearing a tuxedo with a bright-red cummerbund and matching bow tie, a fat Cuban cigar hanging from his mouth. She had never wanted to hug anyone more.

'Frank! How are you? How's Marion?' Kate asked, smiling at her client.

'Of course I'm here, couldn't miss your big night, plus I've put up some of the prize money. As for Marion, she's healing up fine; won't be dancing for a while but she's up and at them, in the ladies doing her make-up at the moment,' Frank informed.

'A woman's prerogative,' Colin responded with a laugh.

'It certainly is. You wouldn't mind if I stole five

minutes with your girl, would you?' Frank asked Colin as he put an arm around Kate.

'Not at all. I'd better see to drinks for the team before the show starts. We'll speak another time, Kate,' Colin spoke with an understanding smile.

'Yes, of course,' Kate replied.

'Trying to chat you up, was he?' Frank asked her.

'No, of course not, Frank!' Kate exclaimed with a laugh.

'Well, I wouldn't blame him. Look at you girl, you look wonderful,' Frank said, admiring Kate's dress.

'Thank you,' Kate answered.

'Right, well, I'll cut to the chase because I know you're just about to dash off and compete for that prize and we can't keep TV land waiting, can we?' Frank began.

'Quite right too,' Kate spoke, trying to concentrate on what Frank was saying and not stare at Marina, who was leaning on Joel's arm and pulling him into her.

'I want you,' Frank stated, his eyes bulging.

Kate just stared at him, wide-eyed and verging on terrified.

'I'm sorry Frank, I must have misheard you. What did you say?' Kate asked gingerly.

'I said I want you. I want to take you away from all this. I want you...'

'Oh dear,' Kate replied awkwardly.

'...as my right-hand man, well right-hand woman, I should say. I'm getting on a bit Kate, losing that sharpness. I need someone to keep me on an even keel, organise me, tell me what to do,' Frank clarified.

'Oh, God, you mean a job; you want to offer me a job?' Kate said, relieved.

'Yes, I've been thinking about it for a while now but with Marion getting laid up, it brought things to a head, made me consider the future. I don't want to let go of the reins yet but my thirty-five-year-old son still acts like he's at university. You know, drinking, different girlfriend every week; he's not ready to take the lead. So, I'm sticking with it for now, but I need help and I want you,' Frank repeated.

'Frank, I do Probate and Wills,' Kate reminded him.

'I know but you have a good head on your shoulders, intuition and common sense. I trust you. That's all I need,' Frank assured her.

'But what would I do? I don't know anything about finance – well, not in the way you mean,' Kate told him, her concentration finally moving from Marina.

'I don't want you to have anything to do with finance; that's my area. You just need to know about me. I like things done a certain way, you know that. I need someone to coordinate appointments, organise meetings, create opportunities. An assistant if you like,' Frank explained.

'Frank, I'm flattered, really I am, but I have Bethan and I'm not sure...' Kate started.

'You could work from home, some of the time at least. I mean, you know my business takes me all over the world and there would be times when I would need you with me but primarily, we don't have to be in the same place. I do a great deal of business by video link these days,' Frank informed her.

'I don't know. I mean, this has come so out of the blue,' Kate began.

'Well, don't rush a decision on the spot. I know better than anyone that decisions need to be carefully considered. I can give you until Wednesday,' Frank answered.

'Wednesday,' Kate said with a gulp.

'It might take me some time to find a candidate as desirable as you and I don't like to let the grass grow once I've made a decision.'

'Frank, I don't think—' Kate started.

'Seventy-five thousand a year plus bonuses,' Frank blurted out.

Kate's eyes went out on stalks. That was more than she could ever have imagined earning at Randall's even if she had made partner.

'Seventy-five thousand a year,' she repeated, the words almost choking her.

'To start with,' Frank added with a smile.

\* \* \*

'Ladies and gentlemen, the time has come, the moment is here, please, be upstanding and put your hands together for our brides and our grooms as we begin the final of *Knowing Me Knowing You* 2011,' Larry Rawlins roared into the microphone.

The already half-cut audience got to their feet and began clapping; cheering, wailing and banging glasses on tables, sounding like a scrum of rugby players on a pub crawl.

Kate took a deep breath, put a smile on her face and then let Joel lead her out onto the stage, following the train of other contestants in front of them. She now had much more on her mind than just trying to win the contest. Frank's job offer was sensational. Working from home would be ideal but jetting off to far-flung countries whenever Frank needed her wouldn't be. She would have to rely heavily on

Hermione and she did that too much as it was. But seventy-five thousand pounds was a hell of a salary and she was in no position to wave it away without serious consideration. Especially as it was money she badly needed; wasn't she competing in the show for that very reason?

'Don't our couples look wonderful? A picture of harmony. But which couple is going to end up victorious tonight and take away the grand sum of one hundred thousand pounds?' Larry continued.

The crowd let out an over the top 'woo' at the mention of the cash and Kate cringed as she noticed the Love Dove loitering with intent at the edge of the stage.

'And, on top of that, there will be spot prizes. Come on Lovey, bring on your golden eggs.'

The Love Dove sprinted onto the stage as fast as his stocking-clad legs would carry him and began to shake his tail feathers for the cameras and anyone else that happened to be unfortunate enough to be looking.

'We have three spot prizes tonight; you could be taking home two tickets for a top West End show of your choice, first-class Eurostar tickets to Paris or a wonderful Mediterranean cruise courtesy of Cruise UK.'

There was more whooping from the audience and Kate's gaze fell on Marina, sat at the table adjacent to Lynn, Darren and most of the Randall's team. She was clapping her hands excitedly and smiling in their direction.

Marina was her other problem. She didn't like the way she looked at Joel. There was something in her expression that spoke volumes about the way she felt about him. She knew she only had herself to blame for losing her chance but she didn't like it and she didn't like being so quickly usurped by someone who could grace the cover of *Cosmo* and probably had.

'Right, without further ado, let's prepare for Racy Cakes!' Larry announced.

With that announcement made, the wedding cakes arrived from stage left. Six decorating stations in a trailer were pulled onto the stage by the Love Dove, who was driving something resembling a golf buggy decorated with sequins identical to those on Larry Rawlins' jacket.

Kate looked at Joel in the hope of receiving some reassurance about the tasks to come but he was smiling out into the crowd, specifically at Marina.

'Do you want to join us or not?' Kate snapped, indicating to him that the other couples were starting to get behind their cake stations.

'Sorry, of course, let's do it,' Joel replied.

'Because if you would rather be down there with her then it's no skin off my nose,' Kate added crossly.

'What?' Joel questioned.

'Marina, the bimbo down there, the one you haven't stopped looking at and flirting with all night.' Kate spat.

She couldn't keep her dislike for her under wraps any longer.

'Kate, I—' Joel began.

'Don't you mess this up for me; I want to win this contest,' Kate told him fiercely.

'Right, *Knowing Me Knowing You* couples, your task is to decorate these wonderful wedding cakes supplied to us by Barnes Cakes of London in two minutes. Once completed, they will be judged by Linda Barnes of Barnes Cakes and her decision is final. One word of warning to you: the cakes must be stacked, three tiers high and if they aren't stacked, Linda won't even give them a second glance. Is that all clear?' Larry spoke, looking at the couples with a serious expression.

'Yes Larry,' the participants bleated.

'Good, then without further ado, I will give you the countdown: five, four, three, two, one – start decorating!' Larry boomed as a loud air horn sounded.

'Hurry up! Roll the icing out! Come on Joel,

smoother than that!' Kate ordered him as she began to arrange the decorations.

'I'm doing my best,' Joel replied, hurriedly rolling out icing and shaping it to fit the cake.

'Yeah, of course, one eye on the icing another on Marina's cleavage – or rather lack of it, actually,' Kate muttered as she began to put baubles and hearts on the bottom tier.

'What's the matter? You've been acting odd since you had that chat with Frank Peterson. What did he say to you?' Joel asked, putting another layer of icing onto the second cake.

'Stop talking and keep rolling, we don't have long left and I wanted to try the bell formation on the top tier,' Kate exclaimed, racing to place the cake decorations on the second tier.

'There's plenty of time, stop rushing; we need it to look right. Not so many balls otherwise there won't be enough to go round.'

'Shut up! Decoration is my job, not yours!' Kate barked.

'Thirty seconds guys!' Larry exclaimed loudly.

'See! Thirty seconds! Get them stacked, get them stacked!' Kate ordered, flailing her arms around and picking up the porcelain bride and groom.

'Hold this and take that,' Joel spoke, passing Kate the rolling pin and some edible roses.

'Never mind those, get them stacked or we don't get any points. Shit, Mark and Gloria's cake looks really good,' Kate exclaimed as she helped Joel hold the cakes steady and get them into position.

'Looks like it's got a lean on to me,' Joel announced, sneaking a look at his competitors.

'Is that central? Joel, are the bride and groom central?' Kate questioned, staring at their cake and trying to measure distance with her fingers.

'I think so. Hold on, this doesn't look good... whoa! Oh dear!' Joel announced as Mark and Gloria's cake toppled over and two tiers fell onto the stage.

'Five, four, three, two, one – OK, time's up. Put down your rolling pins and step away from the cakes.'

'It's not good enough. Look at that couple's over there; the bride with the beehive, theirs looks professional. Linda Barnes from Barnes of London is going to lap that up. Ours looks like something one of Hermione's kids made,' Kate moaned.

'It isn't that bad; the bell formation is sort of working-ish,' Joel told her.

'Oh what would you care? The cakes didn't have your full concentration,' Kate snapped again.

'What's all this about, Kate?' Joel asked her.

'Shh, here comes Linda Barnes,' Kate hissed as the judge, Larry Rawlins and the Love Dove headed over to their table.

'And here Linda we have Kate and Joel. I'd say this is quite a decent effort, wouldn't you?' Larry spoke.

'Yes I would, most commendable. All three tiers stacked up neatly, good use of varied decoration, I like the silver balls in the shape of, I think they're bells, aren't they? Yes, good,' Linda Barnes said, scrutinising all three tiers.

'So how many out of ten for Kate and Joel?' Larry wanted to know.

'I'd say an eight,' Linda decided.

'An eight, wow, that's top marks so far for Kate and Joel. Now let's move on to Martin and Yvonne,' Larry said, moving away.

'Eight, that's great, isn't it,' Joel whispered.

'It isn't enough to compete with beehive girl; they'll get at least a nine,' Kate moaned, folding her arms across her chest.

'What's wrong with you tonight?' Joel asked.

'Nothing a large drink won't fix, or several large drinks seeing as we've blown our chance in the contest,' Kate said, letting out a heavy sigh and looking at Marina, perched on her seat, sucking at a cocktail.

'Don't be stupid, we haven't blown our chances.

We got an eight; that could be good enough to win. Let's listen to the other scores,' Joel suggested.

'What's the point?'

'What's the matter with you?'

'Nothing's the matter with me; I was focussed on the task, unlike some of us,' Kate said.

'I don't understand,' Joel answered.

'No, you don't,' Kate replied, fiddling with the fascinator in her hair.

'...right, so that means, ladies and gentlemen, the winners of Racy Cakes are Claudia and Gerry: five Kissing Gates on the board. And runners-up are Kate and Joel: three Kissing Gates on the board for you. Well done, everyone!' Larry announced.

'Woohoo! Go Kate! Go Kate! Go Kate!' Lynn shouted out, waving her hands in the air from the audience.

'See, we're second, just like we were in the last show. It's a good position to be in,' Joel reassured her.

'Whatever.'

'The next round will be Couples' Catwalk and we'll be back after the break,' Larry spoke to camera one.

'Great, where's the bar?' Kate asked, holding up her wedding dress and striding off the stage towards the green room.

# 34

'Wow, I was so impressed with the way you decorated those cakes, you were like a whirlwind and Joel was a master with that rolling pin. Just a pity he didn't do it naked,' Lynn commented when she had caught up with Kate in the green room.

'You shouldn't be in here. If Becky catches you, she'll have you ejected,' Kate told her, downing a rum and Coke.

'What, me and my poor, disabled husband? She wouldn't dare; you can't be seen to be discriminating,' Lynn remarked, smiling.

'You're helping yourself to the free booze; a disability doesn't give you exemption from being caught pinching stuff.'

'Is something wrong? You don't seem quite right. I thought you would be made up, currently second on the leader board. And having an ex-model strutting his stuff down the catwalk will give you a definite advantage in Couples' Catwalk, then there's free booze and food. What more could a girl want from an evening?' Lynn questioned.

'He isn't paying attention to the games; all he can do is gaze out into the audience at *her*,' Kate stated, looking over at Joel, who was chatting with Darren at the bar. Yes Marina was definitely a 'her'.

'Who?' Lynn asked stupidly.

'Marina of course, bloody ex-girlfriend Marina. Marina with the perfect figure and the even more perfect face,' Kate said, picking up her second drink and gulping from it.

'Oh *her*, yeah, she's a bitch, isn't she? Probably got an eating disorder though, or takes cocaine. What do you think?' Lynn asked.

'I don't know, I don't care, but he does; he can't focus on anything else,' Kate said with a sigh.

'Are you sure? I mean, he might not be looking at her all the time; those lights blind you, don't they? Maybe he's just looking out randomly to give his eyes a rest,' Lynn spoke.

'Thanks Lynn but I need to face the truth: I've lost

him because I was too preoccupied with Matthew. What was I thinking of? Wasting all that time and not noticing the wonderful person under my nose.'

'Well, if that's how you really feel then why are you wasting time here with me? Go and tell him,' Lynn urged.

'No, I can't tell him. He gave me a chance, more than one chance, and I turned him away every time. The way he's looking out at Marina now is the way he used to look at me and I just ignored it because it was like Matthew all over again. I thought it couldn't be genuine. I mean, how could someone like him fall for a single mother like me? I microwave every night for Christ's sake and I have one good suit! Look at her when you're back at the table, look at her in her tiny little designer dress! She's won and she didn't even have to try!' Kate yelled.

'She only rocked up on the scene five minutes ago. If he said he loved you, his head can't have been turned that quickly,' Lynn told her.

'He deserves better than me. I was indecisive; I should have trusted how he made me feel, not buried my head in the sand and moped about Matthew. Another drink please: rum and Coke,' Kate ordered from the barman.

'I'm ringing Hermione; she'll know what to do. We

can't have this depression ruining your chances of winning the contest. This is what you've worked for for the last couple of months; you can't throw it away at the last second, not now you're so close,' Lynn spoke as she got out her mobile phone.

'I don't want to speak to Mione; she'll say the same as you: that I need to talk to Joel but I can't. I'd feel an idiot and—'

'But at least you wouldn't feel like a lonely idiot.'

'I would if he turned me down, which he will,' Kate remarked.

'ATTENTION! Couples' Catwalk is about to start. Can I have Claudia and Gerry, Martin and Yvonne, and Mark and Gloria, please? Ten minutes and I'll be back for the rest of you,' Becky called loudly, holding her clipboard aloft.

'Right then, ten minutes to get this sorted out. Come on, you're going to speak to him,' Lynn announced and she yanked Kate's arm, dragging her over toward Darren and Joel.

'Hello, you two. I hope you haven't drunk too much of the complimentary drink, Darren; I'm not wheeling you back to the room in a luggage trolley again,' Lynn joked, smiling at her husband.

'She's a laugh my missus, isn't she? Nah, we've been having a deep and meaningful, haven't we Joel?'

Darren said, slapping Joel on the back and letting out a hearty laugh.

'Something like that,' Joel replied, looking at Kate.

'Well, we need to get back to our table before the Lady Dragon sells our seats or something. Come on Darren, there'll be plenty of time for celebrating later,' Lynn told her husband, pulling at his arm, keen for him to leave.

'Oh, OK, you're the boss. Good luck with the rest of the show, mate; we'll be rooting for you,' Darren called as Lynn manoeuvred him towards the door.

'See you,' Joel said, waving a hand at Darren.

Kate swallowed as she looked at Joel in his wedding suit. He turned to face her and she wrung her hands together nervously.

'Are you feeling any better now?' Joel wanted to know.

'I'm just a bit nervous, that's all. You know, this is it tonight: the culmination of, well – everything,' Kate said.

'Yeah, I know, it's weird, isn't it? It's hard to imagine we're never going to share the stage with Larry and the Love Dove after tonight. They've become such a big part of my life,' Joel said with a smile.

'I'll be glad to see the back of the big bird,' Kate admitted with a laugh.

'I'll be glad to say goodbye to Larry's sequined jacket; it causes a nasty refraction from the spotlights.'

'Frank offered me a job,' Kate blurted out.

'Wow! Doing what?' Joel exclaimed excitedly.

'Being his assistant, arranging his life and helping him oversee the business.'

'That sounds fantastic,' Joel said.

'It's seventy-five thousand per annum.'

'Kate, that's brilliant, I'm so pleased for you,' Joel said, reaching out and touching her arm.

'I didn't say yes, not straight away. I mean, it sounds like it would be very involved. Frank's business is worldwide; it isn't Mrs Collins' ten thousand in the bank and some premium bonds. I don't know whether I'm adequately equipped for the job in all sorts of respects.'

'Why do you think things are going to go wrong before you've even tried them? It doesn't matter if you make mistakes, you know – try it. If it works out, fantastic. If it doesn't then you try something else,' Joel told her.

'That isn't how I do things. And I have Bethan to think about,' Kate reminded.

'Where's the job based? In Highbridge?' Joel asked.

'He said I could work from home but it would involve some travel, accompanying him to meetings, going to his other offices and stuff,' Kate explained.

'Well it sounds perfect, I'm sure Hermione will be able to help out,' Joel told her.

'I know it sounds like a great opportunity and I know it would get me out of Randall's and away from the Lady Dragon for good but when he was telling me about the job and the great salary and how he wanted me because he trusted me and he thought I was efficient, all I could think about was that I knew he had offices in France. And I started to wonder, in fact, all I could think about was if I could commute from our farmhouse in Marchette,' Kate spoke, looking at Joel intently.

'*Our* farmhouse,' Joel repeated.

'Yeah, I know, stupid,' Kate said unable to keep her eyes from him.

'ATTENTION! Can I have the remaining couples, please! Time for Couples' Catwalk!' Becky shouted out.

'That was a quick ten minutes. God, right, well, do I look OK? This bloody fascinator is itching my head. Is it straight?' Kate asked, brushing down the front of her dress and then tweaking at the hairpiece.

'It's fine,' Joel answered.

'OK, good, right well let's get on with the show,'

Kate spoke jovially and she headed off towards the pink-haired assistant.

* * *

'Right, ladies and gentlemen, let me introduce our next couple: Kate Baxter and Joel Brown. Give them a big welcome,' Larry announced, lights bouncing off his sequined jacket.

Kate and Joel walked onto the stage accompanied by the Love Dove and stood on the mark opposite Larry. The catwalk, set up in the middle of the audience, tables either side, was now lit up like a Heathrow landing strip with red lights down each edge and spotlights focused on it. The Randall's tables were on the left of the catwalk and Lynn seemed to be talking intently on her mobile phone while Darren was pouring large amounts of red wine into his glass. Miranda suddenly caught Kate's eye. The Lady Dragon fixed her with an icy stare, a smug smile playing upon her lips. Kate looked away and then realised Larry had been talking and she hadn't heard a thing he said.

'So, are we all clear?' Larry asked them both.

'No, sorry, I'm not, I—' Kate began.

'They play music, one of us walks down the catwalk like a model, Larry's at the other end, he asks us a question, we answer it, walk back up the catwalk, etc. etc. until we've answered two questions. Then the other one of us has to do the same and if we match answers, it's more Kissing Gates on the board. Oh and there's extra marks for good modelling style; there's a judge,' Joel recapped for Kate.

'Thank you, Joel. Are you after my job, by any chance? OK now, Kate? Know what you've got to do?' Larry asked her.

'I think so,' Kate replied.

'OK, well, so you get a chance to see how it's done, we'll let Joel go first. So, here's your headphones and Gareth – a stool for Kate, please? There you go, you can watch all the action but you won't be able to hear Joel's answers,' Larry spoke.

Kate sat down on the stool and put the headphones over her ears.

'OK, I'll just get into position and – OK, cue the music!' Larry exclaimed, heading down to the end of the catwalk.

It was a sexy, pulsating number and Joel began to work to the rhythm.

Kate watched as he confidently moved down the catwalk; she couldn't see his face but what she could see was him removing his jacket. He threw it to one side and then began to unbutton his waistcoat. She could see Lynn, her mouth wide open, obviously screaming in appreciation and Miranda was clapping enthusiastically. Marina was smiling, watching his every move and Kate chewed her lip, wrinkling up her nose.

By the time Joel had got to the end of the catwalk, his shirt was unbuttoned and the crowd were roaring their approval.

'Nice moves, Joel; have you done this before, by any chance?' Larry questioned.

'A long time ago. I'm a bit bruised and a bit rusty,' Joel responded, indicating his battered torso.

The crowd shouted their disapproval at the statement and Joel smiled out at them.

'Right, well, your first question about Kate is – Kate has fifty pounds to splash out on something. Does she buy a handbag, a pair of shoes or something else?' Larry asked.

'Something else,' Joel replied confidently.

'Something else, good. And do you have any idea what that something else might be?'

'I think she would spend it on her daughter,' Joel replied.

'OK, good. Right, cue the music, off you go, although keep it clean, no full Monty's please,' Larry told him.

This time, as Joel performed his catwalk routine, Kate had the benefit of seeing a frontal view. He strutted down the runway towards her, removing his shirt as he went. Kate bit hard again on her lip as his eyes met hers. He smiled at her then turned and made his way back towards the host.

The audience were shouting 'off, off, off' and it was a few seconds before Larry and the floor manager were able to get them to quieten down.

'OK, Joel, Kate's been told she has to give up something for a month. Which of the following things would she be unable to give up? Chocolate, sex or alcohol?'

'Alcohol, without a doubt. Probably Asda's latest low-price, South African wine,' Joel answered.

'Or any other of the supermarkets own brand wines. Can't favour a particular brand on this show Joel, I'm afraid. OK, that's good, we have all your answers. Time to remove Kate's headphones and see how your answers compare. Gareth, could you remove Kate's headphones, please?' Larry ordered.

Kate was hurriedly relieved of her ear coverings and was ushered down the catwalk to stand next to Joel and Larry.

'OK, let's have some hush please, ladies and gentlemen. Kate, I said to Joel – Kate has fifty pounds to splash out on something. Does she buy a handbag, a pair of shoes or something else?' Larry questioned.

'Oh, er, something else. I'd probably spend it on Bethan,' Kate answered truthfully.

'Who's Bethan?' Larry asked.

'My little girl,' Kate answered, a rush of love sweeping over her as she thought about her.

'CORRECT! That's exactly what Joel said. One Kissing Gate on the board! Well done!' Larry announced excitedly.

Joel smiled at Kate and took hold of her hand.

'OK, the second question we asked was – Kate's been told she has to give up something for a month. Which of the following things would she be unable to give up? Chocolate, sex or alcohol?'

'Oh, that's hard, I don't know,' Kate responded, her mind whirring with thoughts of Dairy Milk, South African wine and mind-blowing sex with Joel.

'It isn't hard, think about it,' Joel murmured quietly.

'No conferring please. Kate, I'm going to have to push you for an answer,' Larry said sternly.

'Um, sex?' Kate asked, not entirely sure it was right.

'Oh no, I'm sorry Kate, Joel said own-brand, supermarket, South African wine,' Larry announced.

'Oh bugger! I mean, oh gosh, sorry,' Kate said, swallowing and looking at Joel apologetically.

'Never mind, you can make amends now. Joel, please take yourself over to the stool and put on the headphones. It's time for Kate to take to the catwalk,' Larry announced.

Strains of 'Lady Marmalade' blasted out over the PA system and Kate attempted to remember some of the dodgy fashion shows she had watched on some even dodgier Sky channel late at night when she couldn't sleep, after Matthew had left her, when she had spent nights alone crying into a glass of own-brand supermarket wine and cannelloni for one.

She had nothing on Kate Moss. She swaggered and staggered in her high heels down towards Larry, hearing Lynn and Darren yelling loudly and clapping their hands together.

'Some nice moves there, Kate. OK, first question. Joel's in a hot air balloon with you, the Queen and a small child. Balloon's going down, Kate; someone has to be thrown out to save the rest. Who does Joel throw out?' Larry wanted to know.

Kate looked over at Joel, who was sat on the stool, the spangled earphones covering his ears. He was everything she wanted. She knew that now, without a doubt.

'Joel wouldn't throw anyone out; he'd jump,' Kate said positively.

'Woo, ladies and gentlemen, did you hear that? He doesn't just look good; it seems like Joel is also a real hero. OK, second catwalk. Perhaps loosening the top a little might earn you some favour with the audience,' Larry suggested, licking his top lip.

Kate walked down the runway, looking at Joel, not interested in swaying her hips in time or flaunting half a calf to the audience. There was something much more important than winning the contest on her mind and it wasn't even the job with Frank Peterson.

She smiled at Joel, turned around, posed briefly and made her way back to Larry.

'OK, final question – if Joel could go anywhere in the world, where would it be? Would it be the Caribbean? Would it be Australia? Or somewhere else completely?' Larry asked Kate.

'France,' Kate said quickly.

'France? Is that your answer?' Larry enquired.

'Yes,' Kate spoke.

'Right, OK, Gareth, if Joel could remove his headphones please and come back down here to join us,' Larry said.

Joel walked back down the catwalk and stood next to Kate.

'OK, Joel, time is running away with us so I'll get straight to it. We said to Kate, Joel's in a hot air balloon with you, the Queen and a small child. The balloon is going down and weight needs to be lost so someone has to be thrown out to save the rest. Who would you throw out?' Larry questioned.

'That's a tough question,' Joel said, letting out a breath of air.

'Kate was very certain about her answer,' Larry told him.

'Was she?' Joel asked, looking at Kate.

'Yes, she was, have to hurry you.'

'OK, well, I couldn't throw anyone out, so I'd jump,' Joel replied.

'CORRECT! A match and another Kissing Gate on the board!'

Kate smiled at Joel and took hold of his hand.

'OK, OK, finally, we said to Kate, if Joel could go anywhere in the world, where would it be? Would it be the Caribbean? Would it be Australia? Or somewhere else completely?' Larry asked.

'France,' Joel told the host.

'France?' Larry queried.

'Yeah,' Joel told him.

'CORRECT! A match! Another Kissing Gate on the

board! So that's a total of three Kissing Gates to add to your score, well done!' Larry enthused.

Kate smiled excitedly at Joel until she saw Marina, preened and puckering up her lips, smiling widely at him from the crowd.

'HANG ON! Who is this?! Oh ladies and gentlemen, here comes the Love Dove! Let's hear it for the Love Dove!' Larry exclaimed loudly, holding an arm out as the bird bounded onto the stage.

'Oh God, not the song, please!' Kate remarked.

The Love Dove's theme music began and he badly juggled with three golden eggs before bringing one over to Larry and putting a wing around Kate's shoulders.

'Kate and Joel, you've won a spot prize. Let's open up Lovey's golden egg and see what you've won – it is – first class Eurostar tickets to Paris. You said France and it looks like you're destined to go there. Well done! Let's hear it for Kate and Joel!' Larry boomed into the microphone as the Love Dove pushed a voucher into Kate's hand.

'France,' Kate spoke, running a finger over the word *Paris*.

'France,' Joel repeated, looking at Kate.

# 35

'We're still second on the leader board; Darren just texted me,' Joel announced, sitting down opposite Kate at a table in the green room.

'Has everyone done their catwalk?' Kate asked.

'I think so; he said Mark and Gloria won the theatre break,' Joel added, taking a sip of his lager.

'Great, she'll want a part in the production; find some way to fit aerobics into *Oliver*,' Kate remarked.

'Now that could be worth seeing,' Joel said with a chuckle.

'Just the mock wedding then, making our vows sound sentimental and gooey,' Kate said, sipping at her drink.

'Yeah,' Joel answered.

'Listen, I'm sorry I went all mental with you during Racy Cakes, I was just trying to keep focused and—' Kate began, unable to meet his eyes.

'It's OK. Look Kate, there's something I need to tell you,' Joel said awkwardly.

'Oh, please don't say anything. Whatever it is, I don't want to know, not yet, not before the end of the contest. Can it wait until the end of the contest?' Kate babbled, fearing it was going to be painful.

It was going to involve Marina and she couldn't bear to hear it. He was probably going to work in Buenos Aires with her on some joint modelling assignment. There would be photos of them barely clad cavorting on the beach, sharing cocktails with a perfect sunset in the background. There would be an attractive Dalmatian and a perfect blonde child with ringlets laughing happily and blowing bubbles into the sky.

'It's about Marina,' Joel continued, undaunted.

'Please Joel, not now. I understand about Marina, really I do and it's fine—' Kate began, standing up and feeling uncomfortable.

'It isn't what you think,' Joel told her.

'Please, not now, I've got to phone Hermione. I

need to check on Bethan and to make sure I didn't look a complete idiot sashaying up and down the cat-walk,' Kate spoke hurriedly and she quickly left the table and dashed towards the exit of the green room.

She knew it but she couldn't bear to hear it.

'No! Kate, wait! Don't call Hermione!' Joel called and he hurried after her, only to have his way blocked by Becky.

'And where do you think you're going? We've done a survey in the audience while the show's been going on and guess who's been voted *Knowing Me Knowing You* resident hottie?' Becky asked him.

'Er, Martin from Martin and Yvonne?' Joel replied.

'No silly, you! Come on, you're needed on stage, there's a prize, chop, chop,' Becky ordered, taking hold of Joel's arm and leading him off.

'Lynn, have you heard from Hermione recent' 've called her at home, seven times and there's one there. I've called her mobile and it's gone it to voicemail? Where is she? Why isn't she the than should be in bed, asleep. Where would sh aken her?' Kate said into the phone in panic.

'Er, well I'm sure there's an explanation. In fact, when I spoke to her last, I'm sure she said something about dropping in on her mum. Yes, that's what she said, I'm positive – staying the night, in fact. Apparently, they're all going to make tents out of bin liners and tea towels,' Lynn replied.

'But that's just stupid; she never stays over at her mother's. What's going on?' Kate demanded to know.

'Nothing! Don't be daft. I told you, Bethan's fine, they're staying at her mum's, don't worry – hang on, Joel's coming onto the stage with his shirt off again, oh deep joy,' Lynn spoke, breathing into the receiver.

'What? What's he doing on the stage? Lynn, what's going on?' Kate demanded.

'Listen for yourself,' Lynn replied.

'...and according to your votes, the winner of the *nowing Me Knowing You* 2011 Hottie Award is – Joel wn,' Larry announced loudly.

Kate listened down the phone as the Love Dove wked and stomped about.

nd your prize Joel is five hundred pounds and a ubscription for *Iron Man* magazine, courtesy of and Health Gyms,' Larry carried on.

let out a heavy sigh, imagining Marina's ile, her heavily made-up face pouting at Joel, o him with her ice-blue eyes.

'The Lady Dragon's had a few, can barely stand in those ridiculous silver mules she has on,' Lynn spoke above the applause.

'You're changing the subject. Hermione has absconded with my daughter and I can't contact her,' Kate exclaimed.

'Now you're really exaggerating and you'd better get off the phone because after the commercial break, they're starting the final part. Virtual Vows, the Showdown of Sincerity,' Lynn told her.

'Is Marina still there?' Kate asked.

'Yeah, she's still here, slapper almost wet herself when Joel removed his shirt,' Lynn answered.

'Keep trying Hermione, will you?' Kate ordered.

'Will do. And good luck. I sense Colin is on the very verge of announcing free champagne for everyone if you and Joel win.'

'I'll do my best,' Kate replied, ending the call.

'So, *Knowing Me Knowing You* resident hottie, eh?' Kate remarked as they stood in the wings, waiting to go on stage.

'Whatever that means,' Joel responded with a laugh.

'It means most of the women in this audience are having trouble keeping their eyes off you – me included,' Kate answered.

Joel looked at her, sensing the sentiment.

'Kate, I really need to tell you something,' Joel repeated.

'I know and you can. I'll listen right after the show, tears or cheers,' Kate said.

'Marina isn't an ex-girlfriend. I hadn't met her before I met her for lunch at the pizzeria. She works for Elite Escorts,' Joel blurted out.

Kate just stared at him, unresponsive.

'Look, I know it was a stupid, ridiculous idea and I should have known better but Hermione said I needed to do something and I would have done anything to keep you interested in me,' Joel continued.

Kate just carried on staring at him, her heart freezing, her breathing laboured.

'I know now that it was wrong, especially because I promised you honesty. Creating Marina was nothing short of deceit but I didn't think it would go this far and—' Joel began.

'Thirty seconds, guys!' Becky announced excitedly, bounding up to them like the Easter bunny.

'Say something Kate, please,' Joel begged.

Kate shook her head.

'I was being selfish, I know, I was being completely selfish, but I was trying to do it for the right reasons. And when I found out Matthew was still seeing Amanda, I had to do something about that too. I knew if I told you, you wouldn't believe me so I told Hermione and she said you needed to see it with your own eyes,' Joel carried on.

'Jesus Christ, the sudden and dramatic urge for a Chinese meal. She knew he was going to be there – that they were *both* going to be there,' Kate announced in horror.

'Kate, I know I said I wouldn't pressure you or force you to make any decisions but, well, I lied about that too. I'm in love with you and I was scared. I didn't want to let you go,' Joel told her.

Kate looked up at him. His enormous, grey eyes were wider than they had ever been and they were filling up with tears as he gazed back at her.

'Ready, you two? And off you go!' Becky announced, giving them both a little shove out from behind the curtain.

'Ladies and gentlemen, let's welcome back our current second-place couple, Kate and Joel!' Larry introduced.

Kate stumbled onto the stage, the lights making her feel completely disorientated. The audience were nothing more than a dark, blurry throng and the light above camera one was flashing like an overactive Belisha beacon.

Her mouth was dry and her eyes were sore. She couldn't focus, she couldn't concentrate.

'Now Kate and Joel, this is where the two of you pledge your truth to one another under the *Knowing Me Knowing You* Arch of Harmony in front of all these beautiful witnesses and our feathered minister, Reverend Love Dove,' Larry spoke.

He waved an arm towards the left of the stage and the Love Dove sauntered solemnly into the limelight dressed in full clerical garb complete with bible under one wing.

The Arch of Harmony resembled a B&Q arbour that had been dressed with white and pink roses, streamers and heart-shaped balloons.

'So, if you two could join hands and come under the Arch of Harmony, we'll get things under way,' Larry said.

'Kate, are you OK?' Joel asked as she stared around as if she didn't know where she was or what was going on.

She didn't reply.

'Kate,' Joel repeated.

'So, if you're ready...' Larry urged.

'Kate, we need to step under the arch,' Joel told her.

'STOP! STOP EVERYTHING!' a voice yelled from the audience.

## 36

The murmuring in the crowd ceased and a stunned silence washed over them.

'Er, ladies and gentlemen, I'm sorry for the interruption, we will try to resolve matters and – could someone get security?' Larry asked, looking uncomfortable.

'No! No security, I need to tell everyone about this farce in order to try and restore the integrity of this competition,' the voice spoke as its owner stepped into the light.

Matthew.

Kate stared out at him. He was standing at the front of the stage, to the right of the Arch of Harmony, all eyes, attention and cameras focussed in on him. His mousey hair was tousled, he was wearing a new suit and a smirk was playing on his lips.

'This "relationship", isn't real. Kate and Joel aren't a real couple; they've been fooling each and every one of you with their cutesy answers and their cake decorating. The truth is, Joel's an escort, he works for Elite Escorts and Kate's paying him to be her partner so she can pocket the prize money,' Matthew said loudly.

Kate felt like a knife had been driven through her and shivers ran up her spine as she heard the audience gasp in horror. It was her worst nightmare; everyone now knew the truth.

'This isn't true,' Joel replied as Larry turned to them looking pale and aghast.

As pale and aghast as someone covered in bronzer could look.

'It is completely true. Check out the website; his rates are very reasonable,' Matthew carried on.

'It isn't true. OK, maybe it was to begin with but *we* didn't enter this competition. We had no idea about the competition until we were in the thick of it and then we couldn't do anything about it; everything just snowballed,' Joel attempted to explain as the colour drained from Kate's face completely.

'And an escort isn't all you are Joel, is it? You were in the Royal Engineers in Afghanistan, weren't you? You're the only survivor of a team of soldiers who were ambushed two years ago. You ran, leaving your friends to die, didn't you?' Matthew continued to rant.

Joel didn't reply, his confidence faded, his mind harking back to the awful day he lost his comrades. He swallowed, trying to force the images out of his mind and regain some composure.

'And who the fuck are you, mate?' Darren questioned, leaping up and leaving his chair.

'Let's just stay calm everybody. I'm sure we can go to a commercial break, can't we Lloyd? Time for an ad break? Do you think?' Larry bumbled, looking for the floor manager.

'I'm someone who wants to see justice done. I don't like the British public being fooled by liars and cheats and cowards,' Matthew shouted.

'Right, that's it,' Darren yelled and he drew back his good arm and thumped Matthew hard on the jaw.

He reeled back into the Randall's table, falling across Andrew Kent and ending up with his head in Miranda's lap.

'You know nothing about Afghanistan, you hear me? Nothing! It wasn't anything like you said. He had to hide for almost thirty minutes in a space half the size of this table until air support came and bombed the bastards,' Darren ranted as he stood over Matthew, his hand clenching his shirt.

'Darren, it's OK, he's right. I am a coward and yes, I was an escort,' Joel said.

Miranda let a satisfied smile wave across her lips as she helped Matthew onto a chair and handed him a napkin for his bloody lip.

'You bitch! This is all down to you, isn't it? You couldn't be content with ruining Kate's life at work; you had to ruin the contest as well!' Lynn yelled, getting to her feet and joining her husband at that side of the table.

'I don't know what you're talking about; this has nothing to do with me,' Miranda spoke as she put on her best mortally offended look.

'Duh! Do you think I'm stupid? This has your hallmark stamped all over it! You vicious witch!' Lynn screamed.

She slapped Miranda hard across the face, making her physically reel backwards on her chair and Andrew Kent hurriedly held onto it to stop it falling over.

'Lloyd! Are we going to a break? Where are the commercials? Where is security?' Larry screamed in a high, camp voice as he tried to take refuge from the situation under the wing of Reverend Love Dove.

'WAIT! Please! Don't go to commercials! I haven't had a chance to explain yet!' Kate shouted from the stage, interrupting Darren and Lynn's dual attack on Matthew and Miranda.

'Kate, we don't need to say anything. It's just a stupid game show and you didn't want to take part in the first place; *she* made you,' Joel reminded, indicating a red-faced Miranda, having her cheek mopped by Andrew.

'But we did take part and I've enjoyed every moment, even the mad burlesque dancing and the catwalk modelling,' Kate answered, tears spilling from her eyes.

'Kate...' Joel began.

'No, you've had your say; it's my turn now. Yes, Joel was an escort I had to pay to attend what I thought was a Peterson Finance dinner. Sorry Frank, I didn't have a boyfriend and I thought I would look silly if I turned up on my own. I had no idea we were going to have to take part in this totally mad couples' competition and I didn't want to, not at first, but then we got through the first round and I saw the prize money and I really needed that money. You see, him, over there, the one in the new suit – he was my husband and he left me and my daughter to the sound of a Coldplay song. You know, the really sad one that always makes everybody cry. And his bags were pre-packed, like he'd been planning it for ages, but I didn't know. I had no idea that he didn't love me any more, that he'd been seeing someone else. And then he didn't pay for Bethan and I was struggling to make ends meet, trying to give Bethan everything she needed, trying to pretend that everything was normal when it wasn't. So yes, in the beginning, I paid Joel to be my date but we never set out to really deceive anyone, it all, just kind of – happened,' Kate spoke, tears rolling down her face.

No one said anything; the audience was silent and Kate looked at Joel.

'But then things changed and Joel and I got to know each other. We practised questions together, we shared omelettes and cheap wine and conversation, like proper conversation, about important things – like the salt content of my favourite meals – and I discovered that he's the most honest and sincere and wonderful person I've ever met,' Kate continued.

Joel just looked at her, oblivious to the audience staring at the stage.

'But it took me until tonight to realise it properly. You see, I thought I'd lost him to someone else, someone blonde and toned and totally more suited to him than me. And I know that she wasn't real and I know I should be angry with you for making her up but I'm not. I'm not because I gave you such a hard time, I never told you what I was thinking or feeling, mainly because I didn't know how I was thinking and feeling myself, but I held you away. I kept you at arm's length because I was scared to let you in. Because of *him*, because of what he did to me and Bethan, because I gave him my faith and he threw it back in my face,' Kate carried on, looking directly at Matthew.

The eyes of the audience fell upon Matthew and he shirked in his seat and tried to ignore their scrutiny.

'But you're not Matthew, and I know that now, without any doubts. You've been there for me these last few months, supporting me, helping me with Bethan, making me laugh, making me happy and I must have been completely blind not to see what was happening between us. When you walk into the room, my stomach turns over like the characters in all those corny Mills & Boon books. When you smile, I feel it on the inside and when you hold my hand, I never want you to let go. I'm in love with you, Joel; I'm ready to move on, properly. That's if you still want me,' Kate spoke, her voice shaking.

The audience were completely silent, the TV cameras were still whirring and everyone was waiting with bated breath to see what would happen next.

'Do I still want you?' Joel asked, looking at Kate.

'Yes. Me and Bethan and everything that goes with us,' Kate said nervously.

Joel took hold of her hand and looked at her.

'More than you could ever imagine.'

A loud cheer went up from the audience as Joel put his arms around Kate and held her tightly to him.

'You *really* want me?' Joel asked as the audience carried on clapping and Larry tried to get his autocue up to speed.

'Yes. I've been a complete idiot, a completely blind idiot,' Kate replied.

'Yes you have, sweetie but you know, you got there in the end which is all that matters,' Hermione spoke as she hauled herself up onto the stage.

'Mione! What are you doing here?! Where's Bethan?' Kate exclaimed as Hermione threw her arms around Joel.

'With Philip, just over there, at the back. Been calling "Mummy" and getting excited since the start, almost had to gag her at one point – that was a joke, by the way,' Hermione spoke, releasing Joel and looking at Kate.

'Can we have some order, please? We've gone to an ad break. Now Kate and Joel, if you could stand under the Arch of Harmony, we can get your vows done – adjudicator has said you can still compete in the competition,' Larry said, appearing at the side of the pair.

'Oh go away you silly little man. They've done their vows; didn't you hear them? And they are more in love with each other than any of the rest of the contestants – especially that ridiculous, star-jumping OAP, Gloria. If you ask me, you need to hand over the cheque to these two now,' Hermione said, turning on Larry.

'Well, I don't...' Larry began, going red and not knowing what to say.

'Do you want to stand underneath the Arch of Harmony and see this out?' Joel wanted to know.

'Damn right. I haven't come this far to give up now,' Kate replied with a determined nod.

'OK, just give me a second, there's something I need to do,' Joel spoke.

He gave Kate's hands a squeeze and leapt from the stage into the audience.

At the Randall's table, Miranda had recovered some composure and was chatting to Andrew and filling up people's wine glasses, including one she had procured for Matthew.

'We had a deal,' Joel said to Miranda, standing in front of her.

'Yes, we did,' she replied, unable to keep the smug expression from her face as she looked him up and down.

'You said you wouldn't tell anyone from the show I was an escort,' Joel continued.

'I didn't tell anyone from the show. I told Matthew. He came into the office, we had a spot of lunch and it just slipped out. Sorry about that. Of course, I had no idea he was going to turn up like he did and try and ambush the show. That really was very mean of you, Matthew,' Miranda responded, smiling at Matthew.

'You're an evil witch! Let go of me, Darren; she needs another slap!' Lynn screamed, trying to get out of her chair and relieve herself from her husband's restraint.

'You're a very, very sad person, Miranda; no wonder Kate calls you the Lady Dragon,' Joel spoke, glaring at her.

'She calls me what?' Miranda questioned, sitting forward in her seat.

Joel put his fingers to his lips and let out a loud whistle which caught the attention of everyone in the room.

'Ladies and gentlemen, just a short announcement. If you just all look this way, at this woman sat just here, the one who got someone to interrupt the show you were so much enjoying – she has a surprise for you all,' Joel called out.

'What's he doing?' Kate asked Hermione.

'I have no idea,' Hermione responded.

Joel reached out, grabbed at Miranda's hair and gave it a mighty tug.

The whole blonde mane came away from her head, revealing a bald scalp spattered with mousey-coloured clumps.

Miranda let out a scream of pain and put her hand to her head to try and cover some of her embarrassment. Andrew Kent gasped out loud, his eyes going out on stalks, Matthew's mouth dropped open in shock and Lynn let out a loud shriek of laughter.

'I promised not to tell anyone you wear a wig; I said nothing about showing them. Now we're even,' Joel told her.

Miranda began to cry, big, sorrowful sobs, involving gulping mouthfuls of air very loudly. She put her bald head in her hands and everyone on the table just stared at her, not knowing what to say or do.

'What d'you think? Is it me?' Darren asked, putting on the wig and twirling around.

* * *

'The winners of *Knowing Me Knowing You* 2011 are...' Larry began, looking at all the contestants who were lined up on the stage.

Kate looked up at Joel and felt his hand in hers, holding it tightly, waiting for the result.

'I sent "Marina" home. By the way, her real name's Sophie,' Joel whispered through the silence which was gripping everyone else who was waiting to hear the announcement.

'She should do acting, not escorting; she was very convincing,' Kate whispered back.

'We're going to find out after the break,' Larry announced after at least sixty seconds of waiting.

Everyone let out a collective groan.

'God, I am so tired,' Kate said with a heavy sigh.

'Me too. It's been some night, hasn't it?' Joel remarked.

'And we're still stood on a stage with a camp bloke in sequins and a seven-foot bird dressed as a bishop,' Kate answered.

'How will you feel if we don't win?' Joel asked her.

'We aren't going to win now. Matthew made sure of that when he hijacked the show. Everyone knows we weren't a couple to begin with, that we lied,' Kate replied.

'But the audience and viewers at home got to vote for the Showdown of Sincerity. I think Matthew might have actually just done us a favour,' Joel told her.

'The actual winning doesn't seem to matter so much any more. It was all I was focused on, all I could think about but now, now I've won something much better,' Kate said, looking at him.

Joel took her face in his hands and kissed her intensely.

Lynn and Hermione let out a whoop of excitement as the couple embraced and Lynn followed it up with a thumbs up.

'I think I need to decide whether I really need secretive friends like those two,' Kate said, watching as they shared out the remainder of a bottle of wine.

'I don't think you'll find any friends better than those two. Anything they kept from you was for a good reason, wasn't it?' Joel asked.

'I don't like being kept in the dark,' Kate reminded.

'I know and you don't like Noel Edmonds or Brussels sprouts either,' Joel added.

'Who told you that?'

'Hermione told me about Noel; Lynn told me about the Brussels sprouts,' Joel replied.

'Yes well, we don't need to know everything about each other any more, quiz is almost done,' Kate reminded him.

'But I still want to know, quiz or no quiz. These things are important. What if I didn't know about the sprouts before Christmas? Dinner could have been ruined,' Joel joked.

'Do they have traditional dinner on Christmas Day in France?' Kate asked.

'We'll have to do research,' Joel said, putting his arm around her.

'Welcome back everybody. We're all waiting eagerly for the results of the competition. OK, I have it through my earpiece, here we go – the winners of *Knowing Me Knowing You* 2011 are...' Larry Rawlins began again.

Kate closed her eyes and wished hard that their names were going to be called.

'KATE AND JOEL!' Larry bellowed at the top of his voice.

Kate snapped open her eyes, her mouth opened and she let out a scream of disbelief.

'Oh my God!' she screeched as the Reverend Love Dove came running towards her brandishing the cheque.

Joel put his arms around her and lifted her up into

the air as Hermione and Lynn stormed onto the stage and grabbed hold of her, pulling her back to the ground and into a group hug.

'We won! Joel, we won!' Kate exclaimed as Hermione and Lynn span her round and round in a circle.

## 37

Kate held the cheque up in front of her face, looking at it, making sure it was real. K Baxter, the sum of one hundred thousand pounds. She smiled and then turned her attention from the cheque to Joel lying next to her in the bed.

It was almost sunrise, they hadn't got to bed until 2.00 a.m. and he had been asleep ever since. A deep, undisturbed sleep.

Bethan had still been awake when Philip had brought her into the green room after the show. Wide-eyed and pepped up on Coke and crisps, she danced around for all the other contestants who 'oohed' and 'aahed' over her and called her 'adorable'. Surprisingly, none of the other contestants were at all bitter about Kate and Joel's victory; Gloria even gave Kate a hug and said their win was well deserved and the bride with the beehive had bought her a drink.

It still didn't seem real, though. The cheque, the hideous, heart-shaped trophy, Joel in her bed in a completely non-platonic way, Frank Peterson's job offer, Miranda's lack of hair being exposed in such a public place. She almost felt a bit sorry for her. Almost.

She got out of bed and walked over to the full-length windows, admiring the view of the London cityscape and the Eye. It was built-up but beautiful, vibrant and full of life. That was how she felt now: vibrant, beautiful, her old self again, Kate Baxter the woman, not Kate Baxter the slummy mummy.

She was just about to turn back towards the bed when a pair of strong arms were around her waist, pulling her into their embrace. She felt Joel kiss her neck and he turned her around to face him.

'I've had almost three hours sleep,' he stated with a smile.

'I know and you never moved; I watched you,' Kate told him.

'Couldn't you sleep?' Joel asked.

'No, too excited,' Kate admitted.

'A hundred thousand pounds is a lot of money,' Joel agreed.

'I'm not excited about that; I'm excited about everything else. I'm excited that I'm going to go into Randall's on Monday morning and hand in my notice, I'm excited about saying yes to Frank's job offer and I'm excited about going on our Eurostar trip to Paris to check out property,' Kate told him.

'Is that what you want to do? You're sure?' Joel questioned.

'Yes, I'm sure. More sure than I've been about anything in a long time,' Kate spoke.

Joel smiled and kissed her.

'Look: a hundred thousand pounds, a real cheque for a hundred thousand pounds, not that stupid big cardboard one we held last night from the Bank of Love,' Kate spoke, getting the cheque and holding it out to Joel.

'I know and it all started because you couldn't book Stephen,' Joel reminded her.

'I am so glad I didn't get Stephen,' Kate assured him.

'Me too,' Joel agreed.

'Really? Truly? Because you could have someone like Marina, I mean Sophie: perfect looking and without any baggage.'

'I like to keep things interesting. Besides, I've just told a room full of people, not to mention a few thousand viewers at home, how I feel,' Joel reminded her.

'And you're standing by that because…'

'Because I want to make sure I get my 40 per cent.'

'Oh.'

'I want to spend it on top of the range chickens.'

Kate laughed.

'I love you, Kate and I want to be with you. And if we're really getting into the realms of baggage here, I should be the worried one. I'm carrying around a whole suitcase full of anxiety, night terrors and flashbacks; we might have to have separate rooms,' Joel told her.

'Never,' Kate replied, putting her arms around him and laying her head against his chest.

'Shh, they're coming! Quiet everyone! You over there, put down that serving tray a minute and stop banging around – the guests of honour are coming! Party poppers at the ready!' Lynn hissed loudly as she ducked back into the hotel dining room and flapped her arms around.

'Mummy! Mummy!' Bethan exclaimed excitedly, waving her arms up and down.

'Shh Bethy, want some more toast, sweetie? Here you go, that's right, all in your mouth at once,' Hermione said, handing Bethan another soldier-shaped piece of toast.

Everyone fell quiet and then the dining room door opened and Kate and Joel came into the room.

Party poppers were let off, everyone in the restaurant cheered and clapped and Kate jumped and clutched at her chest in surprise and excitement.

'Ladies and gentlemen, the winners of *Knowing Me Knowing You* 2011! Kate and Joel,' Hermione announced in her best Larry Rawlins voice.

'God, are you all still drunk?' Kate asked as everyone quietened down.

'Unfortunately no and when I asked for rum with my cornflakes, the waitress looked at me a bit funny. God, you're so loved-up, aren't you? I am so glad Darren and I didn't have the room next to yours or we wouldn't have got any sleep last night,' Lynn remarked as Kate and Joel came to sit down at the table.

'Children present,' Kate said quickly and she sat down next to Bethan in her high chair and gave her a kiss on the cheek.

'Then I'll ask, did you "sleep" well?' Hermione spoke with a big wink.

'Yes thank you, Mione. Did you?' Kate answered, giving nothing away.

'Oh yes, we slept very well, must invest in a queen-sized bed at home. And Bethan slept well too. Bit wet this morning, though – probably the Coke, sorry. Nothing organic behind the bar and the orange juice was pricey,' Hermione told Kate.

'That's OK; it doesn't hurt to have a treat once in a while.'

'Do you want some coffee?' Joel offered Kate.

'Please.'

'I'll go and ask for some,' Joel said, standing back up.

'So, how does it feel to be a hundred thousand pounds better off this morning?' Hermione asked her.

'I can't stop looking at him, Mione; I can't believe I nearly lost out on the chance to be with him,' Kate responded.

'Did you really think that Hermione Wyatt was going to let that happen? I mean, there's only so much the tea leaves and tarot can do; sometimes you need to use your mobile phone and your contacts.'

'And Elite Escorts,' Kate added.

'Hmm, yes, well, I knew if you really cared for Joel,

you would react with good old-fashioned jealousy and I was right, wasn't I? Despite you wrinkling up your nose in disapproval.'

'And I suppose I have Elite Escorts to thank for even meeting Joel in the first place.'

'And who gave you the business card?'

'OK, I get the picture; I am totally in your debt,' Kate answered.

'No, not debt, no more of that with a hundred thousand pounds in your pocket,' Hermione responded.

Joel came back to the table carrying a pot of coffee.

'No Lady Dragon this morning? Probably on the wig hotline trying to order a replacement. Darren put it on one of the yucca plants in the foyer; it's still there,' Lynn announced proudly.

'Great show last night, mate: full of surprises. I loved it, said to Lynn we should enter next year,' Darren spoke, slurping up his tea.

'You must be joking! Have that giant bird shouldering up to me and Larry, a bad Alan Carr substitute, asking weird questions.'

'You're forgetting the green room, Lynnie: free food and drink,' Darren said, biting into a sausage.

'He does have a point and if you get to the final, I'd

be more than happy to make you a wedding dress,' Hermione offered.

'Hey, no stealing our thunder. 2011 is mine and Kate's year; let us enjoy it,' Joel told them, taking hold of Kate's hand.

'Quite right too. A toast! Everyone, please raise your cups and join me in toasting the happy couple – to Kate and Joel,' Hermione announced, raising her cup of mint tea in the air.

'Joel! Joel!' Bethan announced and she banged her spoon on her highchair tray.

'Kate and Joel!' the table repeated.

# ABOUT THE AUTHOR

**Mandy Baggot** is a bestselling romance writer who loves giving readers that happy-ever-after. Mandy splits her time between Salisbury, Wiltshire and Corfu, Greece and has a passion for books, food, race-horses and all things Greek!

Sign up to Mandy Baggot's mailing list for news, competitions and updates on future books.

Visit Mandy's website: www.mandybaggot.com

Follow Mandy on social media here:

facebook.com/mandybaggotauthor

x.com/mandybaggot

instagram.com/mandybaggot

bookbub.com/profile/mandy-baggot

# ALSO BY MANDY BAGGOT

Under a Greek Sun

Truly, Madly, Greekly

Those Summer Nights

In the Greek Midwinter

One Christmas in Paris

One Greek Sunrise

One Hollywood Sunset

One Greek Summer Wedding

Love at First Slice

Mr Right Now

One Wish in Manhattan

**LOVE NOTES**

**LOVE IN EVERY CHAPTER**

WHERE ALL YOUR ROMANCE
DREAMS COME TRUE!

THE HOME OF BESTSELLING
ROMANCE AND WOMEN'S
FICTION

 WARNING:
MAY CONTAIN SPICE

SIGN UP TO OUR
NEWSLETTER

https://bit.ly/Lovenotesnews

# Boldwood

Boldwood Books is an award-winning fiction publishing company seeking out the best stories from around the world.

**Find out more at www.boldwoodbooks.com**

Join our reader community for brilliant books, competitions and offers!

Follow us
@BoldwoodBooks
@TheBoldBookClub

Sign up to our weekly deals newsletter

https://bit.ly/BoldwoodBNewsletter